The key in his hand moved toward the lock.

It wouldn't go in.

In one movement he dove down the steps, behind the flagstone wall, taking the weight of the fall on his right shoulder to spare his hands and knees, then rolled. Instinctively his right hand swept inside his suit jacket. It came up empty. He was unarmed. Had been for three years. Fear gripped him, but took the form of an icy calm.

Awareness of the situation was instantaneous. A stakeout. Very professional. Right out of the manual for intelligence training. Not like the movies or television. No one waited outside in a car. That could be spotted, reported. Instead the house was marked with something casual that had to be moved. The tree limb he'd run over. Yes. The next car which drove by would be them. And entry to the house was denied. Lead, or more likely silver solder, was stuffed in the locks. They wanted to take him outside.

ROBERT A. LISTON

THE SERAPHIM CODE

TOR®

A TOM DOHERTY ASSOCIATES BOOK
NEW YORK

THE SERAPHIM CODE

Copyright © 1988 by Robert A. Liston

A TOR Book
Published by Tom Doherty Associates, Inc.
49 West 24 Street
New York, NY 10010

ISBN 0-812-50616-2   Can. ISBN: 0-812-50617-0

Library of Congress Catalog Card Number: 88-50626

First edition: November 1988

Printed in the United States of America

0 9 8 7 6 5 4 3 2 1

To Robert M. Liston

ACKNOWLEDGEMENTS

This is a work of fiction, although actual places have been used as locales. In particular, there *is* a Brandywine, Maryland. As far as I know it contains no underground facility such as I describe. Short Creek Spring in West Virginia does not exist. There is no Calvert College.

I would like to thank two persons who provided valuable information, Mrs. Eleanor R. Seagraves of Washington, D.C., and Professor Robert J. Doyle of the University of Windsor, Windsor, Ontario. My wife Jean helped with the manuscript and was a most valuable critic.

I would also like to thank those persons who provided information about intelligence agencies.

R.A.L., Santa Barbara, CA

ONE

An *amerikanets* in Moscow was going to die. It struck Pavel Karamasov, trade attaché at the Soviet Embassy in Washington, as strange that he thought of that. His life was ebbing away from a bullet hole in his chest, yet his mind dwelled on the fate of some poor, unsuspecting American *shpion* in Moscow. It would be tit for tat. A Soviet agent dies in America. One must go in Russia.

What did it matter? He should be thinking of home, family, the *Rodina*. Yes, the Motherland. He was giving his life for that. Not the *Kommunisti*. Americans did not understand that. It was their weakness. They believed they alone were—what was the American word?—yes, patriots. He would die as a patriot for the *Rodina*. Or at least try to.

Karamasov stood in the shadow of an American tree trunk in an American night looking at an American house. So far from home. A place called Maryland, named for a bourgeois queen; southern Maryland, not far from the ocean. He would like to see the ocean again, just to know the *Rodina* lay across it. He shook his head. Couldn't be helped. Had to think. A warm evening in April. It would not be so warm in the *Rodina*, not in Leningrad, where he was born.

Pain stabbed at him and he bent over, clutching at the bleeding wound. All this was futile. A .38-caliber bullet at close range. No chance to live. He had accepted that. All he wanted was a little time. One more act for the *Rodina*.

Straightening up, he forced his eyes to focus on the house, now barely outlined in the darkness. Small, one story. Americans called it a bungalow when it was built. He had been there before, remembered it well, a wood frame house, painted white, big porch on the front, windows with little square panes. He was at the back now, looking for light. There was none. No one was home. That was his problem. Someone must come—and quickly. He did not have much time.

Again the pain tore at him, but he didn't even flinch. One last act for the *Rodina*.

The house stood apart, as did its occupant. Had to believe that. Large lot. To the right, from where he stood, was another house, bright, warmly lit, perhaps a hundred feet away. To the left a vacant lot, studded with trees. Anyone could be there. What did it matter? He was a dead man anyway.

Karamasov started forward. He lurched, weaved.

Couldn't help it, no matter how much he tried. At closer range he saw something had changed. A breezeway, connecting the house to the garage. He bent—it helped the pain—felt. Flagstone. Wooden pillars, supporting a roof. Cover to go to the garage. He must have built it. For his wife. In the morning when she went to work in the rain. Loved his wife. A weakness. Or was it? No wife would grieve for *him*. Only the *Rodina*. Or would she?

Come. Please come. I haven't much time. Had to hide. Where? He turned to his left. Garage. Locked. Americans locked everything. Side door. He groped for the knob, found it, twisted. Open. Karamasov stepped inside, leaned against the wall, gasped for breath. The pain. Oh, the pain. *Come. Please come. It is the Rodina's only chance.*

Biggest sale he'd made so far. Corporate pension plan for five young doctors, plus IRAs for their wives. He had checks in his pocket, first quarterly installments, totaling $42,000. Nice commission, now and into the future.

Sloane slowed his Audi—one of the few luxuries he'd permitted himself—as he passed Calvert College where Freddie taught. Only another mile or so and he'd be home. Yeah, big sale. Then why wasn't he more elated? As soon as the question entered his mind, he shoved it aside. There were certain things David Sloane had learned not to think about.

He slowed the car further as he drove through what passed for the heart of town. A clutch of college students emerged from the village watering hole. Through his rolled-down window he heard their squeals of laughter. College town. Dull as dirt, isolated in the sticks of southern Maryland, good place for elite daughters of elite families to feed at the trough of higher education . . . *Stop it!* A bit further on he turned right onto Popular Street.

Quite unbidden, his unconscious mind noted and cataloged the vehicle. Ford Escort, dark green, D.C. plates. Parked in front of the Swallen house. No meaning was attached to these observations, certainly nothing sinister. If his conscious mind had become involved, it would have written off the vehicle as belonging to visitors in the area. The car was simply recorded as something different in an ordered universe.

The reason his observation did not reach his conscious mind was that David Sloane was attempting to stop this sort of thing. He had been retired from the Central Security Agency for almost three years, but the habit of the previous three years—a lifetime really—were hard to eradicate: an intense awareness of everything around him, an instinctive wariness to anything which might be a threat. He had been a top intelligence agent, a field operative who had somehow survived three years of the most dangerous missions, but as he constantly reminded himself, all that was behind him. Not quite. He had a crippled left arm to show for it. Bone was shattered twice by hollowpoints. Elbow bent slightly, little grip in the hand. Doctors had predicted he'd have ninety percent use of the arm. They were wrong. Eighty-five percent, they said. Wrong again. He figured less than eighty. When it ached in damp weather, a whole lot less. No complaints. He could be worse off. Like dead.

At best he could give only a mixed review to his new life. He was David Sloane, citizen, husband, insurance salesman just returning home from work. Freddie would be there. No. She said she'd be late. Wouldn't tell him why. Okay. He'd open a beer, turn on the evening news. Her mental image entered his mind. Beautiful really. Wore well. Brown hair, luminous brown eyes. Gorgeous lips. Good woman. He loved Freddie. She was the brightest, funniest, most fun woman he'd ever known. Helped him to relax. Wasn't that what he wanted—being relaxed, or trying to be, safe, uninvolved with anything except earning money and paying bills? Wasn't that what he and Harry Rogers, his partner now dead, had wanted?

Yet . . . Always there was the yet. If the truth were admitted, as it sometimes was, he felt his life was over, and he was just living out, maybe enduring, the rest of it. He missed the tension, the excitement of high-risk dangers, the feeling his faculties were honed to the fine edge that was vital to survival in the field. He didn't want that life back. He was certain of that. Yet everything was anticlimactic now. He missed Harry. Thought of him a lot. Wondered if Harry wasn't best off, flying through the air from the impact of a bullet to his chest in Munich. Part of himself had died with Harry. David Sloane knew he wasn't a whole man, and he wasn't talking about his bad left arm.

He had not retired as other agents do. Most go into hiding. They take a new name, usually the one they were born with, live under a prolonged cover story which accounts for their past activities, protected by the invisible net the Agency throws around them. The CSA considers them "inactive," but uses them for piddling little surveillance and investigative jobs as a sort of domestic auxiliary to worldwide intelligence activities. If they are not "in" intelligence, neither are they "out," but remain at the beck and call of paper-shufflers at Brandywine, living under the constant threat of being killed if they fail to cooperate.

Sloane had wanted no part of all that. He had seen a way out and taken it. When he unmasked and identified Parsley, the Soviet mole on The Committee, he had done a big favor both for the CSA and the Soviet KGB. Both owed him, so he had cashed in the chips. In return for his silence and total inactivity, he was to be left alone—totally alone. He did not take his real name, David Pritchard, nor did he hide or go under cover. He remained David Sloane, his cover name. Although friends and neighbors knew nothing of his past, people in the business from both sides knew him as a former top agent, almost a living legend. Both sides knew exactly where he was and everything he did—which was to have absolutely nothing to do with the intelligence game. From time to time he ran into people from both sides. But he remained evenhanded with both, detached, uninvolved. He'd have a drink with them, gab about old times, even give a little advice on personal problems. But both sides, having tested him, knew better than to entrust him with classified information or embroil him in any ongoing operation. He wouldn't play the game.

There was a risk in this stance. Other retired ops thought him crazy. Some young hotshot, most likely from the KGB, might plug him just so he could brag that he was the one who killed Liberty Valance. But the risk was tolerable. The alternative wasn't. Freddie simply would not accept the life of the fugitive, all the lies, all the looking over the shoulder. Freddie had become embroiled in the Parsley affair. She knew the intelligence game. She wanted no part of it. Sloane had no doubt she was right. Smart woman Freddie.

Ahead he saw the driveway to his house, Freddie's house, really. He slowed the Audi, preparing to make the turn.

Freddie's office, little more than a cubbyhole, was in the humanities building at Calvert College, the oldest structure on the campus. The trustees apparently believed that since the subject matter was old, the facilities should be too. She stood now at her desk, layered with midterm papers to grade, still holding the phone, although the call from her doctor had been disconnected. She didn't know whether to laugh or cry, so she settled for a watery-eyed smile. The rabbit had died. Blessed animal. Man's, no, woman's best friend. *We are gathered here today for a memorial service to honor one of God's noblest creatures.*

Tears dribbled down her cheeks, and she breathed deeply, swallowing against the stricture in her throat. At last she was pregnant. She had worried so. Her mother had had only one child, her, late in life. And all those years of taking the pill. Half a year past thirty-two now, she had simply wondered if she was ever going to make it, despite all the trying. *I wouldn't exactly call that a hardship.* Which time had it happened? No way to tell. There ought to be flashing lights, neon signs, a stone marker at least. *This commemorates the occasion on which Fern L. Falscape became with child.* Oh, yes! *Thank you, God.*

She started to pat her midsection, then discovered

7

the phone in her hand. She hung it up. *Sloane, you're going to be a daddy. You're going to have to put up with a big, fat, slobby wife who throws up every ten minutes. You're going to be changing diapers so full of number-twos you'll—* She stopped her mental flight. *Sloane.* That was the rub. David Sloane was the cover name given him by his government, the same government which had done its best to make him homicidal, maybe even halfway suicidal. His real name was David Pritchard, but he wouldn't take it. Insisted on Sloane. Okay, she understood why. But no more. This baby wasn't going to live a lie any more than she would. She'd remained Freddie Falscape, rather than be Freddie Sloane. Happily she'd be Freddie Pritchard, but not—*David, be happy now.*

They were—sort of, almost. They laughed and loved. Their fights were not too frequent or serious, never down and dirty. He loved her. No, adored her. She smiled. Sensible man, so perceptive. But it wasn't quite right. He missed his old life. The scars from it were deeper than she ever imagined. Missed Harry, his partner. It was like having a husband who grieved for his former wife. But she understood. Always figured it would be this way when she fell in love and married him. But not so bad or so long. Almost three years. He had to give it up, commit himself to his new life, forget what had happened, forgive himself. This baby would do it. David would make a wonderful father, giving his child all the things he hadn't had. Now she patted her tummy. *Junior—that's right, David Stuart Pritchard, Jr.—you got a heavy load to carry, making a real, honest-to-goodness, caring, loving, committed human being out of your daddy. While you're at it, you can think of a couple things to do for your mama too.*

She turned, went for her coat, put it on. Go home, take David out to dinner, tell him the good news. *You're going to be a father, baby.* She sighed. While she was at it, she might as well confess the letter she'd written. Good for the soul. Maybe he wouldn't be too angry.

President Marvin Grayson was having his quiet time. Every evening he possibly could, he left the Oval Office, said good night to his still-slaving staff, and retired to his study in his private quarters. Alone for perhaps the only time that day, nurturing a bourbon and branchwater, he'd steal some time to do whatever he wanted, read something which interested him, write a letter or two in his own hand to old, trusted friends, take a snooze, maybe just pace the floor letting his mind go where it wanted. After an hour or so he'd join Agnes, whatever children were at hand, whoever had been invited for dinner. Invariably he was refreshed. The quiet time made him a better President. God help the person who interrupted it.

Grayson swallowed generously from his drink, set it on a special cork coaster on his desk, then reached inside his suit coat and extracted a letter, unfolding it before him. Amazing letter. Amazing it had been written. Even more amazing—astounding really—that he ever saw it. He rarely saw any of the thousands of letters and wires sent to the White House every day. All were answered, of course. Squads of people were employed to write some suitable reply—most of them form letters, signed by an autopen which faithfully reproduced his signature. Oh, he received a summary of the mail, so many letters for or against whatever issue was current. Once in a while he'd see a particularly note-worthy letter from some especially noteworthy citizen, invariably fulsome in its praise for his work as Chief Executive. But a letter so thoughtful and so critical as this one? Hardly ever. Mel Stoddard had brought it to him. "Thought this might interest you, Mr. President." It had. Mel Stoddard deserved more confidential and important tasks.

Long letter—four pages, single-spaced, official stationery. Calvert College, Department of Political Science. He read the signature. Fern L. Falscape, Assistant Professor. He'd had her checked. There really was a Fern L. Falscape on the Calvert College faculty. Signed her own name. Simply amazing.

He re-read the letter, slowly, letting the words sink in, stopping frequently to think. With one exception, there was nothing in this letter he didn't already know—or at least suspect. It simply surprised him that a private citizen, this—he glanced at the signature again—this Fern L. Falscape knew of it, then had the guts to write the letter. She was warning him about the Central Security Agency. Through control of all coded information it was able to manipulate the knowledge and thus the actions of the United States Government, including the Joint Chiefs of Staff, Secretaries of State and Defense, and himself as President. This manipulation was orchestrated by an utterly anonymous five-member group in the CSA called The Committee. She wanted him to find some way to gain executive oversight of The Committee, thus to return the United States to constitutional government.

Grayson leaned back in his chair, deep in thought. The letter was full of speculation, innuendo, half-truths, but this Fern L. Falscape only knew the half of it. The simple fact was that every President since Truman had quickly learned the limitations of his power. Those damn blank authorizations, taking responsibility for actions he was not permitted to know. Those "national security briefings"—how often had he realized it was an act of the purest faith to accept what his intelligence chiefs told him was gospel? Gain oversight of the CSA? Return to constitutional government? He shook his head. Every President since Truman had tried, four in particular. And look what had happened to them. Could he hope for more?

He sat forward and leaned over the desk, re-reading the last paragraph of the Falscape letter. Just the other day he had signed a blank authorization. National security. So classified it was best he not know the nature. Another little surprise for the President, another crisis coming. He could do nothing about it—not even refuse to sign. Maybe he could do something now. She had given him a name, something he had never had before. Chances are none of his predecessors had ever had a name. It was something to work with, a place to start. He could only try. Decision made, he picked up the phone, asked for Mel Stoddard, heard the surprise in his voice that he was being summoned to the private study during the quiet hour.

In a few minutes he stood before the desk, tall, thirtyish, black, quite handsome, but far removed from the Presidential inner circle. Was that because he was black? Grayson hoped not. He was going to get his chance now. "How many people have seen this letter, Stoddard?"

"I've checked, sir. Only one, I think. It was opened by . . . Do you want to know the name?"

"No. Just so long as you do."

"She opened it. I don't know how much of it she read. My guess is just enough to realize it needed a special reply. It was passed along to me." He hesitated. "I can check, Mr. President, to see if she paid any special attention to it."

"Unwise, I think. It will just call attention to it." He stood up, reached for his neglected highball. "Would you like a drink?"

"No, sir."

"Still on the job, eh?" He smiled. "Glad to see my people putting in long hours. Makes me feel important." He gave a brief, not very mirthful chuckle. "And I'm glad you brought this letter to my personal attention. Why did you?"

Stoddard wanted to look away from the penetrating gaze of his President, but knew he should not. "I'm not sure, sir. There was something about the letter. I-I . . ." He hesitated. Truth was ingrained in him, no more so than when asked a direct question by the President of the United States. "Sir, I was with the Marines in Nam, an I and R unite—that's intelligence and reconnaissance. I had some . . . some involvement with . . . all this." He swallowed. "Funny things go on, sir. I-I just thought you might like to read the letter."

"And so I have. Stoddard, I have some things for

you to do—for *me*, personally, privately, and in the utmost confidence. You report only to me and in this office when I summon you. You know nothing about this letter or what I'm asking you to do. Do you understand? If you were in I and R, it seems to me you must."

"Yes, sir." Mel Stoddard was impressed. He was not only alone with the President in his inner sanctum, itself unthinkable, but he was being given a personal, private, confidential assignment.

"What is your security clearance?"

"Top secret one, sir."

Grayson shook his head. "I'll never understand all this classification gobbledygook. But if there is any higher classification, you have it from this moment on."

"Thank you, sir." His back became straighter, his shoulders more square, both instinctive from his Marine days.

President Grayson eyed him a moment. "We'll see how much that thanks is deserved. Here is what I want you to do. There is a name in this letter. Find this person. Bring him to me." For the next several minutes he told Stoddard exactly how he wanted it done.

Sloane was aware the streetlight was out. It was some distance to the left of the house, the last at the edge of town, but it ordinarily provided some illumination. The deeper darkness was merely noted, however. He paid more attention to the small dead tree limb which had fallen across the drive. The headlights of the car picked it up, but not in time for him to stop. He heard the crunch and snap of the breaking wood. Must've had a little wind if a limb blew down.

He stopped before the garage, then used the remote control to open the door. He was about to pull inside when he thought better of it. Ought to take Freddie out to dinner, celebrate his good news. They'd go in his car. He backed up, then forward to the side, leaving room for Freddie to put her car in the garage. He doused the lights, shut off the motor, and got out of the car.

His first impulse was to walk back and pick up the branch he'd run over. Orderliness, with everything in its proper place, was instinctive with him. But he didn't. Too dark. He'd do it in the morning. He headed for the house, striding past the open garage door and along the breezeway which led to the side door. He had built it himself and was proud of it. This summer he'd install windows so Freddie would be completely out of the weather on the way to the garage. At the side of the house he mounted three cement steps. Built them too, along with the small landing over which he pulled the aluminum storm door. The key in his hand moved toward the lock.

It wouldn't go in.

In one movement he dove down the steps, behind the flagstone wall, taking the weight of the fall on his right shoulder to spare his hands and knees, then rolled. Instinctively his right hand swept inside his suit jacket. It came up empty. He was unarmed. Had been for three years. Fear gripped him, but took the form of an icy calm.

Awareness of the situation was instantaneous. A stakeout. Very professional. Right out of the manual

14

for intelligence training. Not like the movies or television. No one waited outside in a car. That could be spotted, reported. Instead the house was marked with something casual that had to be moved. The tree limb he'd run over. Yes. The next car which drove by would be them. And entry to the house was denied. Lead, or more likely silver solder was stuffed in the locks. They wanted to take him outside.

"*Volk.*"

The raspy, wheezing voice startled him, even more than hearing his old code name, Wolf, spoken in Russian. He twisted around and looked up. A figure in the open side door to the garage was bent over, clutching his midsection. Again Sloane's hand reached for the weapon he didn't have.

"Help me . . . please."

English now. Slight accent. Wounded. Bad. "Who're you?"

"Pavel . . . Karamasov. Please—" Labored breathing. "Not . . . much time."

The name had meaning to Sloane. Karamasov was perhaps the KGB's top agent in the US, or used to be. Left in place. The devil you know is better than the devil you don't. What was he doing here? Sloane rolled to one knee and rose, starting toward the Russian.

Karamasov lurched forward into Sloane's arms. "You . . . must help. Great—" A deep groan escaped him. He tried to bend over but was held up by Sloane. "Great d-danger. Help . . . me."

Annoyance, a reaction to his rapidly fading fear, welled within Sloane. "You need help, all right. But how can I get to a phone if you stuff my house locks?" He saw Karamasov raise his head, shake it, then felt him collapse more heavily against him. Sloane's arms were around him now, holding him up. His left hand felt the weapon at the Russian's belt. Armed, yet he had not drawn his piece. Sloane did, reaching under the coat. His hand recognized it before his mind. Spanish Llama, 9-mm automatic. Good weapon. "Can you make it to my car? I'll take you to—"

"No, please . . . listen . . . to me." He sucked in air, wheezed it out, gasped it within again. "You . . . your people . . . have . . . broken our . . . code for—" A long, low groan was torn from him.

Sloane held him away at arm's length, trying to see the face. "Pavel, what code are you talking about? You make no—"

"Seraphim . . . Code. You must tell—"

Sloane felt the heavy impact of the bullet into Karamasov's body even before he heard the shot. It drove the Russian against him, knocking them both to the floor of the breezeway.

Sloane lay very still. He was not hit. Damn lucky. The shot came from short range, certainly less than fifty feet. Off to the left, beyond his car. Probably had to move and set up again when he parked the car there. Helluva impact. British Weatherby 300 most likely. With only one shot fired, it was probably bolt action, firing a .30-caliber Horenday dum-dum. Kill an elephant. Hit Karamasov in the back, making probably a three-inch hole when it came out the front. Would've killed *him* too, except the angle was wrong. Came out Karamasov's side. Close call. All he'd felt were the fragments of Karamasov's ribs hitting him.

He waited, holding his breath. His only movement was to release the safety on the Llama. Lucky he hadn't dropped it. Still in his left hand. That was okay. He'd killed many men left-handed. He tightened his grip, waited, mind cataloging what he knew. Not a CIA hit. They did it gangland style. There would have been two cars, five or six men. They'd have driven across the lawn, opened fire in a fusillade, sped off. This was a CSA hit. Two men working as a team. Need to Know kept any more from being involved. Professional, good, well-trained, nice setup. Man with a rifle, a nightscope. Saw everything.

The rustle of grass was barely audible, the sound of straining shoe leather even less so. Coming from the back. *Yes, that is how to do it.* By the book. Have to verify the kill.

He waited, quite unaware of needing new breath for his lungs. The top of a head moved above the breezeway wall. He was sure of it. Yes, a face now. Just visible in the darkness. A hand, reaching over, gripping a weapon, poking at Karamasov's body. Yes, he was dead, most definitely dead.

The weapon came toward him, a further reach, extending the arm.

The Llama bore no silencer. Its noise was deafening.

Yes, I remember how it's done.

He rolled over the back side of the breezeway wall and crept to the body, its skull now exploded. A lifeless hand still gripped a weapon. Sloane removed it. Walther PPK, 9-mm, with silencer attached. So dumb! Finest handgun in the world. Made especially for US intelligence. But no matter how good it was, it marked the bearer as a CSA operative. The KGB was smarter and used a variety of weapons.

He heard voices in the distance. Mrs. Herzbaum

across the street, talking to her husband. Couldn't make out the words, but he knew what was being said. Two unsilenced shots fired. Enough to wake the dead. Cops would be here in a minute. He stood up, looked around. The rifleman would not risk firing again, even if he were still there. Sloane stuck the Llama in his belt, gripped the Walther in his right hand. It felt so good. Comforted him. He had carried a Walther for years.

Awareness of his situation and what he must do flooded his mind. It was an instinctive process of survival and required no thought. He began to run, as fast as he could, across the vacant lot toward Poplar Street. The rented car—he had to get there in time. While he ran, assessment entered his conscious mind. A CSA hit. His old agency, *Mother*, wanted him dead. The rifleman could've picked him off at the car, easily killed Karamasov where he stood in the garage. Wasn't done. Waited till they were together. Two with one shot. Yes. Why? Had to be Karamasov and the Seraphim Code, whatever that was. Think about it later.

He stumbled over something in a backyard, almost fell, but propelled himself forward, past the side of the house. Almost there. He saw the car, heard the motor. Backing up. Somebody had parked him in. Lucky. Just plain lucky. The car was angled away from the curb when he reached it, groped for the handle on the driver's side, pulled. Interior light came on. Weatherby against the seat. Young guy. New man. Could have been himself a half-dozen years ago. Fear, rage in his eyes. His hand reached inside his windbreaker. Mistake. Should have stepped on the gas, knocked him from the open door. *Spit*. The

Walther leaped in his hand. He saw the small entry hole above the ear, the spurt of blood and bone out the other side. Dying eyes held him a moment, then the head fell forward over the wheel.

Sloane shoved the body to the passenger side, slid under the wheel, drove off. Dirty trick on Freddie. But what choice did he have?

Freddie felt like an intruder in her own house. Locks plugged. Had to jimmy the door to get in. Heavy footsteps resounded through the house. Doors slammed. They were searching for her husband.

She stood over the kitchen sink, gripping the edge so tightly her fingers were pressed white. She didn't know whether to retch, cry, or scream. It was happening again. She didn't know how or why or who, but David was ensnared in intelligence again. Damn Mother! Damn the game! Damn, damn, damn! David had tried so hard to stay clean. He'd promised her. And she knew he, of all people, had stayed out of it. Yet here it was again. Goddamn it all to hell!

"Mrs. Sloane?"

She did not turn to the voice. "I've kept my maiden name, Fern L. Falscape. You may call me Doctor, Professor, or Ms. Falscape." *Don't you dare call me Freddie! I most definitely am not your friend.*

"All right, *Ms. Falscape*. Are you certain you don't know where your husband is?"

She straightened and turned to face him. He was in his late thirties, somebody's husband and father. He wore the uniform of the Maryland State Police with captain's bars on his shoulders, but that did not ameliorate her feeling that he didn't know what he was doing. Out of his league. She could see uncertainty in his eyes. *This is the majors, captain. You've never seen curves like they throw up here.* "I told you I don't know."

"You are absolutely certain you don't know either of the dead men?"

She swallowed, as though trying to hold back memory. Fear, terror really, enhanced by déjà vu, had nearly paralyzed her when they asked her to look at the bodies. Once before she had looked at a pair of dead men, certain one of them just had to be the man she loved. Neither was. It couldn't happen again. No life was so virtuous. She didn't deserve it. "They are strangers."

"One face was . . . mutilated. Are you sure?"

She shivered from the visual image. "He was not my husband."

"But that is his car out there, the brown Audi?"

"Yes."

Captain Will Benning nodded, then very elaborately fished a small notebook from his shirt pocket and perused it. Actually there was nothing written on it, at least nothing about this case. "My men have talked to a Mrs. Herzbaum across the street. Do you know her?"

"Yes." Freddie tried to keep her face a mask so as not to reveal her private thoughts. Esther Herzbaum was a nosy gossip of the first magnitude, action recently justified by her membership in the neighborhood watch committee. *Those two have taken their clothes off. I'm sure they are committing a crime.*

"Mrs. Herzbaum—she was the one who phoned the police—saw your husband come home." Benning smiled. "At least she saw someone drive up in your husband's car. She thought it strange that no

20

lights came on in the house. When she and her husband heard two gunshots, they stepped outside. Mrs. Herzbaum believes she saw a man run through the vacant lot toward Poplar Street."

Freddie was so attentive she felt she couldn't breathe. "My husband?"

"Mrs. Herzbaum is uncertain. It was quite dark."

Very soon she will be more than certain. The whole town will be. "What are you saying, Captain? Do you think my husband killed the men out there?"

"I'm not—"

"My husband carried no weapon. I assure you he was unarmed."

"Does he have a gun?"

"Yes. It's kept in the nightstand to the left of the bed—as a security precaution. I'm sure you'll find it there, quite unfired." She watched the captain look at one of his men, saw that man nod, produce the weapon. David's gun. Oh, how she hated it. She'd always hated guns.

"Both the dead—both the deceased wore holsters, one at the shoulder, the other on the hip. We have been unable to find any weapon which might have gone in them."

Freddie blinked, waiting for him to go on. He didn't. "What are you suggesting, Captain?"

"It is just possible your husband"—he cleared his throat—"might have used their weapons to . . ."

"Two men, both armed, my husband unarmed? Don't you find that a little hard to—"

"Yes." Benning's face reddened a little. This was a sharp woman, good-looking and sharp. "The fact remains that two weapons are missing—and so is your husband." He perused the blank page of his

21

notebook again. "We have a report of a strange car parked"—he pointed out the open kitchen door—"over there on Poplar Street. The car is gone now."

Freddie's eyes widened. "What car? Did anyone see—"

"Unfortunately, no one paid any attention to the car, except that it didn't belong there—wasn't from the neighborhood. And no one saw or heard it drive away."

"Why would David—my husband, take that car when his own was parked—"

"I don't know. Do you?"

She looked at him levelly, brown eyes unblinking, and her voice rose a little, taking on an edge. "Captain, forgive me, but I think I'm an injured party. I come home from my office. There are police cars with flashing lights all over my lawn. There are two dead bodies, blood all over hell. I am forced to look at them. My house has to be forcibly entered. My husband appears to be missing. I am worried sick that he may be kidnapped, laying hurt some place, perhaps dying." Tears filled her eyes now. "Given all that, I don't care much for this interrogation. What are you doing to find my husband? Isn't it logical to assume that he was wounded and went to a hospital?"

"We're checking the area hospitals right now."

"Has it occurred to you—since he didn't do the logical thing of taking his own car—that he was forced by someone else to—"

"We are considering that." How in the hell had this woman put him on the defensive?

"Please do. It is more logical to me that David is a victim, not—"

22

"Mrs.—I mean, Ms. Falscape, I'm sorry but I have to ask. Is Mr. Sloane involved in any sort of criminal activity that you know of?"

The question brought her mind back to reality, short-circuiting the emotions welling within her when she realized David might be wounded, abducted. Criminal activity? David Sloane, her husband, the one true love of her life, had once been the equivalent of a paid professional killer. She'd seen him do it. She had once saved his life by killing for him. The forbidden vision of her own hand jerking as it pumped bullets into . . . *Not the pits. Not now.* Criminal activity? Crimes were committed, ghastly crimes, but all were authorized, endorsed, encouraged, applauded, and rewarded by the United States Government, the Central Security Agency, Mother. *Short for Motherfucker. So apt.* Criminal activity? *Wait till you see the major-league knuckleball, Captain. Or the screwball. That's the doozie, the strikeout pitch.* She looked deep into the eyes of the police captain. Better he not know, at least not hear it from her. "Hardly, and I assure you I would know if he was."

Freddie watched him nod, then march out of her kitchen, his men following him. She sagged weakly against the sink, all her strength draining from her, replaced by a surge of conflicting emotions. Worry, anger, despair were paramount, but she forced her mind to a new thought. *Please, God, don't let anything happen to him. Not now, not after . . .* It was honest prayer. Religion had become important in her life. She had made a promise to God the last time David was in danger. Then she began to tremble with fear as a new thought came to her. The letter she had

23

written. Did it have anything to do with all this? *Please, NO!*

Capt. Will Benning ordered an APB for David Sloane. Suspicion of homicide. Black hair, vivid blue eyes. Six-two, 175 pounds. No distinguishing marks. Armed and dangerous. Approach with caution.

By the time Sloane reached the edge of the Patuxent River, he knew just how much his skills had eroded. He actually trembled with fear, not from his narrow escape, but from realization that he was just a shell of his former self. Harry Rogers and he had been in far more perilous situations—several flitted through his mind as mental images—yet he had reached with icy calm, doing what he must to survive, his mind focused entirely on that task. Look at him now, worrying about the men he had just killed. He had never once thought about them, merely swatted them like flies. And he worried about his life, his future, living. *If you worry about living, it's a foregone conclusion that you won't.* He thought about Harry. *We're back in the game, old friend.* Most of all Freddie. God, he loved her. Not until now did he realize just how much. He wanted her. He wanted their life together, a life just getting started. All this scared him. Caring about anyone, wanting anything, thinking about any other blessed thing than survival was a surefire ticket to the mortuary.

He was never going to survive. He was already a dead man.

Sloane slowed for an isolated road, turned right toward the river. Soon he turned right again, this time onto a narrow dirt lane. Lights out, he guided

the car close to the river's edge, stopped under some
trees, and got out, standing there to let his eyes adjust
to the darkness, listening to the night sounds—frogs,
the hoot of an owl, crickets in the distance. Good. He
was alone. He heard the water. High now. Spring
rains. Good. A drop of water fell on his forehead.
Starting to rain. Even better. Wash away the blood.

He walked around to the passenger side and
opened the door. The rifle fell out and he picked it up.
Weatherby 300, bolt action. He had been right.
Sloane's first impulse was to keep it. Valuable rifle,
the nightscope even more so. He might need it. No.
Too bulky to hide. Attract attention. He picked it up
by the barrel and heaved it far out into the river,
heard the splash. What a waste of a fine weapon.

For the next several minutes Sloane worked very
hard, panting from the effort as he undressed the
lifeless body and put his own clothes on it. Then he
donned the dead man's clothes. Fortunately the fit
wasn't too bad, except for the shoes. They were a size
too small and hurt. The shoulder holster with the
Walther felt good. Pockets revealed ID, wallet, money, extra rounds for the rifle, extra clip for the
Walther. Dampness on the front of the windbreaker.
Blood and brains. He stripped it off and walked to the
water, rinsed it, put it back on wet. All set? No. He
bent over the body and removed the papers from his
own inside jacket pocket. Those checks—he could
cash them. Money was important. Anything else?
Sloane hesitated. He didn't want to do it. Bothered
him—a lot. No choice. He removed his wedding
band, the one Freddie had inscribed to him, and put
it on the dead man. Then his watch, also Freddie's
gift.

25

Sloane stood up. He put the Llama in his belt, then gripped the Walther taken from the first man he killed, checking to see the silencer was clicked into place. Bending over the body he began to fire into it, twice more into the head so the face and teeth would be destroyed, then the left arm so his own injury would not be detected, finally into each hand to destroy prints. He dragged the body to the river and shoved it out into the current, sensing more than seeing it drift downstream. David Sloane was dead. Had to hope everyone believed that. *Oh, Freddie!*

The heavens opened up and rain began to fall heavily just as he got into the car and drove away.

TWO

He went to work as he had every morning for years, leaving his home in the Georgetown section of Washington and driving to Brandywine, Maryland, where he parked in a small shopping center. But as he walked past the storefronts and entered a small one-story brick building, somewhat resembling a post office, W. Gordon Adams knew things weren't what they used to be. He was a has-been, a "graybeard"—although he wore no facial hair—a "consultant" on the great events of his time, rather than a participant.

An armed US Marine, dressed as a Pinkerton guard, sat at a small desk. Adams uttered the code words. "Good morning. I have an appointment with Mr. Raybolt," then he waited for the Marine to reply,

"You are expected," and buzz him through the interior doors. Adams turned right down a corridor, walking past various offices, all covers, and stopped before an unmarked door, unlocking it with a key and entering. Another Marine dressed in civilian clothes acknowledged him, then Adams used a red card bearing a magnetic imprint to open still another door. This took him into a small storeroom, where he reached under a shelf, slid back a panel to reveal an array of buttons, four of which he pushed, a numerical code. Then he stood patiently as the storeroom became an elevator carrying him 200 feet underground into the most secure facility operated by the Central Security Agency. It was the nerve center of its worldwide intelligence operations. Its banks of computers decoded and stored the most sensitive information. The top leadership of the CSA worked from here, not the visible CSA headquarters at Fort Belvoir, Virginia.

Adams approached another Marine, this one in uniform, logged in. Using his red card and pressing buttons on a series of cipher locks, he passed through various detection devices and locked doors to finally reach his office. On his desk were various overnight dispatches and memos for his attention, but Adams couldn't bring himself to read them. His mind was on other things.

Once he had been a key man at Brandywine, head of the European zone and a member of The Committee. This had made him one of the five most powerful men in the country, privy to all national security information, able to manipulate nations and their leaders simply by withholding or falsifying that information. He had been in the front lines of the intelligence wars, combating Soviet schemes, concocting our own. It was heady stuff, power such as few men ever know in their lifetimes. He hadn't realized how much he loved it until it was gone.

The damn Parsley affair. He had helped unmask a Soviet mole, code name Parsley, on The Committee, a most dangerous man. But in so doing he had compromised himself. That meant he was off The Committee, out of the European zone, "retired" in his early fifties. Oh, he knew he was lucky he wasn't killed because he knew too much, but there were times like today when he chafed at his role of "consultant." The Committee wanted to use his knowledge accumulated over two decades, but could not permit him to be a participant. He was denied access to codes presently in use by The Committee, nor was he appraised of current operations. Humiliating is what it was.

The buzzer on his intercom rang. Adams listened, said, "I'll be right there." A few minutes later he sat across the desk from Duane Cash, his successor as head of the European zone, his replacement on The Committee. Adams could not be absolutely sure of that. Membership on The Committee was the most closely guarded secret in the world, unknown even to those who worked most closely with it. But Adams believed he was. Cash was reading a memo, so Adams waited patiently. To him Cash was a junior edition of himself, but then being bland and nondescript was an asset in the intelligence game. Cash's hair was a shade darker than his own mouse-colored locks, now graying, his eyes a bit more vivid, and he wore glasses. But he had the same ghostly pallor that came from working underground in this place. Adams had always hated the artificial sounds, the filtered air of Brandywine. He wondered if Cash did.

In truth he felt sorry for Cash. He was in way over his head, especially if he was on The Committee. Three years ago Cash had been his own assistant, in charge of Middle European affairs, a good man being groomed for the future. But in the fallout of Parsley, the future had become now. Two members of The Committee had to be replaced, including himself, and he had been junior. Cash had been pushed ahead, when he really was ten, maybe fifteen years away from being ready. He didn't know enough about past activities and present methods. It must be difficult for The Committee and hell for Cash. Adams knew the reason he was alive and kept on as a consultant was that he was needed to backstop Cash and fill in the information he simply didn't know.

At that moment Duane Cash's thoughts were similar to those of his former superior. He hated these meetings. He hated having to ask Adams for advice. Above all he hated not knowing what had happened to Adams. He did not believe Adams had resigned for health reasons, as he had said. The man looked vigorous enough to him. He could only surmise that Adams had messed up in some fashion. But if he had, why wasn't he dead? All he knew was that Adams was there, imparting his wisdom because The Committee didn't trust his own. It was a shitty situation. He had been elevated to The Committee late last year, yet the group always made him feel like he didn't really belong. Oh well . . .

Cash didn't look up as he spoke. "I wanted to ask you about the operative David Sloane. You knew him, didn't you?"

Adams was shocked, although his expression did not change. Operatives were always called by their code names. This was unprofessional. "Yes, I know Wolf."

Cash looked at him. "I called him Sloane because that name will appear in the newspapers."

"It was a mistake for him to be allowed to keep his cover name. He should've been forced to take another."

Cash read into that an implied criticism of himself, but he let it go. "I believe you have more knowledge of Sloane than anyone else around here."

"Perhaps. He was in a special group I recruited and trained. I was involved in many of his operations. But he's retired now—like myself. Almost three years, I think."

"Is he?" Cash hesitated. Adams was supposed to know nothing of current operations or top codes presently in use, but his knowledge of past agency affairs was to be made use of. Cash knew he'd have to be careful what he told him. "Two bodies were found outside Sloane's house last night—unfortunately by local police. They are very much involved."

Adams said nothing, simply waited him out.

"The police don't know it, but one of the dead men is Pavel Karamasov. I don't need to identify him, do I?"

"His demise can hardly be considered a loss."

"The other body was one of our operatives. The fact is not being blabbed from the rooftops, however." He looked at Adams long enough to note his concurrence. "Karamasov was killed by another of our operatives. At least we think so. He has not yet reported in. It was set up as a standard operation."

31

"The field ops should not have gone up against Sloane."

Cash raised an eyebrow to form a quizzical expression. "Oh?"

"In his day Sloane was the best we had, one of the best there ever was. Should've been dead a number of times. But he was a survivor. I gather he still is."

"Unfortunately."

"You may expect to find the other operative dead too."

Cash glared at him, the only manifestation of his inner annoyance. Some people labeled Adams's foreknowledge as prescience. Cash thought of it as supercilious arrogance. "And why should we expect that?"

"If you used a standard operation, Sloane would have recognized it at once. If the rifleman missed him, which he must have, Sloane would take out the man who came to verify. Then he would go for the rifleman. I would not bet too much that he failed, particularly since the operative has not reported in."

"I wish I shared your enthusiasm for Sloane."

"He deserves respect, however grudging. Even after three years of inactivity, he apparently knew what to do."

And I don't. "What the hell do you think he's up to?"

Adams shook his head. "I have no idea what the operation was or why a hit on Sloane was ordered. But if it was bungled—and I assume it was—Sloane will be a most difficult adversary."

"Explain that, please."

"I told you. Sloane is a survivor. You can neither teach it nor buy it. Unless his skills have withered— and I gather they haven't—he will have radar for everything you try to do. He will know all the Agency techniques and be prepared to counteract them. I assure you he recognized at once that the Agency tried to kill him. He will view himself as in a kill-or-be-killed situation. The demise of two operatives should indicate what you can expect."

"What motivates him?"

"I told you—survival. There is nothing else. Sloane was one of twenty specially selected and trained as Code Word Three operatives. He—"

"There's no such thing."

"Not any more. It was a brief and not very wise experiment in the field. All are dead except Sloane. He was permitted to retire in recognition of—" Adams hesitated. "Just say he did some special work."

Cash grinned at him. "Which you are not at liberty to talk about."

If Cash learned about the Parsley affair, it wouldn't be from him. "Sloane was selected because he didn't care about anyone or anything—not home, family, country, you, me, this agency. It is safe to say he hates us. We are *Mother* to him. He would just as soon kill one of us as look at us. He was trained to be a dispassionate killing machine and that's what he is—particularly if he feels threatened."

"How's he feel about the other side?"

"Insofar as I know, it is the same. He hates both sides equally. He hates the game. He has no loyalties to either side."

"It seems not."

Adams looked at him a long moment, thinking. "Because Karamasov was there?"

"Yes. It seems your friend has turned."

"Sloane is not my friend. I respect him, but we are not friends. I have not seen him in three years." He shrugged. "I find it hard to believe, but people do change."

"Then you think he could have gone over?"

Another shrug, more elaborate this time. "You obviously possess information I do not." He saw Cash nod. "Is your purpose to bring him in?"

"That would hardly serve any useful purpose."

"I see. Chances are Sloane will also realize that."

"You know him. What will he do?"

"If he has turned and wants to go to the KGB, he will know how to do that. But your missing operative suggests he is not doing that."

Again the quizzical eyebrow. "Why so?"

"I suspect you will find his body, quite mutilated to retard identification, with Sloane's ID on him. Sloane has done this before. It gets the cops off his back, and hopefully the KGB will believe him dead and lose interest."

"The Agency too?"

Adams smiled. "He would like that, but I doubt if Sloane will believe life is ever so easy. He will expect the Agency to continue to come for him. His situation is greatly simplified, however."

"You're saying if Sloane is going to the KGB for sanctuary, he would not bother to try to make us think him dead."

"Exactly."

"It seems to me it would aid his disappearance into the embrace of the KGB."

Adams smiled. "But he knows you will not be fooled by the phony body. After all, one of your operatives is missing."

"I see." Cash thought a moment. "The fact Sloane has not gone to the KGB does not mean he is not working for them. It could simply be a clever means to—"

"True."

"What is Sloane trying to accomplish?"

Shrug. "I don't know what all this is about. I can only assume he is surviving."

"I assure you he won't this time." Cash uttered the words coldly, then glanced at the papers on his desk. He did not read them, just gained time to think. "Adams—" Having called him "Mr. Adams" for so long, it bothered Cash to drop the courtesy. But he had to remain in a superior role. "If you wanted to find this Sloane, how would you go about it?" When Adams hesitated, he added, "Do you want time to think about it and make a report?"

"No. Some of the details will have to be worked out, but I can give you the main thrust right now. I'd do two things. First, I'd put his wife under surveillance. He cares about her. It is a weakness and can be exploited. With luck she will either lead us to Sloane or he will come to her."

Cash smiled. "Especially if she is in danger."

"Perhaps. But that is a risky game. She is a civilian, after all."

"It could be made to look like the KGB."

"That's possible, but even more dangerous."

"What's the second thing?"

Adams thought a moment. "I'd bring in Captain Price from Pensacola."

"The director of training?"

"Yes. He knows more about our field ops than anyone else. After all, he trained them. He made a special study of the methods used by Sloane and his ex-partner Rogers, incorporating some of them into the training. If anyone can match up against Sloane, it is Price."

Cash was dubious. "Price is an old man. He's at least—"

"I know exactly how old he is. It is precisely because he is of the old school and unorthodox that he stands the best chance of eliminating Sloane. After all, the two agents you sent last night didn't last very long."

Cash leaned back in his chair. He hated this. Made him feel like a student at the feet of Socrates. But what choice did he have? "All right, Adams. I'm putting you in charge of this. Do whatever you have to. You have full authority. Just find Sloane quickly and eliminate the problem."

"Yes, sir, if that's what you want."

Sir! How strange to hear from this man. "Will this cause you any personal difficulties?"

"You mean because of my past association with Sloane?" He saw Cash nod. "I have no personal feelings toward him, and it wouldn't matter if I did."

"Very good."

Freddie went to her classes at Calvert College the next morning, not out of a sense of duty, but because it was a place to hide. Her phone had rung incessantly all night. One tape on her answering machine was filled and another inserted. To get some sleep, or at least a chance to think, she had turned the ring off, just letting the calls come into the machine.

When she played the tape, she was startled at first to hear David's voice: *This is David Sloane. I'm not in*

*at the moment because I'm wanted for two murders. I'll
return your calls when I finish my life term in . . .* Every
phone call was from a reporter. She neither answered or returned any of them. By first light her
house was besieged by the press, print, radio, and TV,
only the presence of the police keeping them from
breaking inside.

On the way to her car questions were hurled at her.
She gave answers she'd prepared. "No, I don't know
where my husband is." "No, I've not heard from
him." "Yes, I'm worried that something may have
happened to him." "I'm sure the police can answer
that better than I." "I assure you my husband is not a
murderer." If only she could be sure of that. *Okay,
Sloane, the other guy drew first. But I still want you out
of town by sunset.*

Her classes were better, but not much. The press
was kept out, but the eyes of "her girls" told her they
were not learning much in Poli Sci 103. Finally she
said, "I know you all have questions, but I simply have
no answers—like many of your test papers. I also
know many of you are concerned about me and want
to help. The best way to do that is to get on with this
class." *The prime of Miss Freddie Falscape.*

The Dean asked her if she wanted a few days off.
Freddie was so moved tears came to her eyes. *Such a
nice shoulder to cry on.* "Thank you. Maybe later.
Right now I need whatever dregs of normalcy I can
find."

"I understand."

"I'm sorry about all this"—she waved in the direction of the college gates—"this fuss."

Dean Bergen smiled. "I'm sure it'll help enroll-
ment." Then she patted her shoulder in reassurance.

Freddie phoned her parents in Connecticut, Doctor and Mrs. Frederick Falscape. Not too bad. Didn't weep more than a bucket. Didn't break down completely. *I know, Daddy. You warned me not to marry him. If a man kills once, he'll . . . But I love him, Daddy. I killed for him. I felt the gun jerking in my hand, saw the blood. Isn't that proof of love? You just don't know him. He's really a kind, gentle sweetheart, who happens to kill people.*

"I've some good news, Mother. I'm pregnant."

"That's wonderful. I'm so happy for you. Does David know?"

"I was coming home to tell him when . . ."

"Fern." Always called her Fern. Freddie was her husband. "Have faith. Everything will be all right, you'll see."

In her nighttime stalking of her house—*here, ladees and gennulmen, we see how the female of the species remains constantly in motion, evidence of pernicious schizophrenia and bad flossing*—Freddie had come to the same conclusion. She simply had to believe David was alive and all this would turn out well or she would come down with the terminal crazies. *Observe how the screaming and hair-pulling seems to alleviate some inner . . .* If he had survived Munich, he would survive this. Had to believe that, just had to.

They had met when he crawled into the back seat of her car in Munich, when she was on holidays. He'd stuck a gun in her ear, made her drive. He was all shot up. *Freddie dear, I'd like to introduce you to David Sloane. Don't pay attention to all those bullet holes.* Should've died. She saved his life, nursed him back to health, then helped him find Parsley. She'd leaned over the back seat of the car, her hand jerking as . . .

Don't think about it! How many thousands of times had he said that to her. *Yes, David darling, you're right.* It did work. She was able to think constructively about this new problem. There was no doubt in her mind—*well, just a little doubt*—that the two bodies and David's disappearance involved some kind of an intelligence game. That's how David—and she—thought of it, a game played endlessly, chewing up lives, money, and national substance, for no conceivable purpose other than continuation of the game. As David said, the prize for winning is that you get to play again. He had walked away. He would play no more. Apparently the game had found him. Of all the rotten luck. *Snakes keep biting me, doctor, and I don't know why.*

Yes she did. Her letter to the President. The Agency must have seen it, sent men to kill David, silence him forever. She shook her head. Didn't make sense. Why kill David? He knew nothing about the letter, had no involvement in it, would be mad at her for writing it. Maybe they were holding him for questioning. *My wife is an idiot. I'm not responsible for her stupid actions.* Yes, yes, on both counts. *Just release me and I'll beat some sense into her.* Please do. I deserve it. I need it.

No. Couldn't be. Two dead bodies to pick up a man for questioning? Mother didn't leave bodies lying around unaccounted for. She'd seen that with her own eyes. And why hadn't she been approached? She had written the letter, after all. Strange. What had happened? David must have killed those men. He carried no gun. She was sure of that. Yet somehow he had . . . Freddie noted her own reactions. When she first saw David kill a man she had been appalled. All her life she had hated guns, killing—killing anything. She'd be a vegetarian except she could never get enough to eat and rationalized the plant didn't want to die any more than the cow. Look at her now! She was hoping David had killed those men and was still alive. *Class, murder is a perfectly acceptable form of social intercourse. It just depends upon who does the murdering.*

About all she could conclude from her nocturnal pacing was that she just had to believe David was alive, that he had taken off to save his own life—and maybe spare her any involvement. He would do that. All she could do was wait—wait to hear from him, wait to discover what all this was about. Meanwhile, she'd say as little as possible, try to give police no clue to him or what he might be doing. That would be easy enough. *Dr. Falscape, when did you first begin to realize you knew nothing about anything?*

Captain Benning came to her office at midday, fortunately not in uniform. "Ms. Falscape, one of the deceased has been identified as Edziw Kawicki, a Polish businessman. The other is Gerald Sipes, an American, of Fairfax, Virginia. We are trying to learn more about them. Right now I'd like to know if either name has meaning to you?"

She repeated both names aloud, shook her head. "I've never heard of either one."

"You have no idea who they could be?"

Again she shook her head, her brown hair bouncing a little. "I want to be helpful. My husband is in the insurance business. Perhaps they are clients of—"

"We checked with his office. Both names are unknown."

"To me also. I'm sorry I can't be of help."

"Did you hear from your husband last night?"

She smiled. "You know I didn't. You must've tapped my phone."

Benning eyed her. Smart woman. Too smart to tell him anymore than she had to. "I have some news which may or may not relate to this case. Metropolitan Police found a rented car parked at a metered garage in Washington. Ford Escort, similar to the one seen near your home. Would your husband rent and drive such a car?"

Freddie felt her breath quicken, but maintained her calm exterior. "As far as I know he always drives his Audi. He adores the car."

"But might he have rented such a vehicle for some purpose you know nothing about?"

"It is possible, I suppose." She forced a smile. "A wife always thinks she knows *everything* about her husband, but that may be a chimera. Why do you think this car was rented by my husband?"

"We don't, of course. It is just that the front seat was full of blood and"—he hesitated—"the remains of somebody's brains. A bullet hole was found in the window of the passenger side."

"Oh, God!"

Benning watched her, as he planned to do. Her reaction was either natural or she could beat a lie detector with alacrity. He noted the wide eyes first, then the beginnings of tears, the expression of utter disappointment and fear. Damn good-looking woman. "Mrs.—I mean, Ms. Falscape, we have obtained some other information." He saw the brown eyes, especially luminous from tears, blink, her lips purse. She nodded for him to go on. "Your husband's office said he had an appointment yesterday evening with a group of doctors at a medical clinic near Annapolis."

"Yes. He had been trying to sell them a pension plan."

Benning nodded. "Apparently he succeeded. A . . ." Again he fished out the notebook, the cat-and-mouse game he affected. "A Dr. Redding at the Colonial Medical Center says that Mr. Sloane did indeed make that call. He left about six-thirty. In his pocket was a signed agreement for the pension plan and checks totaling forty-two thousand dollars."

Freddie stared at him, trying to comprehend. "What're you saying?"

"I'm not saying anything, at least not yet, Ms.—"

"He was robbed!" She rose from her chair at the small desk, face flushed, voice excited. "Men were waiting to rob him when he came home. He defended himself against two of them, then was—"

"He could do that? He could overpower two armed men?"

Freddie swallowed. "Yes, easily. David was a Navy lieutenant. He'd had combat training—or whatever they call it. Some kind of special training. He was very good at defending himself."

"I see." Benning did his best to keep his face a mask. "You believe he managed to kill two men, then was overpowered and abducted?"

"What else can have happened?"

"To what end?"

She recognized his little game. Slowly she sat back down, then smiled. "You are not dense, Captain. Neither am I. You said *checks*—forty-two thousand dollars in checks. Checks are not money. Obviously my husband will be forced to cash those checks and turn the money over to . . ." She gaped at him. "Captain, my husband is in great danger. As soon as he cashes those checks, he will be killed. You must find him, save him."

Benning heard her out. "Ms. Falscape, your husband went to his bank in Washington shortly after it opened this morning. He cashed checks totaling forty-two thousand dollars."

"*Oh, God!*"

"The manager at the bank reports that David Sloane did not appear wounded or hurt. He seemed normal in every way, except perhaps a little nervous. The manager had no choice but to give him the money. Unfortunately, the manager was unacquainted with last night's events."

"I told you. David was forced to cash the checks, turn the money over to—"

"He was quite alone, Ms. Falscape. No one was there pointing guns in his ribs. In fact he had ample opportunity to tell the manager that he was in danger. He said nothing of the kind."

Again Freddie rose, this time walking over to look out the small-paned window, the view of the campus below. "Are you suggesting that David stole the money?"

"He would not be the first insurance man to find such a large sum irresistible—especially if he has committed murder and is fleeing apprehension."

She turned back to him. "You are wrong, Captain, so very wrong. You don't know him. He is not that kind of man."

* * *

It was early afternoon before Sloane had time to really think. He lay on the sagging cot in the truly disreputable room of the flophouse off 16th Street NW, remembering his actions of the morning—he had been busy—to verify that he had done all that he should. Then he hoped to think about his *real* problem.

He'd left the car in the metered garage shortly before midnight. It wouldn't be found till morning, hopefully even later. Then he'd gone to a dive, managing to spill and drink enough booze so he smelled like the town drunk. His original intention was to hole up in Anacostia, the real ghetto of Washington, but he feared a white man might attract attention. He elected the Adams-Morgan district. Racially mixed. White, black, Hispanic, name it. Nobody's notice him here.

He chose this flophouse after casing it for escape routes and sight lines. Lots of ways out. He could see both the street and alley. He'd "signed" the "register" with a $20 bill. He didn't exist to the clerk. He'd gone to bed and actually slept. There were things to think about, but he forced them out of his mind.

First thing in the morning he bought a razor, shaving cream, and personal items, then attire appropriate to the area from a used clothing shop. Next he moved up the tonsorial ladder, buying new shoes and a serviceable suit to go to the bank. He'd tried to act nervous and evasive. It had gone well. Next he made more purchases, food, a bottle of whiskey, sunglasses, a couple of hats, a variety of makeup in darker shades, a wig, beard, and mustache. He was far from certain he'd need a disguise, but he wanted to be prepared in case he did. Next he took a cab to

Washington National Airport, renting a room at the Marriot Hotel, in back near the service entrance. Signed as George Bell, said he merely wanted the room for storage. No room service would be required. He paid in cash for a week. At the airport terminal he purchased a one-way ticket to Montreal, open-ended. He smiled and flirted with the ticket agent to make sure she would remember him.

Sloane reviewed his actions one more time. Yes, he'd left two false trails. The police probably had found the car and learned he had cashed the checks. When they found the body with his identification, it would be case closed. Robbery-murder. The story would be off the news in a day or so. Mother would know better. Their missing op. They'd go straight to the airport, stake out his rented room. Passengers on flights to Montreal would be under a lot of surveillance. Sloane nodded approval. Should give him a few days to move around a bit.

And do what? Sloane felt his mind moving toward the real problem, which he didn't want to face. He allowed another thought in. His first impulse had been to head for Greece or Turkey, where he knew he could disappear. The hell with Mother and whatever game was being played. He'd always longed for refuge in flight. Harry and he had had it all planned. Then it was too late for Harry. Sloane asked himself why he didn't run. Freddie? Probably. Couldn't do it to her. He'd tried once, but she wouldn't leave family, home, career, be a fugitive. He sighed. Pity the poor field op who's in love. There was another reason for not going. The puzzle was here, in Washington, this country at least. He had to solve it. Couldn't let it go. The bastards! They'd recruited him because, in their words, he was a "highly intelligent problem-solver." Shit! Solving a problem had killed Harry. Was he going to do it again—only this time to himself, maybe Freddie?

Finally he let the real problem in. Karamasov had come to him. Why? He knew Karamasov from his days as a field op. He'd "run into" him in Washington for a social drink. The true purpose was for the KGB to determine for certain that he had really retired. Sloane was sure he had convinced them. Why had Karamasov come to him last night? They were hardly buddies. His wound? Maybe he couldn't get any further.

Sloane forced himself to remember Karamasov's exact words. "Help me, please." "Not much time." Something else. He formed a mental image. Yes. "You must help." Bent over in pain. "Great danger. Help me." Yes, a dying man, struggling to stay alive to gasp last words. So great was Sloane's effort to recall exactly what had happened he could actually feel pain in his own midriff. "Your people have broken the Seraphim Code. You must tell . . ."

Sloane raised his arms, linking his fingers to form a cradle for his head. Yes. Unable to reach his own people with information he considered of great importance, Karamasov had come to him. Why? Chances are he was simply closest. The KGB would know where he lived and be watching his every move. For three years he had done nothing. They would know that. They would also know he hated the game. Even as field ops, Harry and he had tried to be evenhanded. They had never killed unnecessarily. The KGB would know that.

All right. Karamasov, dying, desperate to pass on

his information, had come to him. Sloane reduced the message to its essence. Your people have broken the Seraphim Code. No. He said *our* code. Your people have broken our Seraphim Code. Karamasov had learned, somehow, that the CSA had broken an important Soviet code called Seraphim. It could mean nothing else. "You must tell . . ."

Obviously, it was information of importance to the Soviet Union. "Great danger." Sloane rolled to the side of the cot and sat up. There had to be more. Yes. If Karamasov had come to him, a known if inactive CSA agent, an American agent, a sworn enemy, then he must have believed . . . Yes. "Great danger." Great danger to both sides. Whatever the Seraphim Code was, its being broken posed great danger to both the Soviet Union and the United States. Yes. Karamasov would've died before he revealed information vital to the Russians. By coming to him, he'd shown he believed that what he had learned was of vital importance to Americans too. If we knew what he knew, we would—do what?

"You must tell . . ." Tell whom? Sloane knew he had two choices. He didn't like either one. No point in going to the CSA. There had been two CSA operatives hiding in the dark. One with a nightscope on a Weatherby 300 had tried to kill him along with Karamasov. The second agent had come over to verify and finish the job. The CSA wanted him dead, and if they found him, they would surely finish the job. Why? Because Karamasov had come to him. He could think of no other reason.

The other choice was to go to the KGB. They were probably looking for him already. A veteran agent was killed in his backyard. They'd want to know why.

47

Had he said anything? Sloane nodded. The KGB would want to find and talk to him—a whole lot they would. He also knew the simplest solution to his problem was to go to the KGB. They at least didn't want to kill him.

No, it wasn't. Turning, going over to the other side, was abhorrent to him. More, he wanted out, out of the game—entirely. If he went to the KGB for protection he'd be so deep in the game he'd never get out. And Freddie? That wide-eyed, liberal do-gooder would never forgive him.

Third choice. Find out what the Seraphim Code was, then make a decision about what to do with the information. Sur-r-re! He had about as much chance of finding that out as he did flapping his arms and delivering the airmail. But what other choice did he have? Suddenly he laughed. If Freddie were here and he said that to her, she'd immediately stand up and start flapping her arms.

Sloane began now to think seriously about how he might discover what the Seraphim Code was, unconsciously nodding as he considered and approved his options. He was forming a plan and that made him feel better. The initiative would be his. The CSA and KGB would be reacting to him. He would not be sitting here waiting for them to come to him. Yes.

Deep under Dzerzhinsky Square, Moscow headquarters for *Komitet Gosudarstvennoi Bezopasnosti*, KGB, Dimitri Galenkov sat at his desk reading. His square, fleshy face was now deeply wrinkled. He was old, pained by gout, but beneath his spectacles, made from reindeer horn, his pale blue eyes remained alert. His unconscious pulling on his bushy brows was evidence of how deeply in thought he was.

In a moment he sat back in his chair. Karamasov dead. Mentally he paid his respects. Pavel had been one of the very good ones, loyal, dedicated, resourceful. What made him so very good was that his loyalties were to the *Rodina*, not the Party. Hard to find that any more. So many of the young ones cared only about the Party, proving loyalty, getting ahead.

Dimitri Galenkov sighed. Pavel dead. Not really much of a loss. He had been compromised long ago. His usefulness in recent years had been as a source of American disinformation. Karamasov enabled them to learn what disinformation the Americans were putting out. Knowing what someone wants you to believe, even if it is wrong, can be highly useful. But Pavel had chafed at his role. He insisted he still had good sources of information. It was a mistake not to believe him.

Galenkov leaned forward over his desk, re-read a moment, then leaned back. Karamasov dead. Why? The Americans knew who he was. What was their expression? Yes, the devil you know is better than the devil you don't. Why kill him now? By mutual agreement killing was passé, reserved for only the most extreme circumstances. Why kill Pavel Karamasov?

Had the Americans made a mistake? It was a CSA hit, not CIA. Rifle at close range. Body not removed. Fortunately Karamasov had carried fraudulent papers. That in itself indicated he was working on something.

Galenkov interrupted his thoughts to jot down a note to himself. Didn't trust his memory anymore.

Supervision was to be tightened at once. The fact that Karamasov was a veteran agent and only a source of disinformation was no excuse for not knowing exactly what he was doing at all times. Such carelessness must not happen again.

Instantly Galenkov's mind returned to his previous thought. Body not removed. Strange. Body of a CSA agent—he referred to a file of code names used by American agents—code name Ferret. Also at the scene. Even stranger. Formal police investigation. Galenkov could only shake his head in disbelief.

The residence of David Sloane. Galenkov smiled. Wolf. An old adversary. But he had retired after the Parsley affair. No doubt of that. Yet apparently there should have been doubt. Wolf could do this, kill two men. Had Wolf killed Karamasov? Galenkov picked up a piece of paper, a translation of the official police autopsy report. Two wounds in Karamasov. The wound from the rifle was fatal, but there had been another, earlier wound. Serious, but he had not died from it. Galenkov nodded his craggy head. Wolf had not killed Karamasov. The CSA had, in a formal, by-the-book hit. Wolf had fled. American police searched for him.

Galenkov leaned forward, resting his elbows on the desk, hands cradling his face. He was unaware of the incessant pulling on both his brows. Strange case, disturbing. It could be that Wolf was no longer with the CSA, as he claimed, but it could also be a very clever maneuver to make him think Wolf was not involved when he really was. Perhaps not. Karamasov had gone to Wolf. Why? Had to know.

Galenkov buzzed for Alexei Pavlovich, his executive assistant. He gave two orders. Everyone even remotely associated with Pavel Karamasov was to be thoroughly debriefed in hope of discovering some clue, no matter how small, as to what he was working on. He wanted every memo made by Karamasov sent to Moscow. Every phone call was to be traced. Everyone he spoke to was to be known. What Karamasov was doing would be learned, after which heads would roll. Such lax supervision would not be tolerated.

His second order was to find Wolf—David Sloane. He was to be taken, questioned—chemically debriefed, if necessary. Then Galenkov offered a carrot. Success in this just might reduce the punishment for the bungling in the Karamasov matter to a reprimand.

As an afterthought Galenkov issued a third order. After perusing the list of American personnel in the US Embassy in Moscow, he chose a name almost at random among the known CIA agents. Then he smiled, remembering an expression popular with American comedians. To Alexei he said, "No violence. He is to have a cold, a very bad Russian cold. It is the least we can do for Comrade Karamasov."

When he was alone, Galenkov thought of his order to find Wolf. He could remember not too long ago when such an order would have been foolishness. Wolf would not be taken. But he had been inactive three years. A man's skills erode rapidly. Maybe Sloane would be found.

THREE

The Committee did not meet that often, at least since he had been a member, so it still intrigued Cash how it was arranged. Five men, moving at precise times, made their way via secure elevators to the lowest levels of Brandywine. They never encountered each other until they were inside Space Three.

To get inside, he was first logged in, then required to leave behind everything in his pockets so that he possessed only the clothes on his back. Not even a pencil was carried inside. Since he was a heavy smoker, all this was a hardship. Next, he passed through a battery of rigorous surveillance devices: photo identifier, voice scanner, X-ray, metal detector, weight evaluator, finger-print analyzer. Finally, to enter Space Three he had to pass through two hermetically sealed doors with a passage in between.

At each door he had to press a long series of numerical buttons which both identified him as being authorized to enter and opened the door. The codes were different. One mistake and alarms went off at the first door. He would be at risk of being shot on the spot, no questions asked. At the second door, inside the sealed passage, he would be gassed. He had been told it was lethal gas. He hoped that wasn't so.

Space Three, one of five in the country, measured twelve by fifteen feet. Deep underground, it was made of four feet of reinforced concrete with a lead shield around that. It was indestructible, even at Ground Zero. And it was self-contained, with its own electrical supply, plumbing, air-conditioning, food, water, and other provisions to support a half-dozen people for a year. Space Three guaranteed the survival of the nation's leadership—that is to say, The Committee—if the holocaust came.

The Committee met there because Space Three was wholly secure. There were no communications in or out. No notes or recordings were made. There was no way to learn a single word ever uttered there, except through one of the members. And to speak those words, or even to confirm the existence of The Committee, was the equivalent of an act of suicide.

Being junior, Cash was the last to arrive. He was nominally their equal, yet he remained in awe of them. They were older, far more experienced. They had risen to The Committee simply because over the years they had accumulated and jealously guarded so much information about worldwide military, diplomatic, economic, ideological, and intelligence affairs that no decision vital to national security could be made without their knowledge and participation.

53

Each had in effect appointed himself. Cash was far from certain this applied to him, however. He knew he was in a learning situation and felt inadequately informed next to these men. He didn't belong and wondered how he got there. He knew no answer except that it related in some way to W. Gordon Adams.

This was no social gathering. No pleasantries were exchanged. Wit, any compulsion to self-revelation were frowned upon. He knew none of them personally, not even their names. They addressed each other by code names, Mr. Black, Mr. White, Mr. Brown, Mr. Gray. He was Mr. Green. When they had occasion to speak by secure phones within the confines of Brandywine, it was in code words. They never met outside Brandywine, each filing and slavishly adhering to a rigid schedule which accounted for their whereabouts at all times. The result was that they led extremely dull lives. They were totally anonymous. To give a speech or interview, to have one's photo in the paper, to be identified as a person of importance, let alone an employee of the Central Security Agency, was to be off The Committee and probably dead.

In his months on The Committee it had not yet ceased to surprise Cash just how effortlessly these five men controlled the national security affairs of the nation. They had in place a brilliantly simple system called Need to Know. The CSA had three main powers. First, it was equipped to intercept any message sent electronically anywhere on the planet. Second, it made all codes used by the United States Government. Third, it decoded all messages sent by foreign governments. These three powers combined to put the CSA in absolute control of all encoded information.

The US used hundreds of codes. They were arranged in a hierarchy, each person able to read the message in inferior codes, but none in higher and more secure codes. The Committee sat at the apex of the hierarchy, able to read and possess the information locked in all codes used by the government.

When Need to Know was applied to this system, the results truly startled Cash. Through control of codes, The Committee knew what information another person, indeed every other person, possessed. It was a simple matter to feed that person a little additional information—in the code he was authorized to decipher—which altered his knowledge, thoughts, and actions in a way desired by The Committee. This was Need to Know. A person was told only what he needed to know to think in a certain way or perform a desired task. He had no way to ascertain the significance of that act or how it might relate to the actions of other people, for that information was concealed in higher codes unknown to him. Privates and seamen, generals, and admirals, clerks, cabinet officers, and Congressmen, even the "Chief Executive" in the White House, were told, sometimes in "highly classified briefings" based on "highly classified information"—and none of them had a prayer of determining the accuracy or completeness of the information imparted to them—what they needed to know to think and act in a manner desired by The Committee.

Cash considered all this mind-boggling. The system made instant figureheads out of all persons in government. Rank and title were meaningless. Only security classification and access to coded information had any value. Cash recognized it as a system of thought control. This was not a moral judgment on Cash's part, however. He was just grateful to be on The Committee, one of the manipulators, not the manipulated.

The meeting began in its usual efficient style with each member reporting on the activities of his zone. Mr. Brown, who was in charge of the Asia zone, spoke first. As senior man on The Committee he conducted the meeting, keeping it flowing, but all the members were equal. His report was terse and brief, dwelling only on those matters which might relate to other zones or affect those national security matters which The Committee considered as a whole. It did not concern itself with the nuts and bolts of zonal operations. As a matter of course each man was considered to be on top of all matters in his zone. To suggest otherwise was interference and a discourtesy.

Nonetheless, when Cash's turn, as Mr. Green, came to discuss the European zone, he felt he was asked too many questions, certainly more than the others. His answers were accepted. No one argued with him. But he had the sense he was being watched, or maybe guided more. He tried to attribute this to his junior status and not get his nose out of joint about it.

Mr. Brown now spoke. "Special projects next." These were handled differently. Each man was responsible for an aspect of the plan or operation, regardless of which zone it affected. "Can we set a date for Seraphim?"

Mr. Black: "Not precisely. The Red Navy will

determine that. But it looks at the moment like early or the middle of May. I think we should figure on that."

Brown: "Does this time frame cause difficulties for anyone?" He looked at White. "How about the military?"

White: "Should be okay. Training is going on right now. The first full-scale test is scheduled for Thursday. We should be in good shape by May."

Gray: "Is the target set?"

Black: "If you mean is it aboard, no. But it is prepared. We cannot control exactly when it will be taken aboard."

Gray: "Prepared? Are you certain? It has to be fail-safe."

Black: "It is. It's a guarantee—or as close to one as we're ever going to get."

Brown: "I'm worried about the technology."

White: "I know this laser is new, but it has been tested and re-tested. It has never failed. But if it does, all we have is a no-go on the operation, a scrub."

Cash felt the need to speak. "It's an all-win-no-lose operation."

Black: "Ever hear of Murphy's Law?"

Cash as Green: "The worst that can happen is nothing."

Brown: "What about the White House?"

Gray: "The President signed the blank authorization."

Brown: "Who'd you use?"

Gray: "CIA director. Grayson asked him a lot of questions for which he had no answers."

White: "Except national security." He smiled.

Black: "Did we need the blank authorization?"

Brown: "We decided that at the last meeting."

Black: "I still think we should just do it and let the White House be surprised. The blank authorization alerts him that something is under way."

Brown: "I say again, Grayson is edgy. He's worrying about his place in history. He wants to play President. We can't—"

White: "Is he out of control?"

Gray: "No, but the blank authorization helps. If push comes to shove, he is responsible. It enables us to control the repercussions."

Brown: "What he might want to do after the fact." He looked at Black. "The issue is settled. He has signed."

White: "Mr. Green, have we problems with security?"

Cash: "Not that I know of."

White: "This fracas with Karamasov. Did you order him killed?"

Cash: "Yes."

White: "North America is my zone. It would have been nice to know about it." There was sarcasm in his voice.

Cash: "I am in charge of Seraphim security. I thought it best."

Brown: "Why did you order the hit? Had he breached security?"

Cash: "It was just a precaution. He was meeting Sloane, our former operative. I decided to eliminate both. As I say it was a precaution. Neither will be missed."

White: "It is still my zone. If, as you say, neither knew about Seraphim, you had no business—"

Brown: "You point is noted, Mr. White. Mr. Green, I gather you were not entirely certain Karamasov knew nothing about Seraphim."

White: "Yes. Why the hell did you kill him? He should've been taken, debriefed. The matter would be settled then."

Cash: "It is settled in death." He smiled.

White: "Is it? You failed to get Sloane. He is well-known to us. You've opened up a can of worms."

Cash: "He knows nothing about Seraphim."

Brown: "How can you be sure of that?"

Cash: "Karamasov was already mortally wounded. He could've said nothing to Sloane, even if he had anything to tell him."

A heavy silence fell over the table. It was protracted, unnerving to Cash.

White: "The thing to do is find Sloane and eliminate the problem. It is my zone. I'll—"

Brown: "Mr. Green started this. I suggest he finish it—with your cooperation of course. Any objections, Mr. White?"

White shrugged.

Brown: "Sloane was a wily, canny operative. He will not be easy. I suggest you consult Gordon Adams about him."

Cash: "I already have."

When Cash returned to his office he was shaking and perspiring heavily. All he wanted in life was a shower.

Freddie sat in the back of the police cruiser, Captain Benning in front with the driver. They had gotten her out of her class, saying it was important.

"A body was found early this morning in the Bay, off Cedar Point at the mouth of the Patuxent. We'd like you to take a look at it."

"You think it's my husband?" She looked at Benning. "That's a silly question, isn't it?"

He nodded, then tried to make up for it. "Don't jump to conclusions, Ms. Falscape. We won't know anything till—"

Sure.

She rode in silence, ostensibly staring out the window at the Maryland countryside, lush now with daffodils and tulips and azaleas, among her favorites, but in reality she was struggling to dam a rising flood of panic. She was not succeeding. The dike was breaking. Maybe she should grab a tree limb and . . . How had David put it once? "We're holding on to life by our grubby fingernails." Yes. And she used to have such nice nails—B.S. Before Sloane.

She had begun by saving his bullet-riddled life, then progressed to detesting him and everything he stood for. He was a cynical s.o.b., and that was one of his more endearing qualities. What he was was a killer. She watched him in horror, then crawled into his sleeping bag beside a lake in the Italian Alps, fell in love, and ultimately killed to save his life again. *What I did for love.* She felt the jerking motion in her hand. It was never going to go away, never. But *he* had. Life in the A.S., After Sloane. So be it. A sharp, together girl—*oops, woman*—didn't belong with a cynical jerk who had been trained by his government to be homicidal and halfway suicidal. *God, she'd miss him. We were making it, weren't we, David? Junior, this is a picture of your daddy. He was a field op and went around killing people. When you grow up you're going to be just like him.*

"Turn in there, just ahead on the right."

She turned at the sound of Benning's voice and saw him point to a funeral home. "Where are we?"

"Lexington Park. No morgue near here."

She was led inside, past a flower-draped casket, then downstairs to the business end of the mortuary. *This is where they suck your guts out your asshole and break your legs so you fit in the casket. My, doesn't he look nice. So lifelike.* She shook. *Stoppit, dammit!*

Benning spoke. "Wait here a moment, with Officer Black."

She looked at Officer Black, seeing him for the first time. He really was black. *How strange. I thought all black people were named White. Hi, I'm Fern Falscape. You may call me Freddie. All my friends do. Never been out with a black man. I understand you people have— Stoppit! I'm a widow, you know.*

She watched Benning say something to a short, bald man in a white coat, then pick up something from a table. Wallet. He opened it, pulled out cards. *That's not really his name, you know. He's really David Stuart Pritchard. My son is named after him. Why are my eyes smarting, doctor? You have an incurable eye disease.* "Captain Benning, is it him?" *He, you idiot. Good grammar is important at a time like this.*

She strode the dozen steps to where he stood. *Walking is instinctive in the species. Once learned, it is never forgotten.* He handed her David's Maryland driver's license. *Miss Falscape, when did you first realize you were having difficulty swallowing?* She handed the license back to him. "That's the jacket and pants he wore." *Oh, God!* She picked up his watch, looked at the back. *To D.S.P. from F.L.F.* She'd had it engraved as a not very subtle hint that she wanted him to use his real name.

"Those aren't his initials."

"It's his watch."

Wedding band. It was his. *Do thou, Fern, take this man till death do you part.* She couldn't read the inscription inside. Something wrong with her vision. "M-May I . . . have these?" She wiped at her cheek. "I—I'd like the . . . watch and—" *Oh, God!* "Wedding band. It's the one . . . I g-gave him."

"I'm truly sorry."

She saw it in his eyes, in the hand touching her shoulder. She nodded. "Me too."

"I can't let you have his things right now, but I'll see that you get them in a few days."

"Thank you." She turned away toward the double stainless-steel doors. She knew what lay beyond. "I'd like to see him if I may?"

The undertaker cleared his throat. "Ma'am, I don't think that's wise. The body is . . ." He sighed. "It's not a very pretty sight, ma'am."

She looked at him, then at Benning. "Doesn't someone have to identify the body, Captain? Who else do you have in mind?"

He nodded, then took her arm at the elbow and, accompanied by the undertaker and Officer Black, led her through the double doors. The body lay on a stainless-steel table under a sheet.

"Just like the movies."

She reached to pull back the sheet, but the undertaker stopped her. "Ma'am, there are several bullet wounds to the face and head. Not much of it left to recognize."

She stared at him. Her voice hardened. "What d'you say we stop this pussyfooting around and get on with it?" It was a deliberate act, seeking refuge in anger. Humor wasn't working very well. She lifted the sheet. Gasped. *"God!"* She looked away. It was ghastly, the head just a mass of crumpled bones.

Even Benning was shaken. He had seen a lot, but never this. His arm came around her shoulders. "C'mon. There is no way to tell."

"Yes there is." She lifted the sheet higher, then folded it back. The body was naked, a tag tied to a toe.

On the ride back she kept saying over and over to herself, "Thank God for tears." She would not have been able to pull it off otherwise. Benning thought her bereft, when her tears were really relief and joy. It was not David.

"It's him."

"Are you sure?"

"Every woman knows her husband."

She didn't know how she knew to do it. She had been so sure it was David. The mangled head even had black hair. Then when it wasn't him, it hit her all at once. Thank God for tears. Gave her time to think. He wanted her to say it was him. David was alive! *Thank you, God, oh thank you, thank you.* He'd done it before, buying time by mutilating another body, putting his identification on it. He was counting on her to help him. He needed her.

The hardest part was masking her elation, playing out the role of grieving widow. Then somewhere during the ride back home she didn't have to. Depression struck her almost as a physical blow. Just because that wasn't David on that particular table didn't mean he wasn't on another one. She really didn't know if he was alive—or for how long. Then another thought beat on her. Who was the dead man? Somebody's son, husband, father. Someone was grieving or should be. No. Another MIA. Damn Mother! Damn this *fucking* game! *Welcome to the pits, my dear. You've seen the Marquis de Sade room, and the dungeons, of course. But you haven't visited our splendid catacombs. They extend for miles. I'm sure you'll adore them.*

In his youth Gordon Adams had been in the field. Code Word Two operative. Balkans in the bad old days. Twice inside Russia. Partner killed. He still had scars. After plastic surgery to alter his appearance, he was taken inside, ultimately into Brandywine and The Committee. He always felt his field experience gave him an edge. Helped him understand what could and could not be done. He tried to be a counterweight to the shrinks and code-breakers, computer wizards and pencil-pushers who sat in Brandywine dreaming up harebrained schemes that mostly made fodder out of field men. He suspected there was no one with field experience on The Committee now. Cash certainly didn't have any. Too bad.

Adams had been in the field less than a year, but he had not forgotten. The wariness was instinctive, and he spotted the car as soon as he pulled into his drive in Georgetown. Dark blue Buick Skylark. Two men in front, another in back. Adams drove into his garage, entered his house through the rear door, turned on the lights, opened a can of beer from the refrigerator. Carrying it, he opened the front door and brought in the newspapers. Car still there. Amateurs.

He finished the beer, forcing his mind to read the paper. David Sloane's body recovered from the Bay. Positive ID by his grieving widow. Very good. He smiled. Freddie Falscape was a sharp girl, no two ways about it. He read on. Police now believed Sloane was a robbery-murder victim. They now searched for . . . Splendid.

Adams went upstairs, showered, changed into comfortable sport shirt, slacks, jacket, and loafers, then went out to dinner. Little Italian place he favored. Venetian food. He had rissotto and veal.

They took him outside his garage when he came home. Two men. Skylark roared up. He was shoved into the back seat, blindfolded. Good blindfold. Couldn't see anything. He did not resist. Amateurish. That's what began to worry him. The KGB was not above hiring hoods, even street scum. And there was no question but what they would want tit-for-tat for Karamasov. Then he smelled expensive cologne. It made him feel better.

He was driven around for awhile. That's how he thought of it. Lots of turns. Weren't really going anywhere. Just trying to confuse him. He suspected they were still within Georgetown. After twenty minutes to a half hour the car stopped. Doors opened and he was pulled out. Men at each side, clutching his arms, led him up a walk, through a door. Warmer inside. Kitchen odors. Another door. Carpet, thick and plush. Odors of flowers, or maybe just room deodorizer. Another door opened. Led inside. Musty odor. Books. A library. His arms were released. Whisper of shoes on carpet. Door closing.

"You may remove your blindfold now, Mr. Adams."

He recognized the voice. He pulled off the blindfold, aware now it was a heavy black silk scarf, then blinked against the light. He first looked to see that he was alone. His abductors had gone. Then he met the gaze of the man seated in a maroon leather chair. "Mr. President."

Marvin Grayson raised a tall glass held in his hands. "I'm sorry for this inconvenience. Can I make it up to you by offering you one of these."

"Thank you, Mr. President."

The Chief Executive rose and went to a table behind his chair. It was outfitted with assorted bottles, glasses, an ice bucket. "What will you have, Mr. Adams?"

"Whatever you are, sir."

"Bourbon and branchwater it is. My illustrious predecessor Lyndon Johnson and I have that much in common, at least."

Adams heard the musical clink of ice dropping in the glass. He looked around. Library, all right. Posh. Matched sets of books on shelves. Harvard Classics. Oxford Dictionary. On the wall a Brueghel. Looked genuine. Thick carpet. Furniture genuine leather. Grand mahogany desk. High-back chair. No window. Private home. Bet his last dollar it was in Georgetown.

"It is difficult to obtain privacy in a goldfish bowl, which is what the White House is. I imposed upon a friend to let me use his residence for our little chat. He is not involved in this. If you have any idea who our host might be, I'd appreciate if it you'd keep it to yourself."

Adams accepted the highball. "Yes, sir."

"I'm sure you are very good at keeping things to yourself." Grayson motioned to a chair next to the one he had been using. "Have a seat. Smoke if you wish." He smiled, the same grand spread of orthondontia seen for years on television. "I kicked the habit several years ago. May be the best thing I've ever done."

"I did too, sir." Adams sat, recognizing within himself that he was impressed. With his white hair and square, tanned face, Marvin Grayson was even more handsome than he appeared on the tube. And bigger, both in height and weight, then he had imagined. The celebrated smile was more grand too, but neither it nor his calculated drawl and down-home mannerisms denied the penetrating intelligence of his blue eyes. There was command in them. This man was President of the United States and knew it.

"Let me see what I can remember. W. Gordon Adams. The W stands for Willis, which you dislike. Age fifty-two. Address—well, I guess you know where you live. Divorced, then widowed. Too bad about the second Mrs. Adams. My condolences. Two grown children, a son and daughter, from the first marriage. You don't see much of them. You live alone. Reputation as a workaholic. No close friends or hobbies. Employed as a GS-12 at the Office of Naval Procurement. All that about right, Gordon—if I may call you that?"

"You may, sir. And that is about right."

"In fact, you live a very dull life, don't you?"

"I suppose so."

Grayson smiled. "But you really don't, do you?" He raised his glass, swallowed. "Do you know what really grabs you about being President, Gordon? It's something most people wouldn't think of. It's that moment when you stand up there on the podium before millions of your countrymen, put your hand on the bible, and swear to preserve, protect, and defend the Constitution of the United States. Hits you right between the eyes. All that trust placed in you. That long thin line of men, your predecessors in office, who have each in turn taken the same oath. Some were inferior men. A few were downright scoundrels who obtained the office by means best forgotten to history. But I can tell you right now, the moment everyone of them took that oath he was shaking in his boots that he might fail to measure up. Pundits write about Presidents worrying about their place in history. That's bullcrap from people who've never been there and don't know. What motivates you is the sense of obligation to preserve, protect, and defend the Constitution, to pass it on to the next man in at least as good a shape as you received it."

Adams saw how emotional he was. He knew better than to utter a word.

"That oath of office also contains the words 'to the best of my ability.' That's right. Good words. Madison and Hamilton and others wrote them. Even George Washington helped. Those men knew what they were doing. There are those who say the words are a cop-out. I did the best I could. So the Constitution goes down the drain. Not my fault. But I'm not about to be that way, Gordon. I know I haven't done my best. I'm about to. I'm about to preserve, protect, and defend the Constitution. And whether you know or like it, you are about to help me, W. Gordon Adams."

Suddenly he smiled, broadly, holding it, a characteristic, much-practiced expression. "What say we cut the bullcrap, Gordon? I've made my little speech, so let's get on with it. I know who you are. You don't know enough about Naval procurement to keep a tugboat outfitted in pantyhose. I know the ONP pays your salary, but nobody over there has laid eyes on you in the memory of man. What you really are, Gordon, is a high mucky-muck with the CSA."

Adams felt his eyes boring into him.

"What exactly is it you do over there?"

Adams swallowed, but he refused to look away, no matter how much he wanted to.

"Gordon, this is the President of the United States, Commander in Chief of the Armed Forces, asking you a direct question. We are alone. There is just the two of us. I assure you this room was checked within the hour for bugs. No transcript, either aural or written, is being made. Now I want an answer to my question."

Another swallow. "I am a consultant, sir."

"A consultant." Grayson shook his head. "I don't want to know your cover story, Gordon. I am asking you for the simple truth."

"It is the truth, Mr. President. I retired from active participation in Agency affairs almost three years ago." He tried to smile, not very successfully. "I merely give advice and opinions."

The blue eyes bored into him from under the white brows. Finally Grayson said, "I believe you, Gordon. Prior to your retirement, exactly what were your duties?"

Swallow. "I was involved with Agency activities in Europe."

"I see. Involved? How involved?"

Adams uncrossed, then re-crossed his legs.

"Would you like another drink?"

Adams hadn't touched it. "No, sir, I'm fine. I-I don't drink very much."

"I figured you didn't. What were your duties, Gordon?"

He cleared his throat. "Over the years I had accumulated some expertise in—"

"I'm sure you did. Were you in charge of intelligence affairs in Europe?" He waited, then glared at Adams. "I thought you and I were going to cut the bullcrap."

"Yes, sir, I was."

"Were you a member of The Committee?"

"What committee is that, Mr. President?"

"*The* Committee, Gordon. Were you a member?"

"I'm afraid I don't understand, Mr. President."

"Don't you?" The blue eyes remained on him a moment, then he swallowed the dregs of his drink and immediately rose to make another. "I don't usually indulge myself with more than one of these, but your obstinacy is enough to drive a saint to drink." At once he relieved the statement with a chuckle, but it was dry, humorless.

Adams heard ice drop into the glass, now as a thunk.

"Gordon, just the other day I received a letter from a remarkable young woman. I've never met her, but I hope to one day. She is a patriot, a person who understands what it means to preserve, protect, and defend the Constitution. In her letter she related to me how the CSA uses codes to control the dissemination of national security information and manipulate the beliefs and actions of this government, including me. There was nothing in that letter I didn't already know. Every President since Harry Truman has known it, decried it, lamented it, at least to himself, chafed under what is really a perversion of the Constitution. And each one of them, to the best of his ability, has tried to find a way to end that CSA manipulation and return this land to constitutional government. Four, perhaps five of those men came to know the bitter sting of failure. I don't think I need to identify them to you. Now it is my turn. I intend to rope and hog-tie The Committee. You are going to help me. Sure you don't care for another drink?"

Adams watched him come around the chair and sit down.

"Gordon, that young woman who wrote me, bless her, armed me with something I don't believe any of my predecessors had—a name. *Your* name. Gordon, I went to a lot of pains to set up this little interview. It is just the two of us. No person will ever know a word uttered in this room unless you choose to tell them. I know. I am putting your life at risk in asking you to tell me about The Committee and its activities. But surely you, of all people, realize my life is also at risk in hearing the answers you are about to give me. To borrow that old expression of another patriot, we will either hang together or we will hang separately." He laughed. "I doubt if the CSA uses hanging much anymore, though."

Adams looked at him a long moment, then smiled.

It was a sort of spreading of the lips. He didn't show much tooth when he smiled. "You don't give a man much of a choice, do you?"

The big grin. "I try not to, whenever I can."

Adams nodded and stood up. "Do you mind if I look around. It isn't that I don't trust you, but—"

"Be my guest."

Adams made a quick but thorough inspection of the room. It took about ten minutes. He was still checking out the desk when he said, "What would you like to know, Mr. President?"

"Start from the beginning. It is always best."

Adams hesitated. "It may take some time, sir."

"I have all night."

For nearly an hour Adams related the principal CSA activities since its founding in 1952 by order of Harry S Truman, an order that few people have ever seen. For the sake of brevity, Adams limited himself to those operations which directly affected the Presidency, and even then gave them in summary form. Grayson mostly listened, asking only a few questions to clarify his understanding. Yet his face mirrored his reactions; disbelief, consternation, anger, finally an almost imponderable sadness. When Adams had brought him up to date, Grayson's words gave no hint of what he might be thinking. "Now tell me how The Committee operates."

"It is really quite simple, Mr. President."

"All things that work well are simple. That's what's wrong with our military. They depend on too many gadgets which nobody can figure out."

Adams then described the structure of The Committee and how it used control of coded information, plus Need to Know, to manipulate the beliefs and actions of all others in government.

"In other words, ignorance is not bliss."

Adams saw that he was seething with inner rage. "I guess that is one way to put it, sir."

The Presidential highball was shaking as it was brought to his lips. "It is not very pleasant to know you have been duped, Mr.—I mean, Gordon."

"I wouldn't put it that way, Mr.—"

"Oh yes you would." His voice rose. "The Committee has reduced me, this office, to the level of a figurehead. Why I'm just a damn puppet, a marionette dancing on a string held by that damn Committee." He visibly shook with anger. "I don't like it very much, Gordon."

Adams could think of nothing to say.

Then Grayson smiled. It seemed to be an action which triggered the release of his anger. His voice approached normal. "You say members of The Committee are unknown, anonymous?"

"For practical purposes, Mr. President, they are nameless and faceless. Even when I was a member I could not identify a single member. No one in the Agency, except the members, know for certain The Committee even exists, let alone who is on it."

"Except you."

"I said I could not identify anyone. That is the truth."

"Amazing, simply amazing." He picked up his empty glass and sipped some of the melted ice. "Surely these people know what they are doing is a perversion of the Constitution, that what they are doing may one day get this country into terrible trouble. What on earth motivates them? Is it power? Do they enjoy their power?"

Adams rendered his toothless smile. "I'm sure they do, but they have a higher motive—or believe they do." He hesitated. "I don't believe you'll want to hear it, sir."

"Try me."

Adams sighed, then again, actions designed to give him time to think of the most tactful way to express all this. "The President is elected for only four years, eight at the most. Even if he is intelligent, hardworking, and astute, such as yourself, there is no possible way he can learn enough about what has happened in the past, is going on now, and is likely to occur in the future to make an intelligent decision about national security matters."

"I am not trusted?"

"In a manner of speaking, yes, sir. The White House is a public building. People can virtually walk in off the street."

"Hardly."

"Mr. President, you know how many people work there. Are you certain everyone of them is entirely loyal?"

"Don't go too far."

Adams saw the glint of anger in his eyes. "Put it this way, sir. CSA operations, all intelligence matters, depend on secrecy, not only for success but for the lives of the people involved. Information cannot fall into the hands of people who, if not disloyal, show poor judgment in whom they confide in."

"Are you talking about me?"

Adams realized he was squirming in his chair. "Mr. President, there are always a few people in the White

House who are not above saying a few words to a pet reporter, for example. They may be feathering their own nest. They may believe they are helping you politically.''

Grayson nodded. "Now you make some sense. The White House is a sieve of leaks. Every President has tried to stop it."

"Sir, every President comes to the White House through a political process. The Committee simply feels that the national security of this nation cannot be decided on the basis of what is good politics. The Committee feels it must make hard decisions for the President, decisions he could not make himself."

Grayson bolted out of his chair. "Over my dead body!" Then he gaped. "It might come to that, mightn't it?"

Adams said nothing.

The Chief Executive began to pace the floor, deep in thought. After several trips to the doorway and back to his chair, he said, "The other day I was asked—Ha! Forced is more like it—to sign a blank authorization. Oh, it wasn't blank. It contained a lot of gobbledygook about national security, surveillance of Soviet military activities, testing of communications and national defense capabilities, and so on. But there was no way to read it and make any sense of it." He saw Adams smile. "Is that how it's done?"

"Yes, sir."

"It's a CSA operation, isn't it? One of The Committee's little surprises for me, the country, and the world? I want to know what it is, Gordon."

"I don't know, sir. I've been off The Committee for almost three years. I am deliberately not informed

75

about current operations. Need to Know is applied to me just as it is to you."

Grayson gave his famous smile. "But you can find out, can't you?"

A sigh came from Adams. "I don't know how I could, sir. And if I did find out, I wouldn't live long enough to tell you."

"They play for keeps, don't they?"

"Yes, sir."

"Did you know Richard Nixon used those exact words in his so-called 'smoking-gun tape' during Watergate? He really did know something was going on, but he was powerless to tell anyone." Grayson shrugged. "But that is another matter. Exactly how is it that you are going to help me find out what this CSA operation is?" He smiled. "You are going to help me, aren't you?"

"There might be a way. Would you tell me who wrote that letter which identified me?"

"I'm afraid I can't do that."

"I think I already know. The letter was written by a woman named Fern L. Falscape. She is the only person who can possibly identify me. She was involved in an operation which led to discovery of a Soviet mole on The Committee. In the process she identified me. I was compromised and off The Committee at once."

"Tell me about this Parsley affair."

Adams did briefly, then said, "The agent who found Parsley is now the husband of Fern L. Falscape."

"I see."

"His name is David Sloane. He has been in the news lately as—"

"Don't tell me all that was CSA?"

"One of the dead men was a KGB agent named Karamasov, the other a CSA operative. You will soon hear that Sloane is dead. I wouldn't believe that if I were you, Mr. President."

Grayson shook his head. "You people! I swear! No wonder the public doesn't believe a thing the government tells them any more." He looked at Adams. "You think this Sloane knows something about the current CSA operation?"

"I don't know, sir. Something is going on which I don't understand. The Agency believes Sloane has turned, gone over to the KGB. I don't know why. It may be because he was meeting Karamasov. But in front of his own house?" Adams shook his head. "Doesn't make sense. It is simply out of character for the Sloane I knew to aid the enemy. Impossible for me to believe."

"He's alive, you say?"

"Yes. The Agency ordered both Sloane and Karamasov killed. But it was bungled. Sloane escaped. It is possible, Mr. President, this Sloane-Karamasov incident may relate in some way to this mysterious operation which you"—he smiled—"authorized."

"How?"

"As I say, I don't know. The only way to learn is to find Sloane and get him to tell us."

"Then do it."

Adams's smile was so broad he actually showed some teeth. "That is the second such order I've received. The agency has put me in charge of the hunt for Sloane."

"Really?" The Presidential grin was pure delight. "How wonderful! You'll be using that damn CSA to find the very man we want."

"It won't be easy, sir. The Agency wants him killed on sight. You want him saved for questioning."

"But you can pull it off."

"I can try."

Another Grayson smile. " 'To the best of my ability.' See that it is your best, Gordon. And another thing. You are working for me now, personally and confidentially. I trust that will not create a problem with your loyalties."

"Oh, it will, Mr. President, but what choice do I have? You've blown my cover. Having told you what I just did, I can either work with you and hope for the best or I can be dead."

"Both of us can be dead. Rest assured no one will know of our little discussion. When the time comes, by which I mean after we have discovered this CSA operation and caught them with their hands in the cookie jar, we will decide together what steps are best taken next."

"Thank you, Mr. President."

Grayson lavished his best smile on him. "What's that term you used? Oh, yes, turned. You've been turned, haven't you?"

"I believe that's what they call it, Mr. President."

FOUR

Many times Captain Lawson Jones Price regretted ever going into Naval Intelligence, not that he had much choice in the matter. But it was a career mistake. At age sixty-two it looked like he was stuck at captain. An eagle on his shoulder was nice, but Captain Price simply did not have the ring of Admiral Price, which he surely would have become had he remained a saltwater sailor. Such a disappointment. Through his mother, his lineage went back to John Paul Jones, hence his middle name. His surname came from his uncle, Vice Admiral Lee "Sugarbush" Lawson, famed at Coral Sea. He felt he looked the part of an admiral, crew-cut hair the color of steel, ramrod back. His far vision from gray-green eyes was superb. He exuded command. So much for appearances. Fat lot of good it had done him.

In his early years Naval Intelligence had seemed a good idea. He had come out of World War II with the rank of lieutenant commander. Then in 1952 much of Naval Intelligence, always strategic and worldwide in scope, became the core of the newly formed Central Security Agency. Price figured he'd do well with the new agency, eventually rising to director, a vice admiral at least.

Didn't happen. He was shunted aside to become Director of Training at Corry Field in Pensacola, earning only one more stripe. He came to understand too late why this happened. His classification, Code Word Two, was too high. People with a high classification never achieved much rank. It made them too visible to the Navy brass. Most Code Word two people were junior officers and enlisted men, situated to manipulate admirals by controlling the code machine. Actually Price knew he was lucky to make captain. He did so because he was director of training, which called for some rank. He alone knew the nature of the training done at Pensacola. This called for his high security classification. He sighed. Being in the spook business was no way to make admiral. Fine time to find that out.

He had been hustled from Pensacola to Brandywine, where he was briefed by Gordon Adams, no less. Supposedly retired. Said he had been brought back because he had used Wolf in a lot of operations. But his knowledge of Wolf was nothing compared to Price's. "Guess we old-timers have some use after all." The term annoyed Price. He didn't figure he was ready for that category. Then Adams gave him his instructions. Find and dispose of David Sloane. He was not to be taken and chemically debriefed. Kill him on sight. Adams said he had turned. Hard to believe. But it was something neither of them could question.

Yes, he could find Sloane if anyone could. He had made a special study of the methods used by Sloane and Rogers and incorporated them into the training program. Sloane and Rogers had been the quintessential field ops, absorbing training, then devising methods superior to those they were taught. They'd even developed their own code, which CSA computers had been unable to break. They'd used it to withhold information from the Agency. Maybe that was the real reason Sloane was to be killed, even at this late date. He knew too damn much.

A great mistake had been made, not just with Sloane and Rogers, but with the entire CSA method of field operations. Price was certain of it. Naval Intelligence had long worked—still did—on the principle of the Cell, a group of individual agents performing a mission under supervision. So the KGB used the same method. That was no reason for the CSA to change. He figured the Russians just might know what they were doing. But the Agency became obsessed with secrecy. Everything was Need to Know, and the number of people who really knew the purpose of any operation was reduced and reduced, then shrunk until hardly anybody knew anything. The Cell was discarded in favor of field ops working in pairs. They were recruited and matched, then trained as a team and sent into the field together. They became like twins, only more so. No finer example than Sloane and Rogers. Symbiotic. They could read each other's minds. When Rogers was killed in Munich, the pair was broken. Sloane retired.

He could never work with anyone else. Such a waste. But then there were lots of broken pairs around.

The great advantage of the system was supposed to be that it was virtually impossible for the KGB to infiltrate a pair. And Need to Know could be applied to them, so they could be more easily controlled than a Cell. But field ops like Sloane and Rogers had quickly learned to withold information, thus turning Need to Know back against the Agency. Price figured the Agency lost more information than it gained through use of autonomous pairs. The Cell was simply a more efficient way to run an intelligence operation. He'd prove it to the agency with this hunt for Sloane.

Price sat at a small table in a vacant office in the Federal Court House in Washington. Sparsely furnished, it was a safe house, unbugged and with a secure phone outfitted with a scrambler. He looked at the three men he had chosen—or in the case of one, accepted.

Curt Gillies was a certified psychotic. That fact had gone unrecognized during training. Either that or he had gone around the bend in the field. He simply enjoyed killing, for the hell of it and without reason. He was suspected of killing his own partner. Figured the agency had issued him a license to kill. Big ego. This made him dangerous, and he was targeted to be killed as beyond redemption. By selecting him, Price had postponed his execution. He figured Gillies would be useful in disposing of Sloane. Worked as a paramedic in D.C. Ironic. A homicidal maniac out saving lives? With those gray, vacant eyes, one look at him and you knew he was looney. Code name Cobra. He was that, all right.

Candido "Candy" Mako, short, wiry, catlike. Selected because he was half Puerto Rican and could move among the Hispanics, where Sloane might try to hide. Also, he was a D.C. cop, detective. Worked the ghettos. Lots of stoolies and contacts.

Peter Daugherty. Code name Pigeon, although he was unaware of that. Price wasn't wild to have him, but he had finally given in to Adams's arguments that he would be useful. Daugherty was FBI, a glorified, holier-than-thou cop, who didn't know shit about intelligence methods. There was no way he would fit in with Gillies and Mako. Daugherty had been turned, made into a CSA "shade" inside the FBI, informing on Bureau information and activities. His value to this cell was supposed to be that he would know what the FBI was doing in this hunt for Sloane and could use the FBI if help was needed. After all, the CSA had no domestic police powers, so the FBI had to be manipulated into doing what the CSA wanted. Daugherty's other advantage was that he personally knew Sloane. Years ago he had done the security check on Sloane before he was admitted to field-op training. He knew everyone Sloane had ever spoken to. That could be useful.

Price looked at Daugherty. Short Afro, brush mustache, clear complexion the color of cocoa. Brown, intelligent eyes. "How'd you make out at the airport?"

"One George Bell rented a room for storage at the Marriott. He also bought a ticket to Montreal. It was Sloane. People at both places remember him."

Price nodded. "He laid a false trail."

"Why so?"

Price looked at Mako. "Because we expect him to

go to the airport and run. Sloane knows the book. I taught it to him. Rest assured he will do nothing we expect him to."

Daugherty looked puzzled. "How do we know he's even around here?"

"We don't, but it figures that he is. He met a KGB agent and killed two of our ops, palming one of them off as himself, a technique he's used before. He lays a false trail at the airport. He simply wouldn't have gone to all this trouble unless he is in the area. There's something he has to do. Otherwise he would've taken off immediately."

"Why does Mother want him dead?"

Price glared. "Gillies, you will not use that expression in front of me." He saw the twisted grin of the psychotic. "I am part of the Agency and my sexual proclivities are none of your damn business."

"All right, all right. Why this hit on Sloane?"

"He's turned. We need no more proof than the dead Russian. Actually all we need is the Agency's statement that he is to be killed on sight."

"Shouldn't be too hard."

"Those two dead ops probably said the same thing. Gillies, if he sees you before you see him—any of you—you're dead. If you want to live, believe that. What we have to do is find him, approach with caution, then take him before he knows he's been found. The Agency methods aren't going to work. He's already proved that. So we're going to do something different. We will not work in pairs. He expects that. The four of us will form a Cell."

Gillies looked at him sharply. "That's KGB. Sloane will know how they work."

"But we're not KGB. We'll use our own methods.

84

We'll work as individuals, but in close cooperation with each other. The simple fact we are not working in pairs and using the normal methods will confuse him and force him into a mistake." Price hesitated, watching their faces. Daugherty, an FBI man, accepted it, but the two ex-field ops were clearly skeptical. "Each of us must know what the other is doing at all times. No free-lancing, do you hear? No Buck Rogers. This is a secure phone. I can be reached over it at all times. You'll be expected to report in at regular intervals, more often if you have any leads which look hot. Any questions?"

Again Price saw the doubt and dissatisfaction on the faces of Gillies and Mako. "I know. You weren't trained this way, but believe me, this is the only way to take Sloane." He then began a full review of everything known about Sloane in the last twenty-four hours, attempting to recreate the hit at his home, his flight, dumping the body with his ID on it, the car in the parking garage, going to the bank, dropping out of sight. "He has money, he has knowledge, and he has skill. And he knows we tried to kill him. He is going to be a tough adversary."

Gillies relieved himself of a snorting sound. "So he killed a couple of ops. That doesn't make him so tough. Look, Admiral—"

"Goddammit. You know my rank, Gillies."

"You're not in uniform, are you—Captain? If this Sloane has gone over, he'll go straight to the KGB. We're wasting our time."

"Maybe, but only maybe. We will know when he does. I can tell you he hasn't gone yet."

Mako, who seldom said very much and felt most uncomfortable with this whole discussion, said, "If he's been turned and hasn't gone to the KGB, then what's he doing?"

"I don't know."

Another snort from Gillies. "If we don't know what he's doing, how in the hell are we supposed to find him? He could be anywhere."

Daugherty spoke up. "My guess is he'd try to disappear into one of the D.C. ghettos."

"Where he'll never be found." Gillies shook his head. "He won't stay one place more than one night. He'll stay on the move. If we start knocking on doors and flashing a photo of him—like you G-men do—it will take an army to find him. There are three of us."

"Four." Price glared at Gillies. "But you're right. Trying to find a man like him when he doesn't want to be found is next to impossible. We've got to flush him out, make him come to us."

"And how do we do that—Captain?"

Price heard the sarcasm. "Listen, Gillies, I know you think you're the greatest thing since stretch socks, but you'll show me proper respect. Do I make myself clear?"

"Okay, okay."

"Yes, sir."

Gillies sighed. "Aye, aye, sir." He was tempted to give a salute but thought better of it.

Price glared at him a moment longer, then went on. "Sloane has a weakness." He picked up a manila envelope from the table and reached into it. "You all have a photograph of his wife, one Fern L. Falscape. I suggest you study that face and memorize the pertinent information about her." He waited for them to do so.

"Good-lookin' broad." Gillies flashed an appreciative grin. "Maybe this won't be so bad a job after all."

Price shook his head in disgust but let it go. "I assure you she is no broad. She is a very smart young woman. Sloane met her on a previous operation after his partner Rogers died. She worked with him. I don't know the nature of that operation, but it must be realized she has had some experience in intelligence operations. Apparently Sloane has confided in her."

"Then grab her and let her tell us."

"She has been questioned, Gillies, and will be again. She insists she doesn't know where Sloane is or what he is currently involved in. When I said confided, I referred to past operations."

"Sloane loves her?" asked Daugherty.

"Yes, and that is a weakness we must exploit. Sooner or later Sloane will come to her or she will go to him. She must be kept under tightest surveillance at all times."

Another Gillies grin. "I'll volunteer."

Price shook his head at him. "All this will go much easier if you approach it with some seriousness. Believe me, when Sloane puts a bullet in you, you'll wish you had." He turned to Daugherty. "Surveillance will be by the FBI. That's what Sloane expects. It must appear routine. Can you arrange to participate in that surveillance?"

"I can even head it if you want."

"Even better. Every move she makes must be noted, along with every word she utters—or writes, for that matter. We have to assume the two of them are very clever at exchanging messages. Sloane will be extremely careful in approaching her, both to protect himself and her. My guess is that he will approach her through the college, posing as a maintenance man, delivery man, serviceman of some sort. All these people must be watched. Anyone out of place or who doesn't belong should be picked up at once." He saw Daugherty nod acquiescence. "If Sloane doesn't try to meet her at the college, then it will be in some public place—store, restaurant, any place where there are lots of people. Everyone she talks to must be observed and recorded. Got it?"

"Yes."

"And of course her home, office, and car are bugged. If he does come to her, we should be able to find him."

Gillies had listened to about all he could stand. "And what are Mako and I going to be doing while the G-men do their thing?"

Price looked at him. "I'd hoped you might be able to figure that out. Sloane will approach her only when he thinks it absolutely safe. He will have her under surveillance himself. He will have spotted all the FBI people. I am hopeful you may be able to see him in the act of doing this. You are to stay well away from Fern Falscape. She must never spot you, nor certainly Sloane. Yours must be the larger view. See what Sloane is seeing, act as you think he would. You should be able to find him and take him."

Mako turned down the corners of his mouth, an expression of doubt. "What if he doesn't come to her?"

"He will. Sloane is a hunter, a killer. He knows somebody is after him. He'll try to find out who. The best way to find out is to see who is watching his wife." He looked at both the ex-field ops. "I suggest you two be very careful. Do not act as a pair. Do not coordinate. Sloane will be looking for a pair."

"In other words, if he spots one of us the other may be able to get him."

"Exactly, Mako. He will not be expecting three men or four—a Cell. That is our ace in the hole."

When the three men left, Price sat there shaking. Maybe he was too old for field work, too used to command and respect. Gillies had gotten under his skin—and Mako was little better. For the first time he understood why headquarters personnel are afraid of field ops, especially experienced ones like Gillies and Mako. They are out for number one and would just as soon kill you as look at you. He needed to be careful with these two, keep an eye on them. Then he smiled. That's exactly what was happening. He had set up teams of "watchers" to report back to him every move made by Gillies, Mako, and Daugherty. It was standard procedure whenever a field op was inside this country. The bastards figured they were a law unto themselves. The watchers—and they had no idea who or why they watched this person—were frequently FBI. But because of Daugherty the Bureau couldn't be used. Special "domestic ops" from the CSA had been brought in to watch all three. Sloane would spot the watchers, of course, but he would still think there was only a pair after him, leaving the odd man out.

Being experienced, Gillies and Mako spotted their watchers within minutes. They expected nothing less. But they left the watchers to their job, certain in the knowledge they could lose them whenever the need arose.

Sloane used the Henson driver's license to rent a car from Hertz, then drove it to Anacostia, where he abandoned it on the street. An hour and a half later he found a car with a For Sale sign in the window at College Park, Maryland. Blue '82 Camaro. The owner was a black University of Maryland student from Philadelphia. Sloane paid the full asking price, accepting title under a phony name. He promised to have it registered right away. The kid was delighted.

The flight was endless for Wiley Drake. This P2V with its two prop engines wasn't called the "Truculent Turtle" for nothing. They'd left Lexington Park, the Patuxent River Naval Air Test Center, before dawn and still hadn't arrived over the target. Submarine patrol had to be the dullest duty in the Navy. Drake was glad he was only on temporary assignment and didn't do this for a living.

To amuse himself he'd brought along the *Washington Post*. He'd read about the murders in southern Maryland, but it didn't really interest him until he saw the photo of the dead man fished from the Bay. The caption identified him as David Sloane, but that wasn't the name Drake knew him by. When they served together aboard the USS *Evansville* four years ago his name had been David Packwood. Everybody called him "Packie." Had a black man as a partner. What had he been called? Drake couldn't think of it. Have to work on that.

He looked at the photo again. Same man, no doubt of that. He read the obituary. Insurance agent. Survived by his widow, Dr. Fern L. Falscape, on the faculty of Calvert College. Same old baloney of the day before about the murders in Sloane's yard. He was believed kidnapped for the money he carried, then murdered and dumped in the river.

Drake shook his head. Too bad. He'd always liked Packie. Drank beer, held it too. Good for laughs. The black partner was something else. Kinda scary. You felt he'd just as soon plug you as look at you. Packie—or Sloane—was easier to take. But you never really got close to him. Drake knew why. The man was obviously some kind of spook. No one knew who he was or what he was doing. And the smart thing was never to ask or even wonder. Just do what he asked and talk about beer, baseball, and broads.

Drake understood this because he was in intelligence himself. His Navy rank was CET-1, Communications Electronic Technician First Class. As far as he knew he had the highest security classification there was, Top Secret Three, Cryptographic Code Word One—although he always suspected Packie just might be higher, whatever it was. His own cryptographic clearance put him high in the intelligence game, leaving him always at the beck and call of spooks. And he had to be careful of what he said and whom he associated with. That alone had busted up his marriage. He couldn't blame Vickie. But shoot, he missed his kids. When this test ended, he'd get a few days off to see them—hopefully.

Test. It had been going on almost daily for two weeks. There were two black boxes and a buoy. He'd made them himself, or helped make them, at the Short Creek Spring Test Center in West Virginia. Now there was a really secret facility. Only had fifty people or so, mostly CETs. Few people even knew the place existed. Ostensibly Navy, but it really belonged to the CSA. It was where they built and tested all kinds of top-secret, esoteric gear.

The black boxes were surely that. Laser technology, a way to communicate with a sub deep underwater. Very hush hush. The black box on this plane sent the signal. The other black box was on a US nuclear sub. He didn't even know the name of it himself. His buddy Jerry Hechter, another CET, was aboard and pissing and moaning about it. Jerry was claustrophobic and hated that damn sub. He'd tried the worst way to switch assignments. No way, buster. No subs for Wiley Drake.

He saw the signal from the pilot, Navy Lieutenant Bud Sanderson, and at once slipped on the headset, hearing, "We've located the target. Be over it in a minute."

"Okay, Sandy."

Drake knew there really was no way for a sub, any sub, to hide anymore. Subs were made of metal. Anywhere they went, no matter how fast or how deep, they disturbed the earth's magnetic field. Satellites picked that up instantly. The technology was so sophisticated the satellite could usually identify which particular sub was underwater by the characteristic way it disturbed the magnetic field. Subs sent out decoys, essentially batteries putting out a phony field. At best they confused things, but the sub, being larger, still couldn't hide. Chances are the Russians could do the same thing. If subs of both nations couldn't hide and were sitting ducks, then why keep on building them?

"Drop the buoy when you're ready."

"Buoy away."

Below him Drake heard the bomb-bay door opening, then the release of the buoy. It was outfitted with a plug which would slowly dissolve. The buoy would last five minutes or so, then sink. Couldn't let that little baby fall into unfriendly hands. He flicked the switch on his black box, waited for the ready light to flash on.

Simple gadget really, not hard to build. Basically just a laser sending code. The beam struck the buoy, which in turn relayed it to the sub. Had to do this to prevent the water from refracting the light. They'd been doing it for two weeks. Hadn't failed yet. Jerry Hechter invariably reported receipt of the correct message from the plane. Ah, the wonders of modern technology. But what was it for? Just sending messages to subs? Drake thought not. This was supposed to be a major test today. Test of what? Maybe he'd find out.

"Buoy down. It's all yours."

The ready light was on. Drake pushed the button. The beam of red light lasted less than a second. "Let's get out of here." The plane's tight turning circle over the buoy was making his stomach a little queasy.

"Good God, would you look at that!"

The sharp, excited voice of Sanderson hurt Drake's eardrums. "What's going on?"

"Holy shit! One of the sub's missiles just broke water. It's heading downrange."

"A missile?"

"It wasn't your fairy godmother. Did you do that, Wiley?"

"Damned if I know."

* * *

Dimitri Galenkov angrily pushed the stop button on the cassette player. He had begun with disbelief, quickly reached dismay, and now approached rage. The Embassy in Washington was one of the most important posts in the KGB. It was a plum, good duty, reserved for the best and brightest. The very existence of this tape proved it was obviously too much of a plum. The tape was disreputable, unforgiveable. Demotions were in order. Transfers to Afghanistan were a certainty.

Galenkov shook his leonine head. Imagine! Pavel Karamasov had made a tape, running off at the mouth to some Japanese recorder sold in America. It had been found and brought to Dzerzhinsky Square by diplomatic courier. Unthinkable! Suppose it had fallen into American hands, the CIA or FBI or, God forbid, the CSA. The use they could have made of it!

To calm himself Galenkov half filled a glass with water from a decanter on his desk, drank it all. He would have preferred vodka, but the doctors had forbidden it. This tape was a symptom of a serious problem, involving morale of people in the field. Karamasov had been a top agent, a veteran with a fine record. But he had been compromised through no fault of his own. He had little value in current operations and much of what he learned was disinformation. As a result he was shunted aside. He felt belittled, ridiculed. He was the butt of bad jokes. Worse, no one paid any attention to him or the information he obtained. So he told it to his Japanese machine. Ghastly! Steps would have to be taken to prevent this from ever happening again. Yes, a morale question. He would order an immediate study, then institute the necessary reforms.

Galenkov listened to the entire tape again, carefully, giving Karamasov the attention he deserved in the first place. Karamasov knew he had been compromised and realized he was fed disinformation. But, as he said, "I am not a fool." He felt quite capable of sifting through the disinformation to arrive at a core of truth. He still had good contacts. He would prove it. Pavel Karamasov would prove his worth to the *Rodina*.

"Yes, my friend. I am listening."

Karamasov believed the Americans planned a big operation. He was certain it was a CSA operation, not CIA, and therefore far more secret, more important, more grave, and likely to be directed toward the *Rodina*. He was worried. He was onto something important. Only no one would listen. Damn them!

"Yes, my friend. They will now listen to the falling snow in the Arctic."

He listened to the rest of the tape. Not much there. He replayed the latter portions, seeking any nuance which indicated the nature of the suspected CSA operation. Nothing. Obviously Karamasov didn't know himself. But he was meeting someone who would tell him. The tape concluded with an angry peroration. Maybe then he would be listened to, believed.

Galenkov turned off the machine a final time, then leaned over his desk, unconsciously pulling at his eyebrows. Karamasov had gone to meet someone to obtain information about a CSA operation which posed a threat to the *Rodina*. Was it Wolf, the ex-American agent identified in the newspapers as David Sloane? Again Galenkov was distracted by anger. Karamasov's superiors should have known what he

was working on and whom he was meeting. They did
not. Unforgiveable! Worse was their attempt to attach
no significance to Karamasov's death. It was very
significant. Galenkov was sure of it.

Karamasov had met Sloane. No doubt of that. But
he had not gone directly to Sloane. The earlier
wound. He had been shot by someone else, then had
gone to Sloane for help, or—Galenkov nodded approval of his realization—because the fools in the
Embassy would not pay attention to him. Had
Karamasov trusted an American with information he
would not tell his own superiors? Unthinkable! Perhaps he'd had no choice. Wounded, he could get no
further than Sloane. Yes. Had to be that. Wolf, this
Sloane, was the key to this puzzle. He had to be
found.

Galenkov was interrupted by a gentle rap at his
door. Alexei Pavlovich entered, handed him some
papers without comment. Galenkov read the first.
Captain Price, the director of CSA training, had left
Pensacola and been seen arriving in Washington. He
had not returned to Pensacola. Seen entering and
leaving the Federal Court House in Washington.
Galenkov smiled. So they are using old-timers, a
theoretician and pedagogue no less. There was not a
shred of doubt in Galenkov's mind that Price was
involved in the hunt for Sloane. Good. Simply observe Price, and he would lead them to Sloane.
Splendid.

He read the second summary. The KGB agent
inside the FBI reports that surveillance has been
ordered on Fern L. Falscape. Again Galenkov smiled.
The wife of Wolf. He remembered her from the
Parsley affair. Handsome woman. Much courage.

Both sides had used her as a pawn, hoping she would lead them to Wolf. Hadn't worked. So, the CSA was trying again. He saw little chance for success, but it would be wise to observe the observers.

Alone now, Dimitri Galenkov leaned over his desk, pulling hard on his eyebrows. He had two problems to take care of. The first was to clean up the entire KGB operation in Washington, the second was to find Wolf and discover why Karamasov went to him. Galenkov mentally cursed. If he sent a new Number One Cell from Moscow, the people wouldn't arrive in time or be familiar enough with Washington and American ways to do much about finding Sloane. The solution was to send someone who had already been stationed in Washington, but . . . Again Galenkov cursed. Hardly anyone was ever reassigned to the US. The risk of defection after the second tour of duty was immense. The KGB had been burned too many times.

Galenkov pulled on his brows so hard he actually winced in pain, but he now knew what to do. He would send an entirely new Number One Cell from Moscow. He knew just the person. Experienced, trusted, ruthless, he and his team would clean up the Embassy operation if anyone could. Meanwhile, he would transfer a cell from the UN in New York to Washington with specific orders to find Sloane and interrogate him. They would have authority over all Washington personnel until the new Number One Cell arrived. Yes, yes. New men on the scene. Even if the CSA knew them from New York, they would be confused by their presence in Washington. Yes. He knew just whom to send. Good man. His loyalty was beyond question.

At once Galenkov cut orders to execute his plan. But he was not quite finished. Using a special code, exclusive to him, he sent a private message. When a person is dealing with fools, inept fools at that, it is wise to take every precaution. Of course, if his fellow members of the First Directorate ever discovered he was doing this sort of thing . . . He shrugged. When one is old and has gout there is no point in worrying about such matters.

Freddie's tour of the pits was an extended one. She told herself she must know every nook and cranny of the place by now, but figured she probably didn't. Normally she threw off a depression in an hour or so, even a few minutes. Life was too short. But this time her troubles seemed too real, too ominous. Here she was pregnant, her husband missing, maybe dead, at least being hunted by people who intended to kill him. Didn't she owe herself a nice long spell of quiet desperation? How about a screaming fit or two?

She tried everything to shake it, cold showers, a run long enough to paralyze her legs, a half bottle of imported chablis, and a meal fit for a king—two kings and all their concubines. By the next morning she was trying work, which was a variation on David's constant admonition not to "think about it." She arose early—*doctor, is it really necessary for people to sleep?*—and cleaned the whole house, all the way down to scrubbing out the garbage can, before going off to work.

At her office there was a memo from Dean Bergen. "A Mr. Paul Gorsuch from the Bureau of Immigration and Naturalization is on campus today meeting with faculty about the behavior of foreign students.

Just routine. I've scheduled you for 4 P.M., Room 302. If you can't make it, I'll send someone else."

Freddie made a face. Why check up on foreign students? Are we running a police state? Maybe we are. That's what she'd tell Mr. Paul Gorsuch. It would give her something to do. Her scheduled lecture was on the pernicious effects of the Twenty-Second Amendment to the Constitution limiting Presidents to two terms. She studied her notes, then began to open her mail.

It was a mistake. There were several notes of condolences from friends, former students, and colleagues, a nice letter from her old college prof inviting her for a visit over the summer. All of it depressed her. How much sympathy was the family of the dead man getting? Awful! Just plain awful! *Keep busy. Don't think about it. Yes, David. Where the hell are you? You know I don't even know if you're still alive.* She sighed. *Keep busy.* She set aside the personal letters and opened the business mail. Routine. Invitations to lectures, seminars, and courses, offers to buy the world's greatest book on American government. *You don't know who really runs the government, my friend.*

Several books she had ordered came. She opened and added them to the stack on the table near her desk. She called it her "guilt pile," all the things she never got done. *The college pays good money. You ordered them. The least you can do is read them.* One title ensnared her attention. *Living with Death and Dying*, by Elisabeth Kubler-Ross, published by Macmillan, 1981. She didn't order that. Out of her field. Someone must have sent it to assuage her "grief." She picked it up. No inscription, no note. She leafed through it, even turned it upside down, shaking it. Nothing. She looked at the box it came in. From Waldenbooks in Washington. Nothing. She shrugged and returned the book to the stack. She looked away, then back. Strange. She picked up the book and opened it. Yes. The spine had been broken so the book naturally opened in two places, between 16 and 17 and between 68 and 69. It had been done deliberately. But why?

Her mind leaped at an answer. David? Was he sending her a message? She read all four pages carefully, then re-read them. She read all the pages around them. Nothing. If David was sending her a message, she was too obtuse to get it. Probably just bad binding. Books fell apart these days the first time you read them.

Freddie had trouble concentrating on her lecture, for her mind kept dwelling on the numbers 16, 17, 68, 69. They had some meaning. She tried phone numbers, Social Security. No. She paused in her lecture to look at her credit cards. No. Then, in the middle of explaining how second-term Presidents are lame ducks and lose effectiveness, it came to her. It *was* a message from David. Yes, yes. *Oh thank you, darling, thank you, thank you.* During the Parsley affair they had hidden out in Europe by camping in a VW van. It had Dutch plates, XN-68-17.

She excused herself and ran back to her office, snatching up the book. Yes, 68-17. Had to be from him. *Living with Death and Dying.* Why was she so dumb? Elisabeth Kubler-Ross had investigated the phenomenon of people who die, then are brought back to life, as evidence of life after death. He *must* have sent the book, intending for her to receive it before his "body" was found. It was a signal for her to wrongly identify the body. And he didn't want her to worry. But it had arrived too late. Either that or the body had been found too soon. *Doesn't matter, darling. I got it now. You're alive. I love you. Thank you, God.*

She clutched the book during the rest of her lecture, certain she could feel vibrations from it. *You're next assignment, class, is to read this book. It is one of the most important in the English language—Swahili for that matter.* She carried it to lunch. Other faculty members noticed how ebullient she was. "Life goes on, doesn't it?" *Doesn't it!*

Her euphoria was short-lived, however, Just because David had sent her a book containing a message she alone could figure out didn't mean their troubles were over. He had to have sent the book days ago. He could already be dead by now—or soon. Mother had tried to kill him once. They would keep at it until . . . Yes. Worse, even if he was still alive, there was a real chance she might never see him again, at least for a long time. Back in Munich, when they first met—*great meeting!*—he and Harry Rogers had intended to take off, just disappear someplace. They'd even had the airline tickets. Right now David Sloane could be in some god-forsaken country, bedded down with some cunning, sloe-eyed . . . He wouldn't do *that*, would he? *Ms. Falscape, this is the medieval torture chamber. Here we have the rack. Over there is the Iron Maiden. Just step inside. I know you'll enjoy it.*

The phone call from the local funeral home only made it worse. A Mr. Tydings—*all my friends call me Glad*—wanted to discuss the funeral arrangements.

Oh, God! She hadn't even thought of it. The horror of her situation struck her. The American way of death. Dead husbands are buried. Dead husbands beget grieving widows. She was in charge of burying somebody else's loved one. Lord! She told Mr. Tydings she'd call him back.

Her mental vision of the funeral was appalling to her. She couldn't go through with it. Death was sacred, dammit. God's final gift to mankind, to be shared with loved ones and friends. It didn't belong to some phony "widow," shedding crocodile tears. She would be engaging in the ultimate theft. Stealing death and grief was far worse than taking money. That the United States Government had done it regularly in Vietnam or the intelligence game, calling people they knew were dead MIAs, did not lessen her loathing for it. Damn Mother! Her abhorrence for the Central Security Agency began to approach hatred.

Again she told herself she couldn't go through with it. Then she sighed, deeply, in defeat and resignation. What choice did she have? That body was part of David's cover, designed to gain him time to—to do whatever he had to do. She had identified the body as him. The police believed her. If she now refused the body—*oh, God!* She had to go through with this macabre charade. Maybe she could delay, keeping the body in cold storage until the rightful family became known. "No-o-o." The word escaped her as a long, low wail. If she delayed, it would just raise suspicion, putting David at risk. She had no choice. The Widow Falscape had to do her act. *Step right up, ladees and gennulmen. Watch the fat lady shed real tears.*

She phoned Mr. Tydings. The body was to be

cremated. She could hear the disappointment in his voice. There would be a short, quick private memorial service. It was to be announced in the newspaper after the fact. When she hung up, Freddie promised herself she would do her best to honor this unknown dead man at the service. And she would save the ashes, see that someday they got to the proper family.

Her afternoon class, "The Role of the Press in American Government," one of her favorite courses, had a visitor, one Judy Harkness. Supposedly a stringer for the *Baltimore Sun*, she wanted to sharpen her journalistic skills by auditing Freddie's course— that is, sitting in for information, not for credit. It happened sometimes. But at midterm? Freddie endured her for awhile, then couldn't resist. She marched up to her and snatched her purse from the desk, opening it. When Judy Harkness protested, Freddie said, "Sue me." She fished out her handgun and her identification with the FBI badge. "Get out," she said and pointed toward the door. "None of us have to put up with this sort of thing, you know."

FIVE

In his office in the UN Building, Gregor Azbel read the "his eyes only" orders he had laboriously decoded. It was his second reading, and it did nothing to alleviate his dismay. A major shake-up at the Embassy in Washington was in progress over the death of Pavel Karamasov. The Number One and Two Cells were already on their way back to Moscow, along with the remaining members of Number Six, to which Karamasov had belonged. A new Number One Cell under Vladimir Kastalsky would arrive soon. Meanwhile he and his team were to become the Number Two Cell.

That's what dismayed Azbel. There was no doubt becoming Number Two in Washington was a promotion, but if he failed to find this David Sloane or anything went wrong before Kastalsky arrived, he,

Gregor Azbel, only thirty, darkly handsome, Party member, a brilliant future ahead of him, would be on the next plane back to Moscow and ruin.

Again Azbel read that portion of his orders pertaining to his assignment to find and interrogate this David Sloane, a former CSA operative, code name Wolf. The orders were extraordinary! He had never seen anything like it. He had full authority to take all appropriate action to find and debrief this Sloane—until Kastalsky arrived. Simply unbelievable! It was axiomatic in the KGB that no one was ever given full authority to do anything. No one, but no one made a move—it was a joke that no one even went to the toilet—without approval from higher authority.

Azbel cursed. He was now higher authority, utterly responsible. Only he wasn't. Kastalsky would be there in a few days, second-guessing and disapproving everything he'd done. Guess whose head would roll. Azbel knew he was in what the Americans called the "hot seat." He sighed. Couldn't be helped, but the First Directorate was surely a hard service.

He concentrated on the specific information provided him. This Wolf, this David Sloane, was a former agent of great experience and skill. He had already killed two CSA ops assigned to liquidate him. Subject of a massive hunt by the CSA and FBI. Captain Lawson Price, director of training at Pensacola, believed in charge of the hunt. FBI maintaining round-the-clock surveilance on one Fern L. Falscape, Sloane's wife, in hopes she would lead them to Sloane. Azbel was to join the surveillance on the Falscape woman to identify the agents working with Price. He was also to see that no harm came to her, at least until Sloane was found.

Azbel understood. She was a pawn for both sides. But it was the rest of his orders which dumbfounded him. Sloane was to be taken alive and held for questioning. There was absolutely no room for error in that. This, of course, meant keeping the Americans from killing him. Azbel shook his head. Had ever a man been so cursed?

Freddie remained so angry that the FBI had sent a ringer into her class she almost forgot her four o'clock appointment with Gorsuch. Indeed, she was halfway out of the building when she remembered. Oh, well. She'd give him short shrift. *Our foreign students are some of the best we have, you bigot and racist. Why don't you wear your sheet and burn crosses?* There was a small anteroom with a couple of chairs in front of a closed door. Ellen Wendling, who taught Comparative World Government, was ahead of her and waiting.

Only a few words had passed between them when the door opened. Bert Segal from the French Department came out, then a man stood in the doorway. Freddie saw him look at her. "Dr. Falscape?"

She felt she couldn't breathe.

"I'm sorry. I'm running late. Just give me a few minutes with Dr. Wendling and I'll be with you."

Freddie stared at the closed door. Paul Gorsuch was not Paul Gorsuch. She had first known him as Mr. Green, member of The Committee during the Parsley affair. He had reappeared in her life quite by accident just before Christmas when she was shopping at The May Company in Washington. She was buying wool socks for her father when suddenly there he was, a few feet away from her. They made eye contact. Recognition passed between them. He smiled. Pleasantries were exchanged. He invited her to lunch. She accepted, then waited while he selected three pairs of socks, paying for them with his Visa card.

The lunch was pleasant, casual, as they caught up on their lives since they had last seen each other two and a half years before. They did not speak of Parsley, of the CSA, at least not directly. "Mr. Green" said he had taken early retirement. She expressed condolences on the death of his wife. He accepted it without comment, then asked about her life. Was she still teaching? She told him she was. He asked questions and seemed interested. Was it too late for him to get into college teaching? She thought he might find a spot as guest lecturer somewhere.

Finally, he asked about David. He was well, selling insurance, had bought into an agency. How is he doing? Freddie understood the question had a deeper meaning than finances.

"As well as can be expected. At least I hope that's true."

"Some adjustment problems?"

She made no reply.

"I'm having some myself." He smiled. "I keep telling myself that the quiet life, immersion in the eternal verities, is what I really want."

She nodded. "And you hope that one day you'll convince yourself. It is the same with David."

"It just takes time, I think."

"I hope so. At least his dreams are less frequent and violent. Do you have dreams?"

"Sometimes. They are not debilitating."

She nodded, pursing her lips in thought. "I suspect David had a worse time than you. He was—"

"Very likely."

She understood the interruption. She was not to speak of specifics. "David is younger than you. I think he feels the rest of his life is anticlimactic. And he misses . . ." She caught herself. "You know who I mean." She saw him nod. Outwardly she was calm, but inwardly her emotions rose. "A terrible thing was done to him—by *you*."

"And others."

She sighed. There was no point in these recriminations. A smile came to her. "Put it all together and it spells M-O-T-H-E-R. The truly awful part of it is that he misses her—at least some of the time."

"Yes, I understand."

"I hate her. Always will." Freddie was surprised by her own vehemence.

"A foolish exercise, Dr. Falscape."

She smiled. "Call me Freddie, all my friends do."

And he smiled. "I remember. You told me I could do that once."

She picked at her salad a bit. She wasn't hungry, which ranked as a phenomenon. Eating like a pig and not gaining weight was one of her blessings in life. "And what do I call you?"

"Friend. I like you. I'd like to be your friend— David's too. But you must know it is impossible."

She nodded, forked a wedge of tomato, and inserted it in her mouth. It tasted like wet cardboard. "I'm a very dangerous person, you know. I won't give up. I will find a way."

"I really think it's pointless, Freddie."

"I know. The word is monolithic. Monolithic Mother, impregnable, untouchable, the great manipulator."

He smiled. "An unusual description, but it has merit."

"And so does the Constitution." Again her vehemence showed. "I will find a way to stop The Committee."

"Can we talk about something else?"

They did. Lunch was finished. They walked out into the street.

"Will you be telling David you saw me?"

She looked at him carefully. "I don't think so. He has enough unpleasant memories." Then she smiled. "I didn't mean that as—"

"I understand. I think you might be wise to keep our little meeting to yourself."

"Yes, I will."

He touched her gloved hand. "Good-bye. Good luck."

Freddie watched him walk down the block and turn the corner, then she wheeled and stalked away. She was famished. In McDonald's she ordered two Big Macs, a double order of french fries, and a chocolate shake. She smiled. She had the way. If not, she could at least try.

The name on the Visa card had been W. Gordon Adams.

The door marked 302 opened. Ellen Wendling came out, smiling, saying she hoped she'd been of help. Adams glanced around the room, then said to her, "Come in, Freddie."

She hesitated, suddenly filled with fear, for she knew why he had come. The piper wanted to be paid.

Slowly, clutching her coat and purse, she rose and walked past him into the room. He closed the door, then motioned her to a wooden chair beside a small desk. He sat behind it.

"It is rather difficult to be alone with you in a secure place these days. I had to go to some trouble."

"That is hardly my fault."

"Oh, but it is. The letter you wrote to the President. What on earth possessed you?"

"Oh, God!" Her hands came to her mouth and tears, quite unbidden and unrelenting, filled her eyes. "All this is my fault, isn't it? I knew it. I just knew it."

"How did you get my name?"

She swallowed, tried to order her breathing. "Your Visa card . . . when . . . you bought the socks."

"I thought as much. Very careless of me." He shook his head, a display of despair. "You said you'd find a way. And you did. A letter to the White House identifying me as a member of The Committee."

"Oh, God!" Tears flowed now. "I'm so . . . sorry. I-I brought all this . . . on David, didn't I?"

He stared at her. "What are you talking about?"

"You must know what's . . . happened to David. He's—"

"I know all about him. What's the letter got to do with it?"

"I wrote it. The Agency . . . comes after David. People are . . . dead. David is—"

"Freddie, you know as well as I do David's not dead."

She swallowed, hard. "I know, but he's—"

"Listen to me, Freddie. Your letter has caused a lot of trouble, believe me. But it has nothing to do with

110

the Agency and Sloane. That's another matter entirely."

She stared at him. "It doesn't?"

"No."

She managed another swallow, then wiped both cheeks with her fingertips. "Then why is David—"

"I don't know, Freddie. One of the reasons I'm here is to try to find out. Just calm down and listen to me." He pulled a handkerchief from his pocket and handed it to her, but she refused, dipping into her purse for a tissue. "Your letter reached President Grayson—itself amazing. When you gave him my name . . ." He shook his head at her. "Freddie, I'm in a sea of trouble because of it. Grayson literally had me kidnapped. He confronted me and really put the screws to me. I either work with him against the Agency—or I'm dead. Thank you very much, Freddie."

She saw the cold anger in his eyes, but it did not frighten her. She'd learned to watch the eyes of Agency people. When David was going to kill his were blue ice. Adams had no intention of harming her. "I don't understand. What is the President doing?"

"I think you know very well, Freddie. You got your way. By giving him my name you put the President in the position of being able to reveal and break The Committee. At least he's going to try like hell. And I'm the one in the middle."

Freddie brightened, half smiled. "Is he really? Because of my letter?" She saw him nod. "Then it's a good thing I wrote it."

"Is it? Do you have any idea of the position I'm in? A major manhunt is on for your husband. I'm talking *major*, Freddie. Orders are to find him and kill him on sight. Guess who's in charge of the manhunt?"

She gaped at him. "You?" She saw him nod. "But I thought you'd retired."

"I have, but I consult. Because I know Sloane I was brought in to take charge of finding him."

"Oh, God!"

"That's only the half of it, Freddie. Grayson has also turned me. I'm working for him. I'm to come up with evidence to break the power of The Committee. Wouldn't you say I'm a bit in the middle?"

She only half listened. Adams's problems were of no great concern to her at the moment. "Why do they want to kill David?"

"They believe he's gone over to the KGB."

"That's crazy! He hasn't! He'd never! You know that."

"Yes, I know it, but the fact remains that he met a highly placed KGB agent, Pavel Karamasov, outside your house. The Agency had information Karamasov was meeting a traitor to obtain information. Field ops were there to dispose of both. You know the rest."

"I do *not!* I don't know *anything*."

"All right. They missed David. He got both the field ops, dumping one in the Chesapeake with his ID on it. You saw the body, you know—"

"Don't remind me."

"The Agency believes it is imperative David be found and—"

"But why, dammit?"

"The supposition is that David knew something to tell Karamasov. My own feeling is that it is the other way around. Karamasov told him something. In either event, Sloane must be found."

She stared at him. "I don't understand."

"The agency wants Sloane to kill him. I want to save his life, find out what he knows."

"You're working both sides of the street?"

"Exactly. Freddie, some kind of CSA operation is going down, something big, something so secret even I can't guess. The President knows the operation exists because he signed a blank authorization the other day. You know how that works, don't you?"

"Yes. Go on."

"The President believes—and I guess I do too—that if he can find out what the operation is, he will be able to confront The Committee and break its power."

"And save the Constitution and the Republic." She smiled. "All that from my little ol' letter."

"Yes—unfortunately. Somehow the key is David Sloane. He knows something about the Agency operation. We've got to find him and talk to him before some other people do. Now where is he?"

"I have no idea."

Adams stood up and turned to look out the window behind him. He was slightly claustrophobic and the sight of sky, trees, and grass had a calming effect on him. "Freddie, you're the one who wrote the President. You're the one—to use your term—who wants to save the Republic. Now's your chance. I'm appealing to you for help."

Freddie stared at his back. Her fear had dissipated, replaced by cold analysis. "Mr. Adams . . . May I call you that?"

"Yes."

"Are you really W. Gordon Adams?"

Sigh. "Yes, Freddie, I am."

113

"Please don't call me Freddie. I'm not sure you're my friend."

He wheeled. Anger was in his eyes. *"God!* Now what—*Dr. Falscape?"*

She stood up to his anger. "I saw a credit card with a name on it. How do I know that was *your* credit card? It could've been a phony. I wrote a letter to President Grayson, giving the name of W. Gordon Adams. How do I know the President ever saw it? How do I know it didn't fall into Mother's hands? How do I know this isn't some *halfway* clever ploy to get me to reveal where David is—which I don't know anyway?" She saw the frustration in his eyes. He shook his head. "After all, the FBI has been looking me over like some exotic foreign bug in a sandbox. Ringers have been sent into my class. You admit you're still with the Agency. You admit you're in charge of killing my husband. Why on earth should I trust you?"

He heard her out, then smiled. "Very good, Freddie. Sloane has taught you well."

She started to tell him again not to call her Freddie, then thought better of it. "You people deal in magic. What you see isn't what happened at all. What you believe with total conviction and know with absolute certainty probably never occurred."

He smiled. "I'd have been seriously disappointed if you hadn't taken this attitude." He reached inside his pocket, extracted an envelope, handed it to her. "This is for you. Read it."

The return address was simply THE WHITE HOUSE. There was no address. The flap was sealed in red wax. She broke it, then tore open the envelope with her finger, unfolded the letter. It was bonded

White House stationery. The watermark was the Presidential seal. The words on the page were in longhand, blue ink.

My Dear,

I have received your remarkable letter. I wish to thank you for it and congratulate you on your sense of patriotism and duty. I assure you I share your concerns, as have a number of my predecessors. I am determined to do what I can to correct the deficiency you wrote about. I need your help in that.

I have personally checked on the information you sent me. It was correct. The bearer of this letter may be identified by a small round birthmark on his left wrist. He has a scar from a bullet wound on his left side. I ask that you assist him in any way you can.

I'm sure you understand my need for circumspection in this letter.

I look forward to the pleasure of meeting you in person one day.

Yours gratefully,

As she read the famous signature of Marvin Grayson, her hand came to her mouth and she stared at Adams, watching him pull up his sleeve, show the birthmark.

"Would you like to see the scar?"

She shook her head, swallowed. "That won't be necessary."

He reached out, took the letter and envelope from her. "This is best destroyed." He flicked a lighter and set fire to the paper, held it a moment, then dropped it in an ashtray. When the flame went out, he broke up the ashes with a pencil.

Freddie watched all that, then said, her voice low, "I really don't know where he is."

"Have you heard from him?"

"This morning I received a book. I'm sure he sent it."

"What book?"

She told him. "He was telling me he was alive and I was to wrongly identify his body. Unfortunately the book came too late. That was not a pleasant scene at the funeral home."

He nodded. "How do you know the book came from him?" He saw her open her mouth to answer, then quickly said, "Never mind. If you have some secret code between you I don't want to know it."

She looked at him, her brown eyes wide and luminous. "Thank you. My first loyalty will always be to David. I will do nothing to betray him."

"I know. Where was the book sent from?"

"Waldenbooks in Washington."

He nodded. "We think he's still in the area. What we don't know is why." He looked at her intently for a moment. "Freddie, can you find him?"

"If you can't, I don't know how I can."

"You don't have to tell me where, but don't you have some secret place known only to yourselves, a pre-arranged rendezvous where you'd meet if he—"

"No. We thought we were out of all this. You yourself said we'd be safe—after Parsley was—"

"I remember." He turned away, back to the window.

"Mr. Adams, all I know is that it wasn't David's

body I identified. He was alive at the time that man was killed—may even have killed him. But I don't know if David's still alive. I don't know where he is, what he's doing, or how to find him. I'm sorry."

Still looking out the window he said, "He's alive. I think you can be certain of that."

She swallowed. "Thank you."

"He hasn't approached the KGB. We'll know if he does. As a matter of fact the KGB is looking for him as much as or more than we are. What he's doing is anybody's guess. We have detected no move from him. We're waiting for it."

"What do you expect him to do?"

"That's just it. We don't know. It all depends on what Karamasov told him."

"If he told him anything."

Adams sighed. "We have to assume he did." He turned back to her. "You remember the Parsley affair, don't you?"

"It's a little hard to forget." There was a tinge of sarcasm to her voice.

"Do you remember how you were the pawn? Everyone hunted Sloane. They used you to get to him—or hoped to. You were watched, followed until you—"

"But I didn't know where David was, except somewhere in Washington. He found me."

Adams smiled. "Exactly. It's what you've got to do again, Freddie."

She shook her head. "There's a big difference. Three years ago David and I were working together to trap Parsley. We had a plan. I know nothing of what he's doing now. We are hardly working together. My guess is he won't come near me. He knows I know nothing. As long as I don't I'm safe. I'm sure that's his thinking."

"Perhaps, even probably, but there is a slight chance he might think differently. It is a chance we must take. It is the only one we have." He saw the uncertainty in her eyes. "Think of it this way. You are again the pawn, whether you want to be or not. You are under the tightest surveillance from the CSA and the KGB, both of whom want Sloane for different reasons. Your phones are tapped, your house and office bugged. You are followed everywhere you go. Your every action, virtually your every word, is observed and noted."

She smiled. "I'm hardly surprised—I guess."

"Freddie, our one hope is that someone else is watching you."

Suddenly her eyes filled with tears. The idea that David might be watching her affected her deeply. With some difficulty she said, "He won't come near me, Mr. Adams. I'm sure of it. Not even if I'm in danger. He knows I'll be no good to anyone if I'm dead."

"You don't understand. A pawn works both ways. By observing you, watching who's following you, Sloane will learn who is after him." He saw her eyes brighten, the beginning of understanding. "Whether you know it or not, Sloane needs you, Freddie. I don't mean because you're his wife. You're more than that now, much more. You're his Harry Rogers. Sloane is not used to working alone. He's only half a man. He needs a partner."

She swallowed. "And I'm elected."

"He found you before, Freddie, and he will again. But not if you sit in your house, office, and classroom.

He can't approach you there. You've got to *move*, Freddie, go places, lots of places, public places. Make it easy for him to find you." He gave his lipless smile. "I can't imagine you'd mind if he did."

Her understanding was complete now, visible in her bright eyes. Her lingering depression was gone. "Tell me what you want me to do."

"No. If I tell you, all these people following you, including Sloane, will know it came from me. You're a smart woman. Do whatever comes to mind. Improvise. Sloane is out there someplace and he will find you—eventually."

"Oh, God, I hope so." Agitated now, she rose from her chair and paced across the small office, her mind alive with these new possibilities for the future. She was an activist, a confrontationalist. Always had been. Do something, even if it's wrong. It had to be better than moping around doing nothing. Then a new thought came to her. She wheeled to Adams. "Suppose he does find me. Then what?"

"I don't know. It's a script still to be written. At least you'll be with him, working to—"

"Help him get out of this mess. Yes. I'm pregnant, Mr. Adams. David doesn't know. I'd like to tell him. I'd like my baby"—her voice suddenly broke—"to have a father—a *live* father."

"I'm sure you do." He hesitated. "Freddie, there's another reason I hope you find Sloane—or he you, however it works out. He is a deeply cynical man. He doesn't care about anything, except—"

"You helped make him that way."

He nodded. "I know. But what I'm trying to say is that I'm afraid as soon as he is with you, he'll take off and—"

119

"He knows I won't go. He tried that before."

"At least he'll be motivated solely by survival—his and yours. I'm counting on you to give him a higher motive."

"Such as?"

"The letter you wrote. If Sloane has any inkling of the nature of the secret CSA operation, the President wants to know it. If Sloane can possibly thwart it, that's what the President wants him to do. We are counting on you to get Sloane to do it."

She pursed her lips, nodded. "Just like Parsley. David wanted to run. I made him go for Parsley." She sighed, thought a moment. "Mr. Adams, I won't be put in the position of even trying to manipulate my husband."

"I know that."

"If on the other hand this latest game by Mother turns out to be big, bad, and ugly, I'll probably . . ." She shrugged. "David always calls me a knee-jerk liberal do-gooder."

"That's all we're counting on, Freddie. I'll do all I can to help protect you both."

"Big deal!"

"I understand your sarcasm." He smiled. "I'd be the same way if I were you."

"Can a leopard change its spots?"

"I don't know. All I can tell you is that Marvin Grayson is a tough man, tougher than I ever thought. He's got the screws tamped down pretty tight on me."

"You deserve it." She smiled. "All right. I'll do what I can—which may be absolutely nothing."

"There is one more thing."

"Isn't there always?"

"The need for secrecy is paramount, Freddie. The only people who know about this are the President, myself, and now you. It must remain that way."

"I'm hardly going to blab . . ." She stopped. "I see. You're talking about David."

"Yes. I think it wise he not know of the President's involvement." Adams saw her stare at him, blink, then turn and walk away from him. "Freddie, The Committee will do whatever is required to protect itself. You must know the danger we are all in."

"Yes, even the President. Thanks a lot." She turned to face him. "But that's not why I'm not supposed to tell David, is it?"

"We both know how cynical, how distrustful he is. Would he risk himself, let alone you, to help the President?" He watched her purse her lips, bit at the inner surfaces. "Did you tell him about your letter?"

"I . . ." She sighed. "I was going to the night all this happened."

Adams smiled. "I can just imagine his reaction."

"I hate manipulation—and deception. I hate lies. I don't lie. I survived Parsley because I told the truth. I'm telling only the truth so far in this . . . this *mess*."

"I'm not asking you to lie to Sloane."

"I know. Just apply a little Need to Know to my husband. You people are so *awful*." She sighed, deeply. "All right, if I do see David—which I doubt very much—I'll do whatever seems right to me at the time. That's the best I can do."

"That's all I want, Freddie."

She returned to her office, searched, finally found the bug under her desk. When she left her office and headed for her car, she saw two men in a vehicle further down the faculty parking lot. They followed her home at a respectful distance. In the house she spent an hour searching until she uncovered three bugs, bedroom, living room, and kitchen. She left them in place but got out David's much-hated recording of old-time steam locomotive sounds and played it at full volume. *I hope it breaks your eardrums.*

Over and over Freddie told herself her first loyalties were to David Sloane. Adams simply couldn't or shouldn't be trusted. That letter from the President had impressed her, but she told herself it could still be a fake. What would David want her to do? Stay here? Be safe? Probably. What did she want to do? There was no doubt of the answer. *I'm sorry, darling, but you married a very liberated, very independent bitch. You needed me once. You're going to need me again.* She got her jacket and purse, then went to turn off the stereo. What the hell, leave it on. If they wanted to perform surveillance on her, she'd give them something to surveil. *Is there such a word as surveil? If not, there ought to be. David, darling, find me—please. I'm really very good in bed. At least my husband used to think so.*

On impulse she decided to take David's Audi. If she was going to be followed, she might as well make it easy for them. Her first stop was the public library. Just to be perverse, she took out three books on US intelligence agencies. The fellow sitting in the reading room was terribly interested in *Time* magazine. Her next stop was the dry cleaners, where she picked up two of her suits and one of David's. *Time*-magazine-reader was now in his car parked out front, perusing the *Washington Post. Very literate fellow, truly well-informed.* After paying for the garments, she went to the pay phone on the wall and dialed. It was the number of a friend she knew was at work. While it rang, she had a long "chat" with a non-existent person, trying to look nervous and upset while she did so. *Time* glanced at her a couple of times, dropped his paper, and picked up the car phone. Next stop was the drugstore, where she remained some time, gradually making her way toward the back. When she saw the tail enter the front, she scooted out the rear door, walked down three doors to the pizza parlor, and came out the front, going to the Audi. As she drove away she saw her "friend" in the rearview mirror running toward his car. All this was great fun to her.

The supermarket took some time—she really did need to pick up a few things—but in truth she dawdled. Never read so many labels in her life. *Time* was in the next aisle, very interested in labels too. A minute later she came down his aisle, "accidentally" pushing her cart into his. "I'm sorry."

There was surprise, more than a little anger in his eyes. "That's all right."

Midwestern accent, same as David's. She was good at accents. "Wouldn't happen to know where the Tabasco is, would you?"

"'Fraid not."

He seemed eager to move on, but she held him with her eyes. "Didn't I just see you in the library?" She gave him one of her better smiles. "I hope you're following me." It was a come-on few men could resist. He did.

When her groceries were in the car two different men approached her, flashing FBI badges. "Dr. Falscape, we'd like to ask you to come with us, please."

She looked at them carefully. This now made three men she could recognize. "Do I have a choice?"

Hesitation. "Just come with us, Dr. Falscape. You will not be harmed. Just a few questions."

"I have some frozen haddock in the car. I'd rather it wasn't—"

"This won't take long."

She shrugged, then accompanied them in their vehicle to the post office. They led her inside to stand before an unmarked door. She entered. Three men sat at a small table. Two were younger, the third, wearing a windbreaker, was a little older, perhaps in his thirties. They were bland, utterly nondescript, and she knew at once they were CSA. Funny how she was able to tell. Couldn't pinpoint or describe the difference from the FBI people, but she could just tell. "I guess you don't have badges, do you?"

The older man blinked. "What're you talking about?"

"My husband said the men from Mother don't carry badges. That's FBI or maybe Secret Service."

He eyed her a moment, then motioned to a chair. "Please sit down, Ms. Falscape."

"I'll stand." Suddenly she realized she wasn't afraid. She had been here before. Not *here* exactly, but in a similar situation—at Brandywine. Those men who had grilled her were far worse than these three were likely to be. Nothing had happened to her then. Nothing would now.

"We'd like to ask you a few questions about your husband."

"My late husband."

There was not a wrinkle of reaction from any of them. "Of course. We'd like to ask you about his friends, associates, and recent activities."

"It's none of your damn business."

"I'm afraid it is. Dr. Falscape, the man found dead at your home, the man identified as Edziw Kawicki, was a known Soviet intelligence agent. His real name was Pavel Karamasov. We'd like to find out how your husband happened to know him and why the two of them met."

"Gentlemen, my husband was a retired field operative for the Central Security Agency. Since you three are obviously from the same agency, I suggest you know far more about his friends, associates, and activities than I ever will. This discussion is pointless." Now she saw windbreaker react. Coldness crept into his eyes. It didn't frighten her.

"Did you know this man Karamasov? Had you ever seen him before?"

This came from one of the younger men, the brown-haired one with the freckles. "No. I told the police that and it was the truth."

Windbreaker now. "Then everything you've said has *not* been the truth."

She smiled. "My, aren't we clever today." She turned toward the door. "Good day, gentlemen."

"Miss Falscape, this is a national security matter. We must insist on your cooperation."

She didn't stop, only said, "Stick it up your ass."

* * *

When Adams heard the tape of the interview he burst out laughing, something he rarely did.

To the public it was known as the Cambridge Arms, a desirable, upper-middle-class five-story apartment house with a pool, gym, sauna, and tennis court. Food in the dining room was said to be good, but it was reserved for tenants and not open to the public. At Brandywine, it was known as the BOQ, where bachelor officers and other highly classified CSA employees lived. Security was flawless. The place had everything an employee of Mother could want, including authorized whores hired and cleared by the Agency. Sloane had stayed there once when summoned to Brandywine from the field. The redhead had been nice. Mother believed men in the field ought to relax when they could. He knew the redhead had reported every word he said back to the Agency.

The sybaritic pleasures of the Cambridge Arms, even the good food and opportunities for healthy exercise, would be lost on Dennis Tenpenny, however. Sloane doubted he had ever been with a woman or seriously thought about it for that matter, an attitude Sloane was sure the redhead and the other Agency whores heartily applauded. Dennis Tenpenny seldom bathed. Working in the same room with him qualified as hazardous duty. The pool and other opportunities for healthful exercise would not interest him. As for the good food, Tenpenny existed almost exclusively on a diet of Hershey milk-chocolate bars, no almonds please, and Coca-Cola—the Classic most likely—both of which the Agency supplied him by the case. Indeed, Dennis Tenpenny could have almost anything he wanted, for he was a rarity of rarities, an immensely valuable human being.

Dennis Tenpenny was a master code-breaker, one of the best the Agency had. To even knowledgeable persons, it was an article of faith that computers broke out codes almost automatically. Maybe in the days of letter-number substitutions, but these days ciphers were electronic squiggles on a graph and codes were the equivalent of one-time pads. Even with unlimited time on the finest, fastest computers in the world, code-breaking remained a laborious human task. Computers would spill out "co-relations" by the yard, telling every time and in what context a particular squiggle or code word had been used. The code-breaker had to pick up on that and send the computer off in search of ever finer co-relations until the code was finally broken. It was a devilishly difficult job, involving the most intense concentration imaginable.

There was no one better than Dennis Tenpenny. Sloane had watched him work, gulping chocolate bars and soda, screaming and hollering. It would go on for days at a time. He wouldn't sleep. He'd shit his pants rather than break his concentration to go to the toilet. Sweat would pour off him and blood would run down his face from the pustules of acne he scratched open. There were those in the Agency who considered Dennis Tenpenny a disgusting human being. Others were certain he was an idiot savant, a genius at code-breaking, but mentally defective at virtually everything else. He couldn't even drive a car, and some insisted he didn't read and write. At least no one had ever seen him do it. But Mother loved him.

He was a favorite son, an asset to national security more valuable than a fleet of Ohio-class subs.

Sloane had been waiting for him for two days, certain that sooner or later Dennis Tenpenny would finish his bout of work, return to the BOQ, and collapse. Then he would take a few days off, maybe a couple of weeks before commencing another spasm of code-breaking. Sloane figured to confront him in his apartment at the BOQ. There was a risk in entering, but he had to take risks.

Then he got lucky. He saw a car pull up in front. Two men sat in front. Secret Service. They were assigned to accompany Tenpenny at all times, except when he was inside Brandywine or at the BOQ. They had no idea who this red-haired, pimply-faced kid— actually Tenpenny was twenty-four and held the rank of Navy lieutenant, but he looked and acted about sixteen—was or why they had to guard him. In the Secret Service it was considered the pits as duty. Many a man had resigned because of it. Sloane watched Tenpenny alight from the back seat and go inside. But the Secret Service remained. A few minutes later Tenpenny returned, and the car drove away with him. Sloane followed.

By the time the Secret Service vehicle reached US 301 and turned south, Sloane knew where they were going. Should've thought of it himself. Tenpenny's only idea of fun was playing video games. Crazy! Worked with computers and electronics for days on end, then went out and visited the video arcade. Supposedly a wizard at it. If a game posed particular difficulty for him, he'd take it back to Brandywine and break it out on the computer.

Sloane passed the Secret Service car and arrived a few minutes ahead of Tenpenny, wanting to case the place first. It was a large bowling alley in a shopping center just north of Waldorf, Maryland. To the left of the entrance was the darkened video arcade. To the right was a coffee shop and cocktail lounge with a view of the bowling lanes in the rear. Good. A few minutes later, while seemingly engrossed in the bowling, he saw Tenpenny enter and head for the arcade. The two guards entered the lounge. Sloane watched them take a table with a clear view of the arcade door. They ordered coffee and began a conversation. Dull duty. Like watching a flower open or the nose on a drunk turn red.

Sloane ambled over to the arcade and entered, taking a moment to let his eyes adjust to the near darkness. The whole wall was darkened glass, and he could see the lobby and coffee shop, the Secret Service men still gabbing away, but they couldn't see him. Good. It was a toss-up whether he saw or smelled Tenpenny first, but there he was, intent on some machine, Coke in front of him, chocolate bar in hand. He looked worse than Sloane remembered. Really ghastly acne. And the smell. Sloane went to the machine next to him and inserted a quarter. He had no idea how to play it.

"I see you shit your pants again, Dennis." Sloane was looking straight ahead as he spoke, but from his peripheral vision he saw that he got no reaction, such was Tenpenny's concentration on his game. Still looking straight ahead, Sloane reached over and stuck his finger sharply into the code-breaker's ribs. Now he got a reaction, annoyance first, then recognition, finally fear. That was to be expected. People at Brandywine were afraid of field ops, who would kill and ask questions later if they thought their cover was being blown. When one entered Brandywine, everyone who possibly could made himself scarce. They didn't want to be seen. Once Harry and he had set up shop at an Air Force barracks in Germany. The whole place had emptied. "I said I see you've shit your pants again." He saw the fear, almost terror in Tenpenny's eyes as they darted over to the Secret Service men. "Let them enjoy their coffee, Dennis." He jabbed harder with his finger. "If you call out, I'll kill you where you stand."

"What d'you want?"

The voice was high-pitched, almost squeaky with fear. "Just finish your game, then slowly walk to your right toward the rear. I'll be right behind you." When the game seemed to take too long, Sloane whispered, "Now. Do it now. Walk toward the rear door."

They emerged from the side of the building. The April night had turned chilly, but Sloane knew that wasn't why Tenpenny shivered. "Walk. Toward the cars." In a moment he opened the door to the driver's side of his car, shoved Tenpenny inside, and slid in after him. There was no light. He had removed the interior bulb.

"You do remember me, Dennis."

"Yes."

"Are you sure? It has been over three years."

"I-I re-remember you."

"Then you know I would just as soon kill you as look at your pimply face." He pulled the Walther from his jacket and shoved it under Tenpenny's chin, shoving his head upward with the silencer. "You look awful, pus-face. You really ought to stop eating all that chocolate."

He was shaking all over. There was pure terror in his eyes. "I-I like chocolate."

"I know, but it plays hell with your complexion." He shoved upward with the Walther again, then lowered it away from his chin. "I don't want to hurt you, pus-face. I just want you to tell me something."

In the near darkness the widened eyes darted toward Sloane. "I-I don't know . . . nothin'."

"What's the Seraphim Code, Dennis?"

"Seraphim c-code? Never h-heard of it."

Again Sloane shoved the muzzle against his chin, hard. "Don't lie to me, Dennis."

"Oh, God! That hurts."

"Not as much as it will if you lie to me."

"I-I'm not lying. I-I don't know."

Sloane knew he didn't. Tenpenny broke codes, but he never knew the significance of them or what the broken-out message might mean. He lowered the Walther. "What've you been working on?"

"Russian code, new."

"Tell me about it. Was it tough?"

"Oh yes. A whole new system. They use . . ."

Sloane listened, at least enough to ask a couple of pertinent questions. What he really wanted to do was get Tenpenny talking. He had absolutely no sense of security about classified information, and he liked to brag. When it came to codes he considered himself smarter than anybody on earth, which just might be true. He felt certain he could break any code. He was extremely proud of himself. Trouble was that what he

131

did was so esoteric there were few people he could ever brag to. Sloane pretended to be one of them. "Sounds like some kind of diplomatic code."

"Yes. They use it with their satellites. The message first picked up went to Bucharest."

Sloane was conscious of time. He couldn't keep Tenpenny away too long. "What did you work on before that?"

"Before? You know I can't remember nothin' after—"

"Think!" He shoved his chin with the Walther. Tenpenny had the attention span of a child. Chances were he couldn't remember. But this was the only game in town. "Something important, pus-face. Important and tough." He moved the muzzle away to alleviate Tenpenny's terror. "Something only a genius like you could figure out."

He seemed to mutter to himself, a method of jogging his memory. "Oh, I know. The Naval code."

"Tell me about it, Dennis."

"It was Russian. I mostly work on Russian codes."

"I know." And he did. Tenpenny probably knew more about Soviet codes and code-making techniques than the KGB did. "Was it tough? A real jawbreaker?" The term was code-breaking jargon for a difficult code, meaning it couldn't be said and broke the jaw.

"Oh yeah. Real tough. Whole new technology. Laser communication with subs."

Sloane blinked. "Line of sight?" It was a mistake. Tenpenny looked at him like he was an idiot. Couldn't have him think he was smarter. "I mean was it long-range, from satellite?"

"I think."

Another blink. "How'd Mother intercept it?"

Tenpenny shook his head. "I dunno."

"What was the message?"

A shrug. "Routine. Not worth the fuss. Just ordered the sub to go to such and such coordinates."

"And do what?"

"Dunno. Some kind of maneuvers, I guess."

Sloane felt confused. He needed to think, but he had no time. He glanced at the side door of the bowling alley. The Secret Service men might come looking for Tenpenny at any moment. "You never heard of—"

"The hard part was transposing it."

Sloane stared at him. "The laser message? You transposed it?"

"Sure. I got their transmission down so slick God Himself couldn't tell where it came from." He began to relate in detail the exact aberration in the laser transmission, how he'd spotted it and duplicated it.

Sloane's mind was racing, but he deliberately reined it in. "You can go now, Dennis." The Walther was holstered.

"I can?" He seemed surprised.

"Pus-face, there are people who insist you are a dumb shit, but I know better. You're smart, Dennis, smart enough to realize that if you say one word about seeing me and our little conversation, you are a dead man."

"I know. You'll kill me. I-I won't say a word, I promise."

"Maybe you're not so smart. If Mother gets any idea you told me about this laser technology"—he reached up and pinched the end of Tenpenny's nose —"they'll snuff you out like a candle. The only

133

chance you got of living is to go back in there, play your idiot games, eat your chocolate, drink your Coke, and say not one goddamn word about ever laying eyes on me. Do you understand?''

"Yes.''

"Are you sure? You've told me too damn much. They'll bleed your brains dry, then kill you. It won't matter if you're the world's greatest code-breaker.''

"But I-I haven't t-told you anything.''

"Oh, yes you have, Dennis. Just breathe one word about the Seraphim Code and you're dead. I guarantee it.''

After Tenpenny left, Sloane drove northeast, putting up for the night in a cheap motel in Glen Burnie, south of Baltimore. He was dead tired, too tired to really think about what he had learned. Obviously the Seraphim Code was some new Soviet method for communicating with their subs. Laser technology. Why was it so damn important? Important enough to kill Karamasov and launch this big hunt for himself? Sloane closed his eyes. Never figure it out now. Maybe in the morning.

He tried to fall asleep, but it wouldn't come. If he did learn the importance of the Seraphim Code, what good would it do him? He'd still be a fugitive the rest of his life—or more likely dead. Then he smiled. *That's no way to live*. Freddie'd say that, then burst out laughing. God, he missed her. Couldn't believe how much. Even harder to believe was his thinking about a woman at the very time he was desperately trying to stay alive. Never used to do that. He was a shell of his former self. Freddie. He'd sent her the book, hoping she'd get the message. Apparently she had. She'd identified the body as him. Damn smart female.

He sighed. If he wanted any sort of life with Freddie, he just had to find some way to get these people off his back. Who? Mother doubtlessly. But specifically who? People were hunting him, a pair of field ops, most likely. Maybe if he could take one of them, he could find out who was behind this. Not hardly. What chance did he have? Maybe he could find out why they'd tried to kill him. Maybe he could send some sort of message, figure out some way to bring this to an end. Yes. It was worth a try. How many options did he have?

Sloane then became the hunter, a role he found more comfortable. He began by trying to put himself into the skin of that pair of field ops assigned to find and kill him. What would they do? Find his flophouse? No. They knew he'd never stay there more than one night. He'd left false trails all over Washington. If they fell for them it wouldn't be for long. They'd . . . Yes. They'd go right for Freddie. She was his weakness. They had to figure that sooner or later she'd lead them to him. They'd pick her up, try to scare her. Hell, they might even chemically debrief her. But she didn't know anything to tell them except that he was really alive, and they already knew that. They might even use muscle on her, hoping he might be flushed out if he thought she was in danger. None of it would work. They'd know she wasn't any good to them dead. She was the pawn. And both players of the game use pawns.

Sleep began to come to him now. His last conscious thought was that he wanted to awaken early.

SIX

Freddie emerged from her house a little before eight in the morning. She wore a bright red pants suit and comfortable flats, and she carried an overnight bag and the largest purse, a satchel really, she owned. These she put into Sloane's Audi, then, as though on impulse, she walked back toward the house, lingering to look at some flowers, normally a source of great pleasure to her, and pick up a couple of fallen twigs. What she really was doing was making sure anyone following her got a good look.

Sloane had taken a position a good half mile away, occupying a small copse of trees on a rise of ground. He had approached carefully at dawn and had several times scanned the whole area to make sure he was unobserved. Through binoculars he saw her in the red outfit and was visibly affected. She was so beautiful to him. Then he forced himself to look away. The car down the street, two men, one speaking into a mike. Sloane smiled. She was under surveillance. When he turned the glasses back to the house, Freddie was getting into his Audi, backing out of the garage, closing the door, driving away.

He watched the other car slowly pull out after her. There was no doubt they were FBI. Glorified cops, they would take the direct approach, just like in the movies, tailing her with probably three cars, one dropping out, another picking her up. They'd stick to her like glue. The CSA would never do this. They'd set up a "fence." All her usual movements would be known. She'd be observed at those locations. When she broke out of her usual haunts, the fence would move. Her passage would be reported from checkpoints with new ones being set up ahead of her. But there would be no direct tail. The KGB, who learned the technique from the CSA, now used the same method, especially in the US, where their movements were restricted.

Sloane made another careful visual search of the area, then moved to his car. He'd follow Freddie, but from a long distance. When he figured out where she was heading, he'd take another route. That was his ace in the hole. He knew that brown-haired, brown-eyed female. Did he ever! He could read her mind. He laughed. Her mind was a study in the unexpected, maybe even the bizarre. God, he loved her. *Don't think about it.*

Freddie drove out of town, northwest on Route 5 to Waldorf, then north on US 301. Once she was certain she saw a following car, but it turned off. After that she wasn't sure which car was her tail, but it didn't matter. One of them was. She had to believe that. All of this was a vast waste of time otherwise.

Her first stop was Brandywine, the shopping center where the entrance to the CSA headquarters was. She bought a morning paper, window-shopped a little— just to make sure her tail hadn't fallen too far behind—then walked forthrightly into the lobby of the CSA building. She had been there three years previously during the hunt for Parsley, although never in the underground portion, and knew what to expect. The smile she gave the Marine in the Pinkerton uniform was her very best. "I seem to be lost. Can you tell me how to get to Upper Marlboro?"

She saw him hesitate, glance at the console on his desk. Apparently no red or yellow light came on, for he quickly returned her smile and directed her back to US 301 and north. She thanked him, lavished another smile. "Say, is there someplace around here where you can get a good breakfast?" He recommended the coffee shop further up the shopping center. She lingered a moment, looking up to where she knew the surveillance camera was, making sure she was seen and hopefully identified.

Her visit to the office building was duly noted by Daugherty's men, but they attached no significance to it. The FBI had no conception the building held anything other than offices, nor did the KGB. Sloane was shocked. He had made Freddie promise she'd never go back to that building for any purpose. What the hell was she up to?

Freddie walked to the coffee shop and ordered waffles, eggs, sausage, home fries, toast, and coffee, paying with her order. When she saw two men enter and take a table, she rose and returned to her car.

Driving away she saw the two men emerge from the restaurant. Such a short breakfast!

She drove to D.C. and put the car in a parking garage, emerging with her luggage. Immediately she went to a pay phone and made a seemingly urgent call, doing her best to appear agitated. Then she took a cab, got out of it, window-shopped a little, and took another cab, abandoning it in favor of another pay phone. Another cab and phone call later, she checked into the Capital Hilton under her own name. She went to the room, left her overnighter, then descended the back stairs to the lobby, emerging from a side door to hail a taxi. Three cabs and two phone calls later she was at Washington National Airport buying a one-way ticket to Montreal. She then went to the ladies' room, emerging a half hour later, having missed her flight, wearing a blonde wig and stylishly dressed in heels, beige cotton suit, and floppy hat. Thus disguised, she rented a car and drove to Alexandria, abandoning it on the street. After going in and out of two stores and a restaurant, she took a cab to Arlington National Cemetery, where she mingled with the crowds, twice standing close to men as though secretly conversing with them.

By the time she had made her first phone call and switched to a second cab, Sloane knew what she was doing and reacted with open admiration. He even laughed out loud as he watched her antics unveil. She wasn't going anywhere or meeting anyone, but she sure made it look like she was. Beautiful, simply beautiful!

Actually his attention wasn't on her so much as on her surveillance. She was giving them fits. They lost

139

her almost at once, then picked her up at the Capital Hilton, lost her again, found her at Washington National, only to lose her again. All this was valuable information to Sloane. This tail on her was serious. Nothing casual about it. They were using her as a pawn and expected her to lead them to him. Okay. The tail was FBI, not CSA, and they faced an impossible task in trying to follow someone who didn't want to be followed in a big city. The fence had collapsed. He watched the FBI agents burn up the radio and phone lines, leading to an urgent curbside conference. The black guy was obviously in charge. He looked vaguely familiar to Sloane. Knew him from somewhere. Have to figure it out.

Freddie's confidence was waning. She had been certain David would find her at Arlington. How many times had he told her about making contact in public places where there are crowds and lots of escape routes. Once, near the Kennedy grave, she was sure she saw him and almost couldn't breathe, waiting for him to come to her. He didn't. Then she saw the man wasn't him. *Dammit, David, I'm here. This is safe. A hotshot spook like you ought to at least put in some kind of appearance.* He didn't. Nothing happened, except the man she spoke to came on to her and invited her to lunch. *Lunch.* She remembered the breakfast she'd ordered but not eaten. *I'm starved, David. How about buying me a hotdog. I'll just mosey over there, buy a chili dog. You can walk up beside me and . . .* She ate alone, glancing frequently at her watch. She'd been here over a half hour. No David. Maybe he wasn't anywhere about. She had been so sure. She could *feel* him. She sighed. Maybe not. *Ms. Falscape, we've tested you for ESP and we want to tell you to be careful crossing the street. You're a danger to yourself.*

At the entrance to Arlington she hailed a cab, climbed in back, and sagged weakly against the seat, closing her eyes.

"Where to, lady?"

She sighed. What did it matter? "Downtown, I guess."

"Downtown Arlington?"

The voice was gruff and had a thick accent. And there was condescension in it which annoyed her. She opened her eyes. "You know good and well I mean downtown Washington."

He put the cab in gear and drove away. "Downtown Washington is a big place, lady. Can't you do better than that? You have no idea how hard it is to drive a hack all day and have to put up with dizzy dames who don't know where they're going."

Her anger rose sharply. How dare he? She'd report him. Her eyes swept from the back of his head to the name plate. Lazlo Kucej. She'd remember that. Then she looked back at the driver. He was gray-haired with a heavy gray mustache which covered most of his mouth. His wire spectacles had a heavy tint. She looked back at the name plate. Lazlo Kucej was young, clean-shaven. "Say, you're not the one who's supposed to be driving this cab."

The face was partially turned to speak over the seat. "Do you want to go to Washington, lady, or do you want to argue?"

She gasped. Her hand came to her mouth. "David?" She leaned forward, touched his shoulder. "Oh, my God, it is you!"

"Sit back, Freddie. Don't call attention to us."

141

She obeyed. *Thank you, God.* "You did find me. I knew you would."

"Been following you all morning. I was going to pick you up at the airport, but you rented the car instead."

"I didn't know what to do. I was just hoping—" She turned to look out the back window.

"Don't turn around!" There was sharp command to his voice. "I don't think anyone's following, but I can't be sure."

Suddenly her eyes filled with tears. "Oh God, David. I'm so glad to see you—even in that getup."

He smiled. "You don't look so bad yourself. Are you okay?"

"I'm fine—now." She swallowed, wiped at her lower eyelids, sniffled. "I don't care much for identifying dead bodies, being bugged, followed everywhere, and questioned. Other than that, everything is just fine. Oh yes, I don't like sleeping alone."

"I'm sorry. Can't be helped."

Now the tears really came. A sob caught in her throat and she had a good old-fashioned bawl. Finally she could manage, "I'm . . . sorry. I-I didn't—intend to . . . be this way." She sighed heavily. "Oh God, I-I was . . . going to—"

"I know. You don't have to prove how tough you are."

"Can we . . . go somewhere and . . . talk—or something?" A sound, half sigh, part sob. "I need to be held, David."

The sudden roiling of his loins surprised him. He wanted her—bad. And he was tempted. To distract himself he glanced into both rearview mirrors. No suspicious vehicles. Still . . . "You know I want to, but we'd better not." He sought more distraction. "I gather all this morning's activity was an exercise in losing your tail."

"And allowing you to find me. It worked, didn't it?"

"Why'd you go to Brandywine?"

"No reason. Just making waves. I wanted them to see me."

"Stay away from there, Freddie. I mean it."

"Okay." Then she remembered. "How'd you get this cab?" Her eyes widened. Once before he'd gotten a cab by . . . "You didn't—"

"No. It's a private cab. I paid him three hundred dollars to use it for a few hours."

"What's going on, David?"

"How much do you know?"

She laughed. "Remember the time I accused you of being a psychiatrist because you answer a question with a question?"

"I remember. Tell me what you know so far."

"Okay." She said the word as a long sigh. "One of the dead men in our formerly immaculate yard was a KGB agent named Pavel Karamasov."

"How'd you get that name?"

For an instant she thought of telling him about Adams. "I was picked up yesterday by three men. They told me. I think they were from Mother."

"Describe them." He listened. None had meaning to him. "Do they think I'm dead?"

"I don't think so. But the police do."

"That's all I could hope for."

"What happened, David—at our place?"

"Are you sure you want to know?"

"Yes. I'm a big girl."

"Karamasov was there, waiting for me. It was a CSA hit. Two men tried to kill me. I had to . . ."

She shuddered. Couldn't help it. "You killed both?"

"Had to, Freddie. No choice."

"You dumped one in the river with your ID?"

"Yes."

She exhaled with a long audible sound. "Memorial service is being held for you Monday night. I had you cremated. Do you know who he really is?"

"I have a name, but I doubt if it's the right one."

"I'd like to find out someday—tell his family."

"We'll see."

"David, because of the Russian agent, they think you've turned, gone over. Is that why they're after you?"

"The field ops, maybe. But Brandywine knows better."

"Then why?" She saw him shake his head. "Dammit, it's my husband they're trying to kill. It's my life they're ruining. I have a right to know."

Again he shook his head. "I don't know much myself, Freddie. And look at what's happening to me. You're safe only if you don't know anything."

"What did the Russian want?"

"Nothing."

"Dammit, Sloane, I—"

"If you know anything at all Freddie, you're dead."

She shook with anger and frustration. "Okay, you won't tell me. I'll tell you. The Agency wants to kill you because they think that Russian told you something—or just might possibly have told you something."

"Stop it, Freddie."

"Ergo, the Agency is up to something so bad and so secret they can't have anyone knowing about it—not even their most trusted agent."

"Formerly trusted agent. Listen to me, Freddie. I'm not going to say anything. I want you to live."

"To do what? Enjoy my widowhood? God, this is so *awful!* Can you turn the mirror so I can at least see your face?" He did and she laughed. "Is that how you'll look when you're old?"

"If I get old."

She nodded. "You will. We survived Parsley, didn't we?"

"Hard to believe now."

"I said *we*, David."

"Lord, you're persistent."

"And you wouldn't be alive if I wasn't." She looked at his reflection in the mirror. "Did I go through all that in Munich just for three years of happiness? It isn't enough."

"Don't think about it."

"I knew you'd say that." She shook her head, pursed her lips. "Could you take off those silly glasses so I can see your eyes?" He did. "Nice eyes. Is this the last time I get to see them?"

"Don't think about it."

She knew she was getting to him. She saw the softness in his eyes and felt her own surge of desire. He wanted her. She could tell. "Sure we can't stop somewhere? You used to say I was good in bed."

"Stop it!" To enforce it, he moved the mirror and put on the phony glasses.

She sighed deeply. "All right. I won't tease. I haven't asked how you are."

145

"Scared. I'm not the man I used to be. I care too much about you—and us."

"That's because you *aren't* the man you used to be. David Sloane, the dispassionate killing machine, died three years ago. You're David Pritchard now."

"I suppose."

"What's going to happen to us, David?" She saw the slight shrug of his shoulders. "What're you trying to do? Is there anyway out of this mess?"

"Freddie, I told you I don't want you to know—"

"Can't you tell me *something?* You're a clever man. Give me some tiny ray of hope, *please!*" She saw him shake his head and swore under her breath. "Mother, my real mother that is, told me never to marry a stubborn man who shuts his wife out of his life."

"I'm sorry. I'm doing it because I love you. I want you to live."

"Alone? The Merry Widow Falscape? I thought I was the other day, you know."

"I'm sorry."

"David, if flight is the only way, if taking off for Cape Town or Ouagadougou or some other godforsaken place is the only way for us, take me with you."

"You won't like that."

"I know I won't, but I love you enough to do it—if it is the only way. Is it?"

He sighed. "I dunno. I'm not sure. We may have to."

"Okay, I'll do it, David. For better or worse, remember?"

He swallowed. "Thank you for that. It means a lot. But I'm trying not to run. I'm hoping . . ."

His voice trailed off. She waited. But he didn't want

to tell her. "Please, David. What are you trying to accomplish by staying around here?"

Another, deeper sigh from him. "Okay, I can tell you this much. I'm hoping that I may be able to find out something—about what is going on. If I do, I may be able—hell, I've no idea what good it may do."

"But it's the only sail in the wind, the only hope?"

"That's about it."

"Can I help?"

"Yes. There's a black guy following you. He's your principal tail. I vaguely know him. I'd like to get a better look at him—and whoever his partner is."

"Tell me what to do."

"I'm going to leave you off soon. Take a cab back to the Capital Hilton. Go to your room and change into your red outfit. That's the one they know best."

"Okay."

"Then go to lunch, shopping, whatever you want. The point is to make sure they see you. And don't lose them this time. It's a fine line, Freddie. You want to be seen, but you also want—"

"I know, be furtive. I'm trying to lose a tail so as to meet someone." She smiled. "Am I?"

"Yes. Remember that Italian place in Georgetown we sometimes go to?"

"Trattoria Ponte Vecchio."

"Go there for lunch. I'll pick you up out in front precisely at one-thirty-five. Time it so you just walk out and into the cab."

"It'll be you? In this cab?"

"Yes."

"Then what?"

"I'll tell you then. Any questions?"

"Yes. Why do I love you so much?"

"Just dumb, I guess. Any serious questions?"

"Do you want me to leave my hotel door unlocked in case you want to—"

"Don't even think about it, Freddie."

"You've made me into a wanton." She saw the cab slowing, pulling into a curb. "So this is it—all I get?" She sat forward, grabbed her purse. "I love you, David."

"And I love you. If I'm not there at one-thirty-five, Freddie, you'll know I—"

"Don't *you* even think about it." She reached for the door.

"Better pay me." He turned up the flag. "That'll be five-forty, lady." It was the gruff voice he'd begun with.

"I suppose you expect a tip too."

A moment later she was on the curb, hearing rather than seeing him drive away. She knew better than to look after the cab or attach any importance to it. It was just as well. Her vision was swimming anyway.

"You dumb sonofabitch. She's probably meeting Sloane right now. You let that fucking female make a monkey out of you."

Captain Price heard the anger in Gillies's voice. It was only an articulation of his own frustration.

"We have an exact description of the woman who rented the car found in Alexandria. We'll have her in a few minutes."

"Sure, G-man, sure." Gillies's voice dripped sarcasm. "She goes in the ladies room, changes clothes, and comes out a blonde. Oldest trick in the book and you fell for it."

"I wasn't there. I didn't—"

"The FBI sucks, G-man. It really does."

"And I suppose you could've done better."

"Better believe it."

"All right, all right. This is getting us nowhere." Price glared at both men, and at Mako, who had yet to say a word. "The woman obviously set out to shake her tail and succeeded. There is nothing to do about it. The question is, what is she up to?"

"Meeting Sloane, obviously."

Price nodded at Gillies. "It would seem so. All those phone calls. Must've been pre-arranged. He told her where to go and what to do to meet him. The question is why."

"She's his wife, fer crissake."

"I know she's his wife, Gillies. But the fact remains that meeting her makes no sense. Involving her puts her at risk. He'd never do that. She's safe only as long as she doesn't know anything."

"She knows enough to lose an FBI tail."

The phone rang. Price answered, listened, handed it to Daugherty, who also listened. Handing over the receiver he said, "They got her. She's back at the hotel, went to her room." Daugherty listened, said into the phone, "Okay, don't lose her this time. Let me know as soon as she lands somewhere." To Price he said, "She changed back into her red outfit, no disguise, and left the hotel in a cab. They're tailing her."

"They'd better." Gillies got up and walked over to the coffee pot, half filled a paper cup. "I don't like this dizzy dame making a monkey out of me—or her hotshot husband either."

"I told you not to underestimate him. He's obviously briefed her on what to do."

"But how?" Daugherty's voice was not too defensive. "Her phone, her house, her office, her classroom are bugged. We've had a tail on her—"

"Except for the last hour and a half, dummy." Gillies's voice from across the room ladled on scorn.

"Look, Gillies, I'm not going to take any more of your—"

"Hold it, you two." Price looked sharply at Daugherty. "Have your people got a make on the cabs which have picked her up?"

"I imagine so. Yes."

"Then that's it. Sloane is driving a cab. He's done it before. I'll bet my life he's either picked her up or will shortly."

Mako finally spoke. "Makes sense."

Excited now, Price said, "Watch the cabs. One of them will have Sloane as a driver."

The phone interrupted him. Daugherty answered, spoke a couple of words, then said, "She's gone to the Ponte Vecchio, an Italian restaurant near Georgetown U. She's met a woman there and they've taken a booth, ordered. Apparently it's lunchtime."

"All right, let's go." Gillies set down the cup and headed for the door. "G-man, you take inside surveillance. Don't lose her, for crissake. Take a female agent with you in case she tries that john stunt again. Mako and I will take the outside."

Price had the last word. "Remember to watch the cabs."

* * *

Freddie considered Vivian Styles little more than an acquaintance, yet she latched on to her as a distraction, someone to talk to during lunch. Vivian was on the faculty at Georgetown, a handsome black woman in her forties, very dramatic-looking in her flowered kaftan with a matching cloche on her hair. They chatted about her work in the African Studies program, the political scene in Washington, the possibilities for summer vacation. Vivian didn't know about her "widowhood" and Freddie didn't tell her. Both had cheese ravioli. Freddie hardly ate, a symptom of her nervousness.

Her friend was only a minimal distraction to Freddie. She kept watching the clock and the door. When the black man entered, accompanied by a young white woman, and took a table across the room from her booth, Freddie knew he was the tail, his companion obviously FBI. Freddie made no attempt to ignore him. Indeed, she looked at him boldly, even holding his eyes for a moment. David thought he knew him. She didn't. His face meant nothing to her.

Vivian had to eat and run, leaving Freddie alone now. She glanced at the clock. It just had to be stopped. Her watch wasn't working either, quartz or no quartz. Maybe time was standing still. *Ms. Falscape, it is not natural for persons under stress to lose their sense of time. We'll perform the lobotomy in the morning.* She ordered a gooey dessert and another cup of coffee, then went into the ladies' room, stood in a stall a moment, then flushed. The lady agent was washing her hands at a sink when she emerged. Freddie did not wash her hands. *Dear, you must always wash your hands after you* . . . She returned to the table and actually consumed every crumb of the pastry. At precisely 1:30 she paid the check for both lunches. At 1:33 she rose to leave and walked across to where her tail sat. "Excuse me. I know I've been staring but I'm sure we've met." She watched him rise. Courtesy was ingrained, but he looked nervous.

"I'm sorry, but I—"

"Aren't you on the faculty at Georgetown? Political science, isn't it?"

"I'm afraid you have—"

"I'm Freddie Falscape, Calvert College. I think we met—"

"I'm afraid you have me confused with someone else."

She smiled, one of her better ones. "Do I? Perhaps you're right. I'm sorry to have interrupted your lunch." She turned to go, stopped. "I was just so sure I'd seen you somewhere before."

As she walked to the front of the restaurant, her sense of foreboding was almost unbearable. Why had David wanted her to do this? It was dangerous. She was being tailed too closely. She stopped near the cash register, selected a couple of mints from a bowl. Backward glance. They were on their feet following her. *Don't come, David. Please don't.*

"Did you enjoy your lunch, Dr. Falscape?"

The voice startled her and she wheeled. Antonio, the proprietor, his fleshy Italian face wreathed in smiles. She managed to reciprocate. "Oh yes, Antonio—as always."

"Your husband could not join you today?"

Somehow the question unnerved her. "No, he's—"

"I understand. Man's work is never done." He laughed heartily at his little joke. "Do come another time."

She glanced at her watch. A half minute past 1:35. God! "Yes. You know we will." He held the door for her and she passed out into the sunlight, blinking against the glare. The curb was empty. She looked to her left, up the street. There were lots of cabs, too many cabs. Which one was his? Why didn't she know *his* cab? She felt movement behind her. The black man, the white female agent. They were almost rubbing against her. Too close. *Don't come, David! Please don't come!*

He was less than 50 yards up the street, at the curb, as though stopped for the light. All the doors were locked so no fare would enter. His attention was riveted on the scene ahead. He was aware of Freddie coming out of the restaurant and the black man behind her, but what he really saw were the reactions of two others to her presence, a short, wiry man standing in front of the restaurant, another, taller and blond, across the street. Field ops. He was sure of it.

Sloane's momentary reaction was confusion. *Three* people tailing Freddie? But he had no time to think about it. Quickly he slung a pair of large felt dice on a string over the rearview mirror and started the cab forward, unlocking the right rear door as he did so.

Freddie saw the cab with the dice in the windshield, but it was in the wrong lane. Suddenly it darted through a lane of traffic and stopped perhaps a dozen feet from the curb. She heard the screeching of tires and the crunch of cars colliding. The door to the cab came open. She ran to it. The acceleration of the cab was so great she was propelled against the seat and the door closed.

"God, David!"

The distraction of the collision was only momentary, but long enough for him to get away. In the rearview mirror he saw the two CSA agents react, the black man too. He saw them moving in unison, doubtlessly for a car. He took down the dice and tossed them on the seat.

"Never let it be said you don't make life exciting, darling."

"No time to talk, Freddie." He had already turned the corner and now drove, fast but not too fast, down an alley. "Just listen." He turned onto the street. "I'm letting you out just ahead. There's an empty cab. Take it to the Hilton. Fool around a little—"

"So as to be seen?"

"Yes. Then go sightseeing, Walk or take buses. No cabs."

"I can drive the Audi."

"Okay. Driving around is good. Get to the Lincoln Memorial about quarter to three. Take a good long look around. Come down the steps. I'll be there in this cab, in front, precisely at three o'clock. We'll do all this again."

"Am I still the lady in red?"

"By all means. If there are lots of cabs you'll know this one by the dice in the window. Just hop in as you did before."

She saw the parked cab, felt this one coming to a stop. "I just hope the next ride is longer." She opened the door. "I love you." He did not reply. At least she heard none as she stepped out. Then the cab was gone.

The face of Curt Gillies remained impassive but the rage within him burned at white heat until it seemed to drain even more of the color from his gray eyes, giving him a vacant look. This guy, this Sloane, had made a monkey out of him. He'd seen him, he'd had him, yet he'd gotten away. He had been watching cabs. He'd even seen the cab with the dice, but it was in the wrong lane. He'd looked away. Dammit! Fuckit to holy hell! The G-man was standing right there with the girl. Why didn't he grab her? And Mako. He could've—shit, shit, shit!

But his outburst of rage was quickly set aside as self-defeating and replaced with a quiet determination to get this hotshot field op. No man would make a monkey out of him. This was now *personal*, man to man. That cockeyed Price with his looney ideas of a cell was out of it. He was not in charge of this case. There would be no more pussyfooting around with the girl. If Sloane wanted her, he'd have to come to him to get her. Then he'd kill him.

Gregor Azbel had expected a day or two to get his feet on the ground at the Embassy, but no. This Fern L. Falscape had left her home for Washington. The fence had collapsed and he had spent the entire day trying to keep up with her. One thing was for certain. The ineptitude among KGB personnel in Washington went far deeper than anyone imagined. Only a thorough housecleaning would suffice. He would tell Vladimir Kastalsky that when he came. Maybe it would help ameliorate what he knew was about to be

Robert A. Liston

an immense failure for which he would be held personally responsible.

There really were no excuses. The KGB had the potential to draw upon the services of seven or eight thousand people in the Washington area. Yet they could not keep up with a single woman. He had read her file. She was not in the business. She had no training in intelligence or even police work, yet the finest, most experienced operatives in Washington had repeatedly lost her—even after he ordered direct surveillance. Only the presence of an informant within the FBI had enabled them to find her at all. Unthinkable!

He ran his fingers through his thick black hair and pondered the events outside the Italian restaurant. Azbel knew he now commanded an army of oafs. One of the oldest tricks in the book, and his supposedly crack agents are looking at bent fenders while their prey drives off with his wife. Azbel now knew the depths of his troubles. He might as well start convincing himself just how much he'd enjoy snow and polar bears.

No. Somebody had better start thinking around here and quick. A taxi marked by felt dice. She gets in, goes a short distance, gets out, returns to her hotel. Strange. What is she up to? Even stranger— and this was the only useful information to come out of the debacle at the restaurant—three US agents had reacted to the taxi. Three? It was well-known the Americans always worked in pairs. There were times when he believed the pair system even had advantages over their own five-man cells, but he had never encountered a three-man operation. What was going on? Three men. If the CSA was changing its methods

156

of operation, this would be highly important to Dzerzhinsky Square. It might be enough to save his skin.

The red light on the phone blinked. He answered, listened. The Falscape woman had left the hotel, driven off in the Audi. Americans followed. All were under KGB surveillance. He spoke words into the phone in Russian which translated, "They'd better be!"

Strange. Impossibly strange. This woman, wife of a most hunted man, is moving around Washington like a cyclone, making phone calls, changing cabs, going in and out of buildings, obviously to thwart surveillance. Since she is untrained, she can only be acting under the direction of her husband. Yet the Americans let her go. They do not pick her up! Unfathomable!

For the first time Gregor Azbel's eyes brightened under a glimmer of hope. He knew just what he must do. The next report on the whereabouts of Fern L. Falscape told him just how to do it.

Captain Lawson Price listened to the agitated voice of Mako on the secure phone. He argued that Fern Falscape be picked up right now and grilled. She had obviously been in contact with her husband—that was hardly the tooth fairy driving that cab with the hanging dice—and had to know where he was and what he was doing. Price could not deny the logic. To pick her up now was the accepted procedure. But he said into the phone, "No, Mako. Let her go. She is still the pawn. We want Sloane, not her. She will lead us to him."

"Goddammit, she already has and he got away."

Price knew he was taking a calculated risk, but he had a sense that accepted procedure was exactly what Sloane wanted. Sloane had helped to write the book, therefore the book could not be used. Sloane wanted them to pick her up. He had no fear of it, obviously. She knew nothing to tell them—again obviously. And she had no fear of questioning. Picked up last night she had said, "Stick it up your ass," and walked out. The woman must be left alone at least for awhile.

"She will lead us to him, Mako. I'm certain of it."

"Meanwhile she's driving around in the Audi and he's in a cab."

"Perhaps. I've ordered all cabs with hanging dice to be stopped, the drivers questioned." He laughed. "It turns out there are a surprising number of them."

"A waste of time. He won't do it again."

"Don't be too sure. Because we are so positive he won't, it may be the very thing he does. Where's Gillies?"

"He's with Daugherty following the Audi."

Price bristled. "I did not order that. I want him to report in at once."

SEVEN

Freddie's euphoria lasted but a few minutes. It came from seeing David twice, but more from knowing she was in some way helping him, *participating* in this terrible thing that was destroying their lives. He *needed* her. But her exhilaration quickly gave way to despair. There was danger. David was somehow taking great risks in whatever he was doing. Why was this happening to them?

Don't think about it. Yes. Still the best advice. So she forced it out of her mind. *Ms. Falscape, do you realize how bad repression is for you? It is a primary cause of shingles, tooth decay, and junk mail.* At the hotel she thought about calling Gordon Adams or whatever his real name was. She wasn't about to tell him about the planned meeting at the Lincoln Memorial—*Dr.*

Falscape, distrust is a major symptom of pernicious obesity—but she could report she had seen David and that he was trying to learn something which would. . . Which would what? *My husband is not a traitor, Mr. President. He just has a bad Mother.* She decided not to attempt the call. It was a cumbersome process. Dial this number, wait, give a name, wait for a call. *Vote AT&T. They've been there over a century when you needed them.* The hell with Adams. She wasn't working for him. She was working—*this is gainful employment?*—for David Sloane or whatever his name was. *Ms. Falscape, can you prove your name is Fern L. Pritchard?*

She was now at the Lincoln Memorial, absolutely certain that no one in history had ever *seen* the place as she had. To control her fear and mounting apprehension, she had forced her mind to concentrate on every detail of the monument. She had read the Gettysburg Address and Second Inaugural Address so often she had them memorized. "With malice toward none." *That's easy for you to say, Mr. Lincoln. You didn't have the CSA trying to kill your husband— not to mention the KGB. All you had was a few dumb slave owners and a lot of greedy bankers.* Shameful. There was lint collected in the Great Emancipator's left ear.

It really hadn't worked. She knew she wasn't convincing anyone she was a tourist. Cars had followed her all over town. The black man with his white FBI companion stood just over there. She smiled at him. He wasn't very friendly. There were tourists, all right, some families, but mostly groups of school kids bussed in for spring break. *David, we'll send our son to Washington to learn about life, liberty, and the pursuit of happiness. Pursuit of what?* But she was sure there were just as many minions of the law as tourists. She recognized at least two men from her surveillance. What worried her were all those she didn't recognize.

A little before three she made a trial run, walking slowly out of the Memorial, down the steps to stand at the curb. With her peripheral vision she watched people gravitate toward her. *So many!* After looking expectantly up the street, she turned, smiled at the black man behind her, then walked up to the Memorial. *Four score and seven years ago our forefathers had no idea anything like the CSA would exist. Mr. Orwell, you were right, only it isn't at all like you described it.*

Sloane clicked the shutter, taking a really nice shot of the Washington Monument as seen in the reflecting pool. Then he moved, setting up his equipment again. He had invested in the camera, tripod, and long lens, and a bag to carry it all in. Dressed in a blond wig, brown contacts, droopy mustache, he looked like a seedy and certainly artful photographer shooting photos of D.C. landmarks on speculation. Sometimes he shot the Washington Monument, the Capitol in the background, the D.C. War Memorial, groups of tourists, but more often he turned the lens west to shoot the Lincoln Memorial.

He actually had film in the camera. It was part of his cover, but he also wanted photographs, although he was uncertain he'd ever have them developed. He saw Freddie many times, but most of his attention and photographs concentrated on the people around her. Through the long lens he saw the black man. Why couldn't he think of where he knew him from? *Your mind is going, Sloane. Harry Rogers would never have forgotten a face.* He took a good shot of the short, wiry Puerto Rican. He remained only a few paces from Freddie. Then he got a decent shot of the blond with the vacant eyes. He stood across the street from the Memorial, a study in concentration and wariness. The man was seeing everything and everybody. A CSA op, obviously. The Puerto Rican too. There were other CSA personnel around too, obviously assigned to watch the field ops.

He moved the lens back for a longer view of what was to him a tableau. The blond and the Puerto Rican could be a pair, although there was something strange about the way they interacted. Somehow he had a feeling they weren't a pair. And both worked with the black man. He had seen the blond and black man arrive together shortly after Freddie came. The black man was obviously FBI. Sloane shook his head in confusion. CSA field ops would never, never, never under any circumstances work with an FBI agent. What was going on?

Another bus load of tourists arrived. Good. The place was filling up. Then he saw something which almost made him laugh out loud. They weren't going to do it again? Time to return to the cab. Quickly he packed up his gear and headed for Constitution Avenue.

Freddie felt smothered. There were just too many people. She was being jostled by kids eager for a view of the seated Lincoln. She moved out to the steps. Not much better. Why all these people now? She looked around. The black man, others were close to her, too close. *This isn't going to work, David. You'll never get away with this a second time.*

She looked across the street. A TV truck had just

pulled up. Two camera crews were setting up, one on a tripod shooting the Memorial, the other with a shoulder-carried minicam. They were actually going to do man-on-the-street interviews! Now! God! Tourists gravitated to the cameras and lights, waving, shouting. There wasn't room for a cab to pull up. *Don't come, David, please!*

She glanced at her watch. One till three. Inhaling, then forcing it out deeply, she headed down the steps to the curb. She didn't need to turn around. She knew the black man was right behind her. If she tried to get into the cab they would physically grab her. She didn't have a chance. *Don't come, David. If you love me, don't come.* She saw a cab approaching, slowing. It wasn't David. No dice in the windshield. But she leaned toward it. No one touched her but she could sense the hands unfolding behind her to take her. Across the street she saw men, one a blond with terrible eyes, mirror her movements. They were watching her. If she went for the cab, they would too. *Don't come, David. For the sake of our child don't come.* Another cab. It passed by. Another, another. One stopped, let out passengers, took on fares, drove off. She didn't move. If she was breathing, she was unaware of it.

Far to her left she saw the dice in the windshield, gasped. *Oh, God, no!* She looked across the street at the blond man. He had seen the cab and was turning to look at her, reacting. A twisted smile spread his lips. His right hand entered his jacket. *No, please NO!* The cab angled toward her, slowing, the crazy dice swaying. There seemed to be no other vehicle in the street. *If you love me, God, please don't let this happen.* The cab continued to slow. It stopped in front of her.

"No! Go! Don't stop!"

She tried to wave him away as she screamed, but something held her arms. She couldn't move.

It all happened so fast. At least a half-dozen men surrounded the cab, guns drawn, the blond man on the driver's side opening the door. The driver was pulled out. There was shouting and screaming, some from the camera crew, which rushed to film this real-life drama.

"Come with us, Ms. Falscape, please."

She tried to turn, look at her captors, but she really had no chance as she was forcibly rushed—almost carried—a few feet from the curb and thrust into the back seat of a car. Quickly a man slid in beside her, another in the front seat, and the vehicle sped off at high speed, tires squealing. She turned, looked out the back window. She was aware of the men around the taxi reacting, pointing weapons to fire after them, but she was conscious, truly, of only what she looked to see. She had been right. The driver of the cab wasn't David.

Sloane saw it all from a distance and approved. Probably scared the be-jeezus out of the cabdriver, but he'd be all right. He'd tell the truth. "Some guy—how the hell do I know who he was?—hired my cab all morning. When he returned it he gave me another hundred to go to the Lincoln Memorial at three and pick up some dame in a red suit. He asked me to hang them crazy dice in the windshield. He said it was some kinda private joke. They met at a dice table or something." At least he'd have a chance to explain. There had always been the risk the driver would be shot on the spot, no questions asked. Hadn't happened. Good thing.

He watched the scene at the cab. He couldn't hear what was being said, but he knew what was happening. Men rushed for cars to follow Freddie. It would never work. The blond man was in a rage. He went to the black man, screamed something at him, then he went off with the Puerto Rican.

Sloane watched the scene gradually dissipate. The cabby was led away for questioning. Someone got into the cab and drove it away. It would be dusted for prints and searched for evidence as only the FBI could. The KGB "TV crew"—a stunt they had used once before to grab a person away from US intelligence—was already gone. Lincoln Memorial gradually returned to the tourists. Only then did Sloane begin his next move.

"That was not your husband in the taxi, Dr. Falscape."

The voice was deep, well modulated, the English precise—too precise. Textbook English. The accent was faint, but there. She turned to her left to look at him. Mid-thirties, dark-haired, brown-eyed, dressed in a dark blue suit, white shirt, red tie. Utterly nondescript. Could be a million people in Washington. "Who are you?" She already knew, at least in generalities. People in intelligence all had the same look.

"You expected your husband to be driving the taxi, did you not?"

She looked to the man on her right, the one in the passenger seat, the back of the head of the driver. All were younger, equally indescribable. None of the three seemed to pay any attention to her. She turned back to her interrogator. "I asked who you are." There was firmness in her voice, which surprised her. Part of her mind, the sensible, cerebral part, knew with certainty she ought to be terrified. But she wasn't. Figure that one out, would you?

"Someone trying to help you—and your husband."

She looked ahead at the street. The car had slowed, but it still moved rapidly. She didn't have time to figure out where they were. "Where are you taking me?"

"A place where you will be safe. No harm will come to you, Dr. Falscape."

At least he wasn't attempting to call her Freddie. She looked at him, more closely now. The face was impassive, a mask really. "You're KGB, aren't you?" She shook her head. "My God! I'm a captive of the KGB! In Washington, D.C., yet! Lord!"

"I said no harm will befall you. We have not much time, Dr. Falscape. You saw your husband earlier in the day, did you not?"

She made no reply.

"He was driving the taxi which picked you up in front of the Italian restaurant in Georgetown, was he not?"

No answer.

"He arranged to meet you in front of the Lincoln Memorial. You expected him to be in that taxi."

No reply.

Now he looked at her a long moment, but his eyes lacked the warmth of real interest. "I am trying to find your husband, Dr. Falscape. I would"—he hesi-

tated, as though choosing unfamiliar words—
"*appreciate* any help you can give. It just may save his life."

She nodded. "My husband is not a traitor, sir."

"I know that. No one wants him to be."

"You want to know what your agent Karamasov said to him before he died, don't you?" She was surprised. She had expected some reaction from him, but there was none. She smiled. "I get it. You don't know Karamasov, do you?" She shook her head. "I'm being stupid. Of course you *know* him, but you don't know anything about how he died. Well, Mr. KGB, I don't either—except that he got himself plugged in my front yard by a CSA hit man. But I have no idea what if anything he said to my husband before he died. I really don't. I mean it. You can shove bamboo shoots under my fingernails, fill me full of chemicals, do whatever you do to extract information—you can even kill me—but I have no information to give you."

He looked at her a long moment, almost as long as it took her to utter the words. If there was anything to be read in his eyes, it was that she was a very foolish woman. "You will not be harmed. Dr. Falscape, where is your husband?"

"I don't know. Truly I don't. Somewhere in this city, I suspect. I saw him twice today. You are right. I expected him to be driving the cab just now. I was surprised when he wasn't. I don't know where he is."

"Where did you see him?"

"He was driving a cab both times. He picked me up at Arlington Cemetery and drove me downtown. Then he picked me up in front of the Ponte Vecchio, as you know."

"Where have you arranged to meet your husband, Dr. Falscape?"

"In front of the Lincoln Memorial at three o'clock."

Again he stared at her, then reached into his pocket, removing a small notepad. He consulted Cyrillic letters. "You left your home early this morning, drove to a small shopping center, ordered a breakfast you did not eat, drove to Washington, made a phone call, took a cab—"

"I was making a false trail."

"Why?"

"My house and office are being watched constantly, as you must know. I knew my husband could not come to me. I tried to move around in hopes he might find me." She smiled. "It worked."

"He picked you up at Arlington National Cemetery. Was he disguised?"

Freddie hesitated. She didn't want to say anything which might possibly threaten David. But he had always told her to tell the exact truth when being questioned. Surely he would not use the same disguise again. "Yes. He wore a gray wig, gray mustache, and dark glasses."

"He wore the same disguise when he picked you up in front of the restaurant?"

A mental image crossed her mind, surprising her. "No. He wore no disguise." She hadn't realized it till this moment. He must have wanted the black man and other agents to spot him. He used the dice so they could not help but identify the taxi.

Suddenly she was aware of the vehicle turning, heading downward into an underground garage. She had a sense of a high-rise building above, but couldn't really see it. The car pulled to a stop and three doors opened. Men helped her out, led her to an elevator. It opened. She entered with three men. Buttons were pushed. The door closed. She began to move upward. For the first time she knew fear. *They never do anything in the car, baby. It's after they get you upstairs. You really are going to see the Marquis de Sade room now.*

She kept reading the numbers on the elevator. "Where am I?"

"Where you will be safe."

She shook her head. "I might have known." The elevator stopped at 17. The door opened and she was led down the hall a short distance. They stopped before a door. A button was pressed by a Slavic forefinger. Fear truly gripped her now. She knew she was shaking or about to. The door opened. A large burly man stood in it. She was afraid of him.

"This gentleman will look after you, Dr. Falscape."

She turned to the man who had been her interrogator. "You're leaving?"

"Yes."

Suddenly she didn't want him to go. The devil you know is better than . . . Instinctive understanding came to her. "You're going all the way back to Russia, aren't you? Just because I can identify you as a KGB agent? Such a waste. I-I promise I won't say anything. Then you can stay here. You like this country, don't you?"

They had already turned away from her and she was talking to their backs. Now she turned back to the door. It had opened wider. The man said, "Please come in, Dr. Falscape." She sighed, then she stepped inside.

Peter Daugherty looked around one last time. He had finished here. The whole area had been searched for Sloane, a study in futility at best. He had sent away his men. All that remained was to go to the cell meeting and try to explain how he let the KGB take the Falscape woman from him.

He felt a tug at his sleeve, looked down. A small black boy. Couldn't be ten. A ten-dollar bill was clutched in one fist, a piece of paper in the other. He thrust it toward him.

"I'm to give ya this, mister."

When Daugherty didn't take the paper, he dropped it and ran. Daugherty opened his mouth to shout after him, but knew it was no use. He bent, picked up the paper. It was cheap lined paper, ripped from a spiral notebook, folded in thirds. He unfolded it, read printed words:

IF YOU LOOK AROUND, IF YOU SAY ONE WORD, YOU ARE DEAD WHERE YOU STAND. NOW GO READ THE GETTYSBURG ADDRESS.

He blinked, swallowed, then carefully refolded the paper, inserted it in his breast pocket very slowly, keeping his hands visible at all times, then walked up the stairs and into the Memorial. It was still busy, people still reacting to all the excitement. He took a place, looked up at the bronze lettering as though reading.

"Don't look around. Don't move. Just read."

The voice came from just behind his left ear, *sotto*

voce. He could feel the breath against his skin. "I won't." He felt his jacket flap being lifted, his gun separating from its holster.

"Who are you?"

"Peter Daugherty, FBI."

"How do I know you?"

"I made the investigation when you obtained your security clearance."

Sloane nodded. Yes. He shouldn't have forgotten a thing like that.

"Look, I'm here to help you," Daugherty said.

"Keep your voice down. I'll bet you are."

"I didn't have to let go of your wife just now. I thought it was you taking her."

"Bullcrap! You'd've been dead if you'd resisted. What d'you mean, help?"

"My orders are to keep the others from killing you."

"Who gave you those orders?"

"I don't know."

"What did he look like?"

"I couldn't see him clearly. It was dark."

Sloane thought a moment. His tendency was to believe him. It would be done that way—and this Daugherty was clearly FBI, too inexperienced to know how to lie. "You're not just FBI."

"I'm liaison with your agency."

"Ex-agency." But it had meaning to Sloane. The term liaison meant Daugherty was a paid informer for CSA within the FBI, a "shade," an infiltrator enabling Mother to keep track of the other minions of the law. If he had enough rank he might also exert some control over FBI actions. "Who is the blond with the empty eyes?"

"Curt Gillies. He's the one to watch. He's a psychotic killer."

The name had meaning to Sloane. He didn't know him, but he had heard of him. Cobra. Killed senselessly, even his own partner. He was considered beyond redemption. This is the guy selected to hunt him down? "The Puerto Rican?"

"Candy Mako. He's almost as bad."

Another field op who'd lost his partner. Sloane blinked in confusion. "Those two are paired?"

"There are four of us, Gillies, Mako, myself, and Captain Lawson Price. He's—"

"I know who he is." Price had to be in his sixties. An old fart, always bragging about how great things were in the old days of Naval Intelligence. But he ran a tight ship at Corry Field.

"He says the usual methods won't work with you. He's formed a—"

"Cell, yes. He'd do that. The good old days all over again. Where do you meet?"

"Federal Court House. I'm supposed to be there right now."

"Do you know my wife when you see her?"

"Yes."

"I mean really know her. If you saw several brown-haired, brown-eyed women wearing red suits could you pick out my wife?"

"Yes."

"With absolute certainty?"

"Yes. I've been following her all day. I've stood as close to her as you and I are."

For a moment nothing more was said, then Daugherty realized Sloane must be waiting for a couple of tourists to move further away. Then he heard, "Listen carefully. Your .38 will be returned to you—empty." The FBI man felt the weapon reenter his holster. "I'm also putting a cassette tape in your pocket. You are to return to Price, your cell. Give him the tape. There are instructions for you on that tape. You will follow them exactly, to the letter, dammit, or believe me you will be a dead man."

"Yes. I will. I want to help you."

"For your sake I hope so. You'll get your chance tomorrow morning."

Daugherty felt the insertion into the right-hand pocket of his jacket. For a moment he thought Sloane was gone.

"You may tell the others exactly what happened here. You have my note as proof, and the cassette. You may even tell them you identified the other members of the cell if you want."

"No."

"I thought not."

"I mean it. I want to help you."

"You are. Do as I say. Walk out of here now, but I wouldn't turn around if I were you."

"Yes, sir."

"A word of advice. Try another line of work. You're no good at this. Be a pharmacist. They live a long life."

EIGHT

Gregor Azbel listened to the cassette tape with disbelief, dismay, and apprehension which already bordered on open terror. This was a career-buster if there ever was one. The tape had been delivered to the front door of the Embassy by a paid professional messenger. Happened a thousand times a day in Washington. The plain manila envelope was addressed to Pavel Karamasov. It contained only the tape.

Azbel had played it through once. It was of very poor quality, obviously made on the cheapest recorder with a self-contained mike. The sound was tinny, scratchy, and there were street noises, even other voices in the background. Worse, he did not recognize the voice on the tape. But Azbel's gut feeling was that this was the voice of David Sloane. Of all the rotten luck! He rewound the tape and played it again.

"This is Wolf. I knew Pavel Karamasov, but hardly well. He was your agent in Washington. During my active service I was a CSA field op overseas. Many times he was in Washington when I was in Moscow.

"I met him about three years ago when I retired following the Parsley affair. In that I had done a big favor to both CSA and KGB. Both were grateful. I was to be allowed to live a peaceful life. Karamasov came to me to determine, I'm sure, if that's all I was doing. Apparently he was convinced, for on the two subsequent occasions when I briefly saw him, we discussed family, cultivation of roses, and the joys of retirement into the insurance business. My impression was that he too longed for his homeland and a more pastoral life."

Parsley affair. A big favor to both sides. What was that all about? Azbel had no idea and swore under his breath about it. How was he expected to act independently if he didn't have proper information?

"Last week when I returned home after dark, Karamasov was there, hiding in my garage. He was badly wounded—dying, in fact—as he stumbled into my arms and whispered a few words before a CSA bullet, intended to kill us both, finished him off. The bullet, a dum-dum fired from a Weatherby 300, came at a bad angle. Karamasov's body deflected it enough so I was missed. He saved my life with his own. I am grateful."

Azbel had a sense of truthfulness. Sloane's words fit his own summation of what had happened. This voice was not playing games.

"I've thought a lot about why Karamasov came to me. Obviously, he couldn't go any further. He wouldn't have lived more than a minute or two even without the second bullet. I figure he was shot somewhere nearby and stumbled to my garage. Why he didn't get to a phone and call you people is something you're just going to have to figure out for yourselves."

Again Azbel swore. Yes, so right. Pavel Karamasov so distrusted the members of his own cell, the entire KGB in Washington, that he chose to trust a retired American agent over his own. God Almighty! Impossible! Azbel now understood his own presence here, the eminent arrival of Kastalsky. A major shakeup. Pity the poor bastards who returned to Moscow.

"Karamasov's last words to me were a message to be passed on. Without a doubt it was to you people. He considered it of grave importance."

Azbel shook his head in dismay as he listened, his mind still worrying about the implications for the Embassy staff when this was heard in Moscow.

"There was *great danger*. He used those exact words. He also said *there isn't much time*. That may mean there wasn't much time before he died, but it may also mean there wasn't much time before whatever he was endeavoring to tell me occurred. I also interpret his words *great danger* to mean there exists great danger to both sides. In coming to me I believe Karamasov thought I would recognize the danger to both sides. He knew I had always been evenhanded, and he knew I hate both sides of the game equally. Therefore he believed I would pass on the message he considered so important.

"Events leave no doubt of that importance. An

attempt was made to kill me along with Karamasov. I'm hunted day and night by both sides. My wife has been followed, interrogated, and now captured by you people in the vain hope she knows where I am or what I know. She doesn't. Obviously the CSA wants to kill me to keep Karamasov's message from being passed on. You people want to find me to learn what Karamasov said. My life and my wife's life are in shambles."

Azbel hesitated over the meaning of the last word, then quickly understood it. He was impressed with this voice on the tape and the man behind it. Truth was being uttered by a highly knowledgeable and skillful operative who was weary of the game. This Azbel understood instinctively. He had seen it many times among older agents. He had once or twice had the feeling himself. The next words he heard confirmed this evaluation.

"I truly am sick of the game. I want out, as I always have. I simply want to be left alone. I thought I had insured that. Both sides of the game fear what I know. I have arranged it so that my death will inform both sides of information that cannot possibly be known. Apparently that isn't enough insurance. The attempt on my life proves we are dealing with either utter fools or the information Karamasov gave to me is so important it is worth any risk."

Now that impressed Azbel. The man was a pro.

"I have put Karamasov's message on a second cassette tape. I will exchange it for my wife, whom you hold.

"Listen carefully, for this is exactly how it will occur. It will take place in the Elephant Rotunda at the National Museum of Natural History at the

Smithsonian. At precisely nine A.M. tomorrow—it will be an hour before the museum opens but the doors on the mall side entrance will be unlocked— two men will escort my wife inside and stand to the left of the rotunda as you face the elephant. She will wear her red suit.

"A third man is to enter and stand on the right of the rotunda, facing the elephant. If more than three men enter the deal is off. When the third man has taken his position, he will see a black man standing to the right of the elephant. He will be wearing a shirt with short sleeves to preclude his having a concealed weapon. When he ascertains that it really is my wife you have brought, he will nod to the third man, who will step forward to the elephant.

"He will see the cassette tape in the elephant's mouth, sitting atop a remote-controlled explosive device. A red light will signal the device is activated. If he attempts to remove that tape he will lose a lot more than his hand and the tape will be destroyed forever. When your number-three man has seen the tape, he will turn and signal to the two men holding my wife. They will immediately leave through the Mall doors and depart the area. The black man will now go to my wife and escort her past the elephant, down the escalator, and out the Constitution Avenue side of the building. You will instruct my wife that she is to stand there, make no move until the black man asks her to follow him.

"If these instructions are not followed to the letter and any actions other than these occur, the tape will be destroyed. When my wife is safely down the escalator and out of the building, I will deactivate the explosive device. The red light will go out and your man is free to leave the premises and do with the tape as he wishes. A fair exchange will have been made."

Azbel was already beginning to shake as he listened to the rest of the tape.

"Look, I know how you people think. You believe you have the upper hand because you have my wife. You don't. You can question, terrorize, and chemically debrief her till doomsday, but she knows nothing to tell you. The last time she saw me was in a cab in front of the Italian restaurant. The last thing she knows was that I was to pick her up in front of the Lincoln Memorial at three. Of course, I didn't. It was a setup so I could learn exactly who was on my tail. It worked. I now have photographs of lots of interesting people on both sides.

"There is no sense in your trying to bargain in hopes of upping the ante. My wife is useless to you. If you harm her or kill her, you must know I will both spill everything I know and come after you and everyone else with all the vengeance I possess. If you think I can't do a lot of damage, you are stupid. The tape is not blank, nor does it contain false information. I am not so stupid as to twist the KGB and invite your harassment. Remember, I want only to be left alone.

"If you want Karamasov's message reporting the *great danger* he had discovered, then you must play the game by my rules. You have no choice. Time's awasting. You'd better get at it. I'll see you at nine A.M."

Gregor Azbel's hand shook as he stopped the recorder. This scheme was nothing less than diabolical. This man, this Sloane, was too smart, too good, and only too right. The woman was useless to them.

His own orders were not to harm her but to exchange her for information. This Sloane offered a swap which the KGB itself might have conceived, a public building, empty of tourists, many exits, two men entering with the woman, a third to find the tape. Something similar had occurred many times. But this Sloane had given himself the upper hand, the remote-controlled explosive device under the tape. Release the woman or there would be no tape.

Azbel knew he had no choice. The exchange would be made this way or it would not be made at all. The woman was of no value. The tape was potentially of great value. The risk simply had to be taken. Sloane was clever, cunning. Azbel's admiration was not even grudging. He would like to meet this American one day.

None of this is what made Azbel tremble, however. By declaring the exchange to be made at 9 A.M. tomorrow, only hours away, he was forcing a decision to be made now—*by him*. Diabolical! Sloane had to know no KGB agent ever made such a decision on his own. Such decisions were made in Dzerzhinsky Square, and then only after exhaustive study and consultations. No such decision could be reached in less than days. Nine A.M. tomorrow. This Sloane was surely a bastard.

Azbel paced the floor for several minutes, his rapid pace reflecting his agitation. If he failed to accept the offer and obtain the tape he was ruined. If he accepted the offer, released the woman, and got nothing in return he was likewise ruined. No possible way for him to win. Every rule of Dzerzhinsky Square would be violated. No one, not the Party, the Politburo, or the *Rodina* herself could ask him to make such a decision. He would not. At last he knew what to do.

For the next few minutes he busied himself. First, using the code book, he drafted a message to go by standard diplomatic phone to the Foreign Ministry. The phone conversation, conducted by a pair of minor functionaries in Washington and Moscow, would be scrambled. The Americans would pay attention and quickly unscramble and learn the conversation. What was important in all this was that the Americans not learn that the KGB *expected* them to do this. In other words, we know you do this but we don't want you to know we know it. The conversation, relating to minor personnel shifts, would contain code words alerting Azbel's unknown superior at the KGB that an important, high-priority message was coming.

Azbel now prepared a second message, this one to his superior. His first impulse was just to send Wolf's tape. But the tape was in English. Even if it were greatly speeded up so that the entire tape sounded like a bleep or static to the casual ear, the Americans would learn the content of Wolf's message almost instantly.

Therefore it was necessary to synopsize and paraphrase Wolf's words, translate them into Russian, and then both encode and encipher them into the KGB's premier, most sensitive code. Now, when the static was heard, it would take the Americans days—hopefully forever—to figure out what message was sent. Later he would send a copy of the actual tape to Moscow by diplomatic courier, but it would arrive too late to do any good. A decision would have to be made on the basis of his synopsis.

All this was laborious for Azbel. He could not trust anyone else with the information. But when he finished he felt a little better. He had, as the Americans say, passed the buck. Someone else could make the decision. He had done all that could be expected of him.

Gordon Adams listened to the tape for the second time. Daugherty had transmitted it over a secure line a half hour before. Now, as Captain Price played it for him on a conventional recorder, Adams was prepared for what he must say and do.

"Is that his voice?"

Adams nodded. "Most definitely, I'm afraid."

They were alone in a Space Two at Brandywine, an utterly secure place, unable to be overheard by anyone. The voice of David Sloane droned on: "So, that's the way it's going to be, you sons of motherfreakers. By the time you—and the KGB—hear this, the tape and explosive device will already be in place. If you touch it you get nothing. If anything happens to me you get nothing. If anything happens to Freddie you get nothing. Obviously, you bastards have a problem. How you solve it is part of your problem."

Price shook his head sadly. "Why is he doing this?"

Gordon Adams could barely conceal his admiration. Sloane was performing brilliantly. He expected nothing less from him. "Obviously he's changing the game, Lawson." Adams felt he succeeded in maintaining his face as an unexpressive mask.

"Explain, please."

"All right, but I'm sure you understand. Heretofore

the hunt has been for Sloane. He has now made that tape of superior importance."

"Do you think there is anything on it?"

"Oh, my, yes. He has put on it whatever Karamasov told him. The KGB knows it and so must we. The KGB wants that information desperately. We are now equally desperate to keep them from learning it. Sloane has changed the rules to his advantage."

"You're saying that—"

"Exactly. The tape is more important than Sloane, the woman, or anything else. At all costs we must keep the Russians from obtaining the tape. Sloane knows that. He's forcing us to back away from him." He allowed himself a small, toothless smile. "Very clever, I must say."

"Why not simply let the tape be destroyed?"

"Then we won't know what's on it either, will we? And, we will simply repeat this exercise in another time and place. We must act now, Lawson, in the circumstances Sloane has provided us."

"What does he want?"

"What he has always wanted—survival—for himself and his wife. He wants his wife free from the Russians. And he wants us all to back off and leave him alone. It is that simple."

"You know that will never happen."

"Of course, and so does he. But the game must be played out—which he also knows."

Price sighed. "Will the Russians go along with this?"

"I don't think they have any more choice than we do."

"Yes." Price nodded. "I'll speak to my cell at once."

He was unaware of it, but the gray, vacant eyes of Curt Gillies burned with an inner fire that consumed his diseased brain. He had no words to describe his feeling for David Sloane, the Wolf. It went beyond hatred. Indeed, hatred probably had little to do with it. Sloane, Wolf, his legendary predecessor as a CSA field op, had twice made a fool of him—at the restaurant and, far worse, at the Lincoln Memorial. He not only had failed to kill Sloane at either place, he had lost the woman who was the pawn. No man, but no man, did this to Curt Gillies.

In his psychotic mind Curt Gillies had become the hunter of the Wolf, tracking down a clever, clever animal, an animal that had escaped him and made a fool of him. He had lost sight of the CSA, this idiot cell, the tape, the KGB, everything except the prey. He would find and kill the Wolf. He would be relentless. No man made a fool of Curt Gillies.

As he listened to the tape and then to Price, Gillies knew what he must do. This doddering old man was a fool. Price was the root of their failure. Gillies knew with certainty that he alone knew how to find and kill Sloane.

"We are going to follow the instructions on this tape to the letter." Price felt there was proper command in his voice. "It has already been arranged for the Natural History Museum to be cleared of all personnel by eight A.M. The director has been told it is a matter of national security. The doors on both the Mall side and the Constitution Avenue side will be unlocked. The Russians will find nothing untoward. It will be precisely as they expect it to be."

Gillies could not resist a jibe. "What are we going to do, just let 'em exchange the girl and get the tape? They're running the show, is that it?"

Price glanced at him. His eyes were positively frightening. "Hardly, but it must appear to be so. Sloane has been very clever, but he doesn't know we are working as a cell—and his setup is a perfect arrangement for cell operation. Gentlemen, we are about to prove once and for all the superiority of the cell in intelligence operations. We are about to get Sloane, the tape, and the woman all in one fell swoop."

Price paused for effect. He had at least gained their attention. "Here is what we must do. As soon as the KGB is inside with the woman, we will move in. I will be at the Mall entrance. Gillies, you will be at the Constitution side. Daugherty, you will do exactly as instructed, taking the woman down the escalator and out the Constitution Avenue exit."

"Where will I be?"

Price glanced at Candy Mako. "I was coming to that." He moved a pencil over a large drawing of the Museum floor plan. "You will be in guard uniform here."

"And how do I get there?"

"It has been arranged for you to join the third shift of guards." He returned his attention to the drawing. "As Daugherty walks off with the woman, you will move quietly to her"—he pointed with the pencil eraser—"standing behind this pillar. When the Falscape woman is removed and the destruct mechanism has been deactivated, you will wait until the KGB man takes the tape. Then I'm sure you know what to do."

"Kill him."

"Precisely."

"What about Sloane?" The question came from Gillies.

"Our first priority is the tape. We must obtain it. But it is my belief we should also be able to get Sloane. I am certain he will be somewhere in the building observing everything. He will not risk having his wife fall into our hands. Therefore he will intercept her before she reaches the Constitution Avenue exit."

"I'm to let him have her."

"Yes, Daugherty, by all means."

"And I'm to kill him when he leaves the Constitution Avenue exit?"

"Yes, Gillies. Both him and the woman if need be. I will do the same should they exit on the Mall."

Gillies felt like scoffing, but he managed to restrain himself. "And what about the KGB? Do you think they are going to take this lying down?"

"Hardly. They will have men here, here, here, and here." He pointed to the four corners of the building. "If they also have men outside the two exits, you and I know what we must do. Silencers will be used, of course." He studied the faces of his men. "Coordination is everything in this operation. It should all happen quickly, within a minute or less"—he smiled —"literally bang, bang. It would be nice if we could arrange a dress rehearsal, but we are all experienced professionals. I'm sure we can pull it off and cope with any exigencies which may arise. Any questions?"

There were none.

Price was unaware of the meaningful glances between Gillies and Mako. Within the hour they met over a beer. Both agreed Price was an old fool whose principal accomplishment was going to be to get them both killed. They were not about to let that happen. They decided to act as a pair, not as part of this stupid cell. They would act together to get Sloane, and the key to Sloane was his wife. She was to be their quarry, not the stupid tape. Having so agreed, they quickly decided what must occur. Sloane was not going to dictate their actions.

Freddie was mostly bored. She felt like a bird in a gilded cage. *Fly away, little birdie. Flap your wings and . . .* That wasn't possible. Her keepers included the burly man in a bulging suit. Even if she had a black belt in karate, judo, jujitsu—whatever that was—mayhem, arm-wrestling, and kinesthetic object-throwing, there was no way around him. Forget it.

They served her caviar. Actually it was good, but she declared she was not into sturgeon entrails and asked for a steak smothered in mushrooms and onions and a baked potato. To her astonishment that's what she got. She ate the whole thing, even the bone—well-l. *It is a certified fact, Dr. Falscape, determined by exhaustive research financed by the National Institutes of Health and widely condemned by Senator Proxmire as a waste of tax money, that no condemned person has ever been known to leave a single bite of her last meal.* God! *The bone was delicious.* Oh, Lord! *Now I know what happened to the mastodons.*

There was an exotic TV set, but it only played video

tapes of Soviet English-language newscasts. Now that was perverse. That Soviet news anchor really was an anchor. *I'm sorry, Captain, the ship is stuck. I mean STUCK. It ain't ever gonna move. We are in the rust belt, victims of creeping corosion. The Red Menace isn't what you think, not at all. It's boredom.* Her principal captor was a woman, a real WOMAN, and Freddie knew one when she saw one. Whoever concocted the notion that Russian women were square and burly had never met this blonde, blue-eyed honey, slim, lithe, built, almost top-heavy, chic, sexy, obviously willing to give her all—*I mean ALL*—for the KGB. *Comrades, this model is designed for degenerate American males. We anti-imperialist, save-the-world-for-Commies Commies do not find her attractive. The first man who lays a finger on her will spend the rest of his natural life condemned to someone exceedingly square and burly so that he might better cultivate the joys of democratic socialism.*

"Hi, I'm Freddie."

"You may call me Olga." *The woman was dour.*

"I'm sorry. I know you're going to be sent back to Russia because I can identify you." *Did you know I'm secretly blind?* "You're extremely attractive. Where are you from in Russia?"

She looked at her a long moment. "Kiev. We have strawberry shortcake. Or, if you prefer cherries jubilee or crepe suzettes." *No Twinkies?*

"That'll be fine—all of them." *You see, under capitalism, the body metabolism increases rapidly, permitting a person to . . .* "I was hoping to have some really good borscht."

In truth she was scared witless, using her mental flights to prevent either a screaming fit or crying jag.

Actually, Dr. Falscape, either one is good for you. You can have both at the same time, if you wish. We have a deluxe model of that. David hadn't been in the cab. That much she knew. But where was he? And what was happening? Where was she, for that matter? And what was going to happen to her? *You'll love downtown Minsk. Where the hell is Minsk? You wear it in winter, you dummy. Always wanted one of those.* She had been asked the same questions again and had given the same answers. She knew nothing. *Would you like a little Napoleon brandy with your coffee? Yes, thank you, the magnum will be fine. Tom Selleck is one of my best friends.*

Not for the first time, Dimitri Galenkov thought about retiring. He was too old for these wee-hours-of-the-morning crises. He was tired. His eyes felt like sandpaper. And his nerves were raw. Worse, his gout pained him terribly.

All this was unnecessary, moreover. Gregor Azbel should have made this decision in Washington—or been permitted to. He was on the scene. He was the best judge of the situation. Galenkov shook his head. But he had not. He had sought permission. Deep sigh.

Galenkov could not blame him. This was the way of the KGB, or more accurately, the Party. No one was trusted. Individual initiative was discouraged, and punished even if it succeeded. All decisions had to be made by higher authority, which meant the First Directorate in Dzerzhinsky Square. Americans did not work this way, which was their great advantage. A couple of field agents might well have decided to make the exchange. The cumbersome KGB machinery was at a loss when quick decisions were needed.

The American agent Wolf knew this and exploited it. As he read Azbel's decoded message, Galenkov had open admiration for the man and his methods. Nine in the morning Washington time. Do it now or never. Decide at once. A most clever man.

Part of Galenkov was angry that this solitary American cost him his sleep and made such fools of them and their methods. That part of him wanted not to go for the exchange. Let it pass. They still had the Falscape woman—something Wolf obviously wanted. The exchange could be made another day and on grounds of their choosing. The Russian bear is a patient animal.

But no. That clever American reported Karamasov had said *great danger*. Danger to both sides. It was the carrot dangling before them—and Wolf had correctly surmised the death of Karamasov was chaotic for all the Washington cells. An astute person, this Wolf.

Galenkov knew he had no choice. He must learn what Karamasov said. For a second he engaged his anger at the bumbling fools in Washington, vowing once again to make them all suffer. Then he quickly concentrated on what must be done. By all the rules, the exchange should be approved by the First Directorate. That would take days and he had only hours. Azbel knew this, and had sought to escape responsibility by sending this message.

For the first time Galenkov smiled. He had not risen to the First Directorate by being a fool. He knew how to protect his backside. Young Azbel had much to learn. Thus he quickly scrawled a two-word message to be encoded and enciphered and sent to Azbel. The letters danced before Galenkov's tired eyes, amusing him. The ambiguity was delicious. Everyone's ass was protected.

In English the words read: FOLLOW INSTRUC-TIONS.

Freddie was awakened at 6 A.M. Awakened? She had hardly slept, the dogs of worry and fright baying at her through much of the night. *Don't think about it. David, darling, it doesn't work, not for me.* She showered, then followed instructions to re-don her cleaned-and-pressed red suit. Can't say the KGB isn't neat. Next came a lavish breakfast.

No one said a word to her, and that's when she began to really worry. Something was going on. She could feel it, sense expectancy. But what? The question was answered when she was led from the apartment, down the elevator, and put in the back seat of a car. The big guard sat on her right, one of the men who'd kidnapped her yesterday on her left. She recognized the back of the head of the driver. The man in the passenger seat she didn't know. Russia! They were going to drug her, put her on a plane, and take her to Russia. *Please, really, I was only kidding about Minsk. Oh, David! When will I ever see you again?* Then she thought of the child she carried. No! She'd never let it happen.

"I'm sorry, Mr. KGB, I'm not going to Russia."

The man to her left glanced at her. "I beg your pardon?"

"You heard me. I'm not going to Russia. I'm an American citizen. I have rights." *We the people . . . Life, Liberty, and the Pursuit of Motherhood. Damn you, Mother!*

Despite her panic, it gradually dawned on Freddie that she was not headed in the direction of any airport she knew. They were driving across town and then downtown. "Where are you taking me?" The silence which greeted her was penetrating.

Finally the man in the front seat spoke, his voice flat. He did not turn around to look at her. "It does not matter where you are going, Dr. Falscape. It is what will happen after you get there."

"Listen, buster. You better believe it matters." She was engaging in a familiar process, summoning anger to override fear. "If you think I'm going to sit still for your little games, then you really are dumb Commies. I'll scream, I'll run. You have never heard me scream."

Silence, but only briefly. "If you do either of those, Dr. Falscape, then you are dead. If you follow instructions you will be released, as safe and unharmed as you are now."

Freddie gaped at the men on either side of her, then at the man in front. "Did you say released?"

"I did. Are you now ready to listen to instructions, Dr. Falscape?"

Freddie swallowed. Barely audibly she said, "Yes."

"When we arrive at where we're going, you will accompany the two gentlemen who now sit beside you. You will enter a building and stand quietly between the two gentlemen. If you make a sound or gesture, if you attempt to flee, you will be shot on the spot. Dr. Falscape, I do not believe you are dumb enough to doubt that."

Another difficult swallow. "Then what?"

"The only thing that concerns you, Dr. Falscape, is that you are to stand in your tracks. If you know how not to move or speak, I suggest for your sake that you do it. Ahead of you will be a black man. After a short interval he will step forward and take your arm. If you wish to live and if you wish to go free, I most strongly urge you to accompany this black man. He is a countryman of yours."

Freddie felt she couldn't breathe. "I don't understand. Follow a black man. What is happening?"

"Dr. Falscape, I respectfully suggest you start practicing your silence right now."

"Please. What is going on? Is this some kind of exchange or something?"

Silence. She looked at the men beside her. They ignored her, looking straight ahead, faces impassive. God!

In a few minutes she knew where they were. Constitution Avenue. Ahead loomed the Washington Monument. She was near the Lincoln Memorial of yesterday. Was it only yesterday? To her left was the Ellipse, the White House beyond. *Yes, Mr. President, I got your letter. Thanks for asking me to . . .* The vehicle turned right into the Mall, then left on Madison Avenue. Ahead lay the Capitol. Passing the Smithsonian. The car slowed, prepared to stop.

"Dr. Falscape, if you ever follow instructions one time in your life, may I suggest that now is the time to do it."

She couldn't think. The domed building they stopped at. She should know it. Couldn't remember. *Forgetting familiar landmarks is a surefire sympton of advanced pyorrhea, by gum!* A man—did the Russians choose their suits off the same rack?—stepped forward, opened the back door.

The burly man got out, reached inside, clasped her

forearm to pull her out. In a moment the two men stood on either side of her, very close. She could feel their hips pressed against her. Each gripped her upper arms. Tightly.

They began to walk in tandem, only a few strides, a couple of steps, through doors. Then she knew where she was. Museum of Natural History. Elephant Rotunda. Elegant marble columns rose two stories high. A balcony circled the floor above. In the center stood a gigantic stuffed African bush elephant, so lifelike, its trunk raised as though trumpeting. Long ivory tusks protruded toward her.

In truth she hardly saw the elephant. She had eyes only for the black man who stood to its left. She knew him. Of course she knew him. And that recognition filled her with panic.

Captain Lawson Jones Price saw them enter, their car drive away. Only then did he slide his car forward. It felt good to drive himself, even better to know the surge of controlled excitement through his body. Yes, he could still do it. Lots of life in the old bones.

All was going as he figured. The KGB had a man at each corner of the building. Another stood outside the Mall doorway. It figured another was on the Constitution Avenue entrance, though maybe not. The men at the corners would be able to cover that.

He stopped his car perhaps fifty feet from the Mall entrance. The Russian at the door looked at him warily, but apparently accepted him. Good. Nothing to do but wait. He formed a mental image of what was occurring inside.

The rap on the window surprised him. He turned,

felt annoyance as he rolled down the window. "Gillies, what are you doing here? You're supposed to be—"

Price glimpsed the Walther PPK with silencer attached, but that was the last thing he ever saw. He did not hear the spit, nor feel the impact of the bullet into his forehead, bursting his brain.

Freddie was grateful for the hands holding her arms. She was shaking so badly she wasn't sure she could stand. The black man in shirtsleeves frightened her. Was she being turned over to Mother? She didn't want that.

She saw him look at her. Was that recognition in his eyes? What else? God, she was scared. It drove everything else from her mind.

The third man, the Russian from the passenger seat, stepped forward to the elephant. He bent forward a little, seemed to look in the elephant's mouth. He looked at the black man. Was that a nod?

Silently Sloane stepped forward, Walther in his right hand, approached the up side of the unmoving escalator, mounted a couple of steps in a crouch, then raised his head just enough to peer inside the rotunda.

Everything was as it was supposed to be. He saw Freddie, the two men holding her. Daugherty's back was to him. He couldn't see the third Russian, only his legs as he stood at the elephant's mouth.

Then he saw the two Russians release Freddie, leave, running for the Mall door. Daugherty stepped forward.

Sloane lowered his head and backed down the escalator.

Freddie froze. Her whole body seemed numb with fear. She didn't know even if she possessed a body. She knew only the face of the black man coming for her. He moved aside. She was to follow him.

She couldn't.

He touched her arm lightly. "Come with me, Miss Falscape."

She couldn't move.

He put his arm around her, gently, trying to propel her forward. "Please, Miss Falscape, I won't hurt you."

She looked at the Russian. There was fear in his eyes. His voice was hard. "For God's sake, do as he says."

Then she was moving forward, somehow, past the elephant. Ahead she saw an escalator. The black man moved past her, stood at the top of the stairs waiting for her to go ahead of him.

A sound made her look to her left. She saw a short wiry man step from behind a marble pillar. In truth she saw not so much the man as the gun in his hand. She gaped as it swiveled to its right, fired. Spit! Behind her she heard the Russian groan, fall.

She screamed. The gun swung again, toward her. *Spit!* Another unwilled scream tore from her throat. Then she saw the black man fall forward, roll down the escalator steps.

Her scream now was of pure terror as the man with the gun came for her, grabbed her arm, pulled at her.

She didn't so much hear the new *spit* as feel the

release of her arm. Then for a moment she saw another man, recognized him. His finger came to his lips for silence, then he motioned her to go down the escalator.

"Freddie, come!"

She turned to the sibilant sound of the voice, saw David. She could hardly register his presence before he was reaching up to her, pulling her down the steps, then they were running, as fast as they could. She didn't know where, just down some corridor. She could hardly keep up. Then a door opened, flooding the corridor with light. He pushed her outside.

"The ice-cream truck. Get in. Quickly!" Sloane watched her obey, then stopped in the open doorway, reaching inside his pocket with his left hand. He extracted a small gadget much like a remote control for television, pushed a button, then ran for the truck, got in, and drove away.

Gordon Adams fired again, killing the Russian who burst in the Mall entrance. Then he walked over and bent over Mako's body to make sure it was dead, and descended the escalator, pausing to verify Daugherty's death. He at least shook his head over that in regret. Slowly he made his way toward the Constitution Avenue exit, pausing at the door until he heard an explosion behind him. Bigger than he expected. The Smithsonian was going to need a new elephant. At least there'd be no tape for anyone to listen to. Outside he walked slowly toward his car, aware the Russians at each corner were now reacting to the explosion.

He drove away as though nothing untoward had occurred.

From a distance, using binoculars, Gillies watched the ice-cream truck leave and figured Sloane and the woman were in it. He smiled and his eyes burned bright. A new game now. Mano-a-mano. The Wolf would feel what it was like to be really hunted.

NINE

Senior Captain Ivan Frederyenko remained tense as the *Comrade Molotov* slid beneath the surface of the Black Sea. He would not relax until his ship cleared the pen blasted into the side of a cliff near Sebastopol, exited the harbor, and left behind all the admirals, commissars, and worries of port. Then he would be in his own element, alone with his ship, his men, and the sea. Virtually out of contact. This voyage particularly. There was to be no communication. Not even ELF; the low-frequency, longwave underwater system had been disconnected—until the test was completed. Splendid. Couldn't be better. So the *Molotov* swarmed with technicians and observers. He could live with that.

His orders were burned into his mind. He was to

sail the *Molotov* through the Bosporus and Darda-
nelles into the Aegean, then the Mediterrean, past
Gibraltar into the Western Atlantic, remaining unde-
tected. No problem there. He was to take the ship to a
point west of the Azores where the test of the new
laser communications was to occur. He did not
pretend to understand it, but he knew the procedure.
The *Molotov* raised a buoy. A satellite high overhead
sent a message by laser to the buoy which somehow
reached his ship, causing it to fire a dummy missile
downrange to land in the South Atlantic. Several
such tests were to occur. The number of nuclear
missiles his ship carried was thereby diminished.

Frederyenko looked upon this as more interesting
activity than the usual cruise of a missile submarine.
Still, there was an element to this which dismayed
him. If this test worked, the clear intention was to
replace his own authority to fire nuclear missiles in
time of war with literally a black box. Was man always
to give way to technology? Was a satellite in the sky, a
black box full of wires, to be trusted more than the
decisions a man might make? Apparently. He shook
his head in disbelief. So dehumanizing. Another step
in push-button warfare. All he could do was hope the
damn test failed.

Freddie was surprised at herself. She had just seen
three men shot to death in a matter of seconds, there
had been enough blood to bathe in—and she was
actually functioning. The first time she'd seen a man
die, she had been positively catatonic. *The first time.*
God! *David Stuart Pritchard, Jr., the first time your
Mama saw a man killed was in Munich. Your Daddy
killed him and I ran over him with the car. The second*

*man I saw killed—well, it doesn't matter where it was.
But I saw him, really saw him. I leaned over the front
seat of the car and I pulled the trigger and I can still feel
the jerk of my hand and his eyes, son, his eyes . . .*

She was actually aware of abandoning the ice-
cream truck and getting into a blue 1982 Camaro.
She followed David's instructions to sit in back and
change into clothes he had brought her. They were in
a paper bag. How many dead bodies had she seen?
Let's see, two in her yard, two in Upper Marlboro
three years ago. Oh yes, the one in the funeral home.
God! She couldn't remember. How many had
she actually seen murdered? Well, there were
three just now, the one in Munich, the one she shot.
That's five. Oh, yes, don't forget Parsley. No, no,
couldn't forget that body falling back, almost into
her lap. Six. Not bad. And she was only thirty-
two. Little more than one every five years—on the
average.

"I bought you size six. Hope it fits."

She was a five, but it would do. Blue with white
polka dots. Not her best. She stripped off her suit
jacket. Nudity in the back seat was hardly her major
concern at the moment. Do we become jaded to
anything? *Jade is a semi-precious rock much prized in
the Orient, my dear. It has nothing to do with
murder—I don't think.* She had just seen three men
die before her eyes. *Dr. Falscape, would you like to sign
this petition outlawing the death penalty?* And all she
really cared about was that David was alive and she
was with him. *On your next tour of the dungeons, Ms.
Falscape, we will actually show you men having their
eyes gouged out and their entrails removed by a process
known as rationalization.*

"I wasn't sure you still had your blonde wig, so I bought you a new one, sunglasses too."

It was a sort of pinkish red. Ghastly. *I always wanted to be a strawberry blonde.*

"I bought this car off a kid in College Park. Never had the title changed. He's not going to be too happy when we abandon it at the airport."

The dress was pulled to her waist and she busied herself sliding out of her pants and arranging herself, all the while listening to him talk about how he'd purchased the car. Inane. And David was never inane.

She slid her feet into the heels he'd bought. Not a bad fit actually. "I'm all right, David. You don't need to keep up the silly talk."

"Are you sure?"

Positive. The sun rises in the west, doesn't it? She looked up. He had put on his gray wig and mustache. "What'll I do with my old things?"

"Put 'em in the bag. We'll drop them in a trash can."

Her favorite red suit. Maybe some bag lady would soon be wearing it. *Lady, if you knew where that suit has been . . .* "Can I climb into the front seat?"

"Sure. Good idea."

She managed that, impulsively kissing his cheek as she did so. When she was settled, she leaned over and kissed him again. "God, I'm glad to see you."

He said nothing, only nodded. "Are you sure you're okay?"

"Yes, I told you."

He didn't believe her. "It was a bad scene, Freddie. Anyone would—"

"As long as you're okay and I'm with you."

He made a quick glance at her. "You know you don't mean that."

Sigh. "Oh, David, now's not the time to test my ethics. What ethics?" Words formed in her mind about how many dead bodies she'd seen, but she forbade their utterance.

"I have to know what happened, Freddie. I couldn't see."

"Where were you? I never did see you."

"Down below. I peeked over the escalator once, saw everything was going to plan, but I didn't see the shooting. There were three shots. What happened?"

"You planned all that?"

"I didn't intend all the shooting, maybe only one, but yes."

"God, David!"

"I had to get you back from the KGB. It was the only way." He told her then what he had done, the tapes he'd sent, the third one in the elephant's mouth.

"I thought I heard an explosion."

"Yes. I set it off at the doorway."

"The elephant is gone?"

" 'Fraid so."

Suddenly she felt like crying. Somehow the loss of that dumb stuffed animal seemed so terribly sad, the ultimate tragedy. Her eyes filled with tears.

"It was already dead, Freddie."

"I know. I'm being silly." She exhaled deeply. "So all this was your doing? You let the KGB take me?"

"More or less, yes. I knew they wouldn't hurt you. You knew nothing. They didn't, did they?"

"I don't understand. What were you trying to accomplish?"

"I used you at the Ponte Vecchio, then at the Lincoln Memorial—I was there—in the Mall, taking photos—to identify my tail, Mother's men."

"I mean with the elephant. Why tell the CSA? Why not just make the simple exchange of the tape for me with the Russians?"

"Would you have wanted that? The tape was real. Karamasov's message was on it."

Her eyes brightened. "You mean you didn't want the KGB to know? You were helping—"

"You know me better than that, Freddie. I just changed the game, that's all. The man hunting me is a Captain Price. I knew him from Pensacola. He was director of training. He'd formed a cell. Great bunch!"

"What's a cell?"

"I'll explain later. The point is I had to find out how valuable Karamasov's message was to them. When they showed up at the Smithsonian, I knew it was very valuable. I also wanted to find out whether they knew what the message was. Obviously they don't. What happened, Freddie? I couldn't see. Three shots were fired."

She hesitated.

He glanced at her. "I know you don't want to think about it, but I have to know, Freddie."

Sigh. "There was a short, wiry man. Looked Mexican."

"Candy Mako, ex-field op, now a Washington cop. He killed Daugherty?"

"Who's Daugherty?"

"Peter Daugherty, FBI, member of the cell. He was your principal tail. I turned him at the Lincoln

Memorial. He was there to identify you, make sure the KGB didn't send in a ringer."

"He was helping us?"

"Sorta, I guess."

"God, David, this gets worse by the second. Remember Duane Forbes?"

He swore under his breath. "You got a memory like an elephant."

She smiled. "I'll hit you with my trunk."

"Mako killed Daugherty?"

"The Russian by the elephant, then Daugherty."

Sloane visualized it. Two quick shots. Yes, Mako could do that. "Then what happened?"

Freddie realized how much she'd repressed it already. She didn't want to think about it. "The man—the man you call Mako . . . he came for me. I-I think he was going . . . to—"

"Grab you?"

"Yes, I think so." She sighed. "I'm sure."

Sloane shook his head in puzzlement. It didn't figure. "Someone else was there and shot Mako?"

"Yes."

"Who was it?"

It was her rock and hard place, the thing she didn't want to think about or face. Adams had come. He had helped them, as he promised. He'd asked for her silence. "I don't know."

"Had you seen him before?"

"No." Why was she lying? She'd never lied to her husband. Why now? What kind of a marriage is built on lies?

"What'd he look like?"

She swallowed hard against the lump in her throat.

"Oh, God, David, it happened so fast I—"

"Was he a blond man, average height, gray eyes, kinda vacant?"

"No." How wonderful to tell the truth!

It wasn't Gillies. Price? "An older man, in his sixties, heavy build, gray hair, crew cut?"

"Maybe. I think he might've been older." Isn't a little truth better than no truth at all?

Price? It made no sense. They might have had a plan to seize both Freddie and the tape, but if Mako was doing just that, grabbing Freddie, why would Price kill him, a member of his own cell? "Freddie, this is important. Did the man look like a saltwater sailor?"

"I don't *know*, David." Her voice took on a plaintive tone, rising in pitch. "What's a saltwater sailor?"

"You know, ramrod back, exuding command. Oh yeah, I remember. Price had blue eyes. Didn't wear glasses. He was proud of that."

"God, David! Ease up. I can't remember. I've told you all I know. It was hardly a walk through the park. I wasn't taking notes. Can't you understand I was—"

"Terrorized. I know. I'm sorry." He sighed. "Don't be upset."

She sighed. "I'm not. I'm all right. Where are we going?"

"To the airport, Washington National, then to Canada."

"What's in Canada?"

"A place to hide."

Hide. *Damn Mother.* "Do I get to hide with you?"

"Yes. Either side will take you now. I'll never get you back."

She smiled. "I didn't know you cared."

"I wish I didn't." There was not one shred of humor in his voice. Sloane had never meant anything so much in his life.

She understood. The dispassionate killer she had first met in Munich was gone, never to return. He now cared and loved, and that made his task much more difficult. He was frightened, something he'd never been before Munich. "Do they have a bed in this hideout?"

"What the hell happened?"

Adams knew that Cash was trying to show anger and authority, but he simply wasn't good at it. In fact there wasn't much Cash was good at. He was a number two, not a number one. It figured The Committee would soon realize that and be rid of him—maybe permanently. Too bad. "It seems we have a loose cannon named Curt Gillies. Price never should have included him in his group. In fact he never should've formed the group. We discarded the cell years ago, and wisely so—as events now prove."

"Gillies killed Capt. Price?"

"I don't think there's any doubt of it."

"Then he went inside and killed the others?"

"I don't think so. I doubt if he could have gotten inside. Ballistics shows Mako killed Daugherty and the one Russian. Mako and the other Russian were killed by another weapon."

"Sloane?"

"We don't have the weapon, but it would seem so."

Cash shook his head, slowly, as though it pained him. "Lord, Adams, we're back at square one."

"Far from it. We've made a lot of progress. As you

know I've no idea what this is all about, why Sloane is to be killed, but in any event we now have leisure in which to do it. The rush is over."

"Explain."

"Sloane has what he wants. He's eliminated virtually the entire cell looking for him. The only one left is Gillies, and he's a certified nut. Sloane has to know we'll be after Gillies too, which we are. We'll get rid of the last man for him. Sloane now has his wife with him. I have no doubt the two of them will take off for points unknown. Could be anywhere. My guess is Greece or Turkey. We'll find him eventually. There's no rush."

Cash didn't understand, but tried to conceal it. "I wish I had your confidence."

"Whatever Sloane knows, he's obviously not going to do anything about it. He didn't give it to the KGB. His tape blew up with the elephant."

"Do you know the fuss the Smithsonian is making about that damned elephant?"

"It can't reach you. They only talked to Price. Let me finish. Whatever Sloane knows or doesn't know from Karamasov, he obviously hasn't gone to the KGB. You were wrong about that, as I suspected. He's a survivor. That's all he's ever been. He has no loyalties, none at all, never has had, never will. He's backed the pursuit away, damned near all of it. He's now free to run with his wife. Believe me, he will run." Adams saw his hesitation. "I think you can stop worrying, Cash. If Sloane possesses some knowledge that interferes with some operation, he's not going to use it."

Cash eyed him. "I want him dead."

"I understand. He's a loose end. We'll snip it off, very shortly. Won't take long. Meanwhile"—he rendered his toothless smile—"the world goes on, the house is still in order."

Cash nodded. He wanted to believe him. He had to believe him. Already he could visualize The Committee meeting.

Dimitri Galenkov pondered the ravages of getting old. He truly did feel awful, so tired it would take a week in the Crimea to recover. Intelligence really was a young man's game. But if so, why were the young ones so dumb. Gregor Azbel was being so foolish—much to Galenkov's disappointment in him. He was in a panic after his failure in the museum. He had lost both the woman and the tape. Two men dead. To cover his failure he had dispatched legions of men—almost literally that many—to find Sloane at all costs.

Azbel was so stupid. It confirmed his growing belief there was something seriously wrong with the way the KGB recruited, trained, and motivated its agents. Something would have to be done, but not at the moment.

He had countermanded Azbel's orders. He was to use the net to locate Sloane, all right, but under no circumstances was Sloane or his wife to be approached, spoken to, or picked up. They were to be followed. Azbel's true failure was in not realizing that was the thing to do. He merely reacted to a most clever American agent. He did not anticipate him. Above all he did not make use of what he might do to benefit the *Rodina*. Azbel did not think.

Galenkov had. The scene in the museum with the

stupid elephant was clear in his mind. He understood what had really occurred. This Wolf, this man called Sloane, had used that lousy elephant, not only to get his wife back, but to free himself from all surveillance. Captain Price and all his men were dead—save one, a CSA agent code-named Cobra, apparently deranged. Galenkov now picked up a report from Toronto, read it. He actually laughed out loud. So very clever. It really was too bad Sloane was not Russian. One had to admire him.

He closed that digression out of his mind to return mentally to the museum. Sloane had used the elephant to escape surveillance, both from the CSA and the KGB. Azbel had lost him, at least temporarily. Why? Azbel's failure was in not asking and answering the question. To get his wife back? Hardly. He could have simply made the switch if that's all he wanted. To escape, to run? No. He could have done that at some earlier point when he had her in the taxi.

The only possible answer was that Sloane had something he wanted to do, and he wanted time and distance in which to do it. He was acting on the basis of information learned from Pavel Karamasov. Therefore, my very foolish, young Azbel, let him do it. Let Sloane do for us what we cannot do ourselves. At the very least leave him alone until he tells us what we want to know—tells us by his actions. There was a risk to this. But Sloane left them no choice. He had spoken of *great danger*. He believed the danger was to both sides. He alone had heard Karamasov. The words must be believed. To fail to do so was a far greater risk.

Anticipate. All his career Galenkov had lived by the

word. The intelligence officer must anticipate. Wasn't it a chess game, after all? Galenkov considered himself quite a good chess player. In his youth he had been excellent. *Anticipate*. He arose and went to a map of North America on his wall, pointed to a spot with a pencil. There. Short Creek Spring, West Virginia, twenty miles west of Hagerstown, Maryland. A small CSA facility, security so tight it had never been infiltrated, despite considerable effort. Over and over the woman had said Short Creek Spring. Very well. He had to trust her, as he did Sloane. He would anticipate. Short Creek Spring it would be.

For the first time Duane Cash, as Mr. Green, wondered if it was possible to resign from The Committee. He might have reached the apex of his career, but he was in way over his head. Could he plead stupidity? Might work, but then he already knew too much, if only the existence of The Committee. But surely members must be allowed to resign. They couldn't just stay until they died. Maybe they did—an early death. That's what frightened him. Was there no room for illness? Maybe he could come down with some hopeless contagion. AIDS? No. All known or even suspected homosexuals were eliminated, almost on the spot.

Mr. Brown: "Special projects next. Where do we stand with the Seraphim Operation?"

Black: "The nuclear guided-missile sub *Comrade Molotov* left Sebastopol, destination the Mediterranean and the Azores."

Gray: "Is the software aboard?"

Black: "Yes."

211

Brown: "Are you sure?"

Black: "As sure as we're ever going to be."

Brown looked at White: "Your end?"

White: "All set. No foul-ups. All we need is for the *Molotov* to arrive on station."

Gray: "No failure in our testing?"

White: "That's what I said. The laser has worked every time."

Brown: "Then it's a go."

White: "Except for this business with Sloane, the KGB, and that fucking elephant. What is going on, Mr. Green? Do we have a problem with security or don't we?"

Cash felt himself inwardly buckling, but tried to stand fast. "There is no problem with security."

White: "Does this renegade Sloane know something about Operation Seraphim or doesn't he?"

"I am convinced he does not."

Black: "You're convinced? Mr. Green, we are accustomed to certainties which require no convincing."

"Sloane knows nothing, nor does anyone else."

The four senior members of The Committee exchanged glances during an extremely tense silence. Then Brown spoke. "We would like your evidence for that statement."

Cash struggled mightily not to swallow or avert his eyes, telling himself he was on The Committee, a certified equal to these men. "The possibility existed that Karamasov did meet Sloane to tell him something. It could have been any matter. There is no reason to suppose it had anything to do with our special project at all. Sloane has not gone to the KGB. He has told them nothing. Their continued search for him suggests nothing else. Our security has not been breached."

Gray: "Then what the hell was that little caper at the Elephant Rotunda all about?"

White: "Yes. The damn Smithsonian is acting like they lost the Hope diamond or something."

Cash inwardly heaved a huge sigh of relief. He was going to get out of this. "The KGB had taken his wife. Sloane arranged a trap at the Smithsonian designed to get back his wife and eliminate Captain Price and his team. Unfortunately, it succeeded. He has again escaped surveillance—at the moment. But he will be found."

Brown: "Then it was just a scheme to escape, run?"

"Yes."

Black: "Does anyone else share your view of this?"

"Yes. Gordon Adams has been in direct charge of the manhunt. It is his view. Adams, of course, knows nothing about Seraphim."

Brown: "He has no need to know." He looked at the others, sensed concurrence. Adams was far more likely to be trusted than this new Mr. Green. "Very well. Just get rid of this Sloane as soon as possible. Then that will be the end to the problem."

"It won't take long."

When the meeting was over Cash felt physically ill. It was all he could do to control his vomit. The Committee had bought it. They had not known about the tape in the elephant's mouth. No way they could have known, unless Adams told them. Price was gone, most of the others. Sloane's tape sent to Price was destroyed. Cash felt he had gambled and won. But such a risk. It was the unwritten rule that no member of The Committee ever lied or withheld information from the others. If they ever found out . . . Silly. Sloane knew nothing. Security was not breached. That's all he'd said. It was the truth. Stop worrying. Cash felt better then.

They flew to Toronto, rented a car, and drove northward all afternoon. Sloane fell asleep, having been awake all night in the museum. For Freddie it was a pleasant déjà vu, driving aimlessly over roads she didn't know, a serendipity tour, David asleep beside her. They had done it for weeks three years before while camping in Europe, evading pursuit. They were still the most pleasant weeks of her life. David had healed his wounds. She had healed her spirit.

As she drove along she deliberately let the hobgoblins into her mind, remembering and visualizing all that had happened, finally reaching the Elephant Rotunda and the bullets, blood, and falling bodies. All her life she'd hated guns, violence, and death, and what she had seen was virtually physical pain for her. She accepted it as part of her healing, then asked why so much of what she hated had been visited upon her. Freddie had no answer to the question.

All she knew was that it had to mean something. She simply could not, would not be a participant in something senseless. The dead and dying couldn't be lying around for no reason—no good reason. What truly devastated her was the realization that's probably what it was. Damn Mother! Another stupid, wretched intelligence game, played for no reason but the playing of it. It had happened before with Parsley. She knew all about the game, did she ever! It had come again. Damn Mother! Damn Dzerzhinsky Square!

She glanced at the sleeping David. A good man, really. He had been taken as a teenager, by Mother, his government, *her* government, and trained to be a killer, a halfway suicidal killer. *It's like swatting a fly, Freddie. The fly wants to live, but we all swat them.* She sighed. Yes. She'd killed and knew. But he'd made so much progress. He was now a man, a real man— halfway at least—soon to be a father. He was done with the game. He wanted out. She was sure of it. There was no doubt in her mind. One evening she went to him while he was reading. The Bible. He'd showed her what he was reading. Psalm 51. It was burned in her memory.

> Have mercy upon me, O God, according to thy loving-kindness; according unto the multitude of thy tender mercies blot out my transgressions.
>
> Wash me thoroughly from mine iniquity, and cleanse me from my sin.
>
> For I acknowledge my transgressions: and my sin is ever before me.
>
> Against thee, thee only, have I sinned, and done this evil in thy sight: that thou mightest be justified when thou speakest, and be clear when thou judgest.
>
> Behold, I was shapen in iniquity; and in sin did my mother conceive me.

God, please help him. She had made the prayer. His reading of the Fifty-first Psalm was the answer.

Robert A. Liston

They stopped near dark at a small village beside Georgian Bay, had dinner. The hideout was a small hotel. There was a bed in the hideout. Indeed there was. Of all that transpired there, paramount for Freddie was her sense of renewal, her commitment to this man, this lover, this husband, this father of her child. She was very big on commitment. Oh, my, yes. At their climax she whispered three words into his ear.

Not long afterward he said, "Why did you say that?"

"Did you know that when a woman moves toward the man afterwards it is a sure sign she was satisfied?"

"I asked why you said that."

"*Whither thou goest?* I figure you're planning to leave me here. I don't want that."

"I have to, Freddie. Our escape is only temporary. There are still two men after us, Price and Gillies. The Agency will send more. The KGB still wants me. There is no escape for us."

In sin did my mother conceive me. "What are you going to do?"

"I really don't know. By all that's sensible we should run, but you won't do that."

"I told you in the cab I would—if it's our only choice." Abruptly she sat up beside him, legs tucked under herself. She knew he didn't believe her. "Try me. I might. The last time it was to be Cape Town or Johannesburg. I really don't think I'd like that place. Winnie Mandela I'm not."

"How about Greece or Turkey?"

"Better. Always wanted to see the Parthenon."

216

He squinted at her through hooded eyes. "You'll give up home, family, career, everything you've always wanted?"

"I might. Whither thou goest."

He shook his head, reached out, touched her thigh. "I don't believe you."

"I don't either. But I might—if it has to be. But I have to know why I'm doing it. What did Karamasov say to you?"

"No, Freddie. It won't work."

I'm going to have a child, our child. He needs a father.

"Then I won't go. Everything dies right here, you, me, us, future, dreams, everything. Mother, my real mother, warned me about you."

"Stop it, Freddie."

"You like the game, don't you, David? You've got your gun now, the holster at your armpit. You've got the tension, the stupid machinations, the suicidal danger. It's all come back to you, hasn't it? There's no room for dumb ol' Freddie Falscape. She's just a roll in the hay anyway—like the paid whores Mother used to service you with."

He looked at her a long moment. His voice was unchanged as he said, "Karamasov said the Seraphim Code was broken."

"What's the Seraphim Code?"

"I'm not sure."

"Can you find out?"

"I doubt it."

"But there's just the tiniest sliver of a possibility, isn't there?" He said nothing. "Parsley. We did it before."

"I knew you were going to do this to me."

217

I wrote a letter to the President, David. He wants us to help him. "Then why fight it?"

"If I do anything, I don't need you. You'll just be in the way."

"Wrong. You need a partner. You're only half a man without one. I'm you're Harry Rogers now."

He blinked. She had gotten to him.

"I'm also better-looking. In addition, I have various body processes which are useful." She lay down beside him then and committed herself anew.

"What the hell happened?"

Adams reflected on the fact this was the second time today he'd been asked the same question. "Nothing that wasn't supposed to, Mr. President." It was late at night and they were in the same library of the same house in Georgetown. Adams considered it a mistake. Marvin Grayson either had a severe shortage of friends he could trust in Washington, or he was an ignoramus about intelligence methods. Probably both.

"Lord, Gordon! All those bodies! The elephant destroyed!"

"Couldn't be helped, Mr. President. The KGB had Freddie—I mean Dr. Falscape. To get her back Sloane arranged to swap a tape of the information he had for his wife. It happened in a place and manner of his own choosing."

"But Gordon, the Smithsonian! The elephant destroyed! You have to know what a landmark it is."

"Couldn't be helped. I'm sure the Smithsonian will find another and better elephant." Privately he thought all this fuss about a dumb stuffed elephant positively ridiculous.

Grayson shook his head sadly. "I suppose you're right. What was on the tape?"

"It was destroyed with the elephant, sir."

"God Almighty! You mean all this was for *nothing?*"

"Hardly nothing, sir. Sloane is now free to work in our behalf. His wife is with him. That is precisely what we wanted." *We?* Did Grayson have any glimmer of an idea what was going on?

"*That's* what all this was about? Five dead, a destroyed elephant, just so this man Sloane could—"

"Escape Agency surveillance, yes, sir." He saw the Presidential distress. "It is all being explained away, Mr. President. It will never get back to you. If you wish, I suppose you could mention at a press conference that you are taking steps to prevent defacing of public property, something like that." At once he knew he'd gone too far.

"I don't think I need you to advise me on how to handle the press, Gordon."

"I'm sorry. I didn't mean to be presumptive."

A wave of his hand dismissed the matter. "The upshot is that we are no closer to learning about this secret CSA operation than we were the last time we met."

"No, but I think we'll learn something very soon. Sloane will discover it."

"I wish I had the confidence in him you do."

"Sloane is a very good man, the best I ever knew. And his wife is with him. She can control him."

"You've spoken to her?"

"Yes. She was most impressed with your letter. She will do what has to be done."

Grayson shook his head. "A man and his wife, both very young. Slender reeds for the ship of state, if you

ask me. I don't think I'm going to brag about any of
this in my memoirs."

Sloane arose early and went out to buy a morning
paper. He found the *Toronto Globe & Mail*, then to his
surprise an early edition of the *New York Times*. Both
played the "Massacre at the Elephant Rotunda" as
front-page news, but Sloane restrained himself until
he returned to the hotel so he and Freddie could read
them together.

Sloane was amused by the story. It seems D.C. cop
Candido Mako and FBI Agent Peter Daugherty were
national heroes. Both had lost their lives saving the
Smithsonian from a terrorist attack. Only the elephant had been destroyed, and would be replaced
immediately. The two dead "terrorists" carried phony IDs. The FBI believed they were from a certain
unnamed Middle Eastern country.

Freddie was aghast. "How can they write this
crap?"

"They write what they're told. If the FBI, CIA,
Mother, the White House, and God tell them this is
what happened, reporters have it on impeccable
authority and take pen in hand and—"

"They don't use pens. They use word processors."

"I know that."

"It's still ridiculous, David. You and I know what
really happened."

"Do you think anyone would want to know that?"

"Maybe not, but this"—she waved the paper she
held—"this drivel! How can anyone believe anything
they read?"

"Because it makes them feel good. They've just

read all the news fit to print. It's easier to suspend your brains and believe than to ask questions."

"Like why on earth terrorists would want to blow up the Museum of Natural History in the first place."

Sloane had tuned her out. Something further down in the story had caught his eye.

"This story is garbage, David. I can understand ordinary people believing it, maybe, but the press? They just have to know better. They aren't dumb. They're supposed to have all these contacts. Are they lazy? Have they lost the ability to look beyond the surface facts?"

Sloane read: "The dead man found outside in a car was identified as Captain Lawson Jones Price, USN-retired. The FBI is uncertain whether his death relates to events inside the museum. An FBI spokesperson said it is believed Captain Price just happened upon the scene and was killed by the terrorists to prevent their identification."

"I should know better, shouldn't I? Need to Know. The press is told whatever they can be made to believe."

He shook his head as though clearing it. "What?"

"I said the press is victimized by Need to Know—whatever they can be made to believe."

"That's it." Price dead. That left only Gillies. Awareness of what had happened came at once to Sloane. Gillies had shot Price, set up Mako and Daugherty. The man was free-lancing. He was coming after him one-on-one. He wanted to be the man who shot Liberty Valance. Dumb.

"You'd think some people in the press would figure out how Need to Know works, wouldn't you?"

"And complicate their lives? Don't be silly. Get dressed. I'm buying you breakfast."

"I thought you'd never ask."

Two hours later they were aboard a chartered plane—to Freddie a very old and rickety plane—headed south. Over the roar of the engine and talking into his ear, she asked, "Where are we going?"

He also turned to her ear. "Washington—or near there. A small field in Prince Georges County."

"May I ask why?"

"I thought you wanted to be part of all this."

"I do. But why did we go to Canada in the first place?"

"Because we were expected to."

She shook her head at that and sat back in her seat, thinking about it. Then she leaned over and spoke into his ear. "You really were going to leave me in Canada, weren't you?"

"Yep."

She smiled, one of her best. "I'm glad I changed your mind."

"We'll see."

After landing they rented a car and drove around Washington on the Beltway and into the Virginia countryside.

"May I ask where we're going and what we're doing? Or have I suddenly become your dumb, slobby wife, unfit to know anything more than where the bathroom is? Speaking of that—"

"We're going to West Virginia."

"Lovely state. What's there?"

"Short Creek Spring. A very secret CSA facility. Can you pick up a sailor in a bar?"

"What do you think I did before I met you? I'd just tell them I was Dr. Falscape, assistant professor of political science at a girl's school—excuse me, woman's college—and I'd beat 'em off with a stick."

"You're going to get your chance again."

"Not in this outfit. Red hair and polka dots won't cut it."

He grinned. "You look nice. I bought it for you."

"Which goes to prove you never were much of a sailor. With my vast experience I always knew it. Who am I picking up?"

"His name is Wiley Drake—or it used to be the name he used. He may not be there. This may be a vast waste of your talents."

"There'll be *some* sailor there. Who's Wiley Drake and why do I bat my baby browns at him?"

"Seriously, okay? Wiley's a CT—or in his case a CET, even rarer. We were shipmates together. He may be able to help us."

"Start with the C and progress to the T. I'm still in grade school."

"CT, Communications Technician. The correct terminology is CTT, Communications Technical Technician, but everybody just says CT. They're in the Navy, like Wiley, or the Air Force, Army, or Marines. Only they aren't. They're selected and trained by the Agency at Pensacola. They get their security classification from CSA—usually among the highest in the land. Almost always they have cryptographic clearance. Mother uses them as the pawns in the game. They're the ones trained on all the esoteric gear. They intercept all the messages, break the codes. They send all our coded messages."

"I know about codes. That's how the CSA manipulates the world, concealing the real information, putting out disinformation."

"Exactly. The CTs control the code machines—all the information. Because they're enlisted men, the brass, the politicians, the public, even your buddies on the press—"

"They're not my buddies—not after today."

"—pay them no mind, which is how it's supposed to be. They get away with murder—sometimes literally, although not usually. CTs are a special breed. They have brains or they wouldn't be CTs. And they have special knowledge few others possess. They really, truly won't take shit from anybody. Don't ever cross one or he'll find a way to stick it to you. They walk their own path, go their own way. Their loyalties are to each other—and Mother. *Maybe* Mother."

"They sound sinister."

"Not really. You just have to understand they are *in* the Navy, or whatever, but not *part* of it. The military has never discovered that."

"This Wiley Drake is a CT."

"Not really. He's a CET, Communications Electronic Technician. He repairs and maintains the equipment used by CTs, which makes him even more skilled and important than the CTs."

"I get it. That makes him even more independent."

"It's more than that, and a little hard to explain. CTs and CETs are special and damn well know it. Because of what they know, because of their security classifications and access to classified information and codes, they belong to a special club. I was once a member of the club. I'm hoping Wiley will tell me something I need to know."

224

"And I'm to bring him to you. The poor man won't know what hit him."

"It's no game, Freddie. Short Creek Spring is one of the most secure bases in the country, almost impossible to enter or infiltrate. Most of the action occurs in bars outside the gates. The places are crawling with KGB, all trying to entrap the CTs, and Naval Intelligence, CSA agents, and others watching to see which CTs are talking to whom and about what. There's a lot of very subtle action going on."

"Why do they bother?"

Sloane grinned. "It's part of the fun—a big game of skill and living on the edge. It keeps the CTs on their toes. Wiley will be good at it."

"I think I'm out of my league."

"Maybe you are. But along with the Russian and US ringers are some legitimate hookers and local girls trying to make out with sailors. You're going to have to pass for one of those."

Hooker. The whole image of what she was getting into distressed her. "Why don't you just go yourself?"

"I've an idea some people we don't want to know may be looking for me."

"Gotcha. Freddie the Hooker it is."

"If he does show up and you get a minute alone with him, just say Packie wants to see him."

"Who's Packie?"

"Drake knew me on ship as David Packwood."

"Lord!" *David Stuart Pritchard, Jr., I named you after your father—at least I think that was his name.*

TEN

Alone in the bathroom of their motel room, Freddie surveyed the results of her efforts in the mirror. Maybe a touch more blush. *Baby, the last thing you need is more blush. You got enough naturally.* She added some anyway.

She was dressed as a hooker, at least her idea of what a hooker looked like: white tank top, no bra, lots of cleavage, ridiculous heels, and white satin pants so tight they might have been painted on. *I'm sorry, but I can't sit down and have a drink with you. I mean I really can't. The first hundred bucks is payment for getting in and out of these things. Why aren't they built with a proper zipper?* Her eyes widened. Maybe they are. I goofed. Beneath her platinum blonde wig, she wore enough makeup for the whole cast of *Best Little*

Whorehouse in Texas. Her lips were a bright, shiny red and her false lashes, properly batted, could do at least as well as a Bissel sweeper. She stepped back a couple of paces to get the full effect, stood with her legs apart, hands on her hips. *Maybe you need a whip, just a little one.*

If she'd had it she would have used it on herself. This was the ultimate degradation. *I understand they enjoy it. Some of them? Maybe?* In truth she was petrified. All the while she made her ridiculous purchases, she kept asking herself what she'd do, *really* do, if push came to shove, or better said, grapple came to clutch. She'd decided she would. If that's what it took to bring this Wiley Drake to David, save her country from the Red Menace and Motherhood, that's what she'd do. After all, she'd killed for David. Even now she extended her finger toward the mirror in a shooting motion, felt again the jerking of her wrist. What's a little harmless screwing after that. *Did you know I'm going to be a mother? Isn't there a special term for what you're doing? Mummy, Daddy, I know you sent me to college to become Dr. Falscape, but this is just a little postgraduate work.* Lord! *Junior, did I ever tell you about my experiences as a hooker? There was this one guy. . . .* Wow!

She wheeled, opened the bathroom door, and stepped out into the motel bedroom. He was sitting in a chair, smoking, drinking a can of beer, and watching TV. He didn't even look up. *Godalmighty! You sit there like a slug while your wife goes out on the streets and hustles up the rent money.*

Timorously she said, "I'm ready now."

Sloane turned to look at her. His eyes widened, as though in shock, then he grinned, finally began to laugh. It began as a snicker, turned into a chuckle, expanded into hilarity, and finally reached a guffaw. He spilled his beer and actually doubled over, his head between his knees. For Freddie it was undiluted humiliation. She blushed all over, then her anger came in a surge, painfully so. Her eyes burned and shameless tears filled them. She had never hated him so much. "Damn you, Sloane." She wheeled for the door.

He caught her just as she reached it. "Aw, Freddie, I'm sorry." But new laughter bubbled out of him. "But you're so *funny!*"

"Damn you! You're the one who wants me to turn tramp and pick up some jerk in a bar. You don't have to laugh at me."

He tried to control it, but not with much success. "I'm sorry." More laughter. "I really am but . . . you're so . . . *ridiculous.*"

"Thanks a lot!"

"Jeez, Freddie. What d'you think you're doing?"

"One more damn sound out of you, and I'm not doing a blessed thing."

"Didn't you ever pick up a guy?"

"Thousands. I told you."

More laughter cascaded from him. "I'm sorry. I . . . just can't . . . help it. You're *hilarious!*" Angrily she tried to pull free of him, but he held her arm. "You're gonna pick up somebody all right, but not Wiley Drake." He laughed the hardest he had yet. "My wife, the hooker!"

"The hell with you, Sloane."

He took her in his arms, held her close, feeling his own body pulsate in laughter against her. Then he held her away, looking her up and down. "You are kinda sexy—sort of." Suddenly he kissed that smear of lipstick.

She pushed at him. "Get away from me, you—you—" Then she couldn't say anything for a moment. "Oh, David. I feel . . . so awful."

"I'm sorry. I thought you knew. There may be CTs who will go for a hooker, but Wiley Drake isn't one of them. You'll scare him to death."

She saw the brightness in his eyes. "How about you?"

Again he looked down at her. "The outfit does have a certain appeal."

"Turn you on?"

"Yeah, maybe, kinda."

"I always knew you were a degenerate."

He kissed her with heightened interest. "Take off those stupid lashes. They tickle my cheek."

An amorous half hour later she said to him, "Why didn't you tell me all this in the first place?"

"I dunno. I guess I figured you knew. Wiley Drake is in his mid-thirties. He's serious, studious. The last thing that'll interest him is a hooker."

"Now you tell me—*after* I spent money on these ridiculous rags." Thrift was important to Freddie. "What does interest him?"

"His kids."

"I'm supposed to pick up a married man devoted to his kids?"

"Divorced. That's your edge. Here's what to do."

A short while later she parked across the street from two bars David said were frequented by sailors. One was the Sky Dive. Loud music came from it. No way. The second was The Bulkhead, obviously the classier of the two. When she entered she wore her blue polka-dot dress, the hair and face of Freddie Falscape. But if she had to give a name it was to be Freddie Packwood.

The place was basically one large square room, decorated in late-twentieth-century plastic. There was a long, busy bar and at the far end a small dance floor and stage with a group playing country rock, mercifully not too loud. Closer to the entrance were numerous tables and booths, most occupied. There were almost no uniforms, which surprised her, but lots of young men and even younger women.

She slid onto a stool at the bar, waited for the bartender. His haircut suggested military. Probably worked at the base and moonlighted in this bar. She had a sense he studied her carefully. "Chablis," she said. Then when it came, "Is it too late for dinner? I'm famished." *You're gonna get fat, Freddie. I'll go on a diet sometime when I'm not scared witless.*

He looked at the clock above the cash register. "We can get you something. Wannit here or at a table?"

"Table if I may."

"I'll speak to the waitress. She'll fix you right up."

"Bartender, I'm just passing through town. You wouldn't know the shortest way to Moundsville, would you?"

He blinked, frowned. "Moundsville? That's here in West Virginia, isn't it?"

"On the Ohio River. I think I'm lost."

"Whew! That's tough to get to from here." He started to call out for anyone who knew the way to Moundsville, then thought better of it. "I'll see what I can find out."

David had not explained the significance of Moundsville, a place she'd never heard of. Why didn't he pick Charleston or Wheeling, someplace familiar? The waitress came and led her to a small table near the front of the place. She ordered, then watched the bandstand through a haze of cigarette smoke. *This isn't going to work, David. I'm attracting as much attention as Marian the Librarian. I should look like that singer.* She was blonde, built, bulging out the front of a slinky black dress. She even sang a little in a throaty voice. "Your cheatin' heart . . ." Sure. That was the way to do it. Every time she drew breath she got rave notices from the assembled critics.

Her food came—swiss steak, mashed potatoes and gravy, peas, wilted salad. Good ol' down-home country fare. She ate. What else was there to do? *Did you know the spy racket is one of the dullest jobs on earth? All they do is shoot people, then sit around and eat. It is a known fact that James Bond weighs four hundred pounds and is a permanent resident of a fat farm. He shoulda listened to Dr. No.*

The singer finished her set amid wild applause. *Move over, Tammy Wynette. Crystal Gayle is a slug.* She stepped down among her admirers, then slowly made her way to the bar, smiling, laughing, patting cheeks coquettishly, then accepted a drink. She could've had a whole distillery. Freddie looked away, sipping her wine. When she looked back, she gasped. The singer was looking at her. Olga from Kiev.

Freddie was terrified, but somehow she had the good sense not to avert her eyes. It lasted an eternity. Finally Olga turned away, back to the bar, smiled at one of her admirers. Freddie didn't know whether to walk or run from the place. Her cover was blown. That woman knew who she was, probably what she was doing here. The KGB would be here any second.

Nothing happened. Olga just stayed at the bar, jollying up some sailors. She never glanced her way again. Slowly, Freddie's panic faded. Olga was KGB. Olga was working a bar outside a top-secret Navy base. Of course. David had said the place crawled with both KGB and US agents. And Olga was just as scared of her as she was of Olga. It had been in her eyes, recognition, surprise, then fear. Her cover was blown too. And she was in a lot more trouble than Freddie Falscape was.

"A man at the bar bought you this. Do you want it?"

Freddie looked up, saw the waitress, then the highball glass she held. It was a dark color.

"Rum and coke."

Freddie shook her head. "I don't care for it. Who bought it?"

"Don't look for him. And I'd accept it if I were you. Cause less trouble that way."

Freddie shrugged. "Whatever you say." She let the drink be set on the table, but did not touch it. She tried to concentrate on her swiss steak. Maybe this is how it was done.

"Hiya, baby. Enjoyin' yer drinky-poo?"

She hesitated, bracing herself, then looked up. He was young, blond, hazel-eyed, obviously military, and even more obviously drunk. There could be absolutely no doubt he was on the make. "I'm afraid I'm not into rum and coke. I have my wine."

"Ya like wine? I'll getcha a whole bot'l." He turned, raised an arm toward the bar.

"No, please. I've quite enough, thank you."

He grinned at her approvingly. "Whassyername?"
What was she to do? "Fern."

"Like in the flower? I'm Richard—as in Nixon.
Everybody calls me Tricky Dicky." He thought himself very amusing.

Not everyone calls me Freddie. She turned back to
her food, then thought better of it. Maybe this was
Wiley Drake. Maybe he operated this way. She looked
at him. "Do you know the way to Moundsville?"

"Whassa Moundsville? Never heard of it." He
grinned, or maybe it was a leer. "But ya sure got
mounds. I can tell. Wanna dance?"

Wiley Drake? David said he was serious, studious.
This jerk was serious only about the bottle. But it
could be him. Maybe it was just a way to get her alone
on the dance floor. "I don't know. I—"

"Sure ya do, baby—I mean Fern baby." He clasped
her upper arm, started to pull her to her feet.

Suddenly she was frightened. She wasn't sure she
could cope with this guy. "On second thought, I'd
like to finish my dinner."

"Whassamatter? I'm not good 'nuff to dance
with?"

She saw anger rise in his eyes. Lord! This was
trouble. She twisted her arm free, felt him grab it
again, pull her from her seat.

"I thought you were with me, Dicky."

Behind him stood Olga from Kiev. He turned, saw
her. His eyes brightened as he took in her cleavage.
"This lady doesn't wanna dance wi-me."

Olga smiled. "Well, I do." She actually appeared to
shove out her chest. "I've wanted to all evening." She
took his hand, pulled him away. It wasn't hard.

Freddie stared after them. Olga had not made eye

contact with her. For all the world it appeared she was interested only in the drunken sailor. But Freddie knew better. Olga had come over deliberately to take him away. She was helping her. Why? Slowly Freddie sat back down, tried to eat, but her mind remained on Olga. Why was she here? Why had she helped her?

"You wan' directions to Moundsville, Miss?"

She looked up, startled. Medium height, a little pudgy, steel-rimmed glasses, dark hair halfway back his head. Had to be Wiley Drake. Just had to be.

"Thass my home town, Miss. Li'l hard to get to from here, but I can show ya. Gotta map?" His drawl was pure country.

David, you're so smart. Ask directions to the man's hometown. "I'm sorry. I left it in the car."

"Thass okay. I'll get one from the bar." He grinned, rather nicely, and left her. She looked for Olga. On the dance floor with Tricky Dicky. Lotsa jiggle. She looked toward the bar. The map was being handed over. If this was Wiley Drake, should she let Olga see her talking to him? Too late now. "Do ya mind if I sit, Miss?"

"Please do." She smiled her best, waited for him to pull a chair closer to her left elbow, begin to open the map. "You're so nice to help me. My name is Freddie." She extended a hand. He accepted it.

"How do. I'm Wiley—Wiley Drake."

So easy, David. You're not going to believe it.

"Now here's where we are, Miss, and—"

"Freddie. My friends call me Freddie."

"I'm sorry. Freddie, sure 'nuff. An' over here is Moundsville. I think I can get ya there without too much mountain drivin'."

She let him drone on about highways without listening, then said, "Packie wants to see you. I'm his wife."

He seemed not to have heard her. "West Virginia 19 isn't too bad a road and it takes you to I-79. You can get off at Fairmount. That's here." He pointed at the map. "It's jus' a short drive to Moundsville." He looked at her, smiled. "The tough part is gettin' outta this burg. When yer ready to leave I'll show ya the way."

"I'm ready now. Just let me swallow the last of my wine." She did, then fished in her purse for a ten spot to cover the check and stood up, pulling her sweater around her shoulders. "Are you sure this isn't too much trouble?"

"Not'all, Miss. We hillbillies is always glad t'show folk around."

As he accompanied her out the door, she glanced back. Olga was gone. What did that mean? Was she sending for reinforcements? How about the big burly guy from the apartment?

Freddie was nervous as he walked her across the street to stand beside her car. He carried on a pantomine of pointing, showing her the way out of town. "Lots of ears around, Freddie. Can't be too careful." He had dropped his accent.

"I know."

"I thought Sloane was dead."

"How do you know that name?"

"His picture was in the paper, remember?"

"How do you know I'm his wife?"

"Because you said Packie. Only he could've known that."

"The singer in there is KGB."

"Everybody knows that. You not only get a good lay but a chance to feed her disinformation too."

"She recognized me."

"You probably scared her to death, but we'll play it safe. Four blocks down, turn right. Edge of town is a pizza joint. Vince's. I'll be there." He reverted to his drawl, wished her a safe trip, and walked away toward a car.

She turned, unlocked the car, got in. The light went out when she shut the door.

"I heard what he said. Let's go."

"David!"

"Don't turn around. Just drive."

It was déjà vu. "This was how we met in Munich. You in the back seat, ordering me to drive."

"Don't get romantic. Drive." In a moment she had pulled away from the curb. "How do you know the singer?"

"She was my watchdog in the KGB apartment. Said her name was Olga."

"Drive around a bit. Don't go directly to the pizza place."

"Do you think we're being followed?"

"That's what the rearview mirror is for."

"I gather you checked out of the motel. Why didn't you tell me you were going to be outside in the car? Oh, Lord! I know. Need to Know. I shoulda married a postal clerk."

"You'd be surprised what they do. Any tail?"

"I don't see anyone."

"Figures." He climbed into the seat beside her. "Let's go have a pizza."

"I'm not hungry."

"That's a first."

Sloane felt Wiley Drake had chosen well. The pizza parlor was large, open, with three exits, crowded with a late-night crowd. He picked a corner table. There were good sightlines of everyone entering.

They began as a couple of old shipmates reminiscing, which was true. Finally Drake said, "I gather you're in some trouble, Packie."

"A bit. Want me to tell you about it?"

"Not one syllable."

"I thought not."

"How can I help?"

"Tell me about laser cryptography."

Freddie tried to listen, but soon couldn't. It was simply too technical for her. Her mind wandered back to Olga the singer and Wiley Drake's words: a good lay and disinformation. Suddenly Freddie felt sorry for her. What kind of life did she have, sleeping with sailors in hopes of gaining information? The KGB wasn't a bit different from the CSA, using people, chewing up lives, all for the game. What kind of woman was she? How'd she get into the game? What did she get out of it? And why had she helped her?

"Where'd the black boxes come from?"

"Dunno, Packie. All I can tell you is they aren't ours. They are nothing we ever made."

"Go on."

"We duplicated them—exactly, every detail, every frequency, every modulation."

"Here?"

"Yep. I was in charge." He grinned. "Damn fine work, if I do say so. They test out perfectly. I tested them myself."

"Tell me about it."

Drake looked around and was apparently satisfied, for he said, "One box went on a sub, another on a P2V. That's where I was. Slick as a whistle. You drop a buoy in the water, signal it with the black box. A minute later, there's the missile breaking water, heading downrange. Never saw anything like it."

"Work every time?"

"Every time I did it." Another grin. "Like I say, I do good work."

"I know. You figure your black box made the missile fire?"

"And the one on the sub. What else could it be? But don't ask me exactly how or why it happens. That I don't know. I just duplicated the black boxes."

Sloane's mind craved to assimilate what he had just learned and combine it with Tenpenny's information, but he knew now wasn't the time. "What're you doing these days?"

"Killing time, actually. I wanted to go to Moundsville to see my kids, but I was told to stay available. I'm to go back to Lexington Park in a couple days. I guess they're planning some more tests."

Freddie kept watching David's blue eyes. There was a strange, bright intensity to them. All this gibberish had meaning to him.

"Thanks a lot, Wiley. I owe you."

"Hope I've been some help, but I'm not going to ask how or why. I never saw you or you me."

Sloane nodded. "How old are the kids now?"

Freddie listened to these two old pals talk about the joys of domestic bliss. For her benefit David even talked about getting "his old lady properly trained." She'd show him who was being trained. Did all men have to engage in this male talk?

"Could you do me a favor, Wiley?"

"Depends."

"There's a guy on my tail. Name's Curt Gillies. I'd like to shake him for awhile. Here's what I want you to do." He told him.

Drake laughed. "That's a dirty trick. Can't you do it?"

"I could, but I figure it'd be easier for you."

"No problem. Good as done."

Sloane stood up, reached out a hand for Freddie. "Gotta run, Wiley. Thanks."

"Sure. *Illigitimus non carborundum.*"

Sloane laughed. "Better believe it."

Outside she asked what that meant.

"Don't you know Latin?"

"You haven't trained me in it yet. What's it mean?"

"Don't let the bastards get you down."

"You do have the most interesting conversations —I think."

They flew to Montreal, then to Sudbury, north of Lake Huron, checked into a hotel shortly after daybreak, fell asleep at once. David seemed very quiet the whole trip. Preoccupied, Freddie figured. She just let him be. Her curiosity would wait till morning.

Gillies figured he had plenty of time. He'd give Sloane a long tether. That would make the hunt more savory. Trap him when he least expected it. Still, Gillies knew he wasn't far behind. Trailing them to Toronto was easy. Sloane wasn't so smart. It figured he'd head for Canada. Finding the rent-a-car agency was a little more difficult, but not much. Dumb Sloane had even asked for directions to Georgian Bay. Gillies figured it was a false trail. It surprised him when it wasn't. The key to understanding Sloane was that he wasn't as smart as he and everyone else thought.

Gillies was only a day behind when he found their motel. The rental car parked out front was a dead giveaway. He talked to the manager. Hadn't checked out. Left by cab. Simple legwork, that's all. The cab took them to a dirt airport. Flew to Maryland.

Gillies thought about chartering a plane and following, but he didn't have unlimited funds. They hadn't checked out, paid for another night. The car was there. They'd be back. He'd wait. An hour later he changed his mind. The chartered plane returned without them. Damn! Better get to the airport in Toronto quick.

Freddie slept badly, arose early, and went down to the lobby, buying papers, stopping for coffee while she read them. Nothing really. Not one word about Short Creek Spring, not that she expected there to be.

Why did she feel so rotten? She knew. She was lying to David. She had not told him about her letter to the President, the reaction it had earned. She had not told him about Gordon Adams, nor about running into him in the store, their later meeting. She had openly lied about not knowing who fired the third shot. How could she? David was the brains of this operation. He'd forgotten more about the games Mother played than she'd ever know. How could he function properly if he didn't know the truth? *This is the guilt room, Miss Falscape. It may not look too upsetting, but this is where some of our finer tortures occur. We work on the mind here. As you know, the mind is often the cruelest organ in the body*. Face it. She felt estranged from David and was trying to make it up to him in bed. Little lies, sins of omission destroyed more marriages than the Olgas of this world ever had. *David, I've lied to you. I want to tell you everything.* Yes. *Better tell the biggie.* Yes. *David, I'm pregnant. At least I was a million years ago when the rabbit died.* She ordered more coffee, another to take up to the room to him.

"Mr. Gillies? Mr. Curt Gillies?"

He turned, saw the short, dark-haired man with the fuzzy mustache. Behind him were three others, all wearing dark suits, all looking severe. "Yes."

"Will you come with us, please. I'm Inspector LeClerc." As the words were spoken, a hand entered his jacket, removed his gun.

Gillies eyes darted. There was no escape. He forced a smile. "I'd rather not."

"I think you have no choice."

There was menace—restrained, polite, but there. "What're you? The Canadian Mounties? Toronto cops? I've done nothing. Just got here. You're making a mistake."

"We are Interpol. If you are Mr. Curt Gillies, we are not making a mistake."

The sonofabitch had turned him into Interpol. Of all the goddamned cheap shots!

"We have been asked to hold you for questioning by a United States intelligence agency. We intend to do just that."

Gillies blanched. Mother! The Agency! He knew true fear. "On-on what . . . charge?"

241

The slightest smile spread the mustache of Inspector LeClerc. "We were told only that it was a security matter. Come with us, please."

Gillies trembled as hands clasped his arms. Inwardly he raged at Sloane, but that rage could not override his fear. Mother would kill him. He knew it.

Sloane heard Freddie get up and leave the room, but feigned sleep. He wanted to be alone to think. Now he lay on his back, hands folded under his head, staring up at the ceiling, finally letting into his conscious mind that which had been the subject of dreams during a night of disordered sleep.

A high-level Soviet code, transmitted by laser, probably from a satellite, is broken by Tenpenny. Wiley Drake builds black boxes and a buoy which is dropped from a plane. A laser signal is sent. A minute later Drake watches a missile rise from the water. What did it mean? Obviously, using his black boxes, Wiley Drake could make a submarine fire its missiles. He'd said the equipment wasn't ours. He'd duplicated someone else's black boxes. Soviet? Could Wiley Drake make a Soviet sub fire its missiles? Probably. Maybe undoubtedly.

Why? Sloane's mind returned to Karamasov. Dying, he blurted out words. Sloane forced himself to visualize and remember exactly. "Not much time." "You must help." "Great danger." "Help me." "Your people have broken our code for—" Sloane remembered he'd interrupted to ask what code. "Seraphim . . . Code. You must tell—"

Sloane shook his head. The Seraphim Code. Was that the code which made a Soviet sub fire its missiles? Had Karamasov somehow learned the CSA had broken that code? Was that the message he wanted delivered? Sloane knew he had to believe the answer to all these questions was yes. But what was the "great danger" Karamasov had referred to—great danger to both sides, Sloane was convinced? How could making a Soviet sub fire its missiles pose a "great danger"?

That was the heart of the puzzle, Sloane knew. The missiles on a Soviet sub, any sub, were pre-targeted. Those on a Soviet sub would be aimed for the US most likely, some to Europe, China, Japan, wherever. Why go to all the trouble of having Tenpenny break a code and Wiley Drake build and test black boxes so as to make a Soviet sub fire a missile which disintegrates Washington, New York, or London? Didn't make any sense. Soviet subs, all subs, fire missiles regularly. It is drill for the crew and keeps the missiles fresh. They can't sit in those subs forever. But for the tests the missiles have dummy warheads and are fired down-range to land in the ocean somewhere. Ships fish the missiles out of the water and they are returned to the factory to be re-outfitted and used again. Why make a Soviet sub test-fire a dummy missile downrange? Again Sloane shook his head. Didn't make any sense.

Yet something was going on. A dying Karamasov had warned of great danger and said the Seraphim Code was broken. The CSA had tried to kill them both to keep Karamasov from speaking, himself from hearing—or passing it on if he had heard. This huge manhunt had ensued. What Karamasov had said was of great importance. But what did it mean?

Another thought came to him. Wiley Drake wanted to visit his kids but was told to stand by to return to Lexington Park. He'd expected to go there in a few

days for more "tests." Sloane blinked, an acknowl-
edgement of the fear which suddenly stabbed at him.
Whatever was happening, whatever operation was
planned to make a Soviet sub fire its missile and for
whatever reason, was happening soon.

There was a rhythmic tap at the door. Freddie's
signal. She entered. Carrying coffee in a styrofoam
cup. God, he loved her. At that precise moment he
knew just how much—and just how much he wanted
their life together. He had a sense that if he could just
escape this noose the Agency and the KGB had put
around his neck, he would be able, finally, at long
last, to accept a normal life. All the old fears and
longings would be behind him. About time. Or was it
too late?

As Freddie looked at him, images flicked across her
mind. He was naked. The first time she saw him
naked in Munich he had been so shy about it. That
had appealed to her. She had teased him. Why did
these memories keep coming back to her? Is that
what happened before someone died? "I brought you
some coffee."

"Coffee can wait."

She nodded. "David, I have something to tell you."

"That I have a beautiful body?"

She smiled. "Is that what you've been lying there
thinking about?"

"Among other things." He reached out, took her
hand, pulled her to the bed to sit beside him.
"Wanna?"

"Sure." Never refusing him was a point of pride
with her. "Who needs hot coffee when there are hot
bodies." She set the coffee down, undressed, climbed

in beside him. She really didn't think it would be possible for her, just him, but he surprised her, or maybe she herself. There was an intensity to him—them. A few minutes later she said, "Wow! What makes you so sexy?"

"I always figured that's what everybody would do, one last time, just before the holocaust—or Armageddon, whatever they call it."

He lay on his back, she against him. She pushed herself higher in the bed, raised her head on her crooked arm, looked down at him. "That's heavy, David. Is that what you've been thinking about?"

"Not really. It was just something to say."

He never made idle chatter. He was trying to tell her something—or his subconscious was. "What's the Seraphim Code, David?"

"Not sure." He didn't want to tell her. His only course was to keep her out of it.

"Let me see if I can figure it out." She pursed her lips. "A Seraphim is an angel—a high-ranking angel, as I recall. The Seraphim Code." She thought a moment. "I got it. The Seraphim Code is something that makes angels out of us all."

He turned his head, stared at her. "You really are sharp, aren't you?"

She smiled. "I have my moments."

"Not this time. Code names are spewed out by computer these days, just so no smartie like you can attach any meaning to them." He smiled. "Sorry."

She shrugged. "Okay, I'm a dummy. What's the Seraphim Code?"

"Not sure."

"You keep saying that. Of course you're not sure.

Nobody's ever sure of anything. Einstein wasn't sure about relativity, Darwin about evolution. Hell, the sun only rises in the exact east two days a year. I'll settle for a theory. What do you *think* the Seraphim Code is?" She saw him shake his head. He didn't want to tell her. "David." She made the word a scold. "I have a right to participate in more than we just did. I'm not just a seminal vessel. I'm—"

"Harry Rogers. Okay, okay. I suspect the Seraphim Code is what makes a Soviet sub fire a missile—maybe a lot of them."

She stared at him, blinked, then sat up, tucking her legs under herself. "Then I was right. The Seraphim Code will make angels of us all."

"Why would the Russians want to do that?"

She glared at him, squinting her eyes. "Don't play me for a sap, David. And don't play your little mind games with me—answer a question with a question, find out what the person knows, then fill him full of bull. I may not have understood it at the time, but I heard what Wiley Drake said. He made black boxes. He used one and a missile rose from the water."

"It was an American missile."

"But the next time it could be a Russian missile, right?"

God, he loved her. She was just too quick and sharp to be believed. "Why make a Soviet sub fire its missile?" he asked.

She hesitated, blinked. "I don't know. You tell me."

"I can't. It's what I was lying here trying to figure out when you came in and seduced me."

"You're so easy it doesn't qualify as seduction. You really don't know?"

"No. It doesn't make any sense." He told her his reasons why it didn't.

Her response was a repeated shaking of her head as she reacted to the puzzle. "But it has to make sense to *somebody*. Why build black boxes and test them? Why try to kill you and chase us both over kingdom come? There has to be a reason. And that reason is spelled M-O-T-H-E-R." Adams's words came back to her. *The President signed a blank authorization. Some sort of operation is planned. We must find out what it is. David Sloane is the key to finding out.* "What are they up to, David?"

"I don't know." The words were spoken emphatically, proof that he really didn't know.

"It just seems to me two smart people like us ought to be able to figure it out." She saw him look at her quizzically. He had such faith in how smart his old agency was. She didn't. "There's no sense in the Agency helping the Russians nuke our own country."

"Right."

"Maybe The Committee's turned traitor and is helping the Russkies?"

"Not very likely. Oh, you mean another mole like Parsley? That'll never happen again in a million years, Freddie."

"It might, but I'll go along with you for now." She thought. "As you say there's no point in having the Russians fire dummy missiles downrange."

"Right." She was brainstorming the puzzle. It was a technique he and Harry Rogers had used. Suddenly he was very interested.

More thought. "Maybe it's a way to get the Soviet sub to fire all its missiles," she said. "We pick 'em off as fast as they are launched, leaving the sub just a great big empty sardine can. How about that?"

He laughed. "Possible, I suppose. But it'd be a lot easier just to sink the sub before it launched any of them."

She stuck out the tip of her tongue at him. "You're no fun." Head shake. "Why make a Russian sub fire its missiles?"

He grinned. All this—her, naked above him, playing mental games—was pure fun to him. "That's the problem, dearie."

She looked away, across the room, focusing on nothing, then turned back to him, squinting her eyes a little. "Suppose the missile doesn't go where it's supposed to."

He blinked.

"Maybe it goes to the wrong target. How about that?"

His first thought was what an absolutely uncanny woman she was. Such a mind! Then awareness that she was right flooded his brain. The wrong target. It was possible. Just change the software, the guidance for the missile. It would require a mole inside the Soviet Union. Why not; happened all the time.

"You're thinking. I'm right, aren't I? Change the target."

He looked at her. He couldn't have her know. Had to keep her out of this. "Yeah, I was thinking about it—thinking there is no way to do it." He smiled. "Good idea, Freddie, your best yet, but no cigar. Sorry."

Again she squinted at him, an expression of doubt. "Are you sure?"

"Positive. There's just no way to do it, Freddie. It's impossible." To avoid her eyes he rolled to sit on the edge of the bed, reached for the coffee. "Cold. Let's find breakfast."

"I thought you'd never ask." She scampered off the bed, reached for her bra and panties. "Maybe it's something simple, like . . . I know. Maybe the Russians have a new missile. The Agency wants to see how it works. Maybe they can retrieve it or something."

"Now that's the best idea you've had yet." In truth he only half heard her. His mind was clawing at the problem of changing the target. Easy really—if you had a man inside the software lab. Just dink around with the computer program. A few minor changes and the missile didn't do what it was supposed to. Happened all the time. Supposed to be a big problem the defense contractors and the Pentagon didn't want to talk about. Everything, all the guns, bombs, missiles, damn near everything but a rock and a spear was controlled by computers. The program, the software, controlled the weapon. If the program had been secretly altered, there was no easy way to discover it until the weapon was fired. Maybe the missile sits there, unused for years. Or maybe it tests out fine in drills. But when the time comes to fire it in earnest, it doesn't work. No way to find that out until push comes to shove. It is the Achilles Heel of all this expensive hardware on both sides. Hell, our own weapons could be used against ourselves, the Soviets' against their own country. It was part of what made the arms race so nonsensical.

She knew he was thinking, so she just let him.

Finally, when she was almost dressed, he looked at her. Wherever he had been, he'd come back. "David, do you remember when we first learned about Parsley, the mole on The Committee? You said it was impossible to identify him. I insisted we try. You admitted there was the faintest glimmer of something we might do."

"I remember."

"Is there a glimmer now?"

Images of what must be done flicked over his mind. Impossible really. Virtually hopeless. Probably suicidal. But he also realized he was going to do it. He'd figure out why later. "The remotest possibility."

She smiled. "I think you used those exact words before. What is it?"

"I didn't tell you with Parsley. I'm not about to now. You'll have to accept that."

"We're just going to plug along, do what has to be done. Ol' Freddie will be surprised. Okay. I'll accept that. But we are going to do something? We're going to try?"

"I'll never get any peace around you if I don't."

Delighted, she came around the bed, hugged him. "What're you talking about? You just had a piece."

"You have a very dirty mind, and I'm going to turn you in to the dean of women."

"You should hear her talk."

Both dressed, they headed for the door. Sloane said, "You wanted to talk to me about something. What was it?"

Lord! She'd forgotten. And it wasn't possible now. "I can't remember. Couldn't have been important."

They spent a pleasant day together, even doing the

tourist bit. He seemed particularly relaxed and animated, attentive and affectionate with her. She basked in it. They made love again that night. Such a man! She slept like the dead.

He was gone when she awoke in the morning. There was a note.

STAY HERE. BE BACK IN A FEW DAYS.

Damn him! He had dumped her. He had conned her, led her to believe they were working together. *We*, he'd said. "Damn you all to hell, Sloane. You'd never have treated Harry Rogers this way."

She read the next line: I LOVE YOU, FREDDIE.

The words frightened her. He probably hadn't said those words three times in the last year. He believed in showing love, not in talking about it. Words were too easy. Who could argue with that? Now, going off to God knows where, he'd written it. Realization reached her, quickly followed by fear. It was goodbye, farewell. He was doing something so dangerous, she couldn't go along; something so dangerous he knew he might not come back and was saying goodbye, been good to know you. "Oh David! I'm pregnant, dammit. Don't do this to me, to our son."

All of a sudden she wanted to take everything back. What had possessed her? She didn't want her husband going somewhere, getting himself killed. She wanted life, happiness, him. Oh, why hadn't she run away with him as he wanted? Anything was better than this. Then, not without horror, she knew the answer. She'd done it for that creep Adams. She'd conned David into death because Adams wanted it.

Oh, yeah, the President wanted it. How did she even know that was true? *You're a sap, Falscape. You drip out of trees.* Better believe it. *Damn Mother!*

With difficulty she quieted her agitation by railing at herself. *Think, damn you. You're supposed to be so smart. Think! If you've ever thought in your life, think now.*

Yes. She re-read his note. Stay here. "Not on your life, buster. I'm in this too. Whither thou goest." Be back in a few days. "You betcha. We'll both be back—together." I love you, Freddie. "And I love you, poor, dripping sap that I am."

She began to pace the floor. *You need me.* Yes. She was his Harry Rogers now. Only yesterday he'd made her feel like she was really helping him. Then he dumps her and goes off to play macho. *Wait. Think, dammit!* The eye blink. She'd gotten to him. She knew she had. But he'd passed it off. When had it come? She forced herself to remember, even reconstructing their conversation. She said, he said. When she said the Russians were testing a new missile? No, earlier. She stopped her pace, turned, looked at the empty bed where she had sat. Yes. Change the target. That was it? How on earth did a person change the target of a missile? Could only be done in Russia, big, bad Russia. That's where he had gone. Yes. A place so dangerous he knew he might never return. *I love you, Freddie.* Russia! Lord save us both! She truly meant it as prayer. "David in Russia? Where in Russia? It's such a big damn country." That's when she decided she needed help.

ELEVEN

Sloane flew Sudbury to Quebec, spent a few hours making acquisitions, then flew to Iceland, changed planes for Amsterdam, then took another flight to Tangiers. The last leg was Tangiers to Bursa, Turkey. All were off the beaten track: London, Paris, Rome. He would have preferred to fly into Istanbul or Ankara, but the Turks had been burned so often by US and Soviet agents they were extremely leery. He hoped for an easier time in Bursa.

He had no passport or ticket. He simply snitched a boarding pass, wrote some numbers on it, and walked on the plane, smiled at the stewardesses, and took a seat. If someone looked at him questioningly, he smiled again. If a seat count was made, he had moved. When he left a plane he walked through customs as though he knew where he was going. If anyone had hailed him, which no one did, he would simply have smiled, waved back, and continued on.

All this was aided by the fact his only luggage was a briefcase. It contained his shaving gear, change of socks, underwear, and shirt, his Walther PPK in a lead-lined box, and his purchases from Quebec. The briefcase was chained to his left wrist. In his suit, shirt, and tie he looked like a diplomatic courier. Everyone assumed he was. Diplomatic couriers receive favorable treatment. Diplomatic couriers can carry anything in and out of a country. All they wave is a pass bearing their photo. Sloane had had one made in Quebec.

During the long flights he tried to get as much sleep as he could. He might need it later. Between naps he tried not to think about why he was doing this, but he was not entirely successful in that. There was always a risk in sneaking into Russia, even more so now that he had been inactive for three years. It was not only that he was rusty, going on memory and instinct, but also that things probably had changed. Nothing worse than an old op trying to relive his glory days. Chances are what had worked before wouldn't now.

And he was afraid. That helped to make him tense, alert, careful. Those skills were already back. But the fear was a hindrance in that he now cared about dying. He and Harry had always wanted to live, took great pains to see that they did, but they had always *expected* to be killed. Harry had been. Was his own turn about to come? Three years ago he wouldn't have cared—at least not so much as he did now. That damn Freddie. But she was right. They would have no life together unless he took this chance. But it was going to be the last damn chance. *Stop thinking about it. Think about what you have to do.*

Bursa, Turkey, went as he had hoped. His phony courier's ID was accepted and he left the airport, taking overland transit to Istanbul. Using skills honed long ago and spreading American dollars and Swiss francs, he acquired Soviet papers identifying him as Viktor Potyl, buyer of electronic supplies, from Odessa. Next he had a heavy wooden crate built, filled it with books and rocks, nailed the lid on tightly, then in Cyrillic letters wrote its destination on top: the Soviet Naval base at Sebastopol.

Still attired in his Western suit and jealously guarding his box, Sloane made his way overland to the Turkish port of Eregli, northeast of Istanbul, where he waited for his box to be put aboard a Soviet steamer plying the Black Sea. At this point the box became more important than he. Russian tourists, visiting Turkey or any other country, were always herded about in a group. A single Russian traveling alone had to be a person of some authority, definitely trusted, who went abroad as a buyer of Western goods, frequently technology, which might be useful inside the USSR. This is precisely what his papers showed him to be. His Western suit also left no doubt of his foreign travels. The box was the clincher. Obviously it contained his most recent purchases.

Sloane accompanied the box aboard the Soviet steamer, showed his papers, paid for his ticket, then charged the ship's purser with the safekeeping of his box until he reached Odessa. Then Sloane went to the ship's bar and ordered a vodka. He watched the ship leave Eregli. After several more ports of call he would reach Odessa. Meanwhile he struck up a conversation with Soviet tourists. He wanted to sharpen his skills in Russian. Nobody paid any attention to him.

Freddie had dialed that interminable series of numbers from a Canadian pay phone, then waited. When the return call came, the voice had named a coffee shop near 16th and K in Washington. Four o'clock.

She now slid into a booth, ordered coffee and English, waited. A few minutes later Gordon Adams slid in opposite her. She suddenly realized how little she trusted him. Probably didn't even like the man.

"Sloane has gone off, hasn't he? You wouldn't be here alone otherwise. Where has he gone?" No answer. "Do you know or are you just not saying?" No answer. "Do you wish to join him? I think it would be a good idea if you did. He needs you."

"I'm his Harry Rogers—or so you said."

"At least you have a voice. What has he told you? Did he tell you what Karamasov said?" No answer. "What have the two of you learned so far?" No answer. He sighed, shook his head at her, despairingly. "I thought you and I and someone else were in this together."

"I told you, my first loyalties are to my husband."

"Have you told him of our discussion?"

"No, and I wish to hell I had."

"It is wise you did not. What have you and he learned?"

"None of your damned business."

"You don't trust me?"

"No."

"Did I not help you at the Elephant Rotunda?"

"Yes."

"You still don't trust me?"

"You got it." Then she sighed. "Look, it's not so much trust as . . ." She firmed her lips into a hard line. "I haven't told my husband things I probably should have. Why should I treat you any differently? It's David and I against the world—always has been. If you really want to know, get out your handy-dandy needle and punch me full of chemicals."

He smiled. "That won't be necessary. But I must say, you're getting quite good at Need to Know."

"I wish I wasn't."

He smiled. To him she would always be a remarkable woman. "In any event, you're here and I'm here. Is there anything I can do to help you—whether you trust me or not?"

She remembered. "Tell me about a man named Gillies." She saw him hesitate. "He's after me. I have Need to Know."

"He won't bother you anymore. It seems Sloane asked Interpol to pick him up for US intelligence as a security risk. It is an old trick, using Interpol. Gillies should have known better."

Freddie knew it wasn't Sloane but Wiley Drake who'd contacted Interpol, but she said nothing. She didn't want to tell him about their visit to West Virginia. "What happened to him?"

"It seems Gillies was indeed wanted by the Agency for—well, we need not go into that. I believe Gillies fell overboard while fishing in Lake Ontario off Toronto. Too bad. Such a loss."

Inwardly she shuddered. Knowledge of murder, in whatever cause, always made her do that. "How does a missile work?"

257

"It falls to the earth and goes bang."

"Damn you, don't patronize me. You know what I mean. How does the guidance system work?"

"It was just a small effort at humor, Freddie—if I'm still permitted to call you that. There are a lot of guidance systems. It depends on the type of missile."

"A missile fired from a submarine."

"Ours or theirs?"

"Take your pick."

"Very well. In either case the missiles usually have a fixed target, at least by the time of launch. The targets are built into the missile. After all, the sub is underwater, unable to use radar or other means to guide the missile. Actually, the sub loses control of the missile within a short distance. If the sub wants to destroy the missile, it has a very short time in which to do this, only seconds. After that, the missile is entirely on its own after it reaches a certain velocity or height, maybe both. That arms its warhead and it heads for its pre-set target or, in the case of multiple warheads, targets." He shrugged. "The rest is a nightmare."

"If the missile is on its own, how does it know where to go—what the target is?"

"It is programmed."

She waited, but it seemed an acceptable answer to him. It wasn't to her. She made a face. "Dammit, you want me to help you. So help me. I don't understand 'programmed.'"

"Yes, you do, Freddie. A computer program is prepared, giving the missile all the information and instructions it needs to reach its target. This information is called software. Then it is fixed onto computer chips called *proms*. These are plugged into the missile. The rest is history. Is that enough or do you want to know more?"

"Where is this software made?"

"In the case of submarine missiles, in a very secure place, I'll guarantee you."

"What kind of place?"

"A special lab with special equipment. Do you want me to describe it to you?"

She thought a moment. "No. Where are these labs located?"

"Usually on sub bases. You see, submarines test-fire their missiles. These are picked up from the ocean, refurbished, refitted, reprogrammed, and used again. This is done at a sub base. The software lab would be there."

"Where are the sub bases?"

He hesitated. "I'm sure Sloane went to the one at Sebastopol."

She stared at him. Didn't want to but he'd surprised her. She tried to recover. "How do you know he went anywhere?"

He smiled. "Freddie, I'm trying to help you, whether you believe it or not. I selected Sloane, trained him, controlled him during three years of the most dangerous missions, including several trips into Russia. I know how he thinks, believe me. I could give you all the nuts and bolts of why I believe he's gone to Sebastopol, but I suspect you already know them."

She sighed. It was an act of surrender. The man knew too much and was too smart for her. "I don't know why he'd go to Sebastopol."

"Sloane and Rogers most often entered the Soviet Union from Turkey and the Black Sea area. That is the route Sloane is most familiar with. There is a giant Red Navy sub base at Sebastopol. You're asking me about submarine missiles. It all figures, Freddie."

She nodded. "How do I get to Sebastopol?"

"Buy a ticket. I'm sure Aeroflot needs the money."

"You're kidding!"

"You could join a tour if you like. There's usually one leaving Washington or New York every few days."

"Just buy a ticket? Don't I need a visa or something?"

"I'm sure Aeroflot will arrange all that. Use your own passport. Go as yourself—right up front and in the open. You'll only get in trouble if you try to conceal something."

She blinked, nodded. "That's what I've always done in the past, isn't it?"

"As I recall, yes. It is the safest way. Do you need money?"

She had money, but it was hers and David's savings withdrawn from the bank. The thrift in her would rather have used Agency funds. "No." She wasn't about to take money from this man.

"Very well. Good luck. I'm sure you can find Sloane if anyone can."

"David told me to stay put in Canada. He's going to be awfully upset if I do find him."

"He'll recover. You're doing it because he needs you, Freddie." He smiled. "And you're a lot better-looking than Harry Rogers."

"Which is what I said to him."

He slid out of the booth, rose. "May I say how much I admire your spunk, Freddie?"

"Sure." She handed him her chit. "You may also pay for my coffee and English."

Freddie was surprised at how easy it was. She

boarded the night Aeroflot to Hamburg, then Berlin and Moscow. She was ticketed on to Sebastopol.

In truth it was not usually that easy, but Dimitri Galenkov had greased the wheels. He was letting both her and Wolf come, certain now of his actions. The Russian bear had the scent. These two Americans would lead him to what he wished to know.

He had put out a wide net, loose, nearly invisible, but hopefully tight enough to detect Sloane and his movements. It had failed. Sloane was "lost." Galenkov had grudging admiration for that. This Wolf still had his skills. A worthy adversary—only he was more a compatriot now than an adversary. Galenkov did not worry about where Sloane was. He knew with certainty where he was going. Just let him come.

Now, reading the latest report, Galenkov shook his head in sadness. The box. Boarding the steamer with the box at Eregli. Pitiful in a way. Three years is an eternity in the intelligence game. Methods change constantly. Nothing is ever repeated. Sloane was duplicating an entry he had made years ago when his partner was alive. After the fact, that entry had been researched, the gateway closed. Wolf had been out of the game too long. Sad. Galenkov sighed. As much as he admired the man, he had to use him against himself.

Because he was a careful man, Galenkov reviewed and pondered what he knew, searching for some clue he had missed. The Falscape woman had gone to the Short Creek Spring facility, at least the town where it was. Olga had seen her, helped her escape a drunk. She had met with a communications expert from the base named Wiley Drake. Not much known about him, except age, appearance, etc. A most difficult man, obviously highly classified, circumspect. Neither Olga nor anyone else had made any headway with him. Should he be picked up? No. But he should be subject to heightened interest. He fit into this puzzle somehow.

Sloane had not been seen at Short Creek Spring, but surely he'd been there. Later, he and his wife had arrived in Montreal together, flown north. Then Sloane had disappeared. Falscape returned to Washington and was now on Aeroflot for Moscow.

Galenkov pulled hard at his brows. Short Creek Spring suggested some type of highly secret technology. The involvement of this expert Drake confirmed that. Sloane was on the Black Sea. The Falscape woman was ticketed to Sebastopol. Very well. All this had something to do with the Navy, submarines most likely.

He rang for Alexei Pavlovich, his aide, and said, "You look pale, my young friend. Too long a Moscow winter, I suspect. You need some sun, good warm sun. A few days in the Crimea will do you good."

Alexei Pavlovich was wholly accustomed to his superior's indirection. It was best never to assume anything with him. "The Crimea, sir?"

"Yes, Alexei Pavlovich. I'm sending you there." He saw his puzzlement. "Aren't you glad? The whole world goes to the Crimea."

"Yes, sir. Thank you, sir."

Then Galenkov let out his guttural laugh. "Of course I'm going with you—just for my gout, mind you. We both could use a holiday."

The aide tried not to show his disappointment. "Very good, sir."

A deeper laugh. "I hoped you'd feel that way. I may have need of you, Alexei Pavlovich—and your discretion."

The voyage from Sebastopol had been uneventful. Senior Captain Ivan Frederyenko had enjoyed it. Now he was dismayed. The *Molotov* had reached an area about 130 kilometers west of the Azores and assumed routine patrol. Suddenly, indeed without warning— part of the test, he assumed—control of his vessel had been wrested from him. Those damnable technicians and their black box. A buoy had been raised. Apparently some kind of signal was received from some satellite. Suddenly his Number 16 missile was launched—without his command. He knew only that it had a dummy warhead. But he didn't know where it was targeted or where it landed. No one on board would know until later, maybe not until the cruise ended.

"Very successful test, Captain. The new *mashina* worked to perfection."

Frederyenko nodded acquiesance. The *direktor* of the technical group seemed so pleased with himself. No sense in hurting his feelings. But privately he seethed with rage. What sort of ship captain was he? That machine made a eunuch out of him, a taxi driver. If this was how the next war would be fought, he would resign.

"Is the test finished? Has control been returned to me?"

"Yes, Captain. The ship is all yours until tomorrow when we test again."

* * *

Sloane disembarked the cruise ship at Odessa around midday. Such vessels did not normally go to Sebastopol. Too many military installations. It was necessary to transfer his box and himself to a small freighter carrying cargo to the Red Navy base. This he did in late afternoon, spending an uncomfortable night before arriving at Sebastopol the next morning.

His voyage should have ended at the pier when he turned the box over to a dockworker who would see that it was trucked to the Naval base outside of town. As he handed over the papers for the box Sloane said in perfect Russian, "I want to accompany the box to the end of the journey." The worker, dark, young, highly bored, looked at him. "It is fragile equipment. I want to be sure it does not receive rough handling."

"It will get the best of care."

"But it will be my neck if it doesn't. I'm sure you understand."

"It is simply not possible, *tovarishch*."

Ah yes, comrade. "All things are possible in the *Rodina*." Sloane reached in his pocket and pulled out a significant fold of currency. Soviet rubles were on the outside, but inside were Swiss francs, deutsche marks, even US dollars in sizeable denominations. He did not look at the dockworker, simply unfolded bills slowly.

"As you say, *tovarisch*, all things are possible in the *Rodina*."

Sloane stopped counting, palmed the bills, extended his hand, felt them slide into another.

"On the other hand, some papers will be needed. Do you have anything of interest in your briefcase?"

Sloane smiled. "I did pick up a few things." As he knew it would, the fifth of Smirnoff vodka went at once. The vodka available to Russians was made from potatoes and so vile-smelling and tasting all a person could do with it was get drunk. Real vodka, made from grain, was highly prized. When the Russian hand sought the American blue jeans inside the case, he quickly closed it. To permit more of a bribe would make him look like a fool.

"The truck will be leaving in about an hour, I think."

"Very good." His smile was genuine. Little had changed inside the Soviet Union in three years. Bribery oiled the wheels of government, and in Russia virtually everyone worked for the government.

Freddie felt she was in a perpetual state of fright. It was a chronic condition. *The only known cure, Ms. Falscape, is ginseng root mixed with dried toad warts, followed by years of bed rest—your own bed. You'll be happy to know it also alleviates postnasal drip.* She was alone, on a Soviet airplane, headed deep inside the Empire of Evil. *You were so right, Mr. Reagan.* She felt cut off from everything she had ever known or believed in, surrounded by the Red Menace. Everyone seemed to look at her, and they were all so *big*. Were there no petite Russians? She was certain that any moment would bring rough hands on her. She would be whisked away, never to be seen or heard from again. *They really do have dungeons here, Miss Falscape. The Marquis de Sade is alive and well in Russia.* Yes. That's what truly frightened her, the certain knowledge she was flying to her doom. She would simply disappear from the earth like she never existed. *Freddie Earhart. David, darling, you actually did this for a living?* He was there somewhere. She had to find him. It was all she had to cling to. *Do you know how many people there are in Russia?*

It was a warm, sunny day when she landed near Yalta. Somehow she managed to hire a taxi to drive her to Sebastopol. She tried in vain to relax, enjoy the day, the flowers, scenery. It really was beautiful, just like any oceanside tourist trap. *Did you know the Black Sea isn't black? It's blue and beautiful. The only black thing in it is going to be my bloated body when they find it.*

She checked into the Sebastopol Hotel on Nakhimov Prospect. Might as well go first class. She didn't have the foggiest idea what to do next. *It is a medical fact, Dr. Falscape, that people suffering from chronic fright are incapable of thought. Their brains have turned to . . . David, why didn't I listen to you?*

Entering the Naval base was duck soup. Sloane merely sat in back of the truck with the other workers, who largely ignored him. At the guard gate for the base, the driver simply handed over papers for all those aboard the truck. The vehicle was waved through. No one even glanced at him.

Sloane had been on the base before. But it had been almost four years since he and Harry had entered, using an almost identical method. But their mission had been simple. They were merely to photograph some new antennas used on Soviet subs. It had been largely in and out. This was a far more difficult task. To learn anything about Soviet software he was going to have to get inside a lab where it was made. Difficult. Doubtlessly a highly secure facility. He'd need papers. Even then the lab might not even be at Sebastopol. Software could be made anywhere and shipped here. He'd give it his best shot, then get out.

The truck backed into a loading dock and Sloane climbed out, stretched, looked around. It was a familiar scene, lots of ships in the harbor, busy with sailors and workmen, noisy. The drydocks were full. Long sheds and factories bustled with activity. One well-placed bomb could do a number on the Soviet Black Sea fleet.

"Is this your box, *tovarishch*?"

He turned to the voice. A woman. She wore the blue-gray uniform of the customs service and a badge, carried a clipboard. She was blonde, blue-eyed behind large oval glasses. The male in him noted she was slender, built, pretty, maybe more than pretty. He smiled. "Yes, this is my box."

"What does it contain?"

"Some electronic gear." Another smile. "I doubt if it would interest you." She scared him a little. He had not expected this confrontation, only to get off the truck and walk away.

She extended a hand. "Your papers, please."

He handed them over, watched her read. Then his mind focused on the glasses. Fancy. Designer frames. Not usually available in Russia.

"You are a buyer of electronic goods? You've been abroad?"

"Yes."

Suddenly she smiled. Good teeth. It made her more beautiful. "I would like to go abroad one day. Many interesting things there, I hear."

The glasses told him what he needed to know. The

Soviet system at its best. "There are indeed." He held up his briefcase. "As a matter of fact I brought a few things back with me. Would you like to see them?"

Another smile. Yes, quite beautiful. "I would indeed."

She led him inside the warehouse, behind some crates. They were alone. He opened his briefcase. She almost squealed over the jeans. At once she held them against herself.

"Do you like music?"

"Very much so." Another smile, girlish with pleasure. "I'm a good dancer."

He showed her the cassette tapes. She really did squeal.

"*Chicago. Alabama. Bruce Springsteen.* I never—"

He closed the case, reached for the jeans. She clutched them tight, unwilling to surrender them.

"Is there something I could do for you, *tovarishch?*" It was pure flirtation.

"I have a friend who works in one of the labs. I would like to visit him. Sort of a surprise, you know."

She seemed disappointed. "That is very difficult, *tovarishch.*"

He grinned. "But I'm sure it's possible." He opened the case. "Bruce Springsteen, after all." He held it out to her.

She seemed to waver, took it, looked some more. "Crystal Gayle. I love her." She looked at him soulfully, eyes full of greed and doubt.

He pulled back a fold of tissue to reveal a black lacy peignoir and nightgown.

"Oh, *tovarishch!*" Her hands leaped to its softness, spreading it open.

"I think it might fit you."

"Oh, yes, yes." She looked at him. *"Which lab, tovarishch?"*

Dimitri Galenkov knew her at once. He believed he would have known her even without seeing her photograph. Great character in the face. Intelligence, surely. Integrity, yes. Something more. Courage. She was afraid but still had courage. Remarkable. A most handsome woman.

He bestirred himself and limped across the hotel dining room, stopped at her table, paused to gain her attention—such penetrating brown eyes—then bowed. "Forgive me, young woman, but I cannot help but notice you are American."

She blinked. "Yes."

His grin revealed yellowed, imperfect teeth. At least he still had them. "Having traveled in your fine country many times, I make it a point to impose myself on any Americans I meet. I do so as an admirer—an extravagant admirer. My name is Podorovich, Alexander Podorovich."

Freddie accepted the hand that was proffered, looked at him—huge fleshy face, the bushiest brows she had ever seen, blue-gray eyes, short, stocky body with enormous embonpoint. Had to be in his seventies. His English was good, although his pattern of speech strangely formal. There was only a slight accent. "How do you do?"

"Perhaps you will do me the honor of joining me for an aperitif. It is difficult to get news of America—the straight poop anyway. I believe that is the expression."

He abruptly sat down opposite her. There wasn't much she could do about it.

"Forgive me, but I suffer from gout. Standing is painful for me." Another smile. "Allow me to order. What would you like?"

"White wine, dry if you have it."

He signaled to the waiter. "Some of our Crimean wines are quite good, although not as good as the better California wines. We'll try the Tsinandali Number 1. I'll have some myself." He ordered in Russian, turned back to her. "I'm afraid my English, certainly my American English, is rusty."

"It is quite good actually."

Bow. "You are most kind. May I have the honor of knowing to whom I am speaking?"

Wow! Just like the movies. Charles Boyer had nothing on this fellow. "I don't know how much of an honor it is, but my name is Falscape, Fern Falscape." She paused. What the heck. An old man with gout couldn't do *much* harm. "I'm a professor of political science at a small women's college in Maryland."

"Maryland. I remember it. Lovely state. And a university professor. So young. You must be a remarkable woman, Professor Falscape."

She ignored his promotion of her to a university. "You travel in the United States?"

"I did. Regrettably not any more. I've been retired for some years here in the Crimea. I'm afraid my last visit to your country was almost twenty years ago. But I have fond memories. A most hospitable people. I was treated with courtesy and kindness. That does not happen everywhere."

"Were you a diplomat?"

His guttural laugh broke up into a heavy cough. "No, no. I have no interest in politics. Just a poor peddler, caviar, some of our better vodka and wines, smoked fish, cheese, furs, such things. There is not a great market for Russian goods in America, but we must do the best we can."

"I see."

"I was fortunate to be able to travel widely in your country, more widely than most diplomats, I suspect." It was true. In his younger days he had used sales as a cover while in America. "What brings you to Sebastopol, Professor Falscape?"

"Just holidays. Sebastopol is famous in my country."

"Yes, from the Crimean War, the Charge of the Light Brigade and all that. I understand. Are you enjoying your visit?"

"I've just arrived, but yes, thank you."

"Sebastopol was almost entirely destroyed by the Nazis in the Great Patriotic War. But some notable landmarks still remain. The Peter and Paul Cathedral must be seen. Very nice. Modeled after some Greek temple. Then there is the Vladimirsky Cathedral. Byzantine style. If you are interested in things nautical—after all, Sebastopol has long been a great seaport—you might visit the Black Sea Fleet Museum. It is on Lenin Street, not far from here."

She smiled. "Thank you. I shan't need my guidebook now." *Shan't? People who adopt phony patterns of speech are at high risk of psoriasis. You can look it up.*

"You are traveling alone?"

The question disconcerted her. "Yes." She saw him

look at her wedding band. "I expect to meet my husband here. He's traveling separately . . . on business."

"I see. Trade between our two countries increases daily. It is all to the good. Great tension is unhealthy."

Tell me about it. There was something about the man which didn't quite ring true. She had a sense of him as being, yes, *wily.* "I understand there are Naval bases here."

"Oh my yes. The waters near Sebastopol are the deepest on the Black Sea. This has always been an important Naval base—hence all the wars over the place." He smiled. "The modern facilities have been built a few kilometers from the city—where, I believe, it is more favorable for submarines."

"I see."

"I fear you would not be permitted to visit the facility any more than I would."

"I'm sure it's no place for a woman traveling alone."

"Especially one so attractive." He laughed. "I suspect sailors are much the same the world over. But there is somewhere you can go this evening, if you wish. There is a festival, a combination bazaar and carnival. You will find it most interesting." Smile. "And you will be perfectly safe there, I assure you."

She watched his eyes. They were so—yes, *crafty.* "Thank you. It sounds like fun."

"It is indeed. I urge you not to miss it. There should be local handicrafts on display. You may well pick up a few mementos of your visit to the Crimea."

"Thank you."

He pushed himself to his feet. It seemed to take much effort. Then he remembered his wine, chugged it down. "I must take my leave, Professor Falscape. I have been enchanted by your company. Perhaps we will encounter one another again."

"That would be nice. Thank you"—she smiled her best—"for the guided tour."

He waved her thanks away as of no importance, then reached into his pocket. "Here is my card. If I can be of service to you, please don't hesitate to phone. I can usually be reached at this number."

She nodded, watched him limp away. Strange. An accidental encounter or something more? She shrugged. No way to know. She read the card. Just a name, address, and phone number. Yes, she'd keep it. And she'd go to the festival. He'd made such a point of it.

She took him into a small office, closed the door, phoned. Sloane heard her give her name as Svetlana Koromovsky, wait. Then she began an animated conversation with a man she called *"Doktor* Svetilo." Apparently they were old buddies. Yes, she'd been away but was posted back here. Yes, she'd love to see him. The woman was flirtatious, no doubt about it. She had a visitor, someone he'd like to meet, Viktor Potyl, an electronics buyer. Pause. "Wonderful. We'll be right over." She hung up the phone, turned to him, smiled. "All set. We can go now."

We? He wanted to get rid of her. "No need to trouble yourself, Svetlana."

"It is no trouble. And call me Lana. All my friends do."

"As in Lana Turner?"

Off came the glasses. Big smile. There actually was a sort of resemblance. "She's one of my favorites."

He grinned. "You look better without the glasses."

"I only wear them occasionally when my eyes tire."

He reached out, took them from her. "Nice frames. Most unusual."

"Thank you. A friend brought them to me from abroad."

He held them to his eyes. They were plain glass. "Who is Dr. Svetilo?"

"The director of the lab where your friend works."

Grin. "Another friend of yours?"

"I have some popularity."

Now he consciously looked down at her figure, then back. "I can understand why." A wicked, entirely coquettish laugh was his response. "Thank you for arranging my visit. I can handle it from here."

"If you want to get into that lab to see your friend, *tovarishch*, you will never do so alone."

"But you can manage it?"

Ravishing smile. "Of course. You are a buyer of electronic goods. You must consult with technicians. How else can you make the proper purchases? But you will have to be escorted by someone like me. There is no other way, believe me."

"Are you sure?"

"Positive, *tovarishch*."

He sensed a trap, but he also knew that to protest any more would blow what little cover he had. There was nothing to do but go along and hope for the best. "Very well."

"Just give me a minute."

He watched her fish into her purse for a compact, lipstick, begin to fix her face. She was no customs inspector. It was hard to believe she was even Russian. "What was the name of the lab director again?"

"Svetilo. *Doktor* Andre Svetilo."

Svetilo. The name had meaning to him, but he couldn't figure out what it was. Then he had no time as she turned to him, picked up her purse, and declared herself ready to go. They went out another exit and entered an official vehicle. She drove.

A half hour later he knew she was right about getting him into the lab. Security at the gate was extremely tight. Guards were obviously prepared to shoot anything that moved without authorization. It reminded him of the gate at Corry Field in Pensacola. She obviously knew recognition signals he did not. Even so both their papers were checked carefully, then confirmation obtained by phone.

They drove into an underground garage, had their papers checked again, parked, took an elevator which went only down, had their papers examined once more. Both were given badges.

He was impressed. Security was almost as tight as at Brandywine, yet this woman who called herself Lana had gotten him inside. There had to be more to her than big knockers and a smile. She was far more than a customs inspector. He had to believe she was KGB, but that didn't figure—not at all it didn't. The KGB used women, lots of women, but for seduction purposes. They were "swallows," entrapping the unwary. This Lana certainly qualified as a swallow. But after the seduction the heavies moved in—and they were always males. The KGB would never trust a woman, any more than the CSA would. They certainly would not give her access to a secret facility like this one. Yet here he was. It didn't figure.

As they passed through the final checkpoint, using the badge with its magnetic imprint to gain entry, Sloane had a sense of being trapped. There was no getting out of this place except the way he came in. He was violating the basic rule a field op learns. Always have a way out. His Walther was in his briefcase, back at the warehouse. Nothing to do but carry on and hope for the best. For an instant he realized how afraid he was, but he knew that fear would keep him alert and cautious.

A guard accompanied them to a door bearing the name Dr. Andre Svetilo, *Direktor*. Again Sloane had a sense that name was familiar. It had meaning, but he couldn't plug it in. They stepped inside. Two male secretaries reacted to Lana, then an inner door opened and a man emerged to greet her effusively. "My dear Lana. So good to see you. Lovely as always." He brushed her cheeks three times in the Russian manner. Sloane thought he showed too much enthusiasm. She certainly did.

The man's hair was nearly white, but Sloane suspected he was only in his late forties, perhaps early fifties. He was slender, which made him look taller than he really was, brown-eyed, obviously highly intelligent. The short white coat he wore suggested scientist. Sloane had never seen him before and did not know him. Andre Svetilo. The name was familiar but the man wasn't.

Lana executed the introductions: Dr. Andre Svetilo; Viktor Potyl from Odessa. Hands were clasped.

"I used to know a Gregor Potyl on Kirov Street in Odessa."

Sloane kept his face a mask but inwardly he was dumbfounded. That was the opening of a recognition signal he and Harry had used on their last trip behind the Iron Curtain. Whatever name was given, asked about Gregor on Kirov Street. This man could not possibly know that. No one could. "I know a Gregor Potyl on Potemkin Street."

"Is he short and dark?"

"The Gregor Potyl I know is tall with red hair."

Smile. "Then we do not know the same individual."

"To my great loss, I suspect."

Svetilo ordered tea to be served and ushered him and Lana into his office. As the door closed, Sloane struggled to suppress his consternation. The words were exact. The old recognition signal had been played out precisely. But how did Svetilo know it? Who was he and why was he using it? Who, in God's name, did Svetilo think his visitor was?

No answers were forthcoming. Svetilo sat behind his desk, Sloane and Lana across from it. Her legs were crossed—quite carelessly. Svetilo reacted to that and to her, engaging her in animated conversation about old times. Sloane examined the office quickly. Commodious, even luxurious by Soviet standards. Svetilo was obviously a high-level technocrat, a member of the socialist elite. The tea was served by one of the secretaries, then conversation reverted to himself. Where did his travels take him? What sort of purchases did he make? Sloane felt his senses were so honed he was like an antenna, yet he could pick up nothing. Ordinary gab. Expected gab. That had to be it. The office was bugged. The two "secretaries" were doubtlessly KGB. Sloane played along.

"On your travels, *Tovarishch* Potyl, have you by chance seen any of the newer superconductors?"

Sloane had once had working knowledge of computers. His cryptography skills required it. But he hadn't kept up, except to read an occasional article. He knew he was on thin ice. "You mean those made of some new alloy?"

"Ceramics. The research is done with ceramics."

Sloane bowed to superior knowledge. "I am a mere buyer, *Doktor* Svetilo, not an expert such as yourself. But I was told about a new superconductor capable of a million units per second. Would you be interested in such a device, should I acquire it?"

"Very much so, *tovarishch*. It would be most useful in our work here."

He took a chance. "One of my contacts spoke of a new laser technology. I believe it is useful in submarine communications. Would something like this be useful to you?" He watched Svetilo carefully. He gave no reaction.

"We are in the forefront of laser technology, but there may always be something useful to be learned. Yes, by all means."

Svetilo turned to Lana. "I'm so glad you arrived today, my dear. I'm off tomorrow morning for an international conference in Prague." He looked back at Sloane. "Will you be attending, *Tovarishch* Potyl?"

Sloane sensed it was some kind of signal, but he didn't know what. "I am indeed, *doktor*. Wouldn't miss it."

Big smile, vigorous nod of the head. "Very good. Perhaps I'll see you there."

"I'm sure of it."

Prague? Tomorrow morning? Suddenly Sloane knew. It all came together. *Svetilo*. The name seemed familiar because it was an actual Russian word. It had a meaning other than a name. Svetilo meant *heavenly body* in Russian. *Seraphim*. Karamasov had not been warning him about something called the Seraphim Code, but a *person* code-named Seraphim. Heavenly body. This Svetilo, knowing old recognition signals, had to be a US mole. As director of this lab he could change Soviet submarine software almost willy-nilly. "Great danger," Karamasov had said. Danger to both sides. Yes. This Svetilo, code-named Seraphim, was in a position to be a menace to civilization.

"You're not really going to Prague, Andre?" Her voice was pure petulance.

Svetilo reacted to it. "I'll only be gone a few days, my dear."

Sloane's mind leaped. Prague. Svetilo expected to be contacted by a US agent, thought it was him. *Will you be in Prague?* He expected to be met in Prague. Svetilo was defecting. He had done something in this lab which was certain to blow his cover. He was getting out. Yes.

"Would you like a tour of our facilities, *tovarishch*? You may find it instructive in making your acquisitions."

"Very much so." He arose, followed Svetilo out of the office. Lana accompanied them.

The software lab was amazingly similar to those he had seen in the States, basically a large metal box—necessary as shielding against RF radiation. Without it, the radio frequencies from the programming gear could be played like a tune. The box was divided into

279

two sections. One room contained the array of mini-computers, each roughly four-by-three-by-three feet, kept in one noisy, climate-controlled room with humidity and temperature maintained to exact specifications. In the event of fire, halon gas would put it out, thus preserving the electronic data. The second room, brighter and quieter, contained a dozen consoles each with a keyboard, screen, printer, and tape drive. There was some IBM equipment, but he recognized most of it as a Russian imitation of the VAX system made by the Digital Equipment Corporation.

There was an operator or programmer at each console. Sloane knew what they were doing, but he listened to Svetilo's prideful explanation of how each programmer edited, compiled, and debugged the program by testing it on an in-circuit simulator or CPU. The end product of all this was the "prom," a chip roughly the size of a domino containing the program. Eight of them guided a missile. Altering the program would be duck soup for someone like Svetilo. It might be something so simple as leaving out a parenthesis.

Sloane figured that Svetilo had offered the tour because the metal box prevented the place from being bugged, as his office obviously was. But the white-haired scientist said nothing out of the ordinary. He was just showing off his facility to visiting firemen, indeed reporting nothing which was classified. The same sort of tours were conducted at US facilities daily. Sloane asked questions, hoping to give him opportunity to reveal himself. He did not. The man was not only smart but exceedingly careful. To be a US mole in charge of a software lab rigging

Soviet missiles, he would have to be. Still, the chance was there. Was the presence of Lana restraining him?

"Is there no possibility of error in the program, *doktor*?"

"None. None at all, *tovarishch*. It has simply never happened—not in my lab. Every one of our missiles has been on target. There are tests going on right now, I understand. Preliminary results are excellent, I'm told."

"You must be very proud, *doktor*."

"I am. When I guide a bird, it flies exactly where it is supposed to."

Sloane suspected it was a message, but he couldn't be sure. The words could be only the conceit, even the arrogance, of an elite scientist. But Sloane felt he had to assume it was a message. Tests were in progress. His software never fails. His birds always fly to the target. Yes. And Svetilo was bugging out. One missile was going to miss, but Svetilo would be gone. Yes. Sloane had to assume this was what Svetilo was telling him. Where was the missile targeted? Sloane felt he had little time to find out.

The tour ended. They left the metal box, stood outside the door. Lana resumed her petulance. "My feelings are terribly hurt, Andre. I just get posted back here and you leave at once."

Svetilo shook his head, sadly. "Alas, my dear, duty calls."

Then he suddenly smiled. "But I am free this evening. Perhaps we could do something together."

"I know. There's a festival this evening. Why don't we go. They can be fun." When he seemed to hesitate she said, "I insist you take me, Andre. I won't take no for an answer."

Sigh. "You are a hard woman to resist, Lana. Let me finish up a few things here. I'll meet you there. Let's say seven o'clock—near the puppets. They always have puppets at these things." Still smiling he turned to Sloane. "Will you join us, Viktor?"

He glanced at Lana. "I fear I might be interrupting something."

She smiled. "Please come. What woman wouldn't like two handsome men as escorts?"

They left the lab, returned to the car, and drove out the gate—much to Sloane's relief. They returned to the warehouse, where Sloane picked up his briefcase. He accepted when she offered to drive him to his hotel.

Outside the main gate to the Naval base, he opened the briefcase, took out his Walther, aimed it at her belly, and said in Russian, "Who are you?"

"Put the gun away, Mr. Sloane." The words were in perfect English, surprising him. "If you kill me you have no hope of getting out of this country alive."

He gaped at her, but she did not even glance away from her driving. "I asked who you are."

"Someone trying to help you, so put that foolish gun away."

"Not until I know who you are."

"You are no fool, Mr. Sloane. You must know."

"KGB."

"You have been allowed to enter, Mr. Sloane. You have been observed every step of the way. Your method of entry was closed soon after you used it the last time. You would have been arrested a long time ago except that your presence is desired." Now she glanced at him, then back at the street. "You will not tell us what Karamasov said to you. We decided to let you come and tell us here. Did you learn anything just now? Is it what you came to learn?"

No reply.

"I assure you, Mr. Sloane, that you will tell us, one way or the other. If you wish to return to your wife and child, telling us what we want to know is the only way."

He hardened his mouth, sighed, then put the gun in his suit pocket. "I learned nothing useful. That is the truth. Since you are so well-informed, did you learn anything from the interview?"

"Nothing. Why did you wish to see the director of that particular lab?"

Sloane hesitated. This whole situation was becoming so bizarre he knew he needed time to think. There was something to be figured out, but what? "I'll make a deal with you. I will tell what I've learned in exchange for safe conduct out of the country. But allow me to learn it first. I don't know yet. That is the truth."

"Is Svetilo the key?"

"Perhaps. I'm not sure."

"Very well. You will get a chance to see him tonight. It will be your last chance, Mr. Sloane. You will learn it tonight or never."

Sloane shrugged. "Where are you taking me?"

"To my place. I need to change for the festival." She laughed. "I'm not leaving your side, Mr. Sloane. Whatever you learn, I will also learn. I hope you will not find it too unpleasant being with me."

"Since when did the KGB let a woman like you operate like this?"

"There are many mysteries in this life, Mr. Sloane."
She laughed. "Extraordinary problems sometimes
require extraordinary solutions."

"This is extraordinary, all right."

As the P2V took off from Lexington Park, Wiley
Drake realized he had forgotten to bring anything to
read. This was going to be one long, dull day, that was
for sure. Another test. How many times did they need
to prove this gadget worked?

Wiley had to admit to a different feeling about this
flight. Jerry Hechter, his CET buddy aboard the
submarine, had phoned him from New London night
before last, regaling him with stories about sub duty
and how glad he was to be off the damned thing.
Wiley hadn't thought much about it until this test was
ordered this morning. Jerry Hechter couldn't be on
the sub with the black box. Musta transferred the box
to another sub. Hardly time for that, but it was
possible, he supposed. Funny, though. His reply to his
curiosity was a shrug.

TWELVE

Freddie was exhausted, mentally and physically. She suffered from jet lag, terminal sore feet—*trust me, you can die of sore feet*—agonizing worry, and ruptured hopes. Even her appetite had failed. *When the appetite goes, Ms. Falscape, all is lost. The Eucharist will be administered at once. Forgive me, Father, for I have sinned. I lied to my husband.* She had walked all over Sebastopol—at least twice. *Class, I can certify that Sebastopol is built on a hill. The duplicitous Commie bastards, in their quest for world domination, have concealed the fact it is a hill higher than Mount Everest. Believe me, the Red Menace is the soles of the feet.* She never saw David. She saw a thousand look-alikes, some in disguise, but no David. She wore a bright red dress, almost the same shade as her famous red suit now gracing a bag lady. Any idiot would know the woman in red. *Dillinger, here I am.* She attracted attention. Lots of people approached her, practicing their English. *David, practice your English. I speak, you speak, he speaks. He did not speak.* Oh, Lord! *There is no such person as David Sloane, never has been. You conceived by immaculate conception.* Please, God, help me find him. You cannot have meant for me to love him for no reason.

All she wanted to do was return to her hotel room, collapse into bed, and wait for the life-support system to be turned off. But she forced herself to go to the festival. In fact she felt drawn there. *It is a known fact, Ms. Falscape, your ESP is extraordinary. Please tell us where Jimmy Hoffa is buried. Right next to me.* That old man with the bushy brows had not lied. The festival was a combination bazaar and carnival. But she would have added flea market—with real fleas. Yes, there was a flea circus—and trained bears, jugglers, Cossack dancers, ballerinas, strolling balalaika players, and an inconceivable assortment of goods and wares being hawked—potatoes, veggies, antiques, and a bewildering array of handicrafts. She bought a fancy shawl. *Mummy, you're never going to believe where I bought this. I don't believe it myself.*

She was discouraged. There were just too many people, all jostling and gawking. She'd never find David here. Would he even go to a place like this? She'd watch a little of this puppet show, then leave.

Sloane had sat in Lana's luxurious flat—a KGB safe house, no doubt—in a turmoil of inner rage, itself a symptom of just how much his old skills had deteriorated. In days gone by he would never have given a thought to anything but the task at hand and staying alive. Days gone by. That was the trouble. He was old, blubbery, so out of touch he was Methuselah —worse, an utter fool. The KGB was playing him like a one-string banjo, leading him on, letting him practice his old, out-of-date methods, getting him to do what they wanted. He was trapped. If he wanted to live he would do exactly what they wanted. Pity the ex-field op. Especially a stupid one.

Yes, stupid. He couldn't figure it out. His brain had turned to jelly. Svetilo was obviously a US mole. He had changed the target on missiles now aboard a Soviet sub and was himself bugging out. Yes, obviously. Too obviously. If he could spot Svetilo and figure him out, why couldn't the KGB? This woman was KGB. She'd heard every word said, yet she professed to have learned nothing. Who the hell was she? The KGB simply never gave independence to an agent. They worked in cells, their every move tightly controlled. And a woman? Forget it. In the Soviet Union women were fit only for cooking, cleaning, and screwing. An independent woman like Freddie simply didn't exist. And the KGB was the worst of the lot. Yet there she was, prancing around this apartment in a negligee or less, listening to Bruce Springsteen. Unbelievable! Apparently she was getting some kicks out of trying to seduce him. No way. All he wanted to do was throttle her. But he knew she was right. If anything happened to her, he was a dead man. Probably was anyway.

Sloane made up his mind about what he had to do—or try to do. If Svetilo showed up tonight, and

Sloane was far from confident he would, he would *try* to be alone with him, *try* to wheedle or force out of him the information about which sub, which missile, which target. Then he would *try* a little Need to Know on the KGB, telling them what they might believe without revealing the whole truth. Maybe they'd buy it. But he knew he didn't have a prayer. The KGB would take him, fill him full of chemicals, bleed his brains dry, then get rid of him. Yes. Because of what he knew about past CSA operations, he was under obligation to use his Walther on himself to prevent capture and chemical debriefing. Would he do it? Probably. He was dead anyway. And not cooperating with the KGB was so ingrained in him, he knew he would never be able to live with himself afterwards and might as well be dead.

Lana declared it time. She was attired in a tight blue sweater and skirt. The woman did like to show off her figure. At the door to the apartment she asked for his weapon.

"If you wish me to get the information from Svetilo I may have need of it."

"Very well, but give me the ammo. Andre won't know it isn't loaded." She smiled as she held out her hand. "I wouldn't try anything with me tonight, if I were you. I suspect there will be enough of our people there to give you a very short life span."

He removed the clip from the Walther, tossed it on the couch.

Sloane was pleased by the layout of the festival. He could not have picked a better setting. It was busy, crowded, noisy, a ribbon of activity fronting a park that led down to the waterfront. It would be easy to lead Svetilo into the darkness of the park. With a little luck he might be able to escape himself. *Little* luck!

Svetilo, code-named Seraphim, was there, easy to spot. He stood by an ice-cream vendor, licking a cone, so casual and urbane. The man was smooth. No doubt about it. He embraced Lana enthusiastically, shook his own hand, said how tasty the ice cream was, bought Lana a cone. Sloane refused. He wanted both hands free.

They strolled along, Seraphim and Lana having a big, flirtatious gab. Sloane had eyes for everything, his mind as alert and wary as it had ever been in his life.

"As I predicted, there is a puppet show. Shall we watch? They can be amusing."

Sloane believed he saw Freddie first, but it was a close thing. Probably nothing in his life had ever shocked him so much as seeing her, but from long practice he managed not to show it. Not Freddie, damn her. Her mouth came open in surprise. She even waved to him. She even called out, "David!" He shook his head sharply at her in denial. She called his name again and started toward him.

He had no choice. He turned to his companions. "I see someone I know. Excuse me a minute." In a dozen long, angry strides he confronted his wife. "What the hell are you doing here?"

"Oh, David, that woman you're with. She's KGB."

"I know that. I asked what—"

"She's Olga from Kiev."

He hesitated, momentarily confused. "The woman from—"

"Yes, the bar in West Virginia. She held me prisoner in D.C."

He glanced back at them. They were turning,

walking away from the puppet show. To his wife, as angry as he'd ever been at her, he said, "What do you think you're doing?"

"Helping you. David, there's great danger. We've got to get out of here."

"Tell me about it. Goddammit, Freddie, you're getting us both killed. How did you get here?"

"I flew. Listen, David, there's something you have to know."

He saw them walking around the puppet theater toward the park behind. He was rattled, torn two ways. "Where're you staying?"

"Hotel Sebastopol. Listen to me, David, I—"

He didn't know what to do. "Go back there—NOW. Stay there till I come for you." They were heading into the darkness. He started to follow.

She grabbed his arm. "Wait, David, let me stay with you."

He tore free. "Dammit, Freddie!" He tried to run after them, but the crowds were suddenly heavy. He was pushing and shoving, only halfway to the darkness, when he heard the first shot. It came from ahead of him. He froze. Then the second shot came from the darkness. He looked back at Freddie. Her mouth was open in shock, fear. They had to get out of here—NOW! He started to go back to her, but the crowd had panicked. Screams were all around him as people pushed and shoved to escape the gunfire. He almost fell. His lungs filled with air to scream her name. No sound came out, for rough hands grabbed him, arms and shoulders. Then he was lifted off his feet and carried, slowly at first through the crowd, then faster through the darkness.

Freddie saw in horror, followed as fast as she could,

pushing and shoving her way, barely suppressing screams. She burst through to the edge of the crowd just in time to see her husband being hustled away at a rapid pace toward cars. She stuck her fist into her mouth to keep from screaming. Bright lights suddenly bathed the darkness. Ahead she saw the body of a white-haired man lying on the ground. Blood bubbled from his chest.

Fear more terrible than she had ever known gripped her. She couldn't move. Even when the lights went out and policemen began moving the crowd back, saying something in Russian she couldn't understand, she remained where she was. Only when a hand turned her, pushed her toward the lighted midway, did she find any movement in her legs. She didn't go far, only a few steps, then turned back. The cars were driving away. Which one was David in? Why didn't she know? Where were they taking him?

Again she pushed along. She stumbled a few steps, looked back. Cars gone now. A sense of helplessness and hopelessness seized her. She couldn't think— only feel a sense of incalculable loss. It was like death. All she could do was try to remain there on the grass where she had last seen the man she loved. It was not to be. Uniformed men kept shoving her, and the rest of the curious crowd, back toward the lighted, still-merry carnival. She couldn't understand the Russian words being uttered but they sounded soothing. Probably saying everything was okay, it was all over. Yes. It was all over. But everything wasn't okay.

"Freddie."

The sound of her name startled her. She looked around.

"Freddie . . . here. Come . . . please."

Off to her left. She turned, took a couple of steps. In the shadows behind the puppet theater, a tent really. A couple more steps. Recognition, mostly of blonde hair. "Olga?"

"Help . . . me."

She was there, then, arm around her, holding her up. Her other hand felt wetness at her chest, knew what it was. "You're hurt!"

"Listen. Not . . . much time . . ."

"Stay here. I'll get a doctor."

"No. Listen." She tried to double over, but instead sagged weakly against Freddie. Her breath was against her ear as she gasped, "Target . . . Kabul. From . . . from the . . . *Molotov*. Stop it. Not . . . much time."

Light blinded Freddie. She tried to blink it back, failed. Hands pulled her backwards. Olga slipped from her grasp. She turned her face from the light, saw Olga on the ground, men bending over her. They looked up, spoke in Russian.

"She's dead."

Freddie turned toward the voice which spoke English, but the light blinded her. It had come from a powerful flashlight of some kind.

"What did she say to you just now, Professor Falscape?"

She found voice. "I—I can't see you." Words were uttered in Russian. The light was turned away from her eyes, blessedly so.

"What did she say to you?"

Vision began to return, but she still couldn't see the man who spoke English. "I—I don't know who you are."

Russian words were uttered. They sounded harsh. Apparently they were, for Freddie was picked up bodily by each arm and, feet dangling, carried a short distance, thrust into the back seat of a car, and driven away at high speed.

Dimitri Galenkov had the safe house used by Olga searched thoroughly. Nothing. No clue to what she might have learned. Now he listened on a secure phone to a report on the chemical debriefing of Wolf.

His reaction was a compendium of disbelief, amazement, disgust, and a modicum of fear, which he hadn't felt in a long time. At first he told himself, or tried to, that all this was just an exceedingly clever CSA ploy to interfere with Red Navy submarine operations. Andre Svetilo a US mole? Impossible! This was all just an attempt to force a massive overhaul of the entire Soviet missile-guidance system—a process that might take years, leaving the US at a distinct advantage. The laser system breached? Black boxes which could make a submarine fire on command? It was just a ruse to force the USSR into abandoning a most promising technology. Software changed so a nuclear missile, not a dummy warhead, would explode on a changed target? All speculation on Wolf's part. He didn't know what target, which submarine. Without that what good was his information? All this was a trick to make the Red Navy withdraw all its submarines and tear apart all its missiles. He did not believe it. He, Dimitri Galenkov, was not a fool. He would not be a victim of CSA manipulation.

That was his first reaction. His second was more sober. All Wolf said could be true: a mole called

Seraphim, a broken laser code, black boxes, changed targets. It was all possible. A cautious man would have to recognize that. Worse, and what caused his fear, was his belief—no, certain knowledge—that this was just the sort of diabolical stunt the CSA would dream up and do. If those demented bastards could provoke the Soviet Union into shooting down a plane full of innocent civilians, then what was to stop them from provoking the Red Navy into an "accidental" nuclear explosion? Aloud he muttered, "We would look like butchers, demons. The Red Menace indeed." Secretary Gorbachev's policy of accord with Europe would be in shambles. He sighed. It was possible. All too possible.

Galenkov had just made up his mind that all this was a decision of too great importance for him to make alone—he would have to consult—when the door opened and Alexei Pavlovich entered with the woman.

He saw she was not the same person he had met earlier. She was now terribly frightened. "Won't you sit down, Professor Falscape." She did not obey, so he nodded to Alexei, who forced her into a chair. "Would you care for some brandy? I think it would be a good idea." He limped to a buffet, poured a snifter for her and himself, served her. "I deeply regret this inconvenience, Professor Falscape."

"No you don't."

He shrugged. "Perhaps you're right. We have little time to discuss motives, in any event." He slowly pulled another chair near her and laboriously sat in it. "I know you to be an extremely honest, straightforward person, Dr. Falscape. It inspires me to reciprocate. I wish to confess that I was not entirely forth-coming at our earlier encounter."

"I'll bet it was an encounter." She was again using anger to combat her fear.

"You're right. I had wanted to make your acquaint-ance. I admire you extravagantly. And that is the truth." He smiled, raised his glass, sipped. "As I was saying, I was at one time a peddler in your country. But that was some years ago, as I reported to you. What I failed to tell you, Professor Falscape, is that in recent years I've become a person of some impor-tance in the internal security forces of my country."

"The KGB."

"So we are sometimes referred to."

"David, my husband. Where is he? What have you done with him?"

"No harm will befall him, Professor Falscape"—there was a smoothness to his voice, yet a tone of authority—"if you cooperate and tell me what Olga said to you before she died."

"Where is my husband? I demand to see him."

His impulse was to tell her she was in no position to demand anything, but he didn't wish to threaten her. "You will see him in due course."

"You're asking me to believe that?"

He sighed. "You have my word, Professor Falscape."

"Is that worth anything?"

Inwardly he bristled, but as quickly denied it. "I would like to think it is. As I said, I am a person of some authority. I have used that authority to give orders that the ex-American agent we call Wolf is not to be harmed in any way. I can assure you those orders are being carried out. He is quite safe and unharmed, I assure you."

She was impressed, didn't know why. "Tell me why I should believe you."

"Very well." He motioned for Alexei Pavlovich to leave the room, waited. "There are some things better said in private, as I'm sure you know. In answer to your query, you and I were both acquainted at one time with a person called Parsley, a most dangerous man." He saw her eyes widen in surprise. "I followed you and your husband halfway across Europe. More than once I saved your lives in hopes you might eventually identify Parsley. You did and I am personally grateful for that." He smiled at the pure amazement in her face. "It was I who arranged to have him killed."

"But he was shot by—"

"I know. As far as I was concerned, that woman's usefulness was at an end in any event." He saw her shaking her head in confusion or perhaps disbelief. "I urge you not to ponder the past, Professor Falscape. It is the future that is of importance—I might even say, of vital concern just now. The woman you know as Olga was one of my top agents, very able, most trusted. She worked for me personally, a little device I sometimes use to confuse those who believe they know everything about KGB methods." He laughed, or perhaps it was just a clearing of phlegm from his throat.

"I knew she was KGB."

"And so it was arranged. She helped you in West Virginia, did she not?"

"Yes."

"And you were kept from harm at the Lincoln

Memorial, and again at what I believe is called the Elephant Rotunda."

"Yes."

"It was all arranged, Professor Falscape, as was your seemingly effortless entry into this country. Likewise it was arranged for your husband—a man whom I also admire extravagantly as Wolf—to use an old method of entry, not only into this country, but onto the Naval base here, even into a software lab where he wished to go. Olga did that." He sighed. "A lovely, charming woman. I shall miss her terribly."

She was staring at him, couldn't help it. "Why?"

"I think you know, Professor Falscape. It certainly should be familiar to you from the Parsley incident. We let the two of you lead us to what we wished to know: what Pavel Karamasov said to Wolf and what its importance might be."

"I see."

"No, you don't see. We have questioned your husband, and he has indeed reported Karamasov's words."

"He wouldn't!"

"We have methods which—"

"You chemically debriefed him, didn't you? God!" She stood up in agitation. "But that's *dangerous*. Is he all right?"

"Please sit down, Professor, calm yourself. I assure you he has thrown off the effects of the injection and is quite his old self, although somewhat angry, understandably." He smiled. It quickly faded. "It seems, Professor Falscape, there is a scheme afoot—a quite elaborate scheme—to make it look like the Soviet Union has exploded, perhaps only accidentally, a nuclear missile. Are you aware of that?"

She looked at him. Wily, yes, and crafty. She sat down. "Go on. I'm listening."

"Very well. I merely wish you were cooperating. Perhaps you will. I'm sure you must realize that is a most dangerous scheme. Indeed, Karamasov used the words *great danger*, as Wolf reported to us earlier. You and I owe it to our respective countries, the whole world, to apply our best efforts to prevent it."

"Don't call him Wolf. He's David Sloane." She sighed. "Only that's not his real name either."

He shrugged, a symptom of his growing annoyance and impatience. "By whatever name, your husband was able to report a great deal of useful information about this scheme. Unfortunately he never did learn the most vital information, namely where and when and by whom. We are hopeful that Olga may have learned that information independently. That is why it is of grave importance that you reveal to us what Olga said to you before she died." He smiled. "It seems our agents are making an unfortunate habit of dying in the arms of Americans before we can talk to them." She did not react. His witticism was wasted. "Professor Falscape, I am a patient man, but it does have its limits. If you do not tell me at once what Olga said to you, I will summon a physician from the next room. You will most definitely tell me then."

She heard the edge to his voice. "That won't be necessary, Mr.—What is your name again? I've quite forgotten."

"I doubt if you have. I introduced myself to you as Alexander Podorovich."

"So you did. Mr. Podorovich, please tell me what happened out there in the park."

"I warn you, Professor. I will summon the doctor."

"It is important that I know. I can't tell you if—"

"Very well. I will be patient a little longer. This afternoon your husband, David Sloane, accompanied Olga to the software laboratory at the Naval base. They met with the director of the lab, one Andre Svetilo. Your husband realized that the word Seraphim did not refer to a code, but a US mole in that lab. Since the word *svetilo* means heavenly body in Russian, Sloane perhaps correctly surmised he was the mole. Svetilo believed your husband to be a US agent come to help him defect. This was to occur tomorrow."

"I still don't know what happened in the park."

"We are uncertain at the moment of the precise order of events. But it is obvious that the traitor Svetilo shot Olga. Being a patriot, she returned fire, killing the traitor. It may have been the other way around." He waved in dismissal. "It does not matter now. Both are dead, one a hero, the other a traitor."

"While I was talking to David? Maybe I saved his life."

"Perhaps." He rose, stood over her. "My patience has just come to an end, Professor Falscape. You will tell me now or—"

She rose too. "Please, just give me a moment to think, to remember. I was hardly myself at that exact moment."

"I understand. Take your time."

She strode across the room, looking out a window into the night of a foreign country, supposedly a sworn enemy. What choice did she have? He could make her tell. She had seen David use the chemicals. They did indeed work. And David. What chance did either of them have if they didn't cooperate. And why not? This damnable scheme had to be stopped. She herself had said so. The President had asked her to help. To the window she said, "The target is Kabul. That's what she said."

Behind her came a Russian phrase, clearly conveying astonishment. "Did you say Kabul? Afghanistan!"

She hadn't realized that Kabul was in Afghanistan. "That's what she said." Now meaning began to come to her. He was way ahead, as his flood of astonished Russian words revealed. "They wouldn't! Not all those innocent people!"

Galenkov stared at her, great pain in his wrinkled face. With surprising calmness he said, "They would. It would make us look like savages, barbarians. Our standing in the world would be . . ." He bowed his head, sighed deeply. "All would be lost—forever."

She almost felt sorry for him. "It can't be true. It has to be a mistake."

"It is no mistake."

"But it would start a nuclear war, the holocaust."

"No. We would know it came from our own submarine—an *accident*. We would not retaliate." He raised his head, looked at her sorrowfully. "Very clever. A most diabolical scheme."

"We have to stop it."

"Yes." He nodded, seemed to tap a reservoir of resolve. "Professor Falscape, to do so we must know the name of the submarine which is to fire the missile. Did Olga give you a name of a ship?"

"I don't think so."

"It is vital, Professor. Try to think. Recall every word she uttered."

"All right." She hesitated, trying to re-experience the moment. "First she said not much time."

"As did Karamasov to your husband. Go ahead. Then what?"

"She said the target was Kabul."

She hesitated so long he felt the need to prompt her. "Then what? She must have said something more."

"Yes, but it doesn't make any sense. She referred to Molotov."

"Did you say Molotov?"

"Isn't he the ex-foreign minister? Isn't he dead?"

"One of our nuclear submarines was named for him. It is one of the newest and finest in the fleet. Thank you very much, my dear."

He was at the phone, speaking in Russian, command and urgency in his voice. Freddie watched and tried to listen, all her senses keen. When he paused and seemed to be waiting, she spoke, her voice excited, "I remember now. Olga said *from* the *Molotov*. That must be it, the ship which will fire the missile."

"It is my supposition too."

"She also said *stop it*, stop the ship. She said again *not much time*."

He nodded to her, then abruptly spoke into the phone. Only a few words. Mostly he listened. She tried to read his expression. Surprise? No, dismay. His yellowish complexion was actually lightening. He said a few more words in Russian, slowly hung up.

"Something's wrong, isn't it?"

He was staring at her, but not really seeing her, his mind elsewhere. Then he became conscious of her. "I'm sorry. I must think."

She watched him begin to pace, his arms folded across his ample chest, one hand raised, pulling incessantly at his eyebrow. No wonder they were bushy. "Mr. Podorovich, or whatever your real name is, I insist you tell me what has gone wrong. I think I may be able to help."

He stopped, looked at her sharply. "There are national secrets involved here, Professor Falscape."

"Damn the national secrets!" Her voice rose in anger. "Don't you realize national secrets are about to get Afhanistan nuked?"

He gaped at her a moment, then said, his voice strangely matter-of-fact, "It is impossible to reach the *Comrade Molotov*. All means of underwater communication to the ship were disconnected as part of a test of new . . ." He hesitated. National secrets were still national secrets. "It is not important. You would not understand." The flicking of his fingers was punctuation.

"I think I do understand. The missiles aboard the sub, maybe even the sub itself, are to be controlled by a laser from a satellite. The latest wrinkle in push-button warfare, isn't it?" She saw his noncommittal expression. He wasn't going to answer. "At least tell me where the sub is now."

He sighed. "The *Comrade Molotov* is in the Western Atlantic—in the vicinity of the Azores. Its initial tests have been highly successful."

"I'll bet. Oh, God!" There came a light rap at the door, then the same man who had brought her here entered.

"*Da, Alexei?*"

She listened to the Russian words, but understood only an American name embedded within. "Did he say Wiley Drake?"

Galenkov looked at her guardedly. "That's right, you do know him—from West Virginia."

The thought flashed across her mind. There were no secrets in the world. Why did anyone try to keep them? "Yes. What about Wiley Drake?"

He hesitated, then rendered an elaborate shrug. Painful sigh. Surely resignation. "It seems Mr. Drake left the United States Naval Air Station at Lexington Park, State of Maryland, a little after ten o'clock this morning, Washington time. He was aboard a US Navy P2V aircraft. Our fishing vessels tracked it heading east across the Atlantic."

"God! It's started. It's going on *right now*."

"So it would seem."

"You certainly are calm about it." She looked at her watch. "What time is it in the US?"

"Washington is eight hours earlier. It is a little after two in the afternoon there."

"If the plane left at ten, where would it be now?"

Galenkov nodded, then spoke to his aide, listened to his reply, shaking his head as he did so. "The P2V is an aircraft designed for submarine patrol. It is not the fastest plane in the world. But it must be assumed that after four hours it is somewhere in the vicinity of the Azores."

Freddie gasped. "God, it could happen any minute!"

"Yes. The missile will explode at night. That is not very nice." At once he went to the phone.

"What are you doing now?"

He looked at her with great annoyance. "Steps must be taken. There is perhaps time to save many lives in Kabul."

"You mean evacuation?"

"And deployment of troops."

"But there isn't time for that. We have to stop the missile launch." She saw the annoyance on his face. "Let me use the phone, *please*. I think I can stop it."

"I appreciate your enterprise, Professor Falscape, but I think not."

"*Please!* Let me at least *try*."

"To do what, Professor Falscape?"

She hesitated. It did sound bizarre. "I-I want to phone a man named Marvin Grayson."

He blinked. "The President of the United States? That's absurd."

"It may be, but he is the one man who can stop the launch, the one man who will. I must reach him, warn him."

The leonine head shook violently, making his jowls leap. "I'm sorry. It's impossible."

"No, it's *not*. Please believe me. The President doesn't know about this . . . this scheme. He wants to. He *asked* me to help him find out what was going on. I have to tell him." Suddenly she knew how truly *absurd* she sounded.

"He *asked* you?" His voice was larded with scorn.

"Yes, please believe me. I haven't time to explain, but it's true. It happened after Karamasov was killed."

He hesitated. "Was your husband in on this too?"

"Yes, yes, we both were." It was only a little lie. "Please, at least let me *try*. What other chance do we have?"

He wavered, agonizingly so, then handed her the phone. She took it, held it to her face, then stopped, looked at him, blinked. "Do you happen to know the White House number?"

On Galenkov's instructions, Alexei took the phone from her, spoke into it, waited, spoke again, waited, spoke again. When Freddie received the instrument back, she heard the sound of an American phone ringing in her ear. Second ring. Third. *C'mon.*

"The White House. Good afternoon."

"Whatever you do, don't break this connection. My name is Fern L. Falscape. It is terribly important that I speak to the President."

"I'm sorry. President Grayson is in conference."

Exasperation rose in her, affecting her voice. "Look, President Grayson knows me—at least my name. Fern L. Falscape. Tell him I'm calling from Russia."

"The President is in conference, I'm sorry."

"Look, lady, this is a matter of greatest urgency. It's a national security matter."

"I'm sorry, the President is—"

"Dammit, woman. I'm talking war, nuclear war, H-bombs. If you know what's good for you, you'll—"

"Just a moment, please. I'll connect you."

Freddie waited, realizing just how stupid and hysterical she must have sounded. *Mr. President, there's a screaming woman on the phone wanting to warn you about nuclear war.* She waited and waited. *C'mon.* She waited. Her heartbeat pounded in her ear. *Please! You must answer.*

Click! "Miss Falscape?"

A male voice. "President Grayson?"

"I'm his assistant. My name is Mel Stoddard."

"Oh, please! I must talk to the President. It's a

matter of life and death—lots of lives and death." Her voice broke. She felt like weeping. This bureaucratic delay was unbearable.

"Miss Falscape, I know who you are. Calvert College."

"Yes."

"I know of the letter you wrote the President. I was the one who called it to his attention. I am familiar with"—hesitation—"your situation. Where are you calling from?"

His voice—she detected a Southern drawl—helped calm her. "Sebastopol."

"Russia? Good God. Miss Falscape, this is not a secure line. You used the switchboard."

"Right now none of that matters, Mr. Stoddard. We have maybe minutes, maybe no time at all before Afghanistan gets nuked—*by our side*. I must talk to the President. Only he can stop it." Silence on the line, prolonged silence. "Are you there?"

"Yes, Miss Falscape. Did you hear me say this wasn't a secure phone?"

"Do you want a secure phone or do you want a lot of dead Afghans, or whatever they're called. LET ME SPEAK TO THE DAMN PRESIDENT!"

"It isn't possible, Miss Falscape. He's not in the White House. He's making a speech. It'll take me several minutes to reach him—at best."

"We may not have several minutes."

"It's the best I can do. I'll tell him you called, that it's urgent. Where can he reach you?"

Oh God! "Dammit, he can't reach me." She hesitated, her mind flying. "Look, get to him as fast as you can. Tell him there is a Navy plane, a P2V, from Lexington Park somewhere over the Atlantic, probably around the Azores. Tell him there is a man named Wiley Drake aboard. He operates black boxes."

"What kind of black boxes?"

"Goddammit, shut up and listen! When Wiley Drake activates the black box on the plane, it makes a Russian sub fire its missile. The President must stop Wiley Drake from using the black box."

Prolonged silence. "I don't understand, Miss Falscape."

"You don't have to understand, dammit. Just give him the message. Have you got it down?"

"Yes."

"If Wiley Drake isn't stopped from using that box, the missile he fires is going to nuke Afghanistan. Do you believe that?"

"Miss Falscape, I—"

"Look, the President asked me to find out about this secret operation, to help him stop it. I've found out and I'm helping him. Do as I say—PLEASE!"

"Miss Falscape, you don't know what you ask. You're a voice on the phone. How do I know you're—"

"Godalmighty! Rome burns and . . ." She sighed, struggled for control, remembered. "Tell him Gordon Adams has a birthmark on his left wrist." Another sigh, a warding off of tears this time. "I'm going to hang up. Do it now—I beg you. It may already be too late."

Slowly she hung up the phone, consumed with weariness and hopelessness. He hadn't believed her. The weight of the world was on her shoulders as she said to Galenkov, whom she knew as Podorovich, "Maybe you'd better evacuate Kabul after all."

* * *

307

Marvin Grayson was thoroughly enjoying himself. The National Association of Manufacturers was a wonderfully hostile audience for his speech, "The Bottom Line." He was happily letting them have it for what he termed "pure, good old-fashioned, robber-baron greed" when they had "so-called American products" manufactured abroad by cheap labor. Anything for the bottom line.

He was in the middle of the word "of" when the Secret Service man came to the podium and whispered in his ear. Grayson had no choice but to go to the phone. He did so amid an accommodating murmur from the assembled manufacturers. Was history in the making right before their eyes?

He went to the secure phone available to him at all times, listened, said, "This better be good, Stoddard." He listened, nodding—the only visible display of his growing amazement that he permitted himself. He asked only one question: "Are you sure it was her?" Birthmark on Gordon Adams's left wrist. Very well. Perhaps because he was so full of himself from his speech, he reacted decisively. "Get me that damn fool Drake on the phone. I'll be there at once." Then as an afterthought he gave a second order: "Don't go through channels." He handed over the phone to a Marine, then said to his aide, Billingsley, "Finish reading my speech. Tell 'em I'm indisposed or something. Express my regrets."

During the short limousine ride under police escort to the White House, Grayson took time to reconsider, a characteristic process he used to rein in his tendency toward impulsiveness. A woman he had never met calls from Sebastopol to tell him an American using a black box is going to make a

Russian submarine fire a missile which will nuke Afghanistan. He shook his head. That wouldn't go in his memoirs either.

Why did he believe her? No time to ponder that. He just did, and that was that. The damn blank authorizations had resulted in stranger things. Don't go through channels. He pondered that. The shit would hit the fan. No doubt of that. But he knew what channels meant: consultation, argument, protest, procrastination, foot-dragging, ass-hiding, excuses, delay, and ultimately total inaction. He'd had a bellyful. And if this Falscape woman was right, there was no time. Besides, it was way past time he found out whether the title Commander in Chief meant anything. Was he President or figurehead?

He hurried to the communications room where Stoddard met him. "Sir, do you wish to use the Code of the Day?"

Still pumped up, Grayson barked, "I want to do whatever it takes to get that damn plane on the horn—NOW!"

Stoddard swallowed, an indication of his fright. "It would be the quickest way, Mr. President, but—"

"Then do it, dammit."

Another swallow. "Are you sure, Mr. President?" Hesitation. There is a . . . problem with it. I was about to explain, sir."

Grayson paused. Impetuosity, not thinking things through before acting, was his greatest weakness. It had caused most of his troubles in life. "Go on. Tell me." He forced himself to listen, but his intelligence enabled his mind to leap ahead and grasp the problem before Stoddard had half explained it.

The President of the United States is accompanied

at all times by a marine—he even sits outside the bedroom door at night—who has a black satchel chained to his wrist. The satchel, called the "football,"—not to be fumbled—contains the nation's most precious codes, those which enable the President to order a nuclear strike. With the information in the football he and he alone can send the bombers and missiles flying. Anyone speaking to or touching the marine—or other service person—risks being shot on the spot. If anyone but the marine attempts to open the satchel, it blows up, killing him and others nearby. If anyone cuts it from his wrist and attempts to steal it, long rods burst from it to prevent it from being carried through doors and windows.

The football also contains the Presidential Code of the Day, a five-letter word, frequently a nonsense word, which allows the Chief Executive to automatically intercept all radio traffic to all military installations, including ships and planes. The Presidential Code of the Day takes precedence over all other messages. Grayson knew for a fact it had never been used except for tests.

"I'm sure you understand the problem, sir. Your voice will be heard in the clear, not encoded. That P2V and Wiley Drake will definitely hear you, sir, but so will everyone else."

Grayson nodded his understanding. "Yes. The whole wide world will know." He turned away from Stoddard to think. Even if he was extremely careful in what he said to that plane, mere use of the emergency code would alarm the world. The press would clamor to know what was going on. All this would come out.

The US planning to nuke Afghanistan with a Soviet missile? God! And how could he prove it was true? On the word of a young woman he'd never met phoning him from Sebastopol? He'd be a laughingstock. He wheeled back to Stoddard. "Is there another way to reach that plane?"

"We can try, sir. I've a communications officer at Lexington Park on the phone. There seems to be some sort of problem."

"Let me have it." Into the phone he said, "This is Marvin Grayson."

"Yes, *sir*, Mr. President."

"I want you to put me through to a man named Wiley Drake on a P2V flying over the Atlantic." He listened to Stoddard a moment. "The plane left your base this morning. He's probably near the Azores. It is a matter of highest priority."

"Mr. President, I'm sorry, but—"

"Young man, what is your rank?"

"Lieutenant, sir."

"Very fine rank, Lieutenant. Lots of perks. Nice retirement. But I'm sure you hope for more. Your folks must be proud of you."

"Yes, sir."

"Well, let me tell you something, Lieutenant. This is your Commander in Chief speaking. If you don't want to be a common seaman tomorrow, then put me through to that damn plane."

"But, sir—"

"No damn buts. I'm giving you a direct order!"

"Sir, which P2V? We've got a dozen over the Atlantic, sir."

"The one Wiley Drake is on, you fucking idiot."

"You want me to contact all of them?"

"I want you to do whatever you have to do to get Wiley Drake on this horn—NOW!"

"Yes, *sir*."

Grayson heard voices in the background, then a new voice came on identifying himself as the operations officer. "Commander Lonsberg, do I have to repeat my order."

"No, sir, but I have some information you may want to know. This morning about 1000 hours, a P2V left Lexington Park. It was not part of our regular squadron, Mr. President, and not under our command. It's been operating here for some time, sir. I don't know what its mission is, Mr. President. I was told only that it was classified, sir."

"A damn spook plane."

"I can tell you it bore no markings of any kind, sir. I don't know if it was even a Navy plane."

"That must be it. Put me through to it."

"I can't do that, Mr. President. We have no communications with it."

"Somebody must."

"No one at this station, sir. I'm sorry."

"Doesn't it contact you?"

"No sir. It observes Emcon, sir."

"What's Emcon?"

"Emission control, sir—radio silence. It never communicates with anyone—at least anyone we know about."

Grayson swore under his breath. A spook plane. Secret operation. Doubtlessly the CSA running its own hidden government. Not this time, by God. "All right, Commander. You sound like an intelligent officer. I'm going to give you a direct order as your Commander in Chief. I expect you to carry it out."

"Yes, sir."

"Do we have fighter planes in that area?"

Hesitation. "I don't know specifically, Mr. President, but I assume so."

"So do I. I want those planes armed and scrambled at once. I want them to find that P2V. I want them to shoot it down."

"Shoot it down, sir?"

"That's what I said. That pilot either aborts his mission and turns around at once to return to Lexington Park, or it is to be destroyed on my order. Have you got that?"

"Yes, sir."

"Personally I hope it doesn't, but if by chance that plane does return to your base, I want it impounded. I want the crew arrested and held incommunicado. Absolutely no one is to talk to them about *anything* without my authorization. Have you got that?"

"Yes, sir."

"All right. Get busy. You got five minutes—I hope. Have you enough rank to accomplish all this?"

"I don't know, sir."

"I hereby declare you my personal military attaché with the temporary rank of four-star admiral."

"Yes, sir."

"My man Stoddard will man this phone. Give him a blow-by-blow description of everything you do. Now trot, son."

Bud Sanderson completed his second slow turn over the area. He knew he had the P2V on station, eighty miles west of the Azores, but the S4-R4 had not yet located the target. He turned to his copilot-navigator, Chip Gentilli. "Is that gadget working?"

Gentilli reached out and tapped it with a finger, about all he knew to do with it. "Better be. We're sure not going to find any target if it doesn't."

"I'm going to widen the search." Abruptly he turned the P2V to starboard and settled into a wider turn. Into his mouthpiece he said, "Wiley, we're on station, but don't have target yet. Should come up soon."

"Okay, Sandy. Holler when you got it."

"The name's Bud. Baldheaded men don't like to be called Sandy."

Sanderson looked out the cockpit window on his port side, seeing nothing but ocean. Dull duty this. He'd gone into Naval flight training expecting the glamor of being a fighter pilot. Look at him now. Not only was he flying the Truculent Turtle on sub patrol, he didn't even feel like he was in the Navy. He was in the spook business. Civilian clothes. Taking orders from God knows who. Couldn't even fraternize at the Officers' Club at Lexington Park. What the hell was going on? An unmarked P2V. A crew consisting of himself, Gentilli, and the technician Wiley Drake. Flying over the Atlantic looking for what? He just hoped it was important.

When Marvin Grayson returned to the Oval Office, Admiral Dan "Butch" Hollings, his military advisor, was waiting for him.

"Some kind of crisis, Mr. President?"

Grayson ordinarily liked Hollings. Good man to play a little poker with. But right now Hollings meant channels and channels meant obstruction. "Nothing I can't handle, Butch."

"I gather it's military. Can I be of help?"

"So you think it's military, do you?" He shook his head. "No secrets in this building, are there? Very well, it is military. I've given a direct order to a Commander Lonsberg at Lexington Park. I've even made him a temporary four-star admiral to give him authority. If you or anyone in the damn Navy or DOD says one peep to him or does anything to interfere with his actions, I'll have your asses. Is that clear?"

"Yes, Mr. President, but—"

"No buts. I'm so sick of buts." With delight, he watched the color rise in the admiral's face. "There is something you can do, Butch. There has been an unmarked P2V operating from Lexington Park. Apparently it is part of the Navy but doesn't take orders from the Navy. A spook plane, in other words. I want to know everything there is about that plane and what it's been doing. I doubt if you'll find out much, at least much that's the truth. But it'll give you something to do." He started to dismiss a now angry admiral, then thought of something more to say. "Oh yes, I want to know exactly who controls that plane and what the Navy knows about it. And Butch, I'm not going to be very happy if all you can tell me is that it's classified."

Now he did wave him away. Then he picked up a secure phone and dialed a long series of numbers.

Mel Stoddard's left arm ached from holding the phone to his ear, and he switched to his right hand, shaking out the left. Only a beep every ten seconds told him the line to Lexington Park was still open.

Mentally he kept saying, *Hurry up, dammit. Hurry up. Do it.* The seconds dragged into minutes.

Finally a voice. "Mr. Stoddard. This is Commander Lonsberg."

"Yes." His voice had never sounded more expectant.

"We've located what we think is the P2V. It is circling an area about eighty miles west of the Azores. Do you want the coordinates, sir?"

It struck Stoddard as strange to have an officer call him sir. He'd been an enlisted man. "That won't be necessary. Have we got any fighters in the area?"

"Yes, sir. It seems there is a lot of activity in the area. The Russians have some sort of maneuvers going, so we have the *Admiral Halsey* and its support ships on maneuvers too."

"The *Halsey* is a carrier?"

"Yes, sir, one of the newest. If she's on maneuvers, chances are she already has some birds aloft."

"Send 'em. You heard the President's order."

Hesitation. "Mr. Stoddard, it'll have to be a CRITIC order, direct from the Commander in Chief."

"Do whatever you have to do. Just be quick about it."

In the communications room aboard the *Halsey*, ringing bells summoned Lieutenant Jim Dunninger to the teletype. He read, said "Holy cow," tore off the message, and ran to operations.

Commander "Buck" Wynegar, the ops officer, read, said "Jesus Christ," and phoned the bridge. Fortunately Captain Henry Arlen was on duty.

He listened to the entire order and rendered no expletive, just a question. "An unmarked P2V?"

"Yes, sir."

"Has to be one of ours."

"It would seem so, sir."

"A CRITIC order? From the Commander in Chief?"

"Yes, sir."

The hesitation was brief. "Then execute it. Send the closest fighter group."

"That'll be Bostwick, sir."

"An unmarked P2V? What's going on?"

"I don't know, sir."

"We'd better take no chances."

As Wynegar reached for the mike to call Bostwick, he heard the strident blare of the ship's horn and the words over the 1MC loudspeaker: "ALL HANDS TO BATTLE STATIONS! THIS IS NO DRILL! REPEAT! THIS IS NO DRILL!"

Lieutenant Terry Bostwick, leader of a group of six F-16 fighters, listened to the order. He was astounded. "Did you say CRITIC? The Commander in Chief?"

"Affirmative, Belmont 1. Execute the order."

"You did say shoot it down?"

"Affirmative—if he doesn't abort and turn back at once. Use the guard channel."

"Roger. Out." To his group he said, "You heard him." Then he ordered a spread formation. "The first guy to spot it gets a beer." As he executed the sharp turn to starboard, Bostwick realized that in six years as a Naval aviator, he'd never fired his weapons in anger.

Sanderson heard the beep from the S4-R4, cut his air speed and tightened his circle. His reward was a steady, not unannoying whine from the gadget. "We're over target, Wiley."

"Open the bay doors." He flicked on the black box, waited for the ready light.

Ensign Willie Bright in Belmont 6 was the first to spot the P2V. Excitedly, too loudly, he blurted, "Target below at two o'clock."

"Hold your voice down. I see it." Bostwick put his jet into a steep dive and calculated his difficulties. The P2V was circling at low altitude, probably under a thousand feet. Compared to the speed of the F-16, it was practically standing still.

"They just dropped something. Looks like a buoy."

Bostwick heard the excited voice of Willie Bright. Abort the mission hell. It looked like it was already in progress. "Belmont 2, fire across his nose."

Bostwick had already cut his air speed and dropped his flaps till his fighter was near stall speed. Now he settled into a turn, trying to circle just outside the P2V, and pushed the button on his radio to open the Guard Channel. It was a frequency constantly monitored by all American planes. Supposed to be used only in emergencies. Unauthorized use meant a lot of trouble. He had authorization. And he guessed this was an emergency.

Sanderson had already said, "Hold it, Wiley. We got company."

"Too late. Buoy away. I gotta use it." His ready light was on.

"They're our fighters. What the hell they want?" Gentilli's voice was high-pitched, excited.

"Jesus Christ! They're shootin' at us."

Wiley couldn't believe his ears. "What'd you say?"

"P2V, this is Belmont 1. I know you can hear me." Sanderson looked out his port window, saw one of the fighters trying to stay with him. "I have a CRITIC order. From the Commander in Chief. You are to abort your mission and return to base—NOW. Do it at once or I am to destroy you."

Wiley Drake felt the G-forces of the plane's sharp acceleration and turn. It almost knocked him off his chair. "What's going on?"

"Damned if I know. But I'm not going to argue with those fighters." Then, a moment later, Sanderson said, "Godalmighty, Wiley! Did you fire that missile?"

THIRTEEN

Luxury or no luxury, fatigue or no fatigue, Freddie had slept little during the long flight aboard Air Force One. She was simply too worried about David. Why hadn't she seen him? Why wasn't he on this plane with her? The black man who said his name was Stoddard kept assuring her David was fine and coming home, but she'd believe that when she saw him. Never again was she going to believe *anything*. That was a promise. To her questions about what had happened, Stoddard's answer was the same: "The President wants to tell you himself." Wonderful! Just jolly! All she knew is that if Kabul had been nuked, it was the best kept secret in the world—from her at least.

Air Force One had landed at Andrews AFB, then she was escorted to a waiting helicopter, which was just now dropping to the White House lawn. She climbed out, accepting Stoddard's hand. Just like TV, only she didn't have a dog pulling on her arm. Quickly she accompanied Secret Service men across the lawn and into the White House. At the door to the Oval Office she was greeted by a smiling President Grayson.

"My dear Dr. Falscape. At last we meet."

He was grinning at her. Both his hands were extended in greeting. She was impressed. Should she curtsy or something? She placed her hands in his. "Mr. President." *Junior, let me tell you again about the time I met the President of the United States. Aw, Ma, not again!*

"How are you, my dear?"

She felt the cool, strong grasp of her leader. "Tired—and worried about my husband."

"That we can do something about."

He stepped backwards, pulling her forward into the Oval Office, turned, released her. She gasped. "Oh, God, David!" She rushed into his arms, clutched at him, head against his shoulder. "Are you all right?"

"I think so. You?"

"Heavenly now."

Behind her she heard, "I'm sorry, but it was impossible to bring you both out on the same plane. Some bureaucratic hokum the Russians engage in. But you're both here now, safe and sound." He chuckled. "I must say watching you two does something for my romantic soul."

Sloane had been in a state of anger since he last saw Freddie in Sebastopol. He was angry at her for being here, for her interference just as he was about to learn something. He was angry at being captured and chemically debriefed. He was angry that he had learned nothing and still didn't know what had happened. He had been flown home on a military transport. Lots of MPs. He was far from certain he wasn't under arrest. That made him angry too. Most of all he was angry at being here in the White House. He had scant respect for Presidents under the best of circumstances. These circumstances were the pits.

When he saw Freddie, he didn't exactly melt, but he did realize how much he'd worried about her, how much he loved her, and how damned glad he was to see her. He did clutch at her, but only briefly. The audience embarrassed him. He pulled her arms away. Yes, he was uncomfortable, tense, on guard. Since he had no idea what was going on, that was a good way to be.

They both took seats across the desk from the President. She kept looking at David. He seemed so strange. Was he angry? Maybe just nervous. She hoped he was just nervous.

"First, let me ask again how you both are? The finest medical care in the world is available. Just say the word."

Sloane saw the President looking at him. He knew he'd been chemically debriefed. Just how much he'd been made to reveal he probably would never know. He had to hope the Russians hadn't known enough to ask the right questions. But as far as he could tell, he had no ill effects. It apparently had been done carefully. "I'm fine, Mr. President." He would not admit how dog-tired he was. And he certainly didn't want any White House doctors messing with him.

"And you, Dr. Falscape?"

"I'm fine, just tired."

"I know you're pregnant. Do you wish the services of—"

"Pregnant?"

She saw the sharp, hostile look he gave her. "Yes, David. I found out just before . . . before all this started. I-I couldn't tell you." She forced a smile against the anger she saw in him. Those cold eyes. "I knew you wouldn't let me participate if you knew."

"Dammit, Freddie, I—"

"You have a most courageous wife, Mr. Sloane."

Another forced smile. "I thought you might be pleased, David. I'm sure it's . . . going to be a boy."

Sloane looked at her, back at Grayson, back at her. He felt anger, disillusionment. Coldly he said, "I would like to have found out under other circumstances."

"I know. I'm so sorry, David. It-it couldn't . . . be helped. I did try. . . ."

"We'll talk about it later." The words were almost a threat.

Grayson spread oil on troubled waters. "I'm sure you have a great deal to talk about. I'd like to offer you the use of Camp David for as long as you need to rest up. It's lovely. I'm sure you'll find it a good place to relax."

Freddie watched Sloane. He *was* angry, terribly angry. She turned to Grayson. "Thank you, Mr. President. But if you don't mind we'd just like to go home, get on with our lives."

"Very well. I understand. But if you change your minds, please don't hesitate to let me know. It is not possible for this country to do enough for heroes such as you two. And I mean that."

"What happened in Afghanistan, Mr. President?"

Grayson looked at her, smiled. "Nothing— fortunately. But it was a very close call. When that Soviet missile rose out of the water, everyone thought our efforts had failed. I even used the red phone to warn Mr. Gorbachev. But nothing happened. Under intensive questioning Wiley Drake insists he never activated the laser equipment. The best we can figure is that the Soviet sub, not knowing what was going on above water, coincidentally ran their own test. The missile was a dummy and simply went downrange— thank the Good Lord."

"Was Wiley Drake planning to make the Soviet sub fire a nuclear missile?"

"Dr. Falscape, I don't know the answer to that— yet. But I most definitely do intend to find out. Wiley Drake has been most cooperative, as have the two pilots aboard the P2V. They'd better be. But they can provide little information. It seems they were subject to something called Need to Know. Apparently the whole world is—including me. Drake thought he was just running a test. He had no idea he was contacting a Russian submarine—at least until the Soviet missile broke water. He had no idea what was happening, or was supposed to happen. My tendency is to believe him. What do you think, Mr. Sloane?"

"I'm sure that is correct. Wiley wouldn't have known. Look, Mr. President, I'm still very much in the dark. I really don't know what you're talking about." He looked at Freddie. "Do you know?"

Oh, the coldness in his eyes. It chilled her. "I think so, David. You learned about the mole, didn't you?"

"Yes. Svetilo."

"Apparently he changed the software aboard the

324

Comrade Molotov, a Soviet nuclear sub. He'd changed it so a nuclear missile, not a dummy warhead, would be fired and land, not downrange, but on Afghanistan." She had to look away from those eyes. "Is that about right, Mr. President?"

"We think so, Dr. Falscape, but it may never be known—unless the Russians choose to tell us. I doubt if they ever will."

Sloane was indeed seething, but he wasn't sure why until the door opened and the aide called Stoddard entered accompanied by a mousy-looking man. Grayson stood up, shook his hand, turned to them, said, "I believe you both know W. Gordon Adams."

Sloane did not know that name. He knew him as Mr. Green, a member of The Committee during the Parsley affair. But Freddie did. "Good to see you again," she said. When the hand came to Sloane, he took it, but only out of ingrained courtesy. He stared at Adams, then at Freddie. What was going on?

"Dr. Falscape, you are about to get your wish. Thanks to your letter—a most patriotic letter I might say—constitutional powers are about to be restored to this office and to the Congress and Cabinet. Those blasted blokes on that so-called Committee are about to be roped and hog-tied."

"Mr. President, *please . . .*" She was cringing with fear. Why did this have to come out this way? Why didn't she have a chance to tell David first? She couldn't look at him. She couldn't bear to see those eyes. "David doesn't know. Let me tell him—*please.*" She forced herself to look at him. His eyes froze her. He could kill. Her? Why not? "David, last Christmas,

while shopping in D.C., I ran into"—she sighed—
"the man we both knew as Mr. Green. We exchanged
pleasantries. He asked about you. We had lunch.
Nothing happened." Another sigh. Why was this so
hard? "Nothing happened—except that I saw his
credit card with the name W. Gordon Adams on it. I
knew he had once been on The Committee. As far as I
knew it was the first time anyone ever had a name. I
knew you'd never known one."

He kept looking at her, unnerving her. "David, are
you listening to me? Or are . . . are you just hating
me?"

"I'm listening." His voice was as cold as his eyes.
"You ran into this guy in Washington. He flashed a
credit card with the name Adams on it." His voice
ladled on scorn.

"She wrote to me, Mr. Sloane." The President
wanted to help.

"Let me tell it, please. David, you know how much
I've always hated The Committee, its usurpation of
power, its manipulation of you, me, the President,
everyone. Hadn't I always said I'd try to do something
if I could? When I learned the name Adams, I saw my
chance. I wrote to the President. I-I guess I . . . never
thought anything'd . . . come of it. But—"

"My turn now, young woman. The letter came into
Stoddard's hands. He realized its significance and
brought it to my attention. There really wasn't much
new in the letter. Every President since Truman
organized that damned Central Security Agency has
known something funny was going on over there—
all the lies, all the encoded mumbo jumbo, the
blasted national security briefings, the blank authori-

zations after which some disaster occurs and the President is stuck with a crisis he knew nothing about. Every President has tried to do something about it—and struck out. Mr. Sloane, your dear, lovely, very smart wife gave me something no previous President has had—a name, W. Gordon Adams."

"He really did a number on me, Sloane. He had me literally kidnapped—by Stoddard here. I was forced to tell him about The Committee and its activities. I either cooperated with him or . . ." A shrug finished the sentence.

"You see, Mr. Sloane, I had just signed one of those infernal blank authorizations. I knew something was going on. I told Adams to find out—or else. I was determined to use whatever was going on to break the power of The Committee."

"I was in the middle, Sloane. Karamasov had been shot. You'd killed two agents. The hunt for you was on. The Committee put me in charge of finding and killing you. At the same time, President Grayson had turned me to work for him. I was to—"

"Use me to find out what The Committee operation was."

Adams sighed. "Yes. I used you. I'll admit it. But I knew you were the one person in the world who could discover what the operation was and block it."

"Freddie?"

"I used her too. I knew she was the one person who could control you. I knew she could get you to go for the puzzle and solve it—just like she got you to go for Parsley."

His head turned toward her, so slowly. She dreaded it. How could he look at her that way? "David, I'm sorry. I-I hated . . . lying to you. Several times I . . . tried to tell you. Oh God! This is so *awful*." Sigh. "Adams asked me not to tell you."

"Thanks a lot, Freddie."

She moaned. Here she was, sitting in the Oval Office, watching her marriage being destroyed right before her eyes.

"Mr. Sloane, it was I, not Adams, who enlisted your wife into our little effort. I wrote to her personally, asking her to—"

"That's true, David. I thought I was . . . working for the President."

"You lied to me about the Elephant Rotunda, didn't you?"

Oh, God! "Yes. It was Adams who shot Mako. I saw him, but . . . I'm sorry." She had never felt smaller, more helpless in her life.

"For crissake, Sloane. Don't be so angry. Sure I shot Mako, and the other KGB man who came in the door. I was keeping both you and your wife alive to do what had to be done." Adams grinned, or what passed for a grin with him. "It worked, didn't it?"

"Oh, it did that, all right." His anger was near rage, barely controlled.

"David, *please*. I thought I was—"

"I know, saving the world for constitutional government."

"Which is exactly what's going to occur, Mr. Sloane," said the President. "Thanks to your selfless work—and your wife's—I've caught that so-called Committee with their hands in the national cookie jar. Nuke Afghanistan. My God! Think of it! We can't have it, Mr. Sloane—not in this country. I'm going to put a stop to this sort of thing, thanks to you." He swiveled to his left. "Mr. Adams, as of this moment you are special assistant to the President of the United States. You have full power to do whatever is required to break the back of that Committee— forever. I want you to go into that underground headquarters, wherever it is—"

"Brandywine, Mr. President."

"Yes, Brandywine. I want you to go in there. Use troops if you have to. I want you to find out who sits on that Committee and get rid of them. Charge them with high crimes and misdemeanors if you wish. I'm sure they're guilty of plenty. The day when nameless, faceless, utterly unknown men can manipulate this office, this government, is over. *Over*, I say! We're going to return power to the Constitution. And you're the man who's going to do it for me, Adams."

"Thank you, Mr. President."

Grayson turned to Freddie, grinned. "Does that please you, young woman? You deserve much of the credit, you know."

Freddie really was thrilled. Marvin Grayson certainly was dynamic—yes, Presidential. If only . . . She looked at David, inwardly sighed, then turned back to the President. "Thank you, sir."

"I'll get to work at once, Mr. President. I know at least one member of the Committee, perhaps others. They'll put up a stiff fight, but with your authorization I'm sure we can bring them under control."

"You have that authorization, Gordon, anything else you need."

"There is something else. I'd like David Sloane as my assistant." Adams turned to him. "Sloane, I know you're angry at the moment, but you'll get over that." He smiled. "Between the two of us I think we have enough knowledge about what's going on, how things operate, to really do a number on The Committee. What d'you say? Will you join me?"

Emotions raced through Sloane like a kaleidoscope, so many of them he couldn't separate rage from incredulousness. He felt stabbed in the back by his wife, Adams, this foolish man who was President of the United States. He had yet to figure out all that must have happened, but he knew he had been played for a fool, a colossal fool. *"Not on your life, buster.* I'll only play chump once." He stood up, extended a hand. "Let's go home, Freddie."

The silence was prolonged, full of surprise, from Freddie most of all. "David, I-I don't . . . understand."

"Of course you don't. You were played for the biggest sap of all, although Grayson here is a very close second. C'mon, let's go. I'll explain it to you later."

"Stay where you are, Dr. Falscape. And you, Mr. Sloane, sit down. I don't think I care much for your tone—or your derogatory remarks about me."

"Too bad." Sloane turned to him. "Grayson, I just heard you say how sick you are of being manipulated by The Committee. You damn well should be. You're so easy. Adams has played you like a one-man band, and the cymbal is on your ass. You keep kicking yourself regularly."

"Young man, I warn you. I will not be—"

Freddie felt her husband take her hand, try to pull her to her feet. "David, please, what are you *talking* about?"

"Yes, Sloane, what are you running off at the mouth about?"

Sloane looked at Adams, eyes squinted a little. "Do you really want me to tell them? Or do you want to go on with your game?" He saw the faint flicker of the eyes. "I thought not." He turned. "C'mon, Freddie."

"Young man, this is the Oval Office, *my* office. You are on very thin ice. Gratitude will only go so far."

"Yes, David, please. I don't understand."

He looked at her a moment, sighed, then slowly sat down. "That's been my problem all along. I didn't understand either. None of this made any sense. I couldn't figure it out. But I didn't know about Adams. If you'd just told me about him, Freddie, we could've saved ourselves a lot of trouble."

"I'm sorry, but—"

"I know, I know. He did a real number on you." He turned to his former superior at the Agency. "I got to hand it to you, Adams—or whatever your real name is."

"My name *is* Adams."

"A brilliant scheme, brilliantly executed. You must've spent the last three years concocting it. You have my admiration—however grudging."

"David, *please*."

"I understand. When you work for Mother, play the game with all the tension and danger and risks, everything afterward is anticlimactic. You felt your life was over. I've had a lot of problems with that. How much worse it must've been for you, Adams. You were on The Committee, head of the European zone, at the absolute apex of power in the world. When you came crashing down and had to resign after the Parsley affair, it must have been very hard for you. I can't blame you for hatching a scheme to get back into power. And that, my friend, is all the

sympathy and respect you'll get from me." Sloane
watched the bland face. It was a mask, but he knew
he was getting to him. "It's worked, hasn't it? Beauti-
fully. You're not only back in power, you have more
power even than the entire Committee. Congratula-
tions."

"Young man, are you suggesting that—"

"This whole game, from the very outset, was
concocted by Adams to gain what you just gave him, a
Presidential appointment to wreck The Committee.
He played you, me, Freddie, The Committee, the
KGB, the whole damn world for saps. Fantastic
really."

"It can't be true, David."

"Can't it? You walk into a department store, just
happen to run into Adams, who just *happens* to flash
his credit card with his name on it."

"It could happen."

"Sure, and there could be albino alligators in the
New York sewer system, only there aren't. He worked
you, Freddie. Good ol' Need to Know at its finest. He
knew you were a do-gooding liberal. He knew how
much you wanted constitutional government. He
knew you hated The Committee. He knew you'd
sworn to expose it one day. After all you as much as
said that to him three years ago. Need to Know,
Freddie. It was so simple for him to feed you the little
dab of information you needed to know to do what he
wanted you to do. He let you learn his name. You
wrote what I'm sure was a very stupid letter to the
White House, giving the name you'd just learned. The
rest is history."

"It's not either history, David—not to me."

Sloane turned to Stoddard. "Do you work for Adams?"

"No, sir, I do not."

"Then somebody around here does. For Freddie's letter to get to Grayson is too big a coincidence. Somebody had to help it along."

"Nonsense, Mr. Sloane. I practically had Adams kidnapped."

"Do you really think Stoddard could've kidnapped Adams unless he wanted to be? Do you really think you could've made him tell you about The Committee if he hadn't wanted to? Do you have any idea whether what he did tell you was correct or complete? I'm sorry, Mr. President. I didn't know gullibility was a desired trait in Chief Executives."

"Young man, I warn you."

"No, I should've warned you. I would have—only I didn't know about Adams."

"David, The Committee was planning an operation."

"Yes. I signed the damned blank authorization. I knew somebody was up to something."

"I'm sure they were. A Soviet code, sent by laser from a satellite, was intercepted and broken by Tenpenny. Happens all the time. Somehow the Agency got hold of the black boxes and buoy the Russians used for the code. Wiley Drake duplicated the boxes and buoy and tested them. But what was supposed to happen is anybody's guess."

"They were going to nuke Afghanistan, David."

"Were they? Maybe. I don't know. No doubt it is the sort of thing The Committee'd do. It sure would've given them a great leg up on the Russians. But I don't

know. As Grayson says, we may never know for sure."
He turned to Adams. "Did you con The Committee?
Where did they get the black boxes? How did they
learn about the satellite code? Where did they get the
whole idea, whatever it was?"

"You'll full of shit, Sloane."

"I thought you didn't swear." He smiled. "Getting
to you, am I? When Karamasov fell into my arms,
nearly dead, he said the word *Seraphim*, paused, then
said *Code*. I thought he was just short of breath. I
thought he'd said Seraphim Code. But when I went
into that software lab in Sebastopol and met Dr.
Svetilo—the word means *heavenly body* in
Russian—I realized Karamasov was warning me
about a mole code-named Seraphim. When he said
the word *code* he was starting to say something else,
but got shot." He looked at Adams, his eyes very level,
hard. "A mole, code-named Seraphim, a deep-cover,
high-level mole, head of a lab which made software
for Soviet subs. A most valuable man. Had to take a
long time, years, to get a mole into such a high-level
position—more than three years. Adams, you headed
the European Zone. You just had to know about the
mole called Seraphim. Because he was so high-level,
so vital, not very many people shared your knowledge. My guess is no one did. Seraphim was your
private, personal mole. You controlled him. Not even
The Committee knew about Seraphim. Right, Adams?"

No answer.

"When you were forced to resign from The Committee, you kept control of Seraphim. After all, he
didn't know what your status was—or even that The
Committee existed. He told you about the black

boxes, the whole laser technology. You leaked the info to The Committee. They concocted their little scheme. I'll bet they even dubbed it the Seraphim Operation—not realizing Seraphim was your personal mole, not a code. Clever, Adams, got to hand it to you."

"Bull, Sloane, bull! You got a vivid imagination."

"Do I? I suppose I imagined it when a badly wounded Karamasov fell into my arms in front of my house. How did he get there? Somebody had to lure him to the vicinity, leaving me the nearest person to go to pass on what he'd just learned before he died. Who wounded him in the first place, Adams?"

"The Agency, I presume."

"With a .38 slug, a bullet calculated to wound but not to kill? Not the CSA. They'd have used a 9-millimeter. If they tried to kill him they wouldn't have failed. Karamasov went off, not even telling the KGB, to get top-drawer information that would reinstate him with his superiors. He got it, all right. Then you shot him. Left him to run to me."

"Bizarre, Sloane, bizarre."

"Is it? He said Seraphim. Only you could've told him that."

"I suppose I shot him the second time, tried to kill you."

"No, but it was easy to tip off the Agency so they'd hit Karamasov, me for being with him. That was your biggest risk, wasn't it, Adams? If that bullet had gotten both Karamasov and me as it was supposed to, your whole plan was up in smoke. But you played your luck, got some. The rest was all downhill. I was on the run. You conned Freddie and Grayson. You even got the Agency to put you in charge of the manhunt." He shook his head. "Got to hand it to you, Adams. Damn clever."

Freddie was staring at the two of them. "David, can that be true?"

He turned to her. "Oh, yes, it's true. There's another thing. I never learned that Afghanistan was the target or the missile was to be fired from the *Molotov*. How did you?"

"Olga told me just as she died."

He nodded. "Olga. Very good. And how did she learn that information?"

Freddie hesitated, trying to remember. "I assume Svetilo told her out in the park before—"

"They shot each other? I don't think so, Freddie. If he'd wanted to tell her, he had plenty of opportunities to take her aside in the lab and blab. He was never alone with her. And Svetilo was an extremely careful man. Had to be to work as a mole in such a sensitive position for so long. He would never have told her. Indeed he killed her first chance he got, simply because she was the one person who could finger him. He would never have told the key information to someone he planned to kill."

"You're crazy, Sloane."

"Maybe I am. Had you instructed Olga to kill Svetilo? After all, now that he'd arranged for Afghanistan to be nuked, his usefulness was over. He knew that. He planned to get out. I really don't know—thanks to Freddie's blundering into me at the festival. Did Olga shoot first, or was it the other way around? Only you can tell us that, Adams."

"But David, Olga was KGB."

"She *used* to be—or maybe was part-time. She was a double agent. That's what confused me. I couldn't figure her out, but then I didn't know about Adams. I wish I had."

"The KGB big wheel, Podorovich or whatever his real name was, *told* me she was KGB. She worked for him personally. He used her to confuse people like you who thought they knew *exactly* how the KGB operates. He told me that himself, David."

"I'm sure that's true—or had been at one time. Doubtlessly the KGB guy thought it was still true. But Olga had been turned by Adams. She worked for him." He looked at Adams, grinned. "Got even, didn't you? Three years ago this Podorovich did a number on you. He put a sexy, blonde agent right into your bed as your wife. You had to get even. You turned one of his sexy, blonde agents against him. What'd you promise her? All the money and power in the world after you'd made a sap out of Grayson and gained control of the Agency?"

"David, are you sure?"

"I am, Freddie—now. When Adams was off The Committee, he had a hard time contacting Seraphim. He couldn't run in and out of Russia at will. He needed a contact—Olga, a top KGB agent who had the run of the place. She was the runner between Adams and Seraphim. Freddie, I couldn't figure it out. What was she doing at the loading dock when I arrived? Why was it so easy for her to get me into the lab? Why was she and Svetilo so chummy? How did he know a three-year-old recognition code Harry Rogers and I had used? How come he was expecting me to help take him out? She obviously was helping me. Why?"

"She helped me at Short Creek Spring, remember?"

"Yes."

"And at Sebastopol when she was wounded and called to me, she said *Freddie*." She gaped at Adams. "How did she know that name?"

"Indeed. Tell me, Freddie, did you ever tell Adams you were pregnant?"

She thought. "Yes, yes, I did. I told him. I remember—way back when he came to the college as Mr. Gorsuch. Is that important?"

"I just wish you'd shared the information with the kid's father. Yes. When Olga was threatening me, saying I'd better not harm her or I'd never see my wife and child again, I thought it just a figure of speech. Apparently not. The only way she could have known I had a child was for Adams to tell her."

"Garbage, Sloane."

"I know, but really high-grade garbage." He looked at his wife. "Go back to my earlier question, Freddie. Olga told you about Afghanistan and the *Molotov*. How did she know that? Only Adams could have told her. She was his runner. She told Svetilo what the target was to be. Svetilo selected the sub, told her, probably much earlier. You sure had some hold on her, Adams. Even as she's dying she carried out your plan."

"Don't pay any attention to this, Mr. President."

"But I am, Adams. I find this most interesting. Mr. Sloane, are you suggesting that all this was some plan, some gargantuan plan to—"

"Yes, use us all so Adams could gain control of the Central Security Agency, supplanting The Committee. And it wasn't so gargantuan, just thorough. This sort of thing is done all the time by the CSA. It's a game, Mr. President, the world's biggest chess game, played for the highest possible stakes."

"Like nuking Afghanistan and blaming it on the Russians?"

"Perhaps, maybe even yes. The gain from it would've been immense. The problem with you and the rest of the world, Mr. President, is that you don't think big enough. You have no conception of really high stakes. You don't understand the manipulative power of Need to Know. You're babes in the woods— amateurs playing with pros. When you try to do it, as you did with Adams, you don't have a prayer."

"Mr. President, I insist you—"

"Oh, shut up! I know facts when I hear them. I'm going to see you prosecuted to the fullest extent of the law, Adams."

Sloane laughed. "On what charges, Mr. President? What laws did he break? What actually happened?"

"He just admitted murdering Mako, David."

"Sure, but who's going to charge him and have all this come out? Are you, Mr. President?"

Marvin Grayson looked at him a long moment. "There must be something to be done."

"Oh, there is. And it surely will be done." He turned to his right. "Don't you think so, Adams?" His face had already blanched.

Grayson's mind was elsewhere. "The fact remains, Mr. Sloane, that this office must find a way to gain oversight over that so-called security agency and its Committee. We can't have a group of nameless, faceless men manipulating the foreign policy and military affairs of this country through control of codes and by spreading false information."

"Can't we? There have been some excesses, I'm

sure, but all in all they've done a pretty good job."

"You call planning to drop a nuclear warhead on Afghanistan a good job?"

"Was that their plan or just Adams's plan? Was The Committee about to be as surprised as you were? After all, they probably had no more knowledge that Seraphim was a mole than you did."

"But they were certainly planning something. I signed the blank authorization."

"True, but what were they doing—or what did they think they were doing? They may only have been trying to exert control over Soviet missile subs. Think about it. That might have been a highly useful thing to be able to do. It would've been a defensive capability of the first magnitude. But I can guarantee you that thanks to your buddy Adams it is all out the window now. I'm sure the Russians have abandoned it."

"Adams is not my buddy, Mr. Sloane. And I don't think much of your insulting tone. I am not quite the idiot you think."

Sloane grinned. "I'm sorry, Mr. President, but when it comes to intelligence matters you are. Everyone is. Even Freddie and I were played for patsies."

"Dammit, listen to me. I still think it is important for the President of the United States to have executive oversight of that damned Committee."

"I agree with him, David. I always have. Is there nothing to be done?" She saw him hesitate, make a gesture of disdain. It annoyed her. "Look, David, I know you think Mother is the greatest thing since baked apples, but there are those of us who disagree. The Committee can be wrong, often wrong— whether you choose to believe it or not."

"Yes, well put, Freddie—if I may call you that. Have you ever read the Constitution of the United

States, Mr. Sloane?"

"Please, don't give me a political-science lecture, Mr. President. I get quite enough at home." He sighed. "All right. If you want executive oversight of The Committee, you're never going to do it yourself. You're an amateur. They're pros. If you want oversight, I suggest you round up a group of the most knowledgeable and experienced people from the intelligence field and let them do it. At least let them advise you, then follow their advice. You can even include Adams in the group. He's expert enough."

"Hardly, Mr. Sloane." Marvin Grayson thought a moment. "What you say makes some sense."

"Not really, Mr. President. I don't think such an advisory group has a prayer. The Committee will simply manipulate it, withholding information, applying Need to Know. But you can try."

"Would you serve on such a group, Mr. Sloane?"

"Not on your life."

A year later a most contented Mrs. David Stuart Pritchard sat in her living room suckling David Stuart Pritchard, Jr., at her breast. Her contentment stemmed from more than that most maternal act. She was happy, and she knew David Stuart Pritchard was happy too. He had given up his wanderlust. His life was neither over or anticlimactic. He had accepted real life. He was going to make a splendid father. *Thank you, God.*

She watched him read a moment. "David?"

"Yes."

"Still nothing in the paper?""Nope. You don't expect there to be, do you?"

She sighed. "I guess not, but David, it's like it never happened."

"It didn't—officially. You don't think any reports were filed, do you, records kept? No one is ever going to admit any of this ever happened. How could they?"

"Not even in Russia?"

"Most definitely not there. The KGB is even more secretive and manipulative than the CSA. The Kremlin will never have the first inkling anything untoward went on."

"Lord, what a world!" She was silent a moment, looking down at her son. Gorgeous, simply gorgeous. *Thank you, God.* "David, what would've happened if we hadn't gotten there in time? It was awful close as it was. Would Adams have nuked Afghanistan?"

"Probably. He hoped we'd discover the plan, alert the White House in time. He did everything he could to make it possible for us to do it—or I should say for you to do it. I never did know, remember? But if it didn't work and Kabul was nuked, Adams still had Grayson in his hip pocket. He'd win either way."

"Whatever happened to him, do you suppose?"

"He's gone. My guess is permanently gone. The Committee had no choice."

"And the Committee goes on and on."

"You didn't think it would be any other way, did you?"

She shuddered, couldn't help it. She was still having bad dreams about the whole affair. "What I can't figure, David, is Olga. I sorta liked her. I've never been able to figure her with Adams."

"What's to figure?"

"She really was beautiful. Don't tell me you didn' notice. Sexy too. How does a mousy guy like Adam attract a knockout like her?"

"He must have something. She was the second too

Evelyn Cushman, the wife, was another top-heavy blonde." He shrugged. "Actually there may be something else with Olga. It's just a hunch based on something Karamasov let slip once. But I wonder if Olga wasn't his kid."

"Olga, Karamasov's daughter?"

"Illegitimate, I'm sure. Adams could've played that relationship like an accordian."

"But he killed her father."

"Did she know that?"

"Oh God, David. That's ghastly."

He put down the paper and looked at her. "That's not what's ghastly. Tell me about your KGB buddy, Podorovich. What'd he look like?"

"Old, short, heavy, fleshy face, bushiest eyebrows in the world. Do you know him?"

He shook his head. "Naw, doesn't sound familiar."

"What're you thinking?"

"Something ghastly. Remember way back when? We had two Parsleys in that motel room, Adams and a guy later identified as Mr. White. We didn't know which one was Parsley, the mole on The Committee."

"Yes. You sent both out the door. White was killed."

"What if the wrong man was killed? What if it was Adams all along? What if he and your buddy Podorovich were in this thing together? Two old geezers divvying up the world, playing both sides for saps? Might be. Just an idea, Freddie. How's it sound to you?"

"Ghastly."